GUARDIAN OF MADNESS

NYX FORTUNA—BOOK THREE

MICHELLE MANUS

1

———

Meditation was not a thing Nyx Fortuna had ever been good at. Or been tempted to try more than a handful of times. The last seven years of her life had been spent mostly in her own company, so she hadn't really felt the need to focus even more attention inward.

If she could hear Griff's voice in her head, telling her she was missing the point of meditation, well, that was just further proof that she was once again failing at the exercise. But she didn't know what else to try.

She sat cross-legged on the Station's gym floor, a sleek metal bo staff resting across her thighs. The staff—stuck fast to her palm—was the cause of her most recent meditation attempt. Made of a lightweight, silver metal, it could also collapse to a single foot in length. This should have compromised the weapon's integrity, but since its ability to shrink in length was not by means of interconnected telescoping segments—or any discernible segmentation whatsoever—integrity was not an issue.

It was the perfect compact travel staff, and she wanted it for daily use. Unfortunately, any time she used it for longer than fifteen minutes, it became magically stuck to her hand. Once this happened, the only remedy was to have someone with a longer history of violence take it from her.

Initially, Morgen had tried all manner of spells and enchantments meant to help her overcome this issue, but even he had thrown in the towel a week ago, declaring the project hopeless. Which was how Nyx ended up meditating. Or trying to.

In theory, the staff was reacting to something within her every time it decided to adhere itself to her. One of Morgen's offhand comments had given her the brilliant idea that if she could just "center herself," or whatever, she could will the staff to release her.

It wasn't working. She tried for another twenty minutes before she accepted that today was not the day she solved this problem.

She closed her eyes and felt through the Station's senses, until she picked out the pattern of Morgen walking around in the laboratory she'd built for him. Perfect. She rolled to her feet and struck out for the library.

The Station's library contained secret entrances to every room Nyx had created that she didn't want to be easily accessible to strangers. She liked to think of it as hiding things in plain sight. And, if she was being honest, its abundance of alcoves and hidden areas that one only stumbled upon if one was meant to, and entranceways that only opened for the right person, did appease her inner fantasies of being a dark wizard with a magic castle.

She walked to the classics section and tipped out the spine of *The Strange Case of Dr. Jekyll and Mr. Hyde.* The entire bookcase swung inward, revealing a flight of stone stairs that led down. When Nyx had built Morgen's laboratory, she had leaned heavily on mad-scientist tropes for the décor, starting with this stairwell.

It was made of dark gray stone, rough-hewn to give it an ominous flair. The torches set into the stairwell at convenient intervals might not contain actual fire—stone hallways or no, sentient building or no, she wasn't interested in having a house fire on her hands—but they looked like the real thing, and lent the passageway a medieval feel.

Tuned into the Station's senses, Nyx felt both the stairs beneath her feet, and someone's feet on her stairs. It was a dual-sensory input she was still acclimating to. Much of her down-time had been spent working on her bond with the Station—both manipulating the physical structure and understanding the things she could now attune herself to—but there was so *much* of everything that she still had difficulty.

Especially since the dividing line between which things were a part of the Station, and which things were merely items the Station owned, wasn't always clear. For instance, most people thought the physical building that housed the Station's portal was the entirety of the Station. But while the building was indeed a part of it, so were the grounds, along with the air and vegetation on those grounds.

When it came to Morgen's lab, the floor and the furniture were all a part of the Station, so Nyx could feel them as if they were a part of her own body. The equipment in the room was more of a gray area. The Bunsen burners, lab sinks, and ventilation systems Nyx could feel, but other items—like flasks and graduated cylinders—were regular objects she had no special connection to.

As per her usual ritual for arriving in the lab, she made a great deal of unnecessary noise to announce her presence, which in this case meant loudly tapping the end of the bo staff on the ground with each step. She hit the end of the stairs, passed through the short hallway that existed purely for aesthetic reasons, complete with enigmatic designs etched onto the walls, and entered Morgen's laboratory.

Immaculate tidiness greeted her, each of the lab's six work areas spotless. The only active one held a small cauldron, for lack of a better word. It was a wide, round bowl, approximately the size of a small fish tank, and made of thick, clear glass. Inside, a viscous, indigo blue liquid boiled without aid of any apparent heat source.

A time sphere rested on the counter next to the bowl, slowly shifting color as it counted down. Nyx had tried to convert her alien friends to the awesomeness of the sports watch, but so far she'd failed to convince them the timepiece was superior to magic.

She clanked her way further into the room, staff striking the ground with intentional obnoxiousness.

"I heard you open the door, little Guardian, there's no need to obliterate my eardrums." Morgen's voice filtered out from what Nyx called his mad scientist study. It was a rounded section in the back corner of the lab, where black stone floor and industrial design gave way to thick carpets and comfort.

"Just making sure. I wouldn't want to scare the mad scientist in his lair. You might petrify me or something." She grinned at him as she ascended the stairs to the small room.

This entire section was raised six feet higher than the surrounding area, making the rest of the lab a containment zone for spilled magic or chemicals. This segregated space was surrounded by floor to ceiling glass walls, allowing Morgen to view the entirety of the lab from within its confines. When the door to the study was shut, the walls formed an airtight seal, keeping the ventilation of the room separate from the rest of the lab.

In short, it was the perfect comfortable place to hang out while keeping an eye on experiments that had timed phases—such as whatever was simmering in the glass bowl on the counter—and it was also a safe room in the event something he mixed together made the air unbreathable. Given the sometimes dangerous nature of the magical experiments he liked to perform, he and Nyx had an understanding. If the door to the laboratory was unlocked, it was safe to come in. If it was locked, then even though Nyx could override the lock, it was potentially hazardous to her health to do so.

"Petrification of the human body via magical means is not possible," Morgen replied, without looking up from the small book in his left hand. He held a pen in his right, scribbling notes in the journal that rested on the arm of his chair. The book was the one Seth had brought back from the Shadow Keep, the one they had thought might tell them about the Harvester. Maybe it still would, but Nyx's hope that Morgen, with all his language knowledge, could translate it in a hot minute had proved overly optimistic. According to Morgen, it wasn't written in another language, but in some kind of cipher. An apparently *good* cipher, one which, without its key, might never be broken.

Nyx knew of only one other person who might be able and willing to give her the answers she needed about the Harvester: Jevryn A-Morridahn, member of the All Council and suspected ex of Griff. He had once promised her aid, and she had decided to take him up on the offer.

Since Nyx was never famed for her patience—according to Seth—she had taken to "nagging" Jevryn. Which was to say, she'd picked up the ring he'd given her and spoken his name into it, a lot. Supposedly, he could hear it, and while Griff had reasonably pointed out that Jevryn was a Very Important Person, and therefore probably busy, Nyx was increasingly of the opinion that the ring didn't work.

Or at least, she *had* been, until she and Seth had gotten tipsy a few nights ago and made over an annoying children's song by replacing almost every word in it with Jevryn's name. The ring had zapped Nyx like it held an electrical charge. So maybe he *could* hear her—and find her annoying—but he obviously wasn't going to show up any time soon to offer her his years of All Council wisdom.

Which, honestly, she should probably be grateful for. Figuring out what to do with the Harvester on her own was probably less of a hazard than willingly explaining to Jevryn A-Morridahn that she was in possession of the Harvester, and would like to know how to get rid of it before some theoretical darkness showed up to obliterate her.

"How am I supposed to know that?" Nyx asked, responding to Morgen's tired explanation of the non-possibility of human magical petrification.

"Try reading one of the many magical primers I pointed you toward."

Nyx had read all of the books he'd suggested, so she did, in fact, know that petrification by magical means was not possible. But exasperating him was half the fun.

"So, little Guardian, what brings you to my—" He finally looked up from the book and cut off with a sigh. "You got the staff stuck to your hand again, didn't you?"

"Maybe just a little bit?"

"That's the fourth time this week."

"And?"

"And it's only Monday."

"Well, if a certain brilliant scientist could just figure out *why* it keeps getting stuck, then I could prevent it from happening. Until then, I'll have to keep running my own experiments."

"Or, you could just admit that it's never going to be a functional weapon." He held out his hand, palm up. "Hand it over."

Nyx extended it to him. The very first time she'd gotten it stuck to her, Kaden had offered to take it. He'd explained that weapons that attached themselves to people were attracted to the person most likely to use them often. Kaden had a much longer history of violence than Nyx did, and the staff had promptly abandoned her for him.

Since Evra, Seth, and Morgen also had lengthier histories of violence than she did, and all resided in her Station, Nyx had felt comfortable experimenting with the staff to see if she could find some way past the sticking-to-her-hand thing. She was competent with swords and daggers, and used them when she needed to, but killing was never her first choice, and that was what bladed weapons were designed for.

The bo staff was her weapon of choice, but constantly carrying around a staff that was taller than she was really wasn't practical. Unless, of course, said staff could shrink down to a foot in length and clip into the neat thigh holster Nyx had had made for it.

She'd once shown the weapon to Earth Between's black-smith, Laila, in the hopes the woman could forge her one of a similar nature, but the staff had only mystified the woman. According to Laila—and every other weapons-maker Laila knew —metal of the kind in the bo staff did not exist, and no one knew of any magic that could make regular metal function the way the staff did.

Since Nyx couldn't forge a replica, she wanted to make this one work for her. As she always did when she had to get it unstuck—and thank goodness Morgen didn't know she'd had Seth and Evra unstick it for her twice today already—she tried to feel the magic coursing through the staff as it decided that being with Morgen was better than being with her. If she could just figure out what it was *doing* during the transfer, maybe she could figure out how to make it happen on her own.

It popped free of her fingers, and Morgen set it on the coffee table between them. "If you don't stop doing this, I'm going to talk Griff into dropping it into the endless trunk when he gets back."

Griff had finally decided to use one of his trips off Station. He hadn't said where he was going, and she hadn't pried, because she'd been so excited for him. When she'd first told him she had bargained with the Station to allow him to travel, she'd been afraid he never would. That he'd spent too long here, and was afraid to leave.

Now that he'd been gone almost a week, she just missed him, fiercely. And was starting to get a little fidgety about him coming back, and wondering if he was alright, and she now understood exactly how he must have felt the two times she'd left.

She dragged her mind off missing Griff and gave Morgen her

best wounded look. "You wouldn't." It would take her weeks to find the staff again if Morgen convinced Griff to throw it in the endless trunk.

Morgen drummed his fingers on his thigh. "Wouldn't I, though?"

"After I built you this nice lab? And let you live rent-free in my home? And emotionally supported you when you thought Evra was getting back with her ex?"

A smidgen of guilt crept into Morgen's face, and Nyx pounced on it. "And *all* that I ask in return is for you to occasionally un-bond me from my bo staff and—"

Morgen snapped his fingers. "*Bond.* That's it."

Nyx blinked. "That's what?"

Morgen bent his head over the table, studying the staff. "None of the potential remedies for cursed objects or sentient weapons worked because it isn't a cursed object *or* a sentient weapon."

"Haven't I been saying that for weeks?" She'd lost track of how many supposed curse-breaking spells Morgen had worked over the staff, before he'd gotten fed up with it and told her it was a lost cause.

As for the sentient weapon angle, she'd been pretty certain it *wasn't* sentient, given she was pretty certain the Harvester *was*, and they felt like two completely different things. She couldn't make an immediate comparison, because the Harvester had been impersonating an inanimate object ever since their trip to the Shadow Market, where she had the very bad suspicion she'd awakened its creator.

It had taken three months of ordinary, uninterrupted Station life for her to stop looking over her shoulder every five seconds, expecting some mythic darkness to rear its head and destroy everything. That was one of the reasons she'd taken up this project to make the bo staff usable. It gave her something to think about and puzzle over that wasn't potentially universe-shattering.

She'd thought if anyone could crack the mystery, it would be Morgen. He hummed a low note under his breath, and she felt the staff respond, as if the sound resonated within the metal. As a half-Siren, his magic expressed itself primarily through musical means, though when she'd asked how that was practical, he'd just enigmatically replied, "Music can be a lot of things."

Still, what she'd seen him do so far had been pretty musically straightforward, like the soft tune he was humming now.

Magical ability came in a variety of different stripes and colors, and not everyone could see the underlying structure of magic unless it was their own. Nyx certainly couldn't. But if Morgen sang to an item just right, like he was doing now, he could. Unfortunately, just because someone could see the structure of a magic working didn't mean they could understand it. Like how someone might know where to look to find the blueprints for a construction site, but that didn't mean they would be able to understand or interpret them.

Morgen had said the bo staff's magical makeup was "complex in its simplicity." He couldn't separate what part of its inlaid magic gave the metal its lightweight and collapsible properties, and which part gave it the tendency to adhere itself to its wielders.

She couldn't puzzle out what her saying the word "bond" had clicked into place for him, and wondered if it would really allow him to see the one seemingly-insignificant error in a complex equation. Nyx leaned over the table, her face next to his as they both stared at the bo staff, even though she couldn't see what he could.

"Are you going to tell me what your big breakthrough was?" she whispered. Whispering seemed like the appropriate volume to accompany Morgen's serious, focused expression.

"When we say a weapon is sentient, what we generally mean is that its maker has imbued enough of their own personality into the magical underpinnings to make the weapon bear that personality as a part of its magical existence. There is typically only enough of this personality present to be problematic if the weapon was with its original maker for an extensive period of time—decades, at least—where the maker was continually reinforcing the original enchantment.

"In these cases, the weapon tends to attach itself to people whose goals or ideals line up with those of the weapon's maker. Hence, Kaden's original assessment that the staff would leave you for him, as people who make weapons like this tend to be violence-oriented.

"But what if the staff *isn't* leaving you because it's violence-oriented? After all, a bo staff is not the most deadly of weapons. You typically see that level of sentience with bladed weapons, because they can cause the most destruction."

"Okay," Nyx said, "if it's not violence-oriented, what does it want? Because every time someone takes it from me, I feel like it's rejecting me." She was trying not to get her feelings hurt. Really, she was. It wasn't as if the staff was *actually* alive, therefore it couldn't *actually* reject her.

"It wants a bond," he said, stressing the word she'd started all of this with. "It wants companionship. My guess is that it was with its maker for a very long time. Potentially, that maker was lonely. The staff has now been alone for—" He looked to her.

"A couple centuries," she supplied, having looked up the intake form for the item when Morgen agreed to work on it.

"—centuries," he repeated. "I think it wants some guarantee you aren't going to drop it in a hot second. It isn't throwing you off because of everyone else's history of violence, but because most people who fight for a long time grow attached to a specific weapon. That's what it's after. That's what it wants. It's getting stuck to you in an attempt to force that kind of attachment, and it's throwing you over for literally anyone else because it's sensing a lack of commitment."

"You got all of that from the word 'bond' and looking at its magic structure again?"

"Well I *am* a brilliant mad scientist."

"Uh-huh. So, Mr. Brilliant, how do I go about convincing my bo staff I want to give it a lifelong commitment?"

"Have you considered a marriage proposal?" Seth asked, ambling into the room and dropping down on the couch next to her. "Maybe a promise ring?"

"I'm not marrying a weapon."

"That's what all the ladies say."

Nyx rolled her eyes.

"In that case, there's no help for it. You have to sit it down and tell it you're very fond of it, but you're just not the marrying kind. Promise it a good time when you take it out to play, and that you'll never discuss your time with other weapons in its presence."

"You're ridiculous."

"He actually has a point," Morgen said.

"Right? Thank you." Seth raised his fist and Morgen bumped it in return.

Nyx wanted to ask if the fist-bump was a universe-wide gesture among species that had hands, or if Seth had picked it up on Earth and taught it to Morgen, but she didn't want to get distracted from the main point. Which was, "In what way is Seth possibly right?"

Seth slapped a hand over his heart. "Ouch. You really know how to cut a man."

"Oh, please. You're about as emotionally wounded as a crocodile."

"Crocodiles have feelings too."

"He's right," Morgen cut in, "that you need to try conveying your intentions to the staff. Although, I don't think talking's going to do it. At least not with words. Try talking with magic."

"Right," Nyx said, drawing the word out. "Try talking with magic. I barely know how to use my magic for its very specific intended purpose. How am I supposed to use it to talk with a metal object?"

Morgen shrugged.

"Can't you just Siren-sing it my intentions?"

Morgen canted his head, considering.

"No," Seth said, "he can't." He gave Morgen a pointed glare. "You aren't supposed to be helping the competition."

"*That's* why you've been so annoyed about unsticking it for me?" Nyx asked. "You don't want me to figure it out until after the Hunger Games?"

It had taken Nyx multiple repetitions of the words to be able to spit out "Hunger Games" with a straight face. The event was an annual charity competition run by Every Home, Earth Between's version of a food bank and a homeless shelter. Every year, businesses from all over Earth Between came together to construct a massive obstacle course, complete with very real dangers. The competitors were teams of two, and all proceeds raised from the steep entrance fees were donated to helping the food insecure in Earth Between. Hence the name, "Hunger Games."

Nyx had laughed so hard when she'd first heard it that she'd offended Ankira, Earth Between's Warlock. It had taken her a solid ten minutes of explaining the plot of the *Hunger Games* books—with great enthusiasm, because they were *awesome*—for the pinched expression to leave the Warlock's face. But it wasn't until Nyx had brought her a copy of the trilogy that Nyx had been fully forgiven for laughing at the name of an event put on by a charity Ankira personally chaired.

It was also that laughter that had landed Nyx as a contestant. Ankira had informed her, in no uncertain terms, that after reading the grim landscape of the books, it would do Nyx good to "participate in a fun, community-building event to help others."

Truthfully, Nyx wouldn't have minded competing anyway. A magical obstacle course for adults, in which the champions received bragging rights for the next year, and a few goods and services donated by local businesses, was right up her alley. She'd conned Evra into being her partner, at which point Seth and Morgen had decided the two of them didn't get to have all the fun, and signed up with bold declarations of beating them into the ground.

"Don't you think withholding aid *before* the competition is cheating?" Nyx asked.

"No," Morgen and Seth said in unison.

Morgen gave Seth a look of reprimand. "And while I have been busy discouraging her from pursuing the weapon of her dreams, don't think I don't know you've been unsticking it for her every two hours despite promising not to."

"She gave me puppy dog eyes," Seth defended. "I told you if she gave me puppy dog eyes I was screwed. What's your excuse?"

"If I refuse to help her, any excuse I give makes me appear petty and selfish, and tarnishes my image with Evra."

"So we're even then," Seth conceded. "But you could have held on to your big breakthrough until after the games. Also, you're now late for practice."

Morgen waved a dismissive hand. "There's no need. Evra isn't feeling well and won't be able to attend the games. Therefore, there is no longer any harm in solving this problem, and I get to earn brownie points by making Evra my mother's patented cough syrup recipe."

"That's what's in the bowl?" Nyx asked. "You're making cough syrup? In a *lab*?"

"It's perfectly hygienic. I keep a tidy lab. And that recipe has to be kept at a very precise temperature for a very precise amount of time."

"I can't believe you're making her cough syrup," Seth said. "You know she's playing you, right?"

"She wouldn't." But Morgen's voice held a note of uncertainty as the time sphere floated into the room. It emitted a soft chime and shifted color to a violent red, indicating time was up.

"She absolutely would." Seth followed Morgen from the study to the lab. Morgen removed the cough syrup from the heat, dropped a pinch of something herbal into it, and stirred the concoction with a pensive look on his face.

Nyx grabbed the bo staff, shrank it down, and clipped it into its holster before it could decide to reattach to her. "Thanks for the advice Morgen," she said, as nonchalantly as possible, and headed for the door. "I'm just gonna go work on communicating with my staff."

The choking noise Seth made told her she had succeeded in making her words sound unintentionally dirty, hopefully enough to distract him from—

He jumped in front of her, blocking her exit. "Nyxi," he said silkily. "Care to weigh in on the Evra matter? She's putting him on, isn't she?"

Nyx swallowed. She was a shit liar. She knew it. Seth knew it. As soon as she opened her mouth and said anything along the lines of, "Oh, no, Evra's really sick," he would know without any doubt that the Amazon was in perfect health.

Thinking quickly, Nyx reached for her bond with the Station's senses. Evra was in her room, since playing sick was difficult if you were out and about all over the place. Nyx reached through the bond and grew Evra's bed to twice its original size in the blink of an eye, which knocked Evra onto it. She then hastily erected two temporary walls, enclosing Evra in a doorless room that only had space for the bed, which forced her to stay on it.

"Evra is currently upstairs in her room, in bed. It's two o'clock in the afternoon. Have you ever known Evra to be in bed at two in the afternoon?"

Seth narrowed his gaze at her. "No." He drew the one syllable word out into two, clearly suspicious.

"Well, there you have it." Louder, for Morgen's benefit, she said, "I'll just go check on Evra now. Who's *in* bed at this hour of the day she never sleeps during."

She evaded the arm Seth shot out to hold her back and darted up the stairs, a grin on her face.

2

"What was that for?" Evra growled when Nyx burst into her room.

Nyx took down the temporary walls. "Sorry, but you know I'm a bad liar, and Seth was working very hard to convince Morgen that you were playing him. Unless you want your 'competition strategy,'" Nyx said, using air quotes, "to be ruined, I needed to be able to truthfully tell them you were in your room, in bed."

"Oh, very well."

Speaking of the bed… Nyx started to shrink it back down to its previous size.

"You can leave it like that," Evra said. "It's better."

Nyx raised an eyebrow. "Better for what, exactly? Are you planning to let Morgen nurse you back to health on it?"

Evra turned red. "I have long limbs."

"Uh-huh." Now that Evra had finally agreed to go on a date with Morgen—though stars alone knew when said date would actually take place—Nyx was thoroughly relieved she'd gotten a handle on blocking out the Station's senses. She typically paid the most attention to the premises outside the building, trading nights of "guard duty" with Griff, since she could now gloriously block out every individual's personal rooms. If anyone had a nightmare, it no longer woke her up, and if anyone wanted to get up to *other* activities, she didn't have to know about those, either.

Thank the stars no one had been on amorous terms before she'd learned her blocking skills. Otherwise, she'd likely never have been able to look any of her friends in the eye ever again.

"Well, I hope you're prepared to play the part of the ill and dying. Morgen is making you his mother's special cough syrup recipe. Apparently, it's very involved. He's been working on it for the last three hours."

At that, Evra had the decency to look mildly guilty.

"When are you going to put him out of his misery and finally go on that date with him?"

Morgen had chased Evra for months with outlandish flirting, over-the-top flattery, and expensive gifts, but it was his surviving asking her mother for permission to date her that had had Evra agreeing to go on one. Though, personally, Nyx thought she'd just been looking for an excuse.

Instead of the pretend irritation that usually came over Evra whenever Nyx brought Morgen up, the Amazon's lips thinned into a slim line. She shrugged and said, "Whenever he finally decides he wants to go on it."

Nyx was about to ask what that meant when a soft, silver chiming trilled through the Station. The cafe had a customer, and it was her afternoon to handle them.

She missed Kalvar. She especially missed his love of tips, which had led him to insist on working ninety percent of the cafe shifts. Because, of the four other people who lived in her Station, one didn't have opposable thumbs, one solved her lack of espresso machine competence by trying to beat the machine to a pulp, one refused to put anything less than five espresso shots into a beverage, and Seth had already worked his shift.

"We'll talk about this later," Nyx promised. "You're ready for the competition?"

Evra rolled her shoulders back and down, haughty Amazon superiority overtaking her features. "Of course I am ready. I would not call myself an Amazon were I not prepared for combat."

"That's the spirit." Nyx clapped her on the shoulder and bounded downstairs, tilting her head towards the ceiling in supplication to the universe. "*Please* don't let it be another sad, lovestruck teenager asking where Kalvar went."

Nyx already had a hole in her heart where the kid had been. He was smart, likable, and funny. He should be here, enjoying his youth and some time where he didn't have to worry about anyone killing him. Instead, he was off gallivanting around the universe as part of the Moor siblings' new mercenaries-with-ethics group, and pining after Maruca. At least, that's what she assumed he was doing, since none of them had checked in with her.

Not that she was surprised by the lack of communication. Kalvar didn't seem like the letter-writing type, Maruca hated Nyx with the fiery passion of a thousand dying suns, and Kaden… Well, she *had* very explicitly told him never to come back to Earth. Maybe he'd gotten in touch with Morgen at some point, but Nyx had too much pride to ask. She figured if anything bad ever happened, Morgen would let her know.

She breezed into the cafe. A pretty girl with blue hair that didn't look like it came out of a bottle, perked up when she heard someone coming. She immediately deflated when she saw that someone was Nyx.

"How's it going?" Nyx asked brightly.

"Oh, umm, good." She didn't quite meet Nyx's gaze, turning something over and over in her hands.

"Did you want anything?" Nyx prompted.

The girl's gaze darted to the espresso machine, as if she'd forgotten she'd come to a cafe. "Oh, no. That's okay." She hesitated, then, "I was just wondering if…" She shook her head. "Never mind."

She slid off the barstool, her face such a mixture of nervousness and dejection that Nyx couldn't help but offer, "Kalvar isn't here anymore, if that's what you were wondering."

The girl stopped. "No, I know. He said he was leaving and he might not be back, but..."

Nyx had to work to keep from showing visible surprise. Kalvar had spent the majority of his time at the Station keeping everyone at arms' length, the better to pine after Maruca. Nyx hadn't realized he'd made *any* friends here, much less one he would have told he was leaving.

"Could you—" The girl broke off again, still turning the *something* over and over in her hands.

"Do you need help?"

"No," she said quickly, a distinct deer-in-the-headlights look overtaking her face. "No, I'm fine. Everything's fine. Just, if you could get this to him, that would be great. It's important." The words came out in a rush, practically on top of each other. She dropped the item she'd been holding—a small envelope—on the counter and rushed out.

Nyx ran after her, but by the time she hauled open the front door, the girl was nowhere to be seen. The majority of the Station's grounds were behind the building, so it wouldn't have taken the girl long to leave them—and Nyx's connected senses—via the front, but it was still a fast escape.

Nyx didn't like it. The girl hadn't seemed like a lovestruck teenager delivering an I-miss-you-Kalvar note. She'd seemed like she might be in trouble.

Nyx retrieved the envelope from the counter. It was small, barely the size of her palm, and thin, with Kalvar's name written on it in stylized lettering drawn in blue ink. It was perfectly flat, indicating it probably contained nothing more dangerous than a note.

She tucked the letter into her back pocket—she'd ask Morgen if he could get it to Kalvar—and made a mental note to ask Ankira if she or Diana knew anything about the girl. Nyx didn't even know the kid's name, but she also hadn't seen any blue-haired girls running around Earth Between, so maybe there weren't so many of them that it would be impossible to track this one down.

She was turning for the stairs when the door opened again. The cafe's typical customer base came from travelers as they arrived or departed Earth Between. The Station was too far away from Earth Between proper for it to be a typical destination for most people. Also, her hours were irregular, and her food selection limited.

No, the Station's cafe was basically like the airport bar. If you were getting on or off a plane you might hang out there for a while, but otherwise, there was no reason to make the out-of-the-way trip.

Nyx's only Arrival had been that morning, and it had been a very manageable family of five. Contrary to the tone that had been set on her first day as Guardian, Earth's Station didn't really see a lot of traffic. They weren't an exciting destination—though they were apparently a cheap one, which was why they did see *some* tourism from those interested in the non-magical world of Dead Earth—so Nyx didn't actually have a lot of work. She could sometimes go entire days without Arrivals or Departures.

She didn't have any Departures today, which was usually the only time someone ventured up from Earth Between, unless she knew them and they were coming to see her specifically. She didn't know the man who'd just walked through her door.

He'd stopped on the threshold, looking around as if he wasn't quite sure why he was here. He was unusually tall—maybe six-foot seven? Nyx was bad at gauging height—with an angular jaw, and cheekbones that looked like they could cut glass. The thick, arched brows above hard eyes did nothing to soften his countenance, nor did the gloved hands fisted at his sides.

He looked to be in his late thirties, early forties, and his hair was sheared so close to his skull she could only guess at the true color, though it looked auburn. Slowly, as if just figuring out where he was, he turned to look at her. He stared and frowned. After a few too many seconds, the silence grew awkward.

"Did you need to book a Departure?" Nyx asked, hazarding a guess. Guardians weren't typically as young as she was, a fact that had been drilled into her by the many, many travelers who felt the need to comment on her age. Perhaps the man had come here to book, but didn't realize she was the Guardian? She didn't get a lot of in-person bookings, as they could be purchased from a hub in Earth Between, but the odd person here and there did come all the way to the Station for it.

The man's frown deepened. "No." His voice was as sharp as the rest of him, but the word wasn't hostile. It was just...confused.

"Did you want a latte?" That was usually the only other reason people bothered to trek up to the Station. The wider universe did have coffee, but lattes were a pure Earth invention, and she had the only espresso machine in the Between. She usually got a few customers a week who were residents of Earth Between, and therefore didn't have any typical reason to visit the Station, but had heard about the "strange Dead Earth beverage" and wanted to try it.

"Latte?" He repeated the word in stumbling syllables, sounding them out.

"Why don't you have a seat and try one? On the house. I think you'll like it." Anything to break the odd tension he'd brought into the room with him.

He approached the bar cautiously, choosing the seat at the far end, facing the door. It was the seat anyone with martial experience typically chose, as it was the most defensible position in the room, and the best one for viewing all possible avenues of approach. Despite the choice, she didn't see any weapons on him. Considering Earth Between essentially had open carry laws on every conceivable weapon that was legal in the wider universe, the martially-inclined were usually carrying a blade or two.

Not that this guy especially gave off I-will-kill-you vibes. He carried himself like he knew how to fight, but his clothes, while they were of plain, functional construction, were functional for daily comfort, not daily battle. And he wasn't exactly exuding menace. If anything, the biggest impression Nyx got from him was extreme sadness.

She focused on making the latte, adding a cinnamon syrup, because cinnamon was a scent that always made her feel better when she was sad and, well, she didn't think he'd know what he wanted if she asked him.

She finished making the drink and placed it in front of him. He blinked and looked at her, then at the drink. He reached for the mug, a subtle flare of magic jumping from his gloved fingertips, and Nyx had the absurd notion that he was checking for poison. He waited a beat, then lifted the mug to his lips and took a cautious sip.

His expression gave nothing away as he swallowed and returned the cup to its saucer. "It is interesting." His voice strongly implied that it was not interesting, and furthermore that nothing had been interesting for some time. But he did take another sip. "You are the Guardian here?"

"I am." Nyx braced herself for one of the typical reactions.

You're so young. She'd started telling people she was eighty and daring them to call her on it.

We all really liked Sena. Sena had been the previous Guardian, and Nyx usually replied to those comments with some version of, "Hmm."

We heard Centerian Hyplexia swept through the Station. That was the excuse Griff had come up with to explain why her Station had been shut down when she'd gone off to find Seth. When this came up, she enthusiastically launched into a speech on all of the horrible side effects she had now supposedly recovered from. If the travelers expressed further interest, she added a very technical description of how such an outbreak would have been handled had it occurred. People's eyes usually glazed over pretty quick, after that.

For the most part, Nyx liked talking to the people who came through her Station. She didn't even mind answering the same questions over and over about Dead Earth and technology, and all the other curious questions people had. She'd gone so much of her life starved for human interaction that she had years of patience and emotional energy stored up to talk to random strangers.

But doing that was easier when they actually *talked*. This guy still wasn't.

"Do you live in Earth Between?" she asked. She was good at customer service when other people talked, which they usually did. She had a lot of practice listening. She had not so much practice making small talk on her own. She'd grown up in the-middle-of-nowhere Montana, with two people who never wanted to talk to her and one person who knew her like the back of his hand. Then she'd spent seven years in Dead Earth, where pretty much no one could remember she existed. None of that lent itself to the ability to develop good conversational skills.

The stranger only shrugged in response and took another sip. Maybe he would just finish the coffee and go?

"Are you married?" he asked abruptly.

Say what, now? She was accustomed to being hit on by travelers at this point, because there was apparently a universe-wide obsession with trying to bang a Guardian, but this was a bizarre approach. Or maybe it was refreshing? At least he was getting right to the point. No beating around the bush.

She was opening her mouth to say she wasn't interested when he kept talking.

"I had a wife." That sadness rolling off him intensified. "I lost her. Many years ago, today."

"I'm sorry," Nyx said. His strange behavior made more sense now. If she'd lost someone that important to her, she thought she might end up somewhere like this on the anniversary of that loss. Somewhere she didn't ordinarily go, where no one knew her. Somewhere she could talk about it to a stranger and not have to care what they thought. "What was her name?"

Surprise flashed across his face, as if he hadn't expected her to ask. Maybe he hadn't wanted her to. Maybe she was wrong, and he hadn't come here to talk at all.

"Nyaera." He pronounced it Nigh-era, and he said the name hesitantly, as if he hadn't spoken it aloud in some time. "She was…kind. Smart. Incredibly smart. And no one could tell her what to do." His lips curved in the barest trace of a smile, as if remembering something in particular that she'd done. "And she loved me." The smile disappeared.

"What happened to her?" Nyx asked softly.

"There was an accident with her work. She was lost." His hands clenched and released, clenched and released. "And no one would search for her. No one but me, and by the time I found her, it was too late." He stared at his half-drank cup of coffee and stood abruptly. "I'm sorry. I don't know why I'm telling you this. I don't know why I'm here." He pushed away from the bar and all but ran for the door.

"Well, that wasn't weird at all," Seth said in her ear after the door shut. He'd wandered in shortly after the stranger had, illusion magic tricking the senses into not seeing him. But his abilities weren't good enough to trick the Station's senses—though he kept trying to work out how to do just that—and he didn't get the jump out of her he'd likely been hoping for.

"You know, if you keep sneaking up on people, one day they're going to panic and elbow you in the stomach."

He laughed, the sound easy and mellow, his breath tickling her ear. "Trust me, I have a permanent callus on my stomach from all the times you've elbowed me. So who was the guy?"

Nyx shrugged. "I don't know. I think he was just lonely."

"So long as he keeps it to lonely and doesn't verge into creepy."

"Somehow, I don't think he'll be back." He hadn't really seemed to enjoy being inside the Station. Some people were like that. It wasn't common knowledge that the Stations were sentient, but sensitive people picked up on the something *off* about the buildings—that they were a little more than just buildings—and it weirded them out.

"How's Evra?" he asked casually, moving around her to get to the fridge.

"As well as can be expected in her current condition," Nyx replied evasively.

"Nice," he replied. "Since if her current condition is right-as-rain then she can reasonably be expected to be well."

"If you're so worried about your ability to perform in tomorrow's competition, maybe you should be practicing instead of bothering me."

"My ability to perform is not in question," he said suggestively.

"Uh-huh. That's what all the boys say. Don't worry, when Evra and I kick your asses tomorrow—"

"*Ha.*" Seth jabbed a finger at her in victory. "She's fine. I knew it."

Damn it. Seth had an unparalleled ability to get her to open her mouth and spill anything and everything she ever tried to hide. Spotty memory problems aside, she was relatively certain she'd never successfully kept a secret from him for more than an hour.

Seth pulled half a dozen items out of the fridge and set to work building sandwiches. He finished in record time, despite the high number of ingredients, and magnanimously slid one of the sandwiches across the counter to her.

"Thanks. And yes, okay, Evra's fine. But maybe you could keep it to yourself? Because I don't think her end goal here actually has anything to do with tomorrow's competition."

"I could be persuaded, if you let me in on why." Seth bit off what looked like an entire quarter of the sandwich. The man had an abnormally large mouth. No doubt from all his practice running it.

"I think—and if you ever repeat what I'm about to say to Evra or anyone else, I will murder you for real—that she wants Morgen's attention. You two are BFFs now. Why hasn't he taken her on that date yet?"

Another quarter of Seth's sandwich disappeared, and he impressively managed to talk around chewing it without being disgusting. "We don't exactly sit around painting our nails and talking about our relationship problems."

Thank the stars for that, since if Seth was going to have relationship problems, they would be about her.

Or...would they? An odd feeling settled in Nyx's stomach. They hadn't talked about their non-relationship since he'd come back, hadn't kissed since he'd taken her to see their childhood home in Montana.

Instead, they'd settled into an easy friendship. He was fun to be around. They got along, and if she couldn't remember all of their past, she didn't seem to need to in order to feel the way they fit together. They could move through a space without clashing, each knowing automatically where the other would go.

She loved it and it weirded her out. She loved it because she'd never had that with anyone before. Not even with Kaden. She'd had a relationship—sort of—with Kaden, and she'd known how to exist in his space, but it had always felt like that, she realized: existing in *his* space. When she was around Seth, everything felt like *their* space, and she wasn't the only one moving to accommodate someone else. He moved for her, too.

She'd needed that sense of belonging, of being cared for. Now she had it. The only problem was, she didn't remember where it came from. She had glimpses into it, little snatches of memories that would appear without rhyme or reason, torturing her with a life she couldn't really remember.

It made her reluctant to move forward. How did she know if there was even anything to move forward towards? How did she know what was between her and Seth if she couldn't remember what *had* been there? Did she want to step into him and kiss him right now because that was what she *wanted* to do, or did she want to do that because it felt natural, because she'd done it a thousand times before?

When she'd first reconnected with him, there'd been an intensity that radiated off him every time she was around. That had dimmed somewhat, and she didn't know if that was a good thing or a bad thing, or if it was just a natural, neutral thing.

Kaden had had a similar intensity when she was around him. The difference was, Kaden's had felt more like possessiveness for the sake of possessiveness. Like she'd been his once, so she should be again.

Seth's felt like…love.

The thought stopped her cold.

"Hey, you okay?" Seth asked.

She opened her mouth to say she was fine, but then she stopped herself. She wasn't fine. She didn't know if *he* was fine. They hadn't talked about them, about if there even *was* a them. They'd settled into familiarity, into routines she half-remembered and he wholly did.

It had been soothing and comforting and she thought they'd both needed it, needed these last few months where nothing had been wrong, and they were happy. They hadn't been happy as kids. Happy with each other, most of the time, yes, but not happy in general. She didn't think either one of them had wanted to break that tentative pleasantness by bringing up whatever was or wasn't between them.

But she'd let things go on with Kaden like that for too long after he came back, afraid that whatever she said to him would be the wrong thing. That she'd piss him off and he'd…what? Wouldn't want her anymore? It had scared her, at the time. Because even though she'd finally had connections to other people for the first time in her life that she could remember, she hadn't had a *deep* connection to any of them. Kaden had still been the person she'd known the best. She'd been afraid of losing that.

Just like she was afraid of losing Seth now. But nothing good was going to come from dancing around every person in her life that meant something to her, afraid they'd leave if given half a chance. Seth was important to her, and that importance was more than whatever was or wasn't between them romantically.

To her credit, it wasn't like he'd ever tried to talk about it, either. She'd thought he was just giving her space and time to move past what had happened with Kaden. And maybe he was. But there was also the chance that he'd decided he didn't want to rekindle whatever had been there. Maybe he didn't want *her*, but the Nyx she used to be.

A sharp pinch of pain hit. She accepted it. She had abandonment issues from here to kingdom come. The idea of anyone she cared about not wanting her in any capacity terrified her. She'd been working on that, on recognizing when she was having an emotional response based on fear, and when she was having one based on what she actually wanted.

Right now, she still couldn't tell the difference. Couldn't tell if it hurt to think of Seth not wanting her because it would just be another rejection, or if it was because she wanted *him*. How was she supposed to know? Could she ever know if she couldn't remember all of what—who—she was?

"Nyxi?" Seth prompted, when she didn't answer.

"I think we should talk," she blurted out.

3

—————

At Nyx's declaration, Seth froze, the hand with his remaining piece of sandwich stopped halfway to his mouth. His gaze locked on hers, and she saw the same confusion she felt mirrored in his eyes. He swallowed, dropped the sandwich remnant onto the saucer and pushed it aside, dusting his hands together.

"Yeah, okay. So talk."

Did he look nervous? Seth never looked nervous.

"I..." *You can do this. String words together. It's really not that hard.* She tried again. "I think—"

"How is this *my* fault?" Evra's outraged voice demanded. She was hot on Morgen's heels as he strolled into the kitchen with a look of disbelief on his face. Apparently, the I'm-so-sick ruse had lasted all of five seconds.

"I fought off an entire legion of fanged furies and survived your mother's wrath just to get you to go on a date with me. Therefore, the ball was in your court."

"That saying does not make any sense. What kind of ball? And whose court? Why is someone bringing a ball to court? Or are we talking about the kind of ball that has dancing?"

Morgen gave Evra a hard stare. "Do not even try to avoid the point by pretending you don't understand Earth sayings well enough to carry the conversation."

Evra's lips compressed into a thin line, and Nyx had a feeling she was going to be explaining basketball to Evra later. Wait, was basketball the origin of that saying? Having aliens for friends was eye-opening in terms of the number of sayings whose meanings she understood perfectly well, while having no idea how they'd originated.

"I am not having this conversation in public," Evra argued.

"Neither am I," Morgen said.

"Then why are the two of you in public?" Nyx wanted to know.

"To avoid having the conversation," they replied in unison.

Suddenly, her own decision to have a conversation with Seth didn't seem like such a great idea. If everyone else was avoiding them—and Morgen and Evra looked genuinely pissed off with each other for the first time Nyx could remember—then maybe talking wasn't such a great idea after all.

"You know," Nyx said, carefully taking a step back, "I think I'm just going to go."

Seth gave her a look that said he knew exactly what she was doing. "Me too. Enjoy the kitchen," he told Morgen and Evra. Wrapping an arm around Nyx's waist, he steered her out of the room and into the library.

The library was a comfortable room. It had continued to redesign itself to become even more her favorite version of a library ever, which meant it now boasted two cozy fireplaces on opposite sides of the room, and a number of secretive alcoves perfect for hiding the day away, all of which were complete with comfy chairs and ornate lamps and decor that shifted to match a person's mood.

Right now, the decor was clearly stating that both she and Seth were nervous. She wasn't entirely sure *how* late nineteenth century drawing room décor said nervous, but she was absolutely certain that it did. At least for the two of them.

She paced back and forth in front of the silk-upholstered camelback sofa that horrified her, and that she was going to have removed from the room as soon as was convenient.

"Look," Seth said, "if this is about the other night, I'm sorry."

Nyx froze. Any time a person used a vague phrase like *the other night*, it implied something particularly momentous or awkward had occurred—potentially both—which the person wanted to avoid directly referencing, in case the other person wanted to pretend it had never happened. It was a phrase generally reserved for unreciprocated romantic confessions or awkward one night stands.

The only problem was, Nyx couldn't remember a recent event that qualified as the-other-night material. Or why Seth should need to be sorry about anything.

"And, what exactly are you sorry about?" she asked carefully.

"Pushing you." He dragged a hand through his hair. "I got excited when you remembered Washington, and I was hoping if I talked about it more you might remember something else, even though I know it doesn't work like that. I didn't mean to make you feel like you weren't trying hard enough, or anything. And I really didn't think I *had*, but then you never brought it up again." He finished in a rush, shoving his hands into his pockets.

Something distinctly like panic worked its way into Nyx's chest. "Were we drinking that night?" She doubted it. She hadn't been letting herself go anything past tipsy, in order to avoid making decisions while drunk.

Seth gave her a weird look. "No. Why?"

"I'm going to be completely honest with you. I have no idea what you're talking about."

"No idea, as in, you don't know why I'd think you might be upset about it?" he said hopefully.

"No idea, as in, I don't remember having any conversation like that with you." She hesitated, but added, "And I *don't* remember Washington. I mean, it's a state, obviously, but…" She trailed off.

Seth looked crushed. And almost a little like, despite her well-established inability to lie convincingly, he thought she might be doing just that right now.

Now she felt bad, in addition to being worried. "How long ago was this?"

"Saturday."

Two nights ago. What had she done Saturday night? She ran through a mental checklist of the day, which had wound up with her, Seth, Morgen, and Evra in a four-player game of *Back 4 Blood* in Seth's entertainment room. Morgen and Evra had eventually gotten tired of dying left and right and bowed out, leaving Seth and Nyx to battle it out against the zombie hordes, and—

Nothing. It was like the entire night after that was a blank wall. Just like the one she'd lived with since she was eighteen, separating her from every memory she'd had before then.

The tight feeling in her chest expanded, the chaos thorns in her cheek pulsed, and her arms and hands went light and fluttery with the spike of adrenaline that jolted through her.

"We were playing games," she said, as if reciting it out loud would somehow make the wall come down, "and Morgen and Evra left, and we were still playing and—and—"

Seth's hands settled on her shoulders, rubbing up and down her arms like he was trying to warm up someone who was shivering. Because she *was* shivering. And breathing too fast but still feeling like she couldn't breathe at all.

"I can't remember," she whispered.

"It's okay," Seth said. "It's fine."

She shook her head, her breathing growing even more rapid. "It's not fine, *I can't remember.* Just like I couldn't remember then."

He gave up rubbing her shoulders and tugged her into his chest. She wrapped her arms around his waist because she was cold, and the fireplaces in the room were doing nothing to alleviate it. Because it wasn't the kind of cold that physical heat could fix.

"She can't be fucking with me when she's not even here," Nyx whispered. She didn't have to specify who "she" was. "She can't be making me forget *now*."

It was a fear Nyx hadn't had before this moment. Everything before her eighteenth year had been taken from her, but she'd gotten to keep everything *after*. The idea that her mother could be reaching through whatever broken Hiding still lay over her and taking things away…

"It might not be that," Seth said. "People forget things all the time. I couldn't tell you what I had for lunch yesterday."

Nyx snorted, and it made her feel a little better. "That's because you ate lunch like three times."

"It's an important meal."

"How important was Washington?"

His arms tightened around her. "Important."

Great. So she'd remembered something—something important—and now it was just gone again. Along with the memory of remembering it.

"Why?" she asked softly. "She already took it from me once. Why does she need to do it again?"

"I don't know." There was a hopelessness in his words he couldn't quite hide, the same kind she'd tried not to feel every day since she'd gotten her first memory back, but the rest had failed to materialize. When, instead of getting *easier* to remember, it seemed to get harder, the new memories fewer and farther between.

The hopeless fear that she would *never* get them back. The sense that she wasn't truly herself without them, and that if she couldn't remember, she would never be herself again.

Reconnecting with Seth had made more memories surface, but those had slowed after their initial meeting. Now, she couldn't help but wonder if she had remembered more of them since, only to have them disappear again.

"We'll figure it out." He teased his fingers through her hair, the gesture comforting and familiar, and it made the panic in her chest recede. Now, even when she couldn't remember concrete memories, she had this—the ease of being around him, the knowledge of who he was that just *fit* in her life. She hadn't considered that maybe even that could be taken from her, too.

She tried to force some optimism into her voice. "Yeah. We'll figure it out." She thought she sounded more brittle than optimistic.

"Nyx," Seth said, his hand cupping her cheek, "I—"

A bone-deep thrumming ran through the Station, cutting Seth off and announcing the activation of the Station's portal. Both their heads whipped in the direction of the Arrival Room.

"No Arrivals or Departures today," Seth said. "Which means..."

"Griff." Nyx breathed out. "He's back." A wide grin cracked her face and she ran full out, Seth on her heels, dashing through hallways to skid to a stop in front of the hexagonal portal, its six spheres spinning away atop their posts. The cosmic black floor between the posts turned liquid, and an eagle's head broke the surface.

Nyx danced from foot to foot, and the second enough of her griffin appeared aboveground, she launched herself at him, hugging hard enough she dislodged a few feathers.

"Oh, my." Griff said the words on a forced exhale as she knocked the breath from his lungs. Her feet lifted off the floor as the rest of his body materialized. He was currently draft-horse sized—since the griffin species wasn't actually the housecat size Griff usually maintained inside the Station's walls—and he wrapped his wings around her in a gentle embrace before lowering his neck to deposit her back on the ground.

"I missed you," Nyx said into his feathers before she let go.

Griff ducked his head in that way that indicated he would be blushing if he were human. "I missed you too, Nyx Fortuna." He looked over her shoulder. "And you, Seth Hawthorne." He extended his wing in invitation, and Seth came up to give him a one-armed hug.

"Where are my Station's other two miscreants?" Griff asked.

Nyx and Seth shared a look. "Umm," Nyx said, "Morgen and Evra are having a bit of a disagreement." She filtered through the Station's senses, which Griff obviously hadn't tapped back into yet—and who could blame him? No one wanted to come back from vacation and get straight to work. "The good news is, they're no longer fighting. The bad news is, they wrecked the meditation room before going their separate ways."

Morgen had probably gone in there in an attempt to get away from Evra, who said all the "calming influences" of the room drove her to insanity. She'd obviously followed him there, as all of those calming influences were now in pieces. Nyx could feel the waterfall wall had been shattered, the meditation cushions shredded, and every potted plant had been demolished.

Nyx sent a mental apology to Kaliaris, wondering if her Station could hear the thought. The waterfall wall was already knitting itself back together, the plants and cushions disappearing into the repair room, where Kaliaris stuck the odds and ends of broken things and built others anew.

Griff's eyes grew worried and went a little distant as he tuned back into the Station. "And they are both still upset," he said quietly.

At Seth's questioning look, Nyx said, "Evra's running laps around the Station perimeter fast enough to spark a forest fire, and Morgen's in his music room."

Griff clicked his tongue. "I was gone for *one* week. What happened?"

"From the little bit I gathered before Seth and I wisely decided to not be in their paths when one of them exploded, Evra's upset Morgen hasn't taken her on the date yet, and Morgen's upset Evra hasn't put any effort into making the date happen, since he survived her mother for the honor."

"Oh, dear. I should go check—"

"No," Seth interrupted firmly, "you definitely should not. You don't have to come home and immediately worry about everyone else. The first rule of vacation is that upon return, you pretend you're still on vacation."

Nyx gave him a skeptical look. "And how many vacations have *you* been on?"

"None. But I imagined them longingly and often." Seth clapped Griff on the back. "Come on, I'll make you dinner and you can finally tell us where you went, so we can live vicariously through you."

Griff admitted defeat. "Oh, very well. Will you make the spicy comfort food?"

"Gumbo," Seth supplied, "and of course I will."

<hr>

T he gumbo bubbled on the stove, its rich, aromatic flavor filling the kitchen. It was almost done, only waiting on the handfuls of okra Seth was efficiently chopping through. Nyx had made a trip into Dead Earth for the vegetable a couple days ago, because no one grew it in Earth Between, and she'd missed it.

She finished scraping cornbread batter into a baking dish and popped it into the oven. Dusting off her hands, she jabbed a finger at Griff. "Alright, you've been filled in on every conceivable, boring detail that has occurred in this Station since you left. You are now morally obligated to tell us where you went."

Griff—once more housecat sized and perched on one of the backless barstools—shifted uncomfortably.

Oh, shit. Had he gone to see Jevryn? That seemed like a monumentally bad idea, because Jevryn would then know Griff could leave the Station, and would want to know *how*, but... "Unless," she added hastily, "it's personal, in which case you definitely don't have to tell us."

"It is not personal, merely embarrassing."

Not Jevryn, then. Which was probably best for both her

safety and Griff's emotional health. "Where could you possibly have gone that would be embarrassing?"

"Oh, there are places," Seth said. "There's a couple pleasure planets in—"

Griff let out an indignant squawk, wings flaring wide. "It was nothing like that."

"Hey, no shame man. You've been cooped up in this Station for a few centuries, right?"

Griff quickly said, "I went to the shores of Erilithea." At Nyx's blank look, he clarified, "The beach. I went to the beach."

The sound of Seth's chopping grew louder, the kitchen knife cutting through the okra with far more force than necessary. Nyx frowned. Did Seth have something against beaches?

"What's embarrassing about that?" Nyx asked.

Griff dragged a talon lightly back and forth on the barstool. "You do not think it is a bit cliché? I have been, as Seth stated, cooped up here for centuries. You bargained for the right for me to go anywhere in the universe that I wanted, and I went to a beach."

Most of the time, the centuries Griff had on her were obvious in his sage manner and excellent advice. But sometimes, like now, he lost the air of cultivated wisdom, and he seemed vulnerable and almost young again. Perhaps like he had been before he'd become the Station's Avatar. How old had he been, when he arrived here? Had he been the same age as Jevryn, whose smooth, unlined face made it impossible to guess his age?

Nyx smiled at Griff. "It's a cliché vacation destination for a reason. People like it. Soothing ocean sounds and all that. I'm glad you went where you wanted to go."

Nyx stole a glance at Seth. He'd stopped chopping away with unadulterated ferocity, but he didn't exactly look present in the conversation anymore.

"Well," Griff said, "now that the secret is out, I did bring presents back." He pulled on the Station, summoning a box that had arrived with him from the portal room into the kitchen. He dragged a talon through the adhesive that sealed the seam and dug around inside, pulling out two smaller, gift-wrapped boxes. "This one is for you."

Griff handed her a package in shimmery silver paper with a black ribbon tied around it. She took it, the fancy paper like smooth silk beneath her fingers. Her throat tightened, tears pricking at her eyes.

"Is something wrong?" Griff asked, concern lacing his voice.

Nyx shook her head, trying to get a grip on herself. "No, it's just...Seth's the only person who's ever gotten me a present before." She tugged the black ribbon free.

"It may be disappointing," Griff said as she pulled the lid free. "It is only—"

"Is this naturally blue sand from another planet?" Nyx bounced on her toes as she pulled the glass container of sand free. The glass was blown into the shape of a sea creature she'd never seen before, which looked vaguely like a dolphin and yet...not. It was strange and oddly mesmerizing.

"It has of course been sterilized per necessary travel regulations, and..." He trailed off, looking unsure. "I should have brought you something more interesting."

Nyx shook her head. "It's perfect. I love it. It's like having part of the beach with me." She was struck by a sudden, deep yearning. "I always wanted to see the ocean, but I never got to."

She heard the sound of the kitchen knife as it slipped. Seth cursed and jerked his hand up. Bright red blood welled from a cut on his thumb, crimson liquid splashing onto the cutting board.

"Are you okay?" Nyx grabbed a clean kitchen towel.

"It's fine." Seth stared at the running blood. Just stood there and stared, his face blank.

"How deep is it?" Nyx reached for his hand. He pulled away, splattering blood all over the floor.

"I said it's *fine*." He swallowed, avoiding her gaze. "There's blood on the okra. I need to get more from the cellar." He walked out, wrapping the bottom of his shirt around his hand as he went.

Nyx looked at the mountain of chopped okra on the counter. The only bit of it that had gotten bloody was what lay on the cutting board. They didn't need more, and there wasn't any in the cellar even if they did. And if there had been, the Station would have pulled it for him.

Griff hopped up next to her, hesitating before he asked, "Was it something I did?"

"It's not you. And it's not me, exactly, either." But Seth didn't make mistakes with sharp bladed objects unless something seriously distracted him, and he'd made that slip right after she'd said she never got to go to the ocean.

I got excited when you remembered Washington…

Washington had the shoreline closest to Montana. She closed her eyes. Maybe she'd seen the ocean after all. Maybe he'd taken her to see the ocean.

"Should we go after him?" Griff asked.

"No," Nyx said softly. "It's best to just give him space when he gets like this."

Seth had been dealing with disappointed hopes his entire life, and he internalized his emotions out of a ruthless sense of self-preservation. She would only be salt in the wound right now.

Later, once he'd worked through what he was feeling, he would talk to her. Maybe he'd tell her what was so important about Washington, if she asked. Except she didn't want to ask, didn't want to be told the pieces of her life like they were a story that had happened to someone else.

She wanted to remember them. She *had* remembered this one. So why had she forgotten again?

The pot on the stove hissed, a loud pop sending thick liquid burping onto the stovetop. Nyx broke from her trance and turned the burner down, stirring the liquid.

"Come on," she said, forcing brightness into her voice. "I can finish this from here." She scooped up handfuls of okra and dumped them into the pot.

Griff moved nearer the stove, but she had the impression his focus was elsewhere, his head canted. "Did anything else happen while I was gone?" he asked. "With the Station?"

Nyx slowly stirred the stew, mixing the okra in. "No. Why? Is something wrong?"

"Not...wrong, precisely. Kaliaris is asleep."

"Asleep?" she echoed. Griff had told her once that Kaliaris sometimes slept and dreamed, and that when he did, Griff caught glimpses of those dreams. "I haven't felt anything different."

"You are...not bound to them in quite the same manner I am. You are connected to them, the exchange symbiotic, but you do not feel their emotions, or see what they dream. I do. I always have. They sleep now. Lightly, but they sleep."

"And that worries you?"

He hesitated. "Kaliaris does not sleep often. Once a century, at most, and I can always feel it coming. I received no indication they would do so any time soon, and they are vulnerable while they do. I merely find it surprising that Kaliaris would choose to rest while I was gone."

Nyx searched her connection with the Station, trying to suss out what Griff sensed that told him the Station slept. But nothing felt different to her. When she wanted the Station to act or change, it did. Although, making such alterations felt a little easier than usual. She'd suspected, based on her practice and Griff's instruction, that Kaliaris actively worked to make her use of the bond difficult. So if they were asleep, it made sense that her ability to manipulate things would be easier.

"Maybe they're starting to trust me a little?" she suggested.

"Perhaps." It didn't sound like Griff believed it any more than she did. Kaliaris had not felt markedly friendlier toward her of late.

"Should we be concerned?"

Griff shook his head. "Nothing is materially changed. While Kaliaris sleeps, we are simply in charge of all defenses. My bond to them has never been affected during these periods, and it is not now. Perhaps the addition of your bond, and the larger number of people they have hosted in the past few months, has tired them. You have brought far more excitement to them than they have seen in a few hundred years."

Nyx nodded while her brain helpfully supplied worst-case-scenario possibilities. The darkness Calista had warned her of came to mind first, but nothing was inside her Station. Nothing bad had happened to anyone she loved.

"If you needed to wake Kaliaris, could you?"

Griff considered the question. "I have never tried. But should it prove necessary, I believe so. Are *you* concerned?"

"Just paranoid, probably." The timer dinged. Nyx donned a pair of oven mitts and removed the cornbread from the oven.

Seth walked back in. His injured hand was bandaged, and he gave her a rueful smile, scuffing the toe of his boot on the floor. "So, uh, shockingly, there wasn't any okra in the cellar."

She accepted it for the apology it was. "Well, shockingly, you didn't get blood on much of the okra up here, so I finished everything. Let's eat."

The three of them settled around the bar together, good food working its magic of loosening tensions and easing fears. Seth wasn't upset with *her*, and she wasn't upset with him. Things were just weird, because their situation was weird.

And Kaliaris probably *was* just tired. She'd been putting the Station through its paces pretty much non-stop since she took over the Guardianship. What with opening the Den, adding herself to the bond, and housing a wide array of martially-inclined individuals with hair-thin tempers who'd frequently needed to be separated.

Everything was fine. She would just stay on high alert until Kaliaris woke, and ensure that everything *stayed* fine.

4

"Are you trying to insult me?" Evra demanded of Morgen. She was kitted out in full combat gear in preparation for the morning's charity competition, and if her tone was any more scathing it would start blistering flesh.

"No, I am not trying to insult you." Morgen's voice, while usually calm and measured, had reached heretofore unknown levels of calm that Nyx strongly suspected meant he was on the verge of truly losing his temper. "I am trying to be the bigger person here. If my competing in the event today will be a problem, Seth and I will withdraw."

Nyx and Seth had managed to share one peaceful cup of morning coffee, during which they both pretended that everything was normal, before Morgen and Evra had descended upon the kitchen, bickering furiously.

What was with their sudden insistence on ruining the kitchen peace? If this kept up, Nyx was creating a no-arguing-in-the-kitchen rule, and so help her universe, its institution would come with adorable signs stating the many horrible consequences that would be incurred by anyone who dared break the peace.

"If you are scared to compete against me," Evra said, "you need only say so."

Morgen gripped a handful of the tight braids at his scalp. If Evra actually drove Morgen to ripping out his beautiful hair, Nyx was going to have to intervene.

"For love of all that is holy in this universe, woman, I am not *scared*. I am trying to be considerate."

Nyx shot Seth a pleading, barely-caffeinated glance. Trying to stop this argument with logic was doomed to fail, but if anyone could redirect Evra or Morgen's attention, and make them *forget* they were arguing, it was Seth.

He gave her his, okay-okay-fine-but-you-owe-me look in response, and cleared his throat. "And because we all know that I am the most considerate of considerate people, if you want to back out, Nyxi darling, I completely understand. My record of trouncing you in backwoods survival training is unblemished."

Evra halted the tirade that had undoubtedly been about to come out of her mouth, and spun to Seth with an incredulous look on her face. "*You* did well in survival training?"

Nyx snorted at Evra's skepticism. Seth wasn't just an Illusionist in the magical sense; he'd embraced the idea in every aspect of his life. He had the unparalleled ability to make literally everything he did look lazy and careless, so no one ever took him seriously, or realized just how smart he actually was.

He *looked* like if you dumped him into the woods for survival training, he would wander around aimlessly, whistling a merry tune and waiting for the good hand of fortune to guide him back to civilization. If he happened upon a bear or other dangerous wildlife in the meantime, he might attempt to pat them on the head and share his dinner with them.

Nyx picked up the thread, intent on keeping Evra distracted. "You were good," she admitted, "but you only came out ahead all the time because you layered so many confusion spells over everything that my freaking compass wouldn't even work. And if I tried to look at the sun it was *always* on the left, no matter which direction I turned."

She regretted the words the instant she said them. Normally, when these randomly-remembered bits tumbled out of her unbidden, they made her happy. They made Seth happy. But after the conversation they'd had yesterday, it kind of just hurt.

He opened his mouth, then closed it. Nyx ducked her head to the side, but it was too late to avoid the commingled flash of hope and disappointment and frustration on his face.

The change in mood wasn't lost on the other people in the room and Evra—bless her for snapping fully out of her anger now that she recognized Nyx was in a rough spot—steered the conversation in a different direction. She fell back on the prearranged tactic they'd determined for the Hunger Games competition, looking Nyx over like she'd just noticed Nyx's ensemble. "Please tell me that is not what you were planning on wearing?"

"What?" Nyx looked down at an updated version of the garb she'd worn to the Shadow Market. Her pants and long-sleeved shirt were spelled Talorean cloth that was difficult to rip or tear, exceptionally flexible for ease of movement—such as jumping and running through an obstacle course—and was resistant to staining. "It's perfectly functional. It's a brilliant choice, really."

She'd thrown on the mercury boots from the Station's Den for good measure. Griff had grumbled about it, but it had been a resigned grumble of acceptance rather than one actually intended to keep her from wearing them, since she'd been wearing them a lot lately. For practice, of course.

Evra waved a hand in dismissal. "The clothes are fine. Your weaponry and survival gear is lacking."

"The maximum time to complete any of the rounds is fifteen minutes. It's not like I'm going to be tied to the side of a cliff in a rainstorm for five days, praying for flint to make a fire."

Seth recovered, plastering his happy-go-lucky grin back on his face and clapped her on the shoulder. "You know, it's that excessively optimistic attitude that made living with you in the middle of nowhere both inspiring and irritating beyond measure."

Nyx looked at him dubiously. "I'm pretty sure no one's ever accused me of being excessively optimistic before."

"Well, *I* have," he said, as if that settled the matter.

"You," Evra jabbed a finger at Nyx. "Come with me. Let us see if we cannot scrounge up some appropriate competition gear in the time we have left."

Evra grabbed her wrist and dragged her bodily from the room, which Nyx allowed until they were safely out of sight of Seth and Morgen. Then she rearranged the Station's hallways and brought them to the alcove where they'd stored a pre-packed bag of absolutely everything Nyx might find useful in today's competition.

"Do you think they bought it?" Nyx asked, strapping on an assortment of weapons and other items.

"Difficult to say. Seth seemed like he did, but he does know you well, and he might just be appearing to have bought in an attempt to put *us* at ease, since we *think* he bought it."

"That was exceptionally convoluted."

"Yes, well, strategy comes in two forms: simple and unbearably complex. We're in the latter."

Nyx finished gearing up and led the way to the back of the Station, where two of Earth Between's Gliblin riding birds were waiting to take them to the competitor's check-in down in Earth Between proper. With any luck, they would avoid being seen by Seth or Morgen before the competition actually started.

"You know I detest speaking of relationship issues," Evra said casually, slipping her foot into the Gliblin's stirrup and mounting with easy grace.

"I do. It's one of the things I love most about you."

"But I was recently informed that I have the emotional depth of a rock, and—"

"*Morgen* said you have the emotional depth of a rock?" Nyx asked, outraged as she swung atop her own mount. She scratched its feathers at the apex of its shoulders, right where a horse's withers would be, and was rewarded with a cooing chirrup noise.

"Of course not. He said a lot of flowery language about the stoicism of Amazons, and how noble it is that we have such excellent control over our inner feelings, but sometimes it leads others to be confused about what we want. Which amounts to saying that I have the emotional depth of a rock."

"I don't think that's what he meant."

Evra waved her off. "It is immaterial. The point is, I am attempting to express my concern, as apparently 'normal human beings' are expected to do." Evra had picked up Nyx's habit of using air quotes.

Huh. Nyx gave the Gliblin a gentle squeeze with her legs and it ambled off down the path to Earth Between, Evra's Gliblin falling in step next to it. "And what exactly are you expressing concern about?"

"You and Seth are acting strangely toward one another."

"We're being how we are every day."

"You are forcing how you normally are every day in some strange sort of caricature of the real thing. Did something happen?"

"Apparently. I just don't remember it." Nyx realized how that sounded when Evra's eyes narrowed, and rushed to explain. "What I mean is, apparently I remembered something that made Seth really happy, and then I forgot it again, along with the entire memory of remembering it."

Evra was quiet for a long beat. "Your mother?"

Nyx shrugged. "I don't know, honestly. Look, thanks for asking. It actually means a lot. But I don't really want to talk about it right now. I can't *do* anything about it, so I'd kind of like to just keep faking the happy, if it's all the same to you."

"If that is what you desire."

"Did you want to talk about Morgen?"

"Of course not," Evra said. "I do not care about anything that he does or does not do."

Nyx waited a beat.

"It is just that he is so *infuriating*."

"But you don't care?"

"Absolutely not. I simply do not understand. Why go to all the trouble he went to, and then expect *me* to take the final initiative?"

"Maybe *because* he went to all the initial trouble?" Nyx suggested.

Evra frowned. "Elaborate."

"Well, if you spend a lot of time showering someone with affection, and the end result is that they finally deign to grace you with an acceptance of their offer, it isn't the super encouraging result most people hope for."

Evra thought it over, frowning in a way that seemed to encompass not just her facial expression, but the entire attitude of her body. "So you believe, then, that I have not only hurt his feelings but also made him feel slighted and unworthy?"

"Something along those lines, yes."

Evra heaved a great, discontented sigh. "Shit."

"What did you *think* was going on with him?"

"If you must know—"

"I must."

"—I always feared I was nothing more than a fun chase. That if I ever returned his attention, he would no longer be interested."

"He faced your *mother* for you. I hear she's kind of a big deal."

"He had his pride to consider on that account. He said he would do it, so he did. After, when he never picked a date, I believed I was right all along. Should he not know that? Is he not supposed to be *good* at dating?"

Nyx bit her lip. "If I tell you something, you are sworn to vault it for all eternity."

"Vault it?"

"It means if you ever tell *anyone* I told you, you are condemned to best friend hell."

"That is actually a place?"

"If it isn't, it should be. Do we have a deal or not?"

Evra nodded. "I will give you my oath of silence."

"Okay. Morgen's never been in a relationship."

Evra jerked so hard she pulled on her Gliblin's reins and had to spend a few seconds apologizing and fussing over the poor guy. "What leads you to this belief?" she asked, once the Gliblin was settled.

"He told me. When he was being all mopey because he thought you and Bryn were getting back together. He is experienced in the ways of physical pleasure and innocent in the ways of love."

Evra scowled. "You have the most ridiculous ways of saying things, sometimes."

"It's not my fault you don't appreciate poetic speech. So are you going to fix this?"

Evra grimaced. "Yes. I will...apologize." She bit off the word like it was the most vehemently unpleasant thing a person could be called upon to do. "Are we finished discussing our emotions now?"

Only Evra. "Sure." Nyx nudged the Gliblin into a trot. "Now let's go kick both of our non-boyfriends' asses for the sake of charity."

***

"**Y**ou are nearly *late*," the Warlock hissed as Nyx and Evra finished scratching their names onto the check-in sheet while shooting glances over their shoulders, keeping a lookout for Morgen and Seth.

"I'm sorry, we—"

"No time," Ankira barked. "Over there, in your positions, right now."

The competition space was on the far north side of Earth Between, in a flat, open area that probably would have been the designated fairgrounds or Renaissance Festival space had it existed next to a city in Dead Earth. Bleachers occupied three sides of a rectangular area large enough that two football fields could have fit inside it with room to spare. It was shrouded in opaque black mist that prevented anyone from seeing what lay within, and did so with an ominous flair.

The competitors lined the fourth side of the area, each team standing on a designated square that had their team's number painted on it. Ankira pointed Nyx and Evra to the thirteenth square and shooed them off.

Morgen and Seth were earlier up the line, team number seven. Morgen, still technically being a wanted fugitive and all, had signed up under the name of one of Beauregard's soldiers. Jim Beauregard—Morgen's uncle—was the proud owner of a castle and a standing private army. The soldiers in that army often wore full-face masks in Earth Between, even when they weren't on duty, and thus provided the perfect alias for a man trying to stay off the radar.

Morgen and Seth were surveying the rest of the competition and talking low, their lips barely moving. She noted Seth's hand was no longer bandaged, something she'd missed earlier, and the knife wound was healed over. Griff had sent him down to Ankira's shop last night for a few items, and Tobi had obviously gotten ahold of him.

Diana and Ankira were trying to rein in Tobi's tendency to impulse heal everyone he cared about, but the former prison-planet kid had a near-unstoppable need to heal. It was in his nature, and since he'd taken to Seth pretty quick after they met, no force in Earth Between would have stopped him from fixing the cut once he'd seen it.

Nyx scanned the other competitors. There were fourteen teams in total, and every single one of them looked like they were taking things far too seriously for a simple charity competition. One of the people in team number nine turned, also surveying the lineup, and Nyx realized it was Lauralyn, standing next to Diana.

"Is it legal for the Warlock's wife to compete in her annual charity event?" Nyx joked.

"The Warlock does not own the competition, she simply runs it. Effectively and with great ruthlessness. Still, I believe Diana is only competing because Lauralyn asked her to."

Ankira chose that moment to take her place at the announcer's podium, facing the rows of crowded bleachers. It looked like everyone in Earth Between had turned out for the event. Ankira's fingertips brushed her throat, and even from ten feet away, Nyx could feel the gentle tinge of magic that came with the brushstrokes. When Ankira spoke, her voice was carried as if by the aid of a good microphone and many, many hidden speakers.

"Welcome," Ankira said and, casting a brief glance at Nyx, deadpanned,"to the fifth annual Hunger Games."

She said it so stately, so seriously, so exactly like the actress for Effie Trinket had said it in the movie version, that Nyx couldn't help it. She laughed. She quickly turned it into a snort, then a hacking cough at the glares of literally every other team member in the games.

Well, except Morgen and Seth. Morgen had covered his face with his hand, as if embarrassed that someone might know he knew the laughing woman. Which was ridiculous considering he was wearing a mask that literally covered his entire face already. Seth was giving her his patented half-smile, while his eyes danced with laughter.

She tuned back into Ankira's speech just as she said, "I give you this year's first course." With a flourish of her hand, the mist surrounding the first third of the area vanished, revealing...

"Is she trying to raise money for charity, or kill us?" Nyx whispered.

"Who says she cannot do both?" Evra retorted.

Factually, Nyx understood that no one would die. She'd

looked over the approximately eight-billion safety certifications this event had gone through to be legal. There were dozens of safeguards, highly-trained medical personnel were on standby, and all of the competitors had to pass medical and basic competence exams before being allowed to compete.

Magic could fix a lot of things. It could also break a lot of them. The medical staff were here to do the former, and the course was here to do the latter. Nyx had seen the injury list from the previous four competitions and thus knew that burns, boils, broken bones, and other exciting injuries were not out of the realm of possibility. Examining the course, she moved broken bones to the top of her list of likely outcomes.

A sheer vertical cliff face jutted from the ground, extending one-hundred feet into the air. Nyx listened while Ankira explained that the ground on the other side dropped fifty feet lower , making for a one-hundred-and-fifty-foot fall from the top. Once they reached the precipice, they would need to traverse ten rows of floating beams and planks that traveled back and forth on the other side. Looking at the helpful model image Ankira conjured, the setup reminded Nyx of nothing so much as the vintage *Frogger* game, except that here some of the rows were higher or lower than others.

On the opposite end of the floating log river was another wall, but Nyx couldn't make out what was on the other side of it. Nyx guessed surprise was some part of the challenge of the course, because Ankira didn't elaborate on that section, other than to point out a vague spot in the distance where a row of pennant flags waved in the breeze.

"Remember," Ankira said, turning to the teams. "You have fifteen minutes to reach your team's flag at the end of the first course. Flags will self-destruct unless you have claimed them before the time is up. Every team who claims their flag will advance to the second round, and point bonuses will be given to teams who come in under time.

"I must remind everyone that the first round allows no

personal contact with any competitor other than your own team member. Anyone who breaks this rule will have their team forfeit the competition. May fortune smile upon you, and may the best team emerge victorious."

Was Ankira *trying* to sound ominous?

The competition master stepped to the side and flicked her fingers. A deep, resonant sound, like the striking of a gong, filled the air and the teams took off.

5

___

Nyx sprinted alongside the other competitors, straight for the wall in front of them. Evra reached it a hair ahead of Nyx and scaled it as easily as if the cliff face was horizontal rather than vertical.

Nyx followed. She was less graceful than Evra but she had, at Evra's insistence, spent a lot of time on a climbing wall in the Station's gym leading up to this event. The skill had come naturally, the ability to pick out good handholds and footholds without instruction telling her that climbing things had been some part of her youthful training.

She did not have an ingrained fear of heights, but she also didn't have the daredevil's *lack* of fear of them, and climbing a hundred foot cliff face with no ropes put her inner survival instincts on high alert.

But wind mages were stationed to either side, ready to catch falling competitors, and Nyx shook off natural concern and pressed higher. She was grateful for the thin cloth of her gloves, which allowed maximum dexterity while the well-woven cloth provided protection from the roughness of the rocks. She ignored the desire to look over and see how Seth and Morgen fared, keeping the whole of her focus on finding the next hand or foothold.

She reached the precipice not too far behind Evra, her breathing hard, and swallowed. The precipice wasn't simply narrow, it was knife-thin, and the opposite side of it was not only completely vertical, it was smooth as glass. If she tipped over, there would be nothing to hold onto, no chance of climbing back up. She would fall straight to the netting at the bottom, and she and Evra would be scratched from the competition.

She gripped the top of the wall, found a couple new footholds, and pushed. Her arms extended fully, raising her waist above the precipice. The first row of moving beams floated three feet away, on level with the clifftop. Each beam was approximately six feet long and perfectly round, maybe six inches in diameter. Four feet of empty space separated each beam from the next. They traveled in one direction at a lazy rate until they hit an invisible barrier and reversed direction.

"I do not think going for the same beam is wise," Evra observed. "We work well together, but we do not have the kind of synchronicity needed to do this in tandem. Are you opposed to me heading across first and you following?"

"Nope." She was fully happy to watch Evra conquer, take notes, and benefit from the Amazon doing the trailblazing.

Evra drew both feet onto the thin precipice, her hands resting between her boots. Crouched with the world's best balance, she waited until the next beam floated by. She jumped and caught. Her hands landed near to the center but not quite there, a little to the left, and the beam tipped down to that side, as if it was held up by an invisible string in the middle, and any weight that was not perfectly centered would drag it down. Evra inched her hands to the right, re-balancing.

Below the log Evra hung from, a floating wooden plank moved perpendicular, coming directly underneath the log for a single second before reversing direction. In that second, Evra dropped, landing in a wide-legged stance that centered the plank, which naturally had the same balance requirement as the log.

"Well, fuck," Nyx muttered. Crossing an air lake of floating logs and planks had sounded difficult enough if they were perfectly stable. Gymnastics were not her forte.

"You can always pull that forfeit ribbon," Seth purred an inch from her ear.

Nyx jumped and pitched forward, nearly toppling over the side of the cliff before she regained her balance. Adrenaline shot through her, because *rationally* knowing she wouldn't die if she fell did nothing to convince her body of that fact.

"I hate you so hard right now," she told him. How had he even gotten over to her side of the cliff? There had been six competitors between him and her. Had he gone to the trouble to do a diagonal climb up just so he could arrive next to her to scare the living daylights out of her?

Yes, yes, of *course* he had. It was what Seth did.

He laughed. "If you want me to hold your hand, all you have to do is ask."

Well, considering that if he touched her first, *he* would be the one getting kicked out for breaking the no-contact-in-the-first-round rule... "Would you?"

His hand twitched toward hers, then jerked back. He glared at her. "Nice. Very nice."

"You started it." She swung her legs over the lip, until she was seated rather than crouching, counting the seconds until the next log would be in front of her.

"Technically, you and Evra started it with your psychological warfare." His gaze flickered over her gear. "I notice you don't *seem* last-minute prepared."

Nyx shrugged. "Evra's excellent at picking just the right things in a pinch."

The log neared, and Nyx pressed the soles of her boots to the flat side of the cliff wall, readying. She wasn't confident enough to leap frog off the top like Evra, but the beam was close enough that she could hang off the wall with one hand and make contact with the other.

Beside her, Seth eyed the same log and moved into a similar position. They hung off the cliff, facing each other.

"Don't you even think about it, Seth Connor, that one's mine."

"Don't see your name on it, Nyx Ilera."

The log drifted closer. No way was she skipping this one. She couldn't see past the other end of the log river, which meant she didn't know how long the course was. If she waited the thirty seconds for the next log, she might not make it to the pennants before time ran out.

She readied herself. "Couldn't you have just stayed on your side of the damn cliff?"

"And missed this delightful exchange?"

"I'm taking this one. Back off."

He gave her a wicked grin. "Not a chance."

The center of the log passed between them. They reached for it at the same time. Nyx instinctively went just left of center, and he went just right. As soon as her left hand gripped she shoved off the wall, dangling precariously for a moment before her right hand caught on too.

Seth's movements mirrored hers almost to the second, and they balanced the floating beam like they were on opposite sides of a see-saw.

"See?" He grinned at her. "Fun. We work well together."

She couldn't stop the stupid grin that answered his, but she did snap, "We're competing, dumbass."

She glanced down. The plank row drifted closer. Another two feet and it would be right beneath them.

"The planks have the same balancing issue," she said grudgingly. Because if he insisted on moving with her, his balance affected hers.

"Looks like you're stuck with me," Seth observed.

"Like a cholla cactus," Nyx muttered.

"What's that?"

"Cholla. Jumping cactus that embed their thorny spines in you if you get too close to them, and are then a huge pain in the ass to pull out."

Seth snorted. "If anything in the wider universe is a cholla cactus, it's those things in your face. Ready?"

"Yeah, yeah." The plank came into position and they dropped in tandem, landing on the one-foot-wide plank and dropping into identical crouches for stability, perfectly in sync. She couldn't help thinking about what Evra had said—that she and Nyx didn't have the kind of synchronicity to cross a course like this together.

But Nyx and Seth did, and they weren't even really trying. She didn't have to think about what he would do or when he would do it. She could just feel it.

"You know," Seth observed, "I'm thinking you and I should have paired up for this thing."

Nyx had asked Evra the second the Warlock had conned *her* into competing, and she'd done it because her first instinct had been to ask Seth. But the part of her that was really tired of being risk-averse was coming out. So she said, "Yeah. We should have."

Something dark and hot kindled in his eyes. She wanted to explore it. Just not when she was on a floating plank. And while she'd meant it when she said they should have teamed up, since they *weren't* on the same team, she wasn't any more above using distraction as a tactic than he was. "About that talk we never actually got to have," she said.

"Yeah?"

"I think" —the next beam floated closer and she grinned at him— "you know how much I hate to lose."

"Oh, fuck," he said at the same time she jumped straight up, grabbing onto the other log. She looked down to see him scrambling for the center of the plank, which had tipped straight down on his side and was now wobbling back and forth as he tried to stabilize it.

"You are so dead for that," he yelled.

"Promises, promises," she called back, and put all of her focus into working the rest of the way across the log maze. It was a frustrating course, because there was no way to make any of it go faster. The fastest way to cross it was simply to time every jump perfectly. When she got to the end, the logs were moving so fast that the window to jump from one to the other had dwindled to less than half a second. Twice, she wasn't confident in the timing and waited while the log drifted away and then came back.

But better to be certain than fumble the landing and fail out in the first round. Not to mention she really, really didn't want to fall, safety netting and wind mages or no. She held onto the last beam as it sped toward the wall.

She'd noted from previous observation that it would stop two feet from it and, like the beams on the starting side, it was level with the top of this wall. The easiest thing to do would be to swing herself from the log onto the wall. But since she had no idea what was on the other side, she didn't want to land ass-first and risk tumbling down it.

Which made the best option getting to higher ground on her current ground, so to speak. Nyx repositioned her hands and swung her legs up, ridiculously grateful she lived in a Station full of fitness fanatics, and her core was now in top shape. She crossed her ankles over the beam, inch-worming her position until she was balanced in the center, and then flipped herself onto the top. From her new vantage point she had an unobstructed view of what lay on the other side when the beam drew close.

"Well, shit." She had a split second to decide whether to go for it, or wait another cycle to process and plan. The timer on her watch said she had less than a minute to complete the course.

Besides, Seth was now on the row next to her, having obviously taken first jumps at every opportunity to catch up. So when her window came, she pushed off the beam and onto the top of the wall.

Even calling it a wall was potentially misleading. The side she hadn't been able to see before landing atop it was basically a giant slide. A deep mud pit waited at the bottom, and falling into it would mean instant dismissal. Her goal wasn't to reach the bottom of this wall, but the disconnected, floating island suspended midway down.

The team pennants waved at her from the island. The only way to reach it was to make her way down the slide to one of the ramps that stuck out of its side. She would need to hit the ramp at the right speed and trajectory for it to propel her across the ten feet of empty space between the ramp and the floating island. Standing in the way of her and a smooth glide to one of those narrow ramps were bumpy outcroppings that sprouted from the wall at random. If she hit one, not only would it hurt like a sonofabitch, it would be an almost-guaranteed tumble into the mud pit.

She could slide down on her butt, but she wouldn't be able to avoid those outcroppings. If she grabbed hold of one and tried to drop from handhold to handhold, she wouldn't get to a ramp with enough speed to reach the island.

She considered the slide wall. It was steep, but not *too* steep, and it was smooth. Not smooth like a metal playground slide, where shoe soles would stick, but smooth like ice. Testing, she glided the bottom of her boot across the side. No resistance.

Sincerely hoping she was not about to end up in a lot of mud, Nyx got her feet beneath her. *Just like skiing,* she told herself. Which would be a lot more comforting if she knew whether or not she'd ever been skiing.

She let go of the wall.

She'd expected to slide fast, but fast had nothing on the reality of it. She crouched low, her knees bent, aimed straight at the ramp below. The outcroppings on the wall were all short enough they passed easily between her legs, but she almost lost her balance a couple times when she had to widen or narrow her stance to avoid ones that would have hit her feet.

She'd just recovered from her last adjustment when she approached the ramp. In her peripheral vision, someone on the island—Evra—waved their hands and urgently shouted something. Nyx made out the words just as she dropped to her ass, the ramp narrow enough she could sling her legs to either side of it like riding a horse, and hit it at full speed.

"*You're going too fast,*" Evra shouted.

There was a belly-dropping moment as Nyx went airborne, and then the floating island was flying at her. Or rather, she was flying at it, and she had indeed hit the ramp too fast.

She landed halfway across the six-foot-wide island, which was every bit as slick as the slide wall had been, and kept sliding. Right off the other side. At least, she would have, if Evra hadn't driven an enchanted dagger into the floor of the island, dropped to her knees, and grabbed Nyx's arm as she slid by.

For one horrifying moment Nyx thought the strain would break the dagger's blade and send them both tumbling off the side. The metal flexed alarmingly, then held, and Evra wasted no time in hauling Nyx to her feet. Together, they slipped and slid their way to the ground where their team pennant was planted, and grasped the flagpole with fifteen seconds to spare on the clock.

Their victory was a short-lived affair. So short, in fact, she didn't even have time to look around and see which other teams had made it, and if Seth and Morgen were among them. As soon as the timer on the round wound down to zero, the island plummeted, dropping to the bottom of the mud pit and sliding over, tilting up on its side to dump the round one victors onto the single foot of dry ground between the mud and what looked like multiple cave entrances.

Ankira's disembodied voice floated melodically across the air. "Congratulations teams one, three, four, six, nine, eleven, twelve, and thirteen. Remember that in rounds two and three, inter-team interference is allowable, though the use of bladed weaponry on fellow competitors is strictly forbidden. When you hear the gong, begin round two by entering the caverns. Good luck."

Her voice had barely cut off when the gong sounded, and Nyx and Evra darted into the cavern entrance directly in front of them. Complete darkness engulfed them.

"Bless you, Shadow Market," Nyx muttered as she pulled a penlight from the side-pocket of her pants. Her brief stint in the universe's dark underworld—literally, as much of the city had been belowground—had made her realize the wisdom of always traveling with a flashlight.

She clicked it on. At the same time the bright white of her flashlight illuminated the cave, a softer, hypnotic blue light flared to life. The magic pulsing through that light beckoned. Unable to help herself, Nyx took a step toward it just as a tall form appeared silhouetted in the blue.

"Nyx!" Evra yelled and lunged for her.

Nyx knew she should move, but she couldn't. The magic called to her too strongly, emanating the same, euphoric promise the ley lines held. Her mind screamed at her to flee, that this wasn't a part of the games. Her body leaned in, starved for the magic's touch.

The silhouetted form grabbed her arm, yanking her into them and out of Evra's reach. Portal magic wrapped her in its embrace, and the already dark world dissolved as she fell through to somewhere *else*.

6

———

Seth emerged on the other side of the caverns, unable to shake the feeling that something was wrong. That feeling had nothing to do with the maze of traps they'd navigated their way through to complete the second round. He didn't know *what* it was from. He was fine, Morgen was fine, and yet the belief that something terrible had happened persisted.

When Evra stalked up to them, her face grim as she pulled her forfeit ribbon, the nagging worry in his chest coalesced into a hard knot.

"Where's Nyx?" he asked.

"She's gone."

Seth yanked his own forfeit ribbon free. "What do you mean she's gone?"

"Not dead," Evra said quickly, but the way she said it didn't do anything to reassure him.

"Then where is she?"

"I don't know."

"How can you not know? Is she in the caves?" He moved for the cave mouth they'd just exited, and Morgen moved with him. Evra grabbed both their wrists, hauling them back.

"She is not in there."

His frustration mounted, the beat of his heart too heavy, too fast. "Then where?"

She leaned in, her voice low, as if she was afraid someone would hear even though no one was around. The other competitors had long since left them in the dust. "Someone portaled into the caves. Right in front of her. They portaled her out within seconds."

Seth heard the words, but they didn't compute. "Portal stones aren't that accurate. They don't just take you where you want to go, they're specified to locations. Certainly not to people. This is...something to do with the game." It was the only explanation that made sense.

Evra didn't contradict him, but her silence spoke volumes. It wasn't that he doubted what she *believed* she'd seen. But he understood how well illusion could trick, and he'd spent the last seven years of his life navigating the universe via portal stones. He knew damn well how they did and didn't work. *Something* had happened, and it was clearly something that had gone wrong with the games. Something that could be fixed. "I'm going to find the Warlock."

This part of the course was level with the rest of the ground, and exiting the competition was as easy as walking past the painted boundary that meant an immediate forfeit if you hadn't already done so. Morgen and Evra followed on his heels, the crowd murmuring around them, no doubt speculating on why three apparently uninjured contestants had just quit. And where their fourth member was.

He didn't have to look for the Warlock. She found him, her expression grave, and oddly enough that made him relax. It meant she already knew something was wrong. Something she could presumably fix.

"Are you searching the caves?" he demanded. "What happened? Where is she?"

Ankira was silent for a beat. "She isn't in the caves. She isn't anywhere on the course."

"She has to be."

"Every inch of the course is monitored by energy mages, and the identifying signature of each competitor was recorded prior to the start of the games. After Nyx and Evra entered the caves, the energy mage monitoring that section of the course reported a third, unknown individual. Before another mage could arrive to verify the report, the unknown individual and Nyx were gone."

Her eyes demanded an answer, as if *he* was somehow more likely to have an explanation than she was. What she'd said wasn't possible. Except...except Nyx had held the portal open when they'd come back from the Shadow Market. She'd used portal magic in a way he'd never seen it used before.

She'd been excited by that aspect of her magic, something she hadn't known she had. Excited by Morgen's theory that portal witches originally had to have been able to travel by some other means than spelling stones, else they never could have gotten to another planet in the first place. She'd never gotten to test the theory, because she hadn't had any portal magic with which to test it, but if Morgen was right, then who was to say there wasn't a portal witch out there who still knew how to travel that way?

The Warlock's eyes flicked to Evra. "Were you with her? What did you see?"

"A practical joke," Seth said smoothly, before Evra could respond. "One that resulted in both my and Nyx's teams being expelled from the competition."

The Warlock wasn't stupid. She understood exactly what he wanted from her with that explanation, but she also clearly didn't trust him. "Evra?"

Evra's eyes narrowed on him, but she agreed. "A practical joke. Seth has a tendency to take them too far."

The Warlock let out a frustrated sigh. "What do you expect me to tell the very confused energy mage who witnessed her disappearance?"

"A good Illusionist can fake an energy signature." Seth wiggled his fingers, and a copy of himself did the same, close enough to the Warlock to make her jump. "I'm a very good Illusionist. Tell them whatever you have to, and if they need a demonstration to be convinced, I'll oblige them. But right now I need to go find my—" He cut off. "Nyx. I need to find Nyx."

"Is she going to be all right?" the Warlock asked.

"Yes," he answered, even though he had no idea if it was true. It *had* to be true, so he would make it true. "I need back in the caves."

"Why?"

He didn't answer.

Her shoulders slumped a fraction. "Very well."

She beckoned to one of the goblins who was monitoring the second round and he trotted over. His head barely came to Seth's waist, pointed ears extending above his head. He interlaced his long, spindly fingers, the triple-jointed digits forming an intricate weave that he extended toward them.

Seth, Evra, and Morgen inclined their heads in return. Double-jointed fingers couldn't make the pattern Nijahl just had. Goblins were understanding of this shortcoming of base Human species, so long as they were given some form of polite greeting in return.

"Nijahl," Ankira addressed him, "please escort these three into the caves where contestant twenty-five disappeared."

Nijahl seemed perfectly happy to carry out this request, and unconcerned with the reasons behind it, which was likely why Ankira had chosen him as their guide.

Evra walked alongside him as they followed the goblin, her voice dropping to a low whisper. "I have already told you she is not in the caves."

"And I believe you."

"Then why are we wasting time?"

"I wasn't lying about a good Illusionist being able to fake—or mask—an energy signature. I need to make sure you didn't just *think* you saw her portaled out. If an Illusionist was involved, there will be residual magic I can pick up on."

"And if it was not an Illusionist?"

He didn't answer, and when Evra led him to the spot where Nyx had disappeared, he found nothing to indicate illusion magic at work. "Morgen?" he asked tersely. The half-Siren had a way of seeing magic not all people could, and he'd been studying portal magic.

Morgen hummed a low note, frowned, and shifted a couple notes up before settling on one. His melodic voice filled the cavern, growing in intensity until the very air seemed to drink in the sound and send it back. He repeated the note through a couple breaths, then let it fade.

"I'm sorry, Seth. Evra saw what she saw."

E vra and Morgen were quiet beside him on the way back to the Station. They reached the border and found Griff, pure black and buffalo-sized, pacing agitatedly along its edge. With the chaos thorn linking him to Nyx, and Nyx to the Station, he would have felt it the second she disappeared.

His great eyes were worried. "Nyx?"

It didn't take long to fill the Station's Avatar in, because they didn't truthfully know much. By the end of it, Griff had gone from worried to grave.

"Portal stones don't work in this manner," Seth said, repeating his earlier conviction. "So if she *was* portaled out of that cave, it had to have been by another portal witch."

Morgen hesitated. "I know it was my theory that portal magic must once have been used differently than it is now. But if someone was alive who could do so, don't you think we would have heard about it?"

Seth considered the question. Morgen's theory was that this had been a form of travel before the construction of the ley lines. Before the Stations. *Griff* was from before the Stations. He didn't talk about that time much, and surely if he knew something that could help he would have said so already. But the silence from that side of the room was a little too loud.

"Griff?" Seth asked. "You wouldn't know anything, would you?"

Griff's beak opened, then clicked shut, a garbled noise leaving his throat. "I cannot say."

Seth's eyes narrowed. "What do you mean you can't say?"

"I mean just that. What I *can* say is that I have been alive for a very long time. If you suspect I might know something, consider where I am likely to know it from, and draw your own conclusions."

"The All Council?" Evra asked, a frown in her voice. "But I cannot see one of them—even one acting alone—needing to come after Nyx in such a clandestine manner."

"Neither can I," Morgen agreed.

Seth shook his head. "Right now, the most important thing isn't who took her, but *where* they took her." He hesitated over his next words. Trusting people didn't come easily to him, no matter how much he liked them. But Nyx trusted Evra and Morgen, and Seth needed their help if he was going to get her back. "I have portal stones to every planet in the verse."

For a minute, both of them just stared at him. Then Evra said, "No wonder Bryn wanted to murder you."

"While that is admittedly impressive," Morgen said, "as you've pointed out, we have no idea which planet she's on."

It took Seth a minute to get his next words out. Because he didn't want to say them. He knew of only one potential way to find Nyx. One highly unpleasant, self-absorbed, walking pain in his ass he'd hoped to never see near her again.

He squeezed his eyes shut, and even though he *knew* it was the only chance Nyx had, he almost choked when he said, "How fast can you get Kaden here?"

Nyx tried not to panic. But she couldn't see. She felt herself come out on the other side of a portal, felt it as rough hands dropped her. The clang of a door clicking shut sounded in the darkness, and she ran forward, straight into a row of cold metal bars.

Blinking furiously did nothing to improve her vision, and a momentary fear that she'd somehow gone blind took her. She spun in a slow circle, and her eyes caught on four glowing blue rings. That was when logic cut through and she realized she wasn't having any problem with her vision; she was simply somewhere that didn't have *any* natural light, aside from the rings of blue.

She fumbled for her penlight and nearly dropped it, because it had been clutched in her hand the whole time, her thumb still pressed over the on/off button. She must have turned it off by accident when she was dragged through the portal.

She clicked the button and a sphere of light bathed the stone floor of a prison cell, stretching just beyond the bars to illuminate a pair of black boots.

Nyx jumped back on instinct, even though the boots were on the other side of the cell. Her back hit another set of bars—it was a small cell—and the abrupt hit bumped the path of her light up.

The four glowing blue rings were a set of armbands on a man's forearm. She jumped again when the penlight swept up to the man's face. Not because she recognized him, which she did —it was the man who'd come into the Station's cafe yesterday— but because he was staring directly at her, as if he'd known right where she was in the absolute darkness.

There was something off about him. In the cafe, he'd just seemed like a man saddened by the loss of his wife—a little confused, maybe, but not *too* weird. Now, it was like all the humanity had fled him.

He stared at her, unblinking, his gaze hollow and expressionless. She waited for him to speak, to move, to do anything, but he didn't.

It was so quiet in the space that all she could hear was his breathing and her own, and as the seconds stretched out with no movement from either of them, and no sound to indicate that anything else was alive in the space they shared, the eeriness grew.

Then Nyx felt the familiar tug of her Station's portal. Except it was a thousand times fainter, and it wasn't her portal at all; it was portal *magic*, a thin stream of it the man siphoned from one of the bands. Nyx barely felt the hypnotic pull before it enveloped him and he vanished, leaving Nyx utterly alone.

Nyx didn't need to sweep the flashlight around to know the man was *gone* gone, but she did it anyway. She wished she hadn't.

The penlight she'd purchased boasted one-thousand lumens which, according to the research she'd done after visiting the Shadow Market, was overkill suitable even for caving activities, and should theoretically stretch as far as three-hundred meters, or nearly one-thousand feet. Nyx recited those facts in her head, because it was more calming than looking at what those one-thousand lumens revealed.

What horrified her wasn't the fact that, not only was she in a prison cell, but a full-on prison—row after row of cells stretched to either side of her and, if what she saw across from her was any indication, above and below her as well—it was that her earlier assumption that she and the man had been the only people in this place wasn't entirely accurate. They'd simply been the only *living* people in the place.

The dead were all around her.

7

———

Skeleton after skeleton filled the cells, as if Nyx stood in ancient catacombs rather than...wherever this was. The bones lay on the floor, some with placement indicating the person had died in the fetal position, others laid out flat as if they'd gone to sleep and never woken up.

She stood, rigidly facing the front of her cell, unwilling to turn and discover that hers might be similarly occupied as well. But after a minute of staring at the sheer volume of cells—she counted fifty in the row parallel to hers before they got too far away to accurately count—seeing the number of dead that surrounded her seemed worse than seeing the dead that might be in the cell with her.

Swallowing, she turned in a slow circle. The skeleton in her cell wasn't neatly stretched out. It was a collection of bones in one corner, as if the person had been sitting huddled against the wall when they died, and once time had destroyed the connections between bones, it had fallen into a heap.

Ironically, seeing the skeleton in her own cell calmed her. The rows and rows of them surrounding her were too much, but this one, in here with her, was a clue.

Yes, she ordered herself, *think of it just like that. This is not a pile of bones that was once a person who was left here to die. It's a clue to where you are, and hopefully how you can get out, so treat it like those forensic shows you were so obsessed with a few years ago.*

Thanks to said forensic shows, she knew she had very little likelihood of figuring out with any precision how long ago these people had died. Even in the absence of insects or other small creatures—of which she saw no evidence—the body's own bacteria would start breaking it down upon death, and continue doing so until nothing but the skeleton remained.

As for the bones themselves, they had probably been here a long time—for whatever definition of *long* one chose. This was a sheltered environment in which there was no light, the temperature was cool—maybe sixty-five Fahrenheit—and it was neither overly humid nor overly arid. In short, it felt like any climate-controlled building.

In conditions like these, bones could conceivably last several centuries. Especially if the place held some small preserving magic and, given the pristine condition of the cell bars, Nyx was guessing it did.

Running through all that didn't really help her, aside from getting her brain to run in a more analytical mode. She was in a prison that had likely been abandoned for centuries, and whoever had run it had left all of the inmates here to die. Since no one had ever come here to claim the bodies, the location was most likely either difficult to reach, or it was a very well-kept secret and, once abandoned, had never been rediscovered.

The sense of isolation, the oppressive weight of the place, closed in around her. Despite the gut certainty that she was alone, she found herself calling, "Hello?"

Her voice echoed once before the darkness swallowed it. The only reply was the heavy thud of her pulse in her ears. She gripped the bars of the cell and called again, then again, unable to stop herself. Unable to stop from wondering if she would end up like the person who had been in this cell before her, huddled into a corner until she too was nothing but bones.

The fear of dying, alone and forgotten, was not a new one to her. She had lived with it every day on Dead Earth. But since coming to the Station, that fear had faded. It swamped her again now, the old dread and panic clawing its way up her throat. The knowledge that no one was coming to save her because no one knew she was here.

Nyx gripped the bars so tight her fingers ached, the world narrowing to the rush of blood in her ears, the harsh quickness of her breath.

Just breathe, Nyxi darling. Seth's voice. He wasn't with her, but she heard his words as if he was, the familiarity of them calming.

Think. Her own voice this time. It wasn't quite true that no one knew she was here. *She* knew. The only question was, *where* was here? Because as she released the cell bars and made herself sweep the flashlight's beam over the tattoo on her left hand, the black ink that had formed a five this morning now showed a four.

Wherever Nyx was, it wasn't on Earth.

I f it weren't for Nyx's deep and abiding love of the sports watch, she might have already gone insane. It felt like she'd been trapped in here for days, while the date and time on her watch informed her it had been less than three hours.

Three hours in which she had carefully rationed her use of the flashlight, as the batteries in it would only last for approximately seven. She'd checked every inch of the cell, looking for weak points, but the bars were as shiny and pristine as if they'd been installed yesterday. She'd tested them all anyway, nearly spraining her ankle kicking at the bottom bars, hoping to find one that wasn't anchored properly.

Nothing she'd had on her for the competition—six throwing stars, a thin but very strong length of rope, a few daggers, and the bo staff—were going to help her get out of this cell. It didn't even have a visible lock to try and pick, which was all to the good since she didn't actually know how to pick a lock should the cell have one.

A small sphere hovered high above her reach. It was probably a light source of some kind, but even when she climbed the bars and messed around with it, she couldn't get any light to come on. She sat alone in total darkness, occasionally hitting the button on her watch to light up the dial, taking comfort in the soothing glow of the numbers.

But there was only so much comfort to be had. She was on another planet and, this time, she hadn't the faintest idea which one. She hadn't *planned* to leave Earth, so she had no plan to get back, no portal stone waiting to take her home. She had no idea where the Station on this planet was, or if there even was one. No idea if the planet was even inhabited.

She tucked her knees against her chest and banged her forehead against them, trying to think of something intelligent to do. A burst of portal magic rent the air and she scrambled to her feet, clicking the penlight on as the last flare of magic died. Her abductor stood once more on the other side of the cell, and one thing suddenly became very clear to Nyx.

There—right there—was her means of escape. A person who knew she was here, and who was capable of taking her away.

The man looked more mentally present than he had before, albeit not by much. She resisted the urge to scream at him, because she suspected it would only earn her another vanishing act on his part. She needed a way out of this cell, and she needed a way home. *He* was both of those things.

She took a deep breath and said, "Hi. I'm Nyx. Nyx Fortuna." If she could get him to see her as a person—one with a name and a life—maybe she would have a better chance of coming out of this alive.

"Nyx. I am Laiveran." He responded as if by rote, sounding more like a computer programmed to spit out a response than like a person exchanging a greeting. Then, as if startling from a dream, he shook himself and looked at her like he was seeing her for the first time. His brows knitted together in obvious confusion, and he said, "What are you doing here?"

Her earlier urge to scream at him intensified, but she said, calmly, "You brought me here."

Laiveran canted his head to the side, still staring at her as if she were a puzzle he couldn't put together. "Did I? But why would I—" He broke off, and she wasn't sure if it was because he'd remembered the why, or if he'd just lost the thread of the conversation.

"There was something I needed. There was a girl," he said slowly, "in a shop. I went there... I think I went there." He broke off, then looked directly at her. "There was a girl in a shop," he said again, even slower this time, as if he wasn't telling *her* something, but himself.

His gaze dropped to her chest, to the exact space where the Harvester rested under her shirt. As if he could see it, *feel* it, through both clothing and Hiding.

Realization dawned on her with painful obviousness. Maybe Calista's darkness should have been the first thing she thought of upon being abducted. But then, having never been abducted and dropped in a prison before—at least that she could remember—she'd been a little caught up in the visceral terror of the experience.

She had also, in all her apprehension about the darkness, morphed it into some kind of horrific monster in her mind, one that would come at her straight on, with obvious intent. She hadn't expected it to be a *person*, one who might resort to something as mundane as abduction instead of bludgeoning her over the head with supreme magical force.

As soon as she had the last thought, she wished she could take it back. *Supreme* magical force might not be happening, but some kind of magic was. Strange, whiplike appendages slowly unfurled from the man's chest.

She had no doubt that they were an extension of the man in

some way, but while they originated from his chest, it didn't look like they were attached to his skin. They weren't physical appendages, they were...psychic? The longer she stared at them, the more certain she was that she wasn't even seeing *them*, but the imprint his power left, and her mind was simply forcing that imprint into a shape she could understand.

She backed up to the far wall. The tentacles followed. They did it slowly, waveringly, as if Laiveran still wasn't sure *why* he was doing whatever it was he was doing. But despite the practically glacial pace of the tentacles' progress, they were going to touch her soon and there was nothing she could do about it, nowhere she could hide.

Hide.

Nyx reacted on instinct, following the thread that had shoved the memory at her, and drew in on herself. She didn't even fully realize what she'd done until Laiveran blinked, the momentary clarity that had come into his eyes disappearing. The psychic tentacles vanished and he looked around, searching. Searching for *her*, but not seeing her, just as had happened time and time again to her on Dead Earth.

Swallowing, Nyx took a moment to figure out exactly *where* she had retreated. It had been a mental movement, not a physical one, and she realized, as she poked and prodded at the net of magic she huddled inside, that she had finally discovered, by accident, what she'd been trying to find for months: the physical shell of her mother's Hiding.

It was a fine mesh net, so light and pretty and gossamer thin Nyx wasn't surprised she hadn't found it before. It was the type of thing that would be more difficult to see the more intensely you looked for it, the kind of thing that was more easily felt than seen, even with magical sight.

Jagged holes gaped here and there, where either the Guardian bond, or the chaos thorns, or the unmaking she'd experienced on the ley lines had ripped through sections of her mother's Hiding. She wasn't surprised to see them. She *was* surprised to see them repairing.

Hot fury pulsed from the thorns in Nyx's cheek, a rage that rippled through the net, searing the edges of a tear that had been mending itself back together. She felt another's magic recoil at the hit, as if—as if her mother was *here*. As if Elena Fortuna had some connection linking her to her own Hiding from wherever she was.

When Nyx had made the comment to Seth about her mother fucking with her again, she hadn't actually believed it. Once she'd had time to think about it, she'd assumed the Hiding had been built with some sort of self-repairing capabilities, and that was why her memories never returned with any speed, was how she could have forgotten something she'd only just remembered.

Now, it was all too clear that they weren't returning because, wherever Elena Fortuna was, she was actively pouring everything she had into sewing up those tears. No doubt she'd been sure to concentrate her efforts on keeping from Nyx those parts of her memories that would have been the most useful to her. Like, say, how her Hidden magic functioned.

It must have been hard-won, painstaking work, fighting against Nyx's desperate desire to remember. But now—with Nyx voluntarily inside that web of Hiding, Elena's magic raced along the tears, weaving at a rate that made Nyx dizzy.

Panic clawed at her throat. She couldn't forget again. She *wouldn't*. She wanted to burst out of the net, to run and hope that not too much damage had been done yet. But if she went back out *there*...

The confusion in Laiveran's eyes had gotten worse, and he muttered angrily under his breath, pacing from side to side. Every now and then she caught snatches of words. "...girl... lost...so long..." Then, the one that made her blood turn cold. "Harvester."

He stopped on that final word, staring straight at her even though the weight of her mother's Hiding told Nyx he *didn't* see her. Any feeble hope she'd had that Laiveran wasn't the darkness Calista had warned her of died.

He stalked to the cage, his eyes wildly roving the cell. "Here, she was here, *it* was here."

Go, she thought, *just go.* The holes in the net she huddled inside were repairing so quickly, more quickly than the anger from the chaos thorns could rip them anew. How many memories had she lost in the scant minute she'd unwittingly given her mother free reign to do repairs? Did it even matter? If Laiveran left and she stopped her mother's progress, Nyx was still going to die in this cell. Looking at Laiveran, it was painfully obvious she wouldn't be able to convince him to take her out of here. That hopeful ship had sailed the moment she'd realized he wanted the Harvester.

The glowing bands on his arms caught her attention. *He* wouldn't take her...but he wasn't the only portal witch present. She could manipulate that power too, and those bands—that was portal magic. That was her way home.

Carefully, quietly, she clicked the penlight off. Laiveran didn't react. Or at least, the glowing blue bands on his arm, which were now the only thing she could see, didn't shift position, so she assumed he didn't react. She held her breath and crept forward, until she stood directly in front of him. She squinted—the glow of the bands was so bright up close that it made it difficult to see past it, to see how the bracelets attached, and if one had a clasp that could be flicked open.

If she tried to steal a bracelet and couldn't get it off, she'd catch his attention even inside her Hiding, like the way jumping up and down in front of someone in Dead Earth had allowed her to gain their notice. If she fumbled the theft, Laiveran would know, and she would never get another chance. She stood there waiting, thinking, her lungs screaming with the need to breathe, but she was too afraid to inhale.

Another six small holes closed up in the net of Hiding.

She couldn't afford to let her mother keep working. How far

would Elena take it this time? Would Nyx wake up on the floor of this cell in an hour like she had in that apartment at eighteen, no memory of who she was? No one to explain anything to her?

She steeled herself and reached for the nearest bracelet. But as if he sensed her movement, Laiveran spun in a wild circle, out of reach. The psychic tendrils burst from his chest again, bathing the outside of the cell in soft light. Laiveran stood, shaking, his head gripped between both of his hands.

The top bracelet on his arm glowed brighter, and a thin stream of portal magic flowed out, wrapping around him. Shit. He was going to leave. He might not come back. Nyx might not remember what to do if he did.

She latched onto that part of herself that was drawn to portals and reached for that flow of magic. It was slippery and didn't want to respond, because it already answered the call of another. But a small bit, barely larger than a cotton ball, broke off and floated to her hand just before Laiveran disappeared.

Nyx sucked in a deep lungful of air, clutching the small bit of portal magic to her chest. High on wondrous oxygen, she grasped the largest hole in the Hiding net with metaphorical fingers, ripped it open, and hurled herself out.

Nyx felt like someone had jabbed an ice pick straight through the base of her skull. She dropped to her knees, panting and shaking from tearing at the net to escape its confines. She remembered Seth's words when he'd casually told her he'd taken all his memories back at once. *Knocked me out cold,* he'd said. If she was stubborn enough to want to tear at the net again despite the pain—and she was—she had enough sense not to do it here.

She couldn't afford to be knocked out. Besides, it wasn't as if tearing that section of the Hiding open had flashed a camera-roll of memories before her mind's eye. She was certain she'd regained some, in the way she felt a little more *her*, a little more whole. But people didn't remember things the way film recorded them. People stored memories, and when something happened to make them think of them, they pulled that bit of life out of their brain and relived it. She just had a little more access to that reservoir now.

Even knowing she couldn't dismantle the Hiding right now, she was reluctant to let it go. Especially when, studying the edges of the net, she realized her mother was *still* trying to mend it. Her work was slower now that Nyx was no longer resting complacently inside it, but Elena Fortuna was still trying. And as Nyx followed each strand of carefully-woven magic, she realized just how much her mother had *been* mending it in the last few months.

Everywhere Nyx looked, she found little sections where the magic was newer, shinier, in the same way an actual net, if patched, would show a disparity of color and quality in the patched sections, the newer areas not worn by time and use. It was glaringly obvious that ever since Nyx had punched that first hole and regained *any* sense of who she was, Elena had been actively trying to erase it once again.

It made more than a little sense. She'd never understood why, since she'd broken through the Hiding in the first place, her memories hadn't come back more quickly. Or why the only ones she'd gotten back had been about Seth, and practically none about how her own magic worked.

She was locked in a magical battle of wills with her own mother, and Elena had been strategically letting her win ground in the area most likely to make her happy enough to be distracted: Seth. All the while, her mother had been judiciously guarding the areas pertaining to Nyx's abilities, running along behind and closing up everything she could.

It made Nyx wonder why her mother had taken back the memory Seth said she'd gotten about Washington. Had it been a mistake, or was there something about that memory Elena didn't want her to have?

It didn't matter, Nyx decided, because this ended now. She might not be able to take the risk of bringing the entire net down this instant—she had a feeling doing so would put her out of commission for more than the day Seth had suffered, since his only Hidden memories were of *Nyx*, and Nyx's were eighteen whole years of her life—but she was done letting Elena give her ground only to take it back.

She tied a tether of her own magic to the net, ensuring she could find her way back to it, even if she didn't remember it was there. But she was pretty certain she *would* remember. She settled back against the bars and went to work on the area her mother was busily patching. Nyx traced her finger along the torn edges. In the wake of her touch, the frayed bits cauterized, curling in on themselves and melding together into a whole. They wouldn't unravel anymore on their own, but neither was there anything for Elena to grab hold of and knit back together.

Nyx swore she could feel Elena's frustration from across the galaxy, and laughed. "Fuck you, Mom." The words, spoken to an empty room stars-alone knew where, were oddly liberating. She didn't stop smiling the whole time she moved from tear to tear, cauterizing bits and locking her mother out. It was *Nyx's* own damn mind—her mother had no business there.

She worked until her eyes were dry and grainy and her throat scratchy. Her body ached, and a push of the light-up button on her watch had her blinking at the numbers, certain they couldn't be right. Because if they were, she'd been cauterizing magic fraying for nearly ten hours.

No wonder she felt like shit. She was thirsty, she was hungry, she was tired, and she was mildly surprised Laiveran hadn't reappeared.

She gave the net around her memories one final going over. Her repairs wouldn't stop her mother from trying to close the gaps, but instead of being able to reattach the damaged bits, Elena would have to fabricate wholly new patches to weave in. It would be time-consuming, power-consuming, and it would look ugly. If there was one thing Elena Fortuna hated above all else, it was ugliness. She might make progress, but it would be slow-going, and it wouldn't be enough to stop Nyx from ripping the whole thing apart once she got back home, and it was safe enough to do.

Home. That thought jerked her away from her righteous fury at her mother and centered her squarely back in the present. She looked down at her hand, where the small tuft of portal magic she'd stolen glowed in her palm.

This was her way out. She just had to figure out how to use it. And she had to do it before Laiveran returned.

8

———————

Seth Hawthorne was not a man who liked to wait. It was never an activity he'd been good at. If something had to be done, he preferred to do it himself. Even if it took him longer to do than it would take someone else, at least he was busy with the doing, instead of sitting around on his ass waiting and hoping nothing went wrong.

But some situations in life required delegation. Or rather, there were some situations where his personally doing something was guaranteed to achieve a result opposite of the one he wanted. Convincing Kaden Moor to return to Earth was one such situation. Seth knew that. It hadn't made giving Morgen the portal stones needed to retrieve the Moors, and staying behind while Morgen did the convincing, any easier.

"If you pack anything else in that bag, it will not close," Griff said. The words were spoken in his usual chiding tone, but they lacked true censure.

Seth's fingers stilled on the bag. It was filled with every conceivably-useful medical supply known to mundane and magical existence, because preparing for the worst-case scenario was the only useful thing he could do right now. He wanted to be ready to leave the second Morgen returned.

Whenever that was. It had already been sixteen hours. Seth had dressed in the bootleg set of enforcer armor he'd spent years making aftermarket modifications to. He might not like the enforcer institution, but they had the best armor available. He'd also packed and re-packed everything he considered vital to the trip. About the only other thing he'd done was glamour Griff to look like Nyx, so the Avatar could handle the scheduled batch of Arrivals that had come through an hour ago.

Apparently, the new bond Nyx had created with the Station made it so Griff was capable of fulfilling the Guardian's duties, though letting him do it looking like himself would have raised a red flag from every traveler that came through. Shutting down Arrivals again had seemed like something also guaranteed to raise a red flag and draw the All Council's attention, so Seth had crafted the illusion that Griff *was* Nyx.

It had been so disturbing that the second the Arrival was finished and all the travelers were out the door, Seth ripped the illusion away. Griff was Griff again, and Nyx was still gone.

Griff's wingtip touched Seth's hands where they clenched the bag. "She will be fine."

Seth forced his hands to relax. "Yeah." He tried not to think about what he would do if Kaden refused to help. Or what he would do if Kaden did—could—help. "Yeah, I know."

She would be fine because she was always fine. She would be fine because she was Nyx, and she was clever and stubborn and she totally *would* have beaten him at backwoods survival training if he hadn't cheated. She would be fine because she *had* to be fine, because he didn't know what he would do if she wasn't.

"You should sleep," Griff said. "I will wake you when—" He broke off, his eyes holding that faraway look that both him and Nyx got whenever they were paying attention to something that was happening in some other part of the Station. "Never mind. It appears that *when* is *now*. Morgen has returned."

"Is Kaden with him?" Seth slung the medical bag over his shoulder and picked up another, slimmer bag.

"Yes," Griff answered, as tersely as Seth had asked.

They left Seth's room, pausing to knock at Evra's. The speed with which she answered, and the fact she was completely dressed—which for Evra included having a walking arsenal strapped to her body—told him she hadn't intended on getting any more rest than he had that night.

"Have they returned?" she asked.

He nodded and the three of them descended the stairs, reaching the cafe as the door swung open. Kaden strode in like the world was on fire behind him. He looked pissed. Granted, Seth's limited experience with Kaden Moor was that he always looked pissed. His expression did, however, have an exceptional extra-pissed-off quality to it today.

Morgen followed him through the door, along with a teenage kid Seth would bet money was the Kalvar that Seth, while working the cafe, had disappointed multiple other teenagers by not being.

"You *lost* her?" Kaden demanded.

Seth's hands twitched. If Nyx's fate didn't literally rest in this asshole's hands, he would punch him in his obnoxiously handsome face and enjoy every second of the ensuing throw-down.

"Since Nyx is not an object capable of being misplaced, no, I did not *lose her.*"

Kaden crossed his arms, his stance widening. "What happened?"

It was Evra who rehashed every detail Morgen had undoubtedly already shared. When she was finished, she said, "Do you know who might have taken her?"

It was a question Seth had returned to over and over in the last few hours. Who would have—could have—taken her? *Why* had they taken her? And when none of the answers he could come up with made any sense, he'd assured himself that it didn't matter, so long as they got her back.

Kaden shook his head.

Seth unrolled the slimmer of his two packs and grudgingly slid it across the counter to Kaden. "There's a portal stone in there to every planet in the verse. Tell me where she went."

Kaden didn't respond. Seth knew exactly why—at least, he *suspected* exactly why—but Morgen didn't. Or rather, Morgen probably thought the failure to answer was for other reasons.

Morgen cleared his throat, almost apologetically. "He can't track someone through a portal. No tracker can. I told you that. I only asked him here to help us form a plan of investigation."

Seth locked Kaden's gaze. "Is that right? You can't track her through a portal? Because you did in the Shadow Market. You also found her after the flaying winds. I *know* good tracking. I know there wouldn't have been anything left of her scent, magical or otherwise, to follow after that. Unless, of course, you weren't tracking her in the typical sense at all."

Kaden held Seth's stare, a muscle ticking along his jaw, but he still didn't answer. Morgen looked uneasy, as if he finally understood where Seth was going with all this, and he didn't like it.

"Did you fucking Link to her or not?" Seth's breath caught and held. If Kaden hadn't, Seth had no way to find Nyx. But if he had, Kaden had a connection to Nyx that could never be broken. Once a tracker Linked to something, they could always find it. It was an obsession to them, and they never managed to stay away from that obsession for long. If Kaden had Linked to Nyx...

"He wouldn't do that," Morgen protested. But he said it at the exact moment Kaden said, "Yes."

Seth had guessed. That moment when Kaden and Maruca had shown up in his home in the Shadow Market, he'd guessed.

"Did you tell her?" Seth demanded.

Kaden lifted his chin. "No."

Seth shouldn't be surprised. It didn't seem like Kaden had ever told Nyx anything unless she'd pried it out of him first. With her memories such a mess, she'd never have even known to ask him about this.

"You Linked to her without asking?" The disbelief in Morgen's voice—the reproach—eased a little of the tension from Seth's shoulders. He liked Morgen. But if he'd thought this was okay, their budding friendship wouldn't have survived the fact.

Kaden ran a hand through his hair. His eyes were still hard, and if there was any guilt in him, it didn't show. "Don't make it sound worse than it is."

"When?" Morgen asked.

Kaden shrugged. "Arkadia."

"Why?" Morgen asked.

"It was Arkadia. She could have gotten herself killed going there." He shook his head. "You never should have brought her."

Kaden acted like Nyx was a child who had no idea what she was doing. He underestimated her.

"If she got lost or taken from the group, I needed a guarantee I could find her quickly."

Seth snorted. "And it had nothing to do with the fact the Harvester was hanging around her neck?"

Kaden's eyes narrowed. "How do you know about that?"

"Nyx and I don't have secrets. Maybe you should try it sometime."

Kaden shook his head. "I don't have time for this. What's done is done. Let's just find her." Kaden pulled the pack of portal stones to him. It unrolled into a flat mat with little pockets, each small pouch containing a stone.

"Don't lose them," Seth gritted out. He had duplicates of most of them—but not all.

Kaden started at the first row, running his fingers over each square. Seth was all too familiar with the look Kaden had in his eyes right now, burning hot with the all-consuming need to find what he viewed as *his*. It was the same look Seth's father had gotten every time Elena Fortuna up and disappeared from their lives for a while. It would intensify the longer she stayed gone, until Viktor Hawthorne couldn't take it anymore, and he left to find her and drag her back home.

Knowing what he knew now—what Nyx had told him about what her mother had done—Seth wondered which had come first—his old man Linking to Elena, or Elena using her powers to make him obsessed with her.

What was it with Hounds and the Hidden, anyway? Were they cosmically drawn to each other, or did Seth just have the misfortune to be smack in the middle of two unhealthy relationships of the type?

Kaden was halfway through the portal stones now, and Seth was growing anxious. They were organized in order of planets most visited to least, and while it didn't necessarily mean anything that she wasn't on a well-trafficked planet, he couldn't stop the sense of foreboding it brought. A kidnapper wouldn't have qualms about going to the far reaches of the universe, but every stone Kaden's fingers passed over without so much as a twitch felt like one settling into Seth's gut.

Kaden was almost through them all, and the planets his fingers were passing over now...calling them seedy was being polite. If Nyx was on one of them...

But then Kaden's hand was passing over the final stone and he was shaking his head, shoving the pack back at Seth. "She's not there."

"What do you mean she's not there? It's every planet in the verse." He'd been exceptionally thorough in his ransacking of the Shadow Keep's stores. "She has to be on one of them." Unless...he felt the blood drain from his face. "Is she—" He couldn't finish the sentence. Because she couldn't be dead. He would know, wouldn't he? He might not have some magical Link to her, but the universe would feel different without her in it. And the Station—Griff. If Nyx was gone, they'd be showing signs, they would be—

"She's not dead," Kaden said sharply.

Some measure of feeling returned to Seth's limbs. "Then where is she?"

"I don't know. I just know that she's not here, and she's not *there*." He pointed at the portal stones.

"She has to be on one of them. I already told you, it's every planet. Look again." Seth *knew* it was pointless, knew it by the resigned look on Kaden's face as he turned back to the pack.

But Griff interrupted him. "That is *not* every planet." Before Seth could even open his mouth to argue, Griff continued, "That is every ley-line-connected planet."

"What else is there?" Evra asked.

"The rest of the universe," a cool voice said.

Jevryn A-Morridahn stood in the doorway. Seth hadn't heard the door open, and gathering by the looks on everyone else's faces as they turned to stare, neither had they.

For a moment, Seth didn't react. He couldn't. To him—and almost everyone else in the verse—the people that comprised the All Council were more myth than reality. He only recognized Jevryn because he'd looked him up after Nyx told him she'd reached out to the councilor. Which must be why he was here now, only Nyx wasn't around for him to speak with.

An amused smile curled Jevryn's lips, and that was the moment Seth realized he *had* reacted—everyone in the room had. With the exception of Griff, everyone had a weapon of some kind in hand. Well, technically, Kalvar had just unsheathed his claws. So he didn't have a weapon in hand, so much as his hands *were* weapons.

They had all done about the stupidest thing they could do in the presence of a councilor—threatened him—and none of them could seem to make themselves stop doing it. Not that Jevryn appeared concerned. His fingers twitched a fraction, a small spark at their tips, and Griff—who until that moment had been completely unconcerned—exploded into motion. He leaped off a chair back, landing between Jevryn and everyone else. As he landed he grew, until he was large enough that anything Jevryn did would inevitably hit him before anyone else.

Through the gap between Griff's wings and his head, Seth could just make out the expression on the councilor's face. It was nearly inscrutable, but it reminded him of when Nyx was thoroughly exasperated and very much trying not to show it.

"I am not here to harm her, Arradin. You must realize I could have come to do so long before now, had I wished. I did not need her calling in the favor I offered, were that my intent."

"At the moment, she is not the one I am concerned you will harm. And my name is Griff."

Jevryn exhaled an audible breath, as if seeking patience. "Hide behind a different name all you want, Arradin. It will not change the past. Or the present. Or the future. But I did not come here to debate the nature of your name. I came here to keep a promise. *Not,*" he continued, with a nod to where Kaden and Morgen stood behind Griff's wings, "to concern myself with matters that might otherwise be of interest to a councilor."

Seth glanced at Kaden and Morgen. Nyx had warned Morgen, after his return, that she had tried to summon Jevryn. She'd called in the promise when Morgen hadn't been at the Station, and she'd had no reason to believe that her doing so would put anyone other than herself in danger. And after, she had expected to be here if and when Jevryn did show up, fully capable of protecting Morgen from prying Council eyes.

Something Griff should *also* have had enough prior warning to be able to do. Unless Jevryn was somehow capable of circumventing the Station's—and therefore Griff's—senses.

"I would have your word," Griff said, still holding himself as a physical barrier between them, "that you will not harm any of them. That you will not take any of them against their will, and that you will not reveal their presence here to anyone, either directly or indirectly."

"I can give it," Jevryn said easily enough. "Though I confess surprise that you consider my word to be worth anything, when you hold me in such contempt."

Griff didn't answer for a long while, and Seth wished he could see the expression on the Avatar's face. Nyx had told him there was some history between Griff and Jevryn, though she hadn't known anything more than that. "You possess many faults," Griff said finally, "but going back on your word is not one of them. Promise me that you will do no harm here, either directly or *indirectly*, and I will let down my guard."

"Very well. You have my word, Arradin Thesrani, that I will do no harm here, by any means within my power. I shall speak to no one of what I have seen. Is this vow acceptable to you?"

Griff didn't make an issue of Jevryn using his full name, and inclined his head. He did not shrink in size, but the room grew to better accommodate him, and he prowled back to sit at Seth's side.

"I have come to speak with you Guardian. If her obsessive summons can be considered indicative, it is apparently of some urgency."

Jevryn was here for Nyx. She was missing, and Seth had no idea wether it was prudent to let the councilor know that. If his word could be trusted, he had promised not to reveal anything he learned today. But would that promise hold in the face of a Guardian who had altered the bond of her Station so significantly that she could leave it without causing injury?

And if they didn't tell him she was missing, how precisely were they supposed to *hide* it? If he demanded to stay until she was back from whatever fictional engagement they concocted, there would be no hiding her absence. Seth didn't think a member of the All Council who had traveled all the way here would take well to being denied the thing he had come for.

Seth debated how best to phrase his response. He needed to evade a direct answer while simultaneously getting some indication of what stance Jevryn might take on the situation.

Then Kaden opened his mouth and ruined any chance of careful planning or manipulation. "She's gone."

Was Kaden *trying* to get Nyx killed? Or was he simply incapable of not damaging everything he touched? On some level, Seth knew that Kaden had been high up enough in the Enforcer ranks that he'd had contact with the individual councilors. Perhaps he had some reason to believe that what he was saying to Jevryn wouldn't have negative consequences. But Seth didn't have a good enough opinion of Kaden to trust in that possibility. And Jevryn's gaze, when it landed on Kaden, was cool.

"What do you mean, *gone*?" Jevryn asked.

"She's out," Seth said. "I'm not sure when she'll be back."

"Is that so?" Jevryn turned his gaze back to Kaden, as if expecting a different answer from him. Which he received.

"She was taken from here approximately sixteen hours ago. We don't know by whom, or why."

Jevryn's gaze flashed to Griff even as Seth was running through how to do damage control, how to—

"Is this true?"

Griff wouldn't sell her out like this, Griff wouldn't—but then he did.

"Yes."

Jevryn's gaze fell on the pack of portal stones before flashing back to Kaden. "You attempted to track her through them?"

Kaden nodded.

"And that is something you are confident in your ability to do?" There was steel in his gaze, at that, challenge in his words.

Kaden looked vaguely uncomfortable answering Jevryn, as he had not looked answering Seth. "If she were there, I could find her. But she's not on any of those planets. And..." He hesitated—fine time for the prick to be hesitating *now*—before he continued, "and whoever took her had no need of stones to manage a portal."

"I see." Jevryn pondered the pack of portal stones. But there was nothing hungry or angry in his gaze, and those were the two emotions Seth would have expected from someone looking at what amounted to a fortune in black market resources, an unaffordable means of escape. That pack was a ticket to the universe, to any planet a person wanted to see. At the least, he expected Jevryn to confiscate it. He hadn't promised Griff he wouldn't do *that*. But in the end, all he said was, "Then we will need to find her wherever she *is*."

Jevryn shoved up the sleeve of his shirt, revealing a row of metal bands traveling from his wrist up to his elbow. Each band gleamed with neon blue light. The same light that had spun from Nyx's fingers when she'd held open the portal from the Shadow Market to Earth Between.

This was portal magic. Jevryn was using *portal magic*. And he had no need of stone, or portal magic well, to access it. It hovered in the air in front of him, between him and Kaden, though it had not yet opened any rift in reality, hadn't created an actual portal.

"I am going to cycle through possibilities," Jevryn said, as if what he was doing was common. "I need you to search for her, and tell me when you find her."

"No," Seth said. Quietly, but firmly. Jevryn and Kaden both looked at him like he was an inconvenient cockroach they'd forgotten was around, and would now like to squash.

"You wanted her found," Kaden said. "We're finding her."

"Why?" Seth's gaze was trained on Jevryn. The sane part of him demanded he shut up and not question a councilor for any reason. Not bring undue attention to himself. But the part of him that wanted Nyx found *safely* was stronger than any sanity. He could rationalize Jevryn giving Nyx a promise—a promise he perhaps hoped would gain him some inroad with Griff. But overlooking two All-Council-wanted fugitives, a fortune in black market goods, and volunteering to *find* Nyx with one of those fugitives? What incentive did Jevryn have to do any of that? "Why would you help her? Why do you care if we find her or not?"

"Why do *you* care, Seth Hawthorne?"

Seth didn't react to Jevryn's knowing his name. He was getting the sense that Kaden and Jevryn were more acquainted with each other than anyone might have guessed before this moment, and Kaden had known that the last of the Hidden had fled to Earth with Seth's father. It wasn't too much of a stretch for Jevryn to guess who he was.

"Because I care about her," Seth said.

"I see."

"It's your turn to answer."

Jevryn shrugged, careless. "I never said that I would."

"Jev." Griff's voice was tired. Seth thought it was his use of a shortened version of Jevryn's name, more than anything else, that made the councilor respond.

"Suffice to say that it is in my best interest for her to return here, alive, with no one on the Council any the wiser that she was ever missing."

"You aren't surprised," Seth challenged. "That she *is* missing, and the Station still stands."

"It would be more accurate to say that I was…aware that she might be capable of leaving the Station, if I do not understand the mechanism behind *why* she is able to do so." He didn't offer anything more than that. "Your suspicion is understandable, if misguided and ultimately pointless. Let me put this in terms I believe will speak to you. I am the only possible person who could both take you to Nyx and is willing to do so, and I do not require your approval to do either. If you wish to be involved in her retrieval, you would do well to find the silent side of your tongue."

9

———

Nyx didn't have time to attempt to use the small portion of portal magic she'd gained. She had only just finished cauterizing the holes in her mother's Hiding when Laiveran reappeared, the now-familiar row of blue rings giving away his presence. He paced back and forth in front of her cell, then abruptly stopped and snapped his fingers. The sphere above Nyx's head, the one she'd thought might be a light source, proved to be just that as it buzzed to life, bathing the cell in a soft yellow glow.

Laiveran's eyes were red. Not been-awake-all-night red, but vampiric-fiction-novel red, and they were filled with a mad kind of hatred.

"What are you *doing* to me?" he demanded.

Nyx took an involuntary step back. "Nothing." She answered before she could stop herself, before she could remind herself that silence was probably safer. It was difficult to *exist* in the amount of fury rolling off him.

"Why are you here?" he demanded. "Who brought you in?"

She didn't answer, since he had already asked her that question the last time he was here, and her answer had made him remember the Harvester.

He drew himself up, seething. "You refuse to answer?"

She definitely did. If he got angry enough at her silence, maybe he would open the door. He reached for something next to her cell. She couldn't tell what exactly, but it was clear he expected something to appear, or happen. Nothing did.

His annoyed gaze swiveled back to her. "You aren't in regulation clothing. Where are your intake papers?"

She shrugged, hoping it would make him a little angrier. This version of Laiveran seemed to think this was still a fully-functional prison, and she was just one of its inmates.

His gaze dropped to her wrists. "How did you remove the suppressing cuffs?" He scanned the rest of her cell, as if expecting to find the aforementioned cuffs lying somewhere. Instead, his gaze landed on the skeletal remains in the corner.

The psychic tentacles shot out of his chest, but this time they weren't reaching for her. They flatted to form a barrier in front of him, as if he thought *she* was the cause of the pile of bones, and might attempt to reduce him to the same state. One tendril broke from the shield to hit what looked to Nyx like a random part of the cell. The prison exploded into brilliance. Lights came on everywhere, flashing in various colors in the apparently universal signaling of an alarm.

"You can't be Salyrian." He said it more to himself than her. "Half, perhaps? You have the look, though the eyes aren't quite right."

Note to self, Nyx thought, *if they make skeletons out of people, don't meet a Salyrian.* It was a race name she didn't remember coming across in any of the reading she'd undertaken to make herself less ignorant about the universe. Given that this place was ancient, and Laiveran had theoretically been asleep for centuries, maybe all the Salyrians were dead.

She didn't have long to wonder what would happen when no one responded to Laiveran's raising of the alarm. He looked to his left impatiently, and saw the skeleton in the cell next to hers.

And the one next to that, and the one next to that. He turned slowly, the shield shifting to cover his back, and saw the rows and rows of skeletal remains on the other side. The tentacles in his shield writhed with unease, then quieted, slipping back into his chest

When he turned back to her, she had no doubt he was rooted firmly in the present once more. Especially when he reached out and turned the alarm lights off. He looked at her coolly. "You have something that belongs to me."

Nyx couldn't jump inside the net of her mother's Hiding again. She'd sealed the edges of the tears too well for it to be of any use this time. Without it to hide inside, when Laiveran's attention focused on her, searching for the Harvester, the only protection she had was her own magic.

She had made a promise to Kaden to keep the Harvester Hidden, and her magic was intent on fulfilling it. Power flooded out of her, wrapping around the Harvester.

"I don't have anything," she said. As if her words aided her work, her magic flashed hotter. Something squeezed painfully in her chest. Too much. It was too much magic being pulled to Hide the Harvester.

Her mother's voice, cold and dispassionate, rose up. *There are two kinds of magic. That which is innate to us, and that which can be drawn from the world around us. Hidden magic is innate and, as such, it is finite. The body produces it, and the body can to some degree store it. Any long term Hidings represent a constant draw on your physical resources.*

We teach you, as children, to access your power via a promise. But there is a reason the promises you make in these exercises are finite. 'I promise to Hide this apple for five minutes,' etcetera. A promise made with no end can kill a Hidden. If you promise to Hide the apple forever, but someone knows you hold it in your hand, the amount of magic required to make your promise true is increased exponentially.

In that way, our magic is very similar to an Illusionist's. It is why

we are better suited to Hiding secrets than objects. For an object, an Illusionist is almost always a better choice. But in either case—Illusionist or Hidden—if someone knows you have what they desire, and your magic is trying to convince them that you do not, the magic draw is immense. If their will is stronger than your magic's, you have to make a choice. Either give up the working, or your magic will eat your body to fuel what amounts to a suicide attempt.

This is why you should never make an open promise. For a Hidden's promise can never be broken. If you promise an unachievable goal, your magic will kill you in an attempt to make it true.

Sweat broke out along Nyx's temple. As if the brief memory had unlocked the knowledge connected to it, Nyx suddenly recognized the feeling in her chest, the lassitude in her body. She *remembered* it. Her mother had made her make the very promise she'd warned her of, albeit *before* she'd explained the consequences. She had handed her an apple, told her to hold it in her hands, and Hide it. No restrictions, no time limits.

The difficulty had been insurmountable, because her mother's *will* had been insurmountable. Elena Fortuna hadn't been able to see the apple once Nyx made her promise, but she had known it was there. The next fifteen minutes of Nyx's life had been pure hell as her magic ravaged through her body for fuel, trying to convince Elena the apple was gone, when her mother knew beyond a shadow of a doubt that it wasn't.

Only when Nyx had been on the verge of passing out had her mother said, carelessly, "I release you from your vow."

By the time her mother had spoken those words, Nyx had been curled up in the fetal position, her body so wracked with muscle spasms she could barely move, and she had been determined to never promise to Hide anything ever again.

Too bad she'd forgotten that vow. Because the man before her was convinced she had the Harvester of Worlds. She had made a promise to Hide it that she couldn't take back, and Kaden wasn't here to release her from it.

But the pull on her magic, while strong, was not as strong as it had been with the apple. Laiveran only *thought* she had the Harvester. He didn't know for certain, which made her chances of success marginally better. And even if he was convinced the Harvester was in her possession, he couldn't know it hung around her neck. The object lay, as it always did, beneath her shirt. If he'd known it was there, he would have ripped it from her the second he'd brought her here.

She looked him in the eye and put all the force of her power behind her words. "I don't have what you want."

Pain radiated from her chest as the words tore another chunk of magic from her. The agony rippled out to her shoulders, her stomach, until her body prickled all over with pins and needles as physical warning signs screamed at her to quit doing what she was doing.

Laiveran canted his head to the side, a look on his face like he was listening for something. She remembered how the Harvester had fought her going into Calista. How absolutely silent it had been since then. She remembered what Calista had said about her Hiding the Harvester from the darkness being like a bird hiding in the forest. If the bird chirped, one might be unable to find it in the vastness, but they would still know it was there.

Laiveran looked like he had come into the forest listening for a bird, and had only just realized he hadn't heard one chirp. That there might not be a bird in the forest at all.

She suspected that, were it not for her Hiding, the Harvester's efforts at silence would not have been so successful in keeping it from Laiveran's notice. But the two together? Its cooperation and her magic? They let no trace of the Harvester's presence escape.

Laiveran straightened as her magic strained, wiping away his confusion. "Of course you do not. I felt it on Kaliaris. You...you were simply in the way."

A beat later, he vanished.

Simply in the way. He was going to her Station.

T he need to get out *now*, to get home, hit Nyx hard. But she didn't need experience with portaling to know that what she held in her hand was not enough magic to carry her to another planet. She doubted it was even enough to portal her out of this cell. But maybe she didn't have to portal *herself* out. Maybe…

She gathered the magic in her hand and wiped it over one of the cell bars, willing it to stay. She had enough to coat one bar, from the floor to about two feet up. The magic remained there sullenly, like a dog grudgingly obeying a command to sit when it wanted to go chase after a squirrel.

She thought about how the portal stones worked, how they opened doorways into other worlds. She didn't need a doorway. She just needed the magic-coated section of the bar to be some-where *else*. So she thought of the vast emptiness of space and tugged on the magic.

There was a corresponding tug on *her*, and the bar vanished. For half a second she couldn't believe it had actually worked. Then the alarm lights returned, accompanied this time by a noise that sounded like a whale groaning in the depths of the ocean. The prison, it seemed, knew she was trying to escape.

Logically, she understood the flashing lights and repeating, ominous whale-noises didn't mean anything bad for her. There were no prison guards here, ready to apprehend her and shove her back into a cell. Illogically, the combination of the two did what they were designed to do: they sent her body into a state of panicked high alert, insisting she needed to *move move move*.

This was fine. Everything was fine. She would get out of this cell, find a door out of this prison, and hope against hope her instincts were wrong, and there was a Station on this planet.

She dropped to the ground and angled onto her side. The bars were close enough together that, even with the missing piece, she was barely going to fit through. She went feet first, palms flat on the floor to help wiggle her way back. Suddenly, her feet dropped as the floor outside the cell gave way to empty air. Panic lurched through her and she jerked her feet back, nearly impaling herself on the cut-off portion of the bar above her in the process. The tips of her boots hit the bars of the neighboring cell, contorting her body into an *L* shape.

She took a couple deep breaths. She'd known the landing outside the cell only extended so far, but given the ease with which Laiveran had paced it, she'd thought it was a little wider. Forcing herself to relax, she carefully wriggled the rest of the way out.

Holding onto a cell bar with her left hand, her right fished out her penlight and clicked it on. Pointing the beam at the edge of the landing, she looked down. Her vision was hampered by the strobing lights of the alarms. They made her feel like she was in the middle of a rave, flicking on and off between the periods of darkness.

When her vision finally focused, her stomach tried to drop out of her body, a quick pulse of adrenaline surging through her limbs. The prison stretch into infinity below, so far that the vast darkness swallowed up the beam from her penlight. She couldn't see a bottom. If she fell, it was a long trip to a certain death.

She took a deep breath and firmed her grip on the bars. "Right. Don't fall. Just find the stairs." Her voice was swallowed up by the vastness of the prison, written over by the groaning of the audible alarm. She looked left and right, but couldn't see the end of the row to either side. The penlight went back into her pocket, and she picked her favorite direction and headed to her left, keeping a hand to the cell bars at all times.

The flashing lights and alarms messed with her sense of time and distance. When she finally reached the end of the cell row, there was…nothing. The walkway ended at the wall. No door marred the seamless perfection of that wall and no stairway existed to take her up or down. There wasn't even a walkway to reach across the divide to the cell rows opposite.

Resisting the urge to bang her head against the cell bars, she ran her hands over the smooth surface of the wall, searching for cracks that might indicate a door, or hidden levers, or *anything*.

She was about to give up when she found it. Along the outer seam of the walkway was a slight depression that, when pushed, caused the tile she stood on to slowly blink with purple light. It reminded her of a "waiting" signal. So she waited. It was over a minute before she heard the faint hum that had her looking down. A square tile floated steadily up from below, sliding to a stop on this level, perfectly even with the walkway she stood on.

She saw no evidence of pulleys or other mechanical components connecting the square to the wall that would allow it to move up and down. Which meant whatever its means of control and movement were, they were likely magical.

Nyx wasn't sure if that made things better, or worse. On the one hand, she wouldn't trust an elevator whose mechanical components had been sitting for what was probably a few centuries, lack of obvious degradation in this place or not. On the other hand, where did the magic that ran the elevator come from? More importantly, was there enough of it to get the elevator all the way down to the bottom, however far that was?

She debated her options, but there weren't that many. Either find another way down, or take this one. Out of an abundance of thoroughness, she moved back along the walkway, to her cell and then past it, all the way to the other end. It was identical to the one opposite. No doors, no stairs, no nothing.

She could probably call an elevator from here, but, in the event there *was* a limited supply of magic to work them, she didn't want to spend more of it calling another one up here. Resigned, she returned to the opposite end of the row and the waiting elevator square.

Holding onto the cell bars, she stretched a foot out and

tapped her toes to the square. When it didn't move, she drummed her heel down on it. Stable.

"I would kill for stairs," she muttered. Only the flashing lights and the alarm answered.

"Fuck it." She let go of the cell and stepped onto the square.

10

———

Nyx's breath whooshed out of her in a rush when she did not immediately plummet to her death. This was fine. Everything was fine. Even if something happened to the elevator, she could jump off and grab whatever row of cell bars was nearest.

She crouched down—the lack of safety features or handrails was mildly disturbing—and felt along the side for operational controls. She succeeded in first going up, then sideways, before bringing the square back alongside the walkway and managing to go down.

The floors slipped by interminably, one after another, level after level of death. She blocked it out because she had to, and kept her focus on ensuring her ride wasn't about to drop out beneath her. But in the end, it wasn't any mechanical or magical malfunction that almost had her falling the remaining floors to her death.

The ground came into view below and as she passed the sixth floor, the call of magic hit her hard. The pull was stronger than when she'd first encountered her Station's portal, stronger than the draw of the portal magic well in the Shadow Market. She leaned toward it before she could stop herself and tipped right over the platform.

Fear knocked her out of her stupor. She scrambled and caught the platform edges, dangling now like she had from the floating logs in the charity competition. Stars, that seemed like a lifetime ago. But unlike in the competition, no benevolent wind mage waited below to catch her if she fell.

The elevator, which apparently didn't have *any* safety features, was unperturbed by her near-death experience and continued its descent. She didn't try to swing back atop it. The ground was close enough that she held on until her boots were only a couple feet from the bottom, and dropped.

She landed lightly, the platform settling onto the floor a few seconds behind her. Without the fear of falling to distract her, resisting the magic that dragged her to the right was impossible. She took three stumbling steps and then she was running, heedless of anything around her, until she came to a set of metal doors. They were carved with planets and stars, solar systems and galaxies, the deep thrum on the other side of them beckoning.

She ran her fingers over the carvings, searching for a handle. When she found none, she tried pushing on them. They didn't open. At least, not from her physical exertions. As if the magic beyond the door recognized her, she felt it flow to the door, to *her*, blue light filling in the indentations carved into the metal. Small gears along the right and left sides of the seam, ones she had thought were merely decorative, spun, a series of clicking noises issuing forth as the door unlocked.

What waited inside exceeded her wildest imaginings. This wasn't a portal, like the one in her Station, nor a well, like the one in the Shadow Market. It was a *lake*.

The flashing lights and alarms were not present in this room, and as the doors snicked softly shut behind her, they were blocked out entirely. The room lay bathed in the soft blue light of the lake. It stretched from wall to wall, like an in-ground pool that covered all space save the narrow ledge that ringed it. Another set of doors lay on the other side.

Six stairs led into the pool. Nyx wanted to strip her shoes off and descend them, to feel the magic against the bare soles of her feet, and only the fear of losing the mercury boots kept her from taking them off. Instead, she walked down the steps until the magic lapped at the toes of her boots, crouched, and drew her fingers across the surface.

The liquid—and it *felt* liquid here, where the magic in the Shadow Market had felt like fine-spun cotton candy—was cool and soft against her skin. The air above the pool was coated in a fine blue haze, as if whatever the pool was made of held the magic in this liquid state, and what was on the top misted like steam in a sauna.

She drew off her gloves, tucked them into her pocket, and drew her fingers through the lake. The magic was cool and soothing against the frazzled edges of her nerves. Unable to help herself, she dove in.

The need to *go* gripped her. Go anywhere, everywhere, it didn't matter, and as she thought it a map unfurled in her mind. She no longer saw the lake, but bright silver points in a sea of black, like looking at constellations in the night sky.

Were they planets? And if they were, how could she know which ones? How did she know which one was home? She tried to hold back, to think, but the magic inundating her demanded use, and she could no more resist reaching for the point closest to her than she could choose to stop breathing. Magic hooked through her, leaping from her body to that point. The map disappeared as a portal yawned opened.

Holy shit.

The space on the other side of the portal was not Earth. At least, she was pretty certain it wasn't Earth. The landscape was dry and barren, which some of Earth's surfaces certainly were, but... Hesitant, she stretched her fingers to the opening, just pushing through the surface.

Heat singed her fingers, like sticking them in a heated oven, and she yanked her hand back. The tips of her fingers were red and blistered from less than a second of contact with the planet's atmosphere. If she went through that portal, she would be dead in a handful of seconds, and it wouldn't be a pleasant way to go.

But the portal wasn't closing. For one horrifying moment, she considered that it might never close unless someone went through it. Her body was a conduit, pouring the lake's endless magic into holding the pathway open.

Her lungs burned, and she realized she was still beneath the lake. She kicked, swimming in a vertical line until her head broke the surface, and gulped down air. She shook her head and swam to the ledge, heaving herself onto it and pulling her feet clear.

The portal magic hadn't soaked her through, like water would, but it clung to her skin, her clothes, her hair. And it still flowed through her to the open portal below. She concentrated and tried to reverse that flow. The magic resisted. It wanted to be used, and it had been a very long time since anyone had been here to use it.

But it obeyed. Finally, it obeyed, and she broke the connection between the magic and the portal. The pathway fizzled out a moment later, the rift in space shrinking until it dwindled into nothing. The tips of her burned fingers throbbed, and Nyx shuddered. If she'd blindly jumped through that portal, instead of testing it first...

Hesitantly, she swung her legs back into the pool. She wanted to go *home*, and as she thought it, the constellation-like map reappeared. But it was a map she had no context for. It was like waking up in the middle of nowhere with a piece of paper that had four dots on it labeled Place One, Two, Three, and Four, and whoever had left the map hadn't even had the decency to place an X labeled, *You Are Here*, on it.

If she stepped through a portal into a place that looked safe but wasn't, could she find her way back to wherever she was now? There were no distinguishing marks on any of the points in her mind. They just hung there, glowing, waiting for her to choose one.

But what choice did she have? It was either stay here or try to get home. No one was coming for her. Unless… Her first instinct had been to assume that, because the prison had obviously been abandoned for centuries, the planet was too. But if it wasn't, if the prison had been intentionally forgotten, maybe Seth could get to her.

If she could find her way to this planet's Station, she could get a message to him. He had a cache of portal stones capable of getting him to her and getting them both home. Traveling via the Station itself would be an option of last resort on her end. Her name was attached to the Station on Earth, as its Guardian, and she wasn't kidding herself that if she booked passage home, the All Council wouldn't find out about it. She would take that route if she had to, but she didn't relish the ramifications of making that choice.

She glanced at the number four tattooed on her hand. If she didn't make it home within one Earth week, that four would become a three, and so on down until she had nothing left. If she didn't make it back before she hit zero, she was pretty sure that she, Griff, and the Station would die.

The lake beckoned hypnotically, and all she wanted to do was slip beneath the waters once more and let the universe unfurl before her. But she'd just proven how wrong *that* could go. Staying here, finding a Station, had to be the better option.

Determined, she skirted the ledge of the pool and headed for the doors opposite the ones she'd entered through. These also had no handles, and were immune to shoving and pulling. And the portal magic clinging to Nyx's skin didn't leap to activate the door gears. After she gave them a particularly hard shove, a voice spoke, startling her.

"No insulating atmospheric spells detected. The air of Lehine is toxic to all mammalian species. Exit doors will not open until the proper insulating spells are detected."

Nyx lifted her hands from the door, suddenly more afraid they *would* open than that they wouldn't. Insulating atmospheric spells were something she had no idea how to produce. Furthermore, they were something neither Morgen nor Seth had ever mentioned to her in all her asking about other planets. If an "insulating atmospheric spell" was necessary for travel to any of the ley-line-connected planets, she thought Seth or Morgen would have mentioned it.

She walked back through the ground floor, seeking out non-cell rooms. She located what had probably been the break room, if the arrangement of chairs and tables were any indication, and flung open every drawer and cabinet she could find, hoping for water. Given some of the magic here was still functional, if there were preservation spells on the water storage, it should be safe to drink.

But the cabinets were all empty. Attached off that room was another, smaller area that had probably once been the bathroom. It looked like the kind of pit-style toilet you could find at some camping sites. She availed herself of the facilities, hoping it was indeed the bathroom and not a laundry chute, or something else she couldn't even fathom. Though in the end, it wasn't like anyone was here to inform her of the error if she was wrong.

The final room she found looked like it had been used for storage. It contained a few packages that crumbled to dust as soon as she touched them, and nothing else useful. Like, perhaps, a pre-made insulating atmospheric spell that might have conveniently survived the passage of time to help her out of this desperate situation. The room certainly didn't contain any water.

It seemed the only things still around were the cells themselves, the bones of the people who'd been in them, and the lake of portal magic.

Faced with the conclusion that she had nowhere—absolutely

nowhere—else to go, she returned to the portal lake. She considered the planet that had singed her fingers. Could anything really live in an environment that hot? Anything other than bacteria, anyway? And if nothing could, if the planet was uninhabited, then that meant it wasn't connected to the ley lines.

In all of her theorizing with Morgen about portal magic and its uses, it hadn't occurred to her that witches who could portal without an anchoring stone might be able to portal to planets that were not livable. How many had died doing just that before the ley lines were created? Was that *why* the Stations had been created, why no one portaled simply by using the magic itself?

She stared at the lake. She had two choices: stay here and wait for Laiveran to return, or take her chances with a new planet. If she stayed, there was no telling how much time would pass before Laiveran returned. She was relatively certain he would come back as soon as he realized the Harvester wasn't on Earth, but who knew how long it would take him to realize that? He'd been more than half mad. And if he was stuck in the past again when he came back, and thought she was an escaped prisoner, would he kill her before he remembered she had something he wanted?

There was no food here, no water. She had, what? Three days before dehydration killed her? Even supposing Laiveran returned here in time to prevent that outcome, she had no guarantee she could convince him to take her away from here. She had less of a guarantee that she could convince him to return her to Earth, and no guarantee that he wouldn't simply kill her outright.

She had to leave. On her own. There had to be *some* smart way to do that other than jumping blindly to a planet that might or might not kill her. She didn't have to go through the portals she opened, as she'd just proved, and she had an entire lake of magic at her disposal. So she would just open the portals one at a time and pick the best option.

She stepped back into the pool, this time staying in the

shallow end. Magic wrapped around her, curling lovingly up her legs, and as she fed the magic her desire to return to Earth, the constellation map reappeared. She wondered idly if the map was something only she could see, or if it was a physical thing she brought up, something anyone else around her would also see.

Thinking back to when she'd been snatched in the caves, she thought it was probably the former. She hadn't seen any map then, and if this was how portaling without stones worked, then Laiveran had to have been able to see something like this.

She walked between the silver points suspended in the air, noting their positions, the shape they made. There were seven in total, forming no true pattern she could distinguish. She walked to the point farthest from her, hoping more points would appear once she reached it, but none did.

These were her options then. Seven points. Seven planets. Six, really, since she'd already determined one was thoroughly inhospitable. Her throbbing, blistered fingers were only too happy to remind her of that fact.

She returned to the start of the map, bypassed the first point, and reached for the second. As magic flowed through her and the portal opened, she didn't have to stick her fingers through this one to prove it wasn't a viable option. The scene through the portal was nothing more than an ocean of bright, orange-red lava. She cut the flow of magic, drawing it back to her.

The third and fourth planets proved equally undesirable in the opposite direction, both frozen solid. Planet number five was a shifting mass of storms. Of planets six and seven, neither looked promising. The landscapes were barren, neither one pointing towards signs of life. She didn't see a single plant, animal, or anything in between. Of course, that was how the first planet had looked, the one that had blistered her fingers in a fraction of a second.

She walked back and forth between the two points, hesitant. If there were no visible signs of temperature and atmosphere, how was she supposed to guess them without sacrificing her extremities to potential loss? There wasn't anything living in the space she currently occupied to toss through and see if it survived, even if she was willing to expend the life of something else as a test. She'd never been on board with sacrificial mine canaries.

Nyx pulled one of her knives. She might not have any way of testing the breathability of the air on the other side, but the metal of the knife would heat or cool with the planet's temperature. She reopened the portal to the sixth point. She felt a little sluggish as it opened, and it occurred to her that, while her body might not have to make the magic she was using, it probably still cost her something to channel it.

She stuck the point of the knife through. Strong winds wrenched it, and she let go before the pull could drag her hand into the other world. The knife went flying. It disappeared in a matter of seconds. She frowned at what *looked* like a perfectly placid planet on the other side. She couldn't see the wind...because there was nothing loose on the planet for the winds to blow.

She mentally marked the sixth planet as non-viable, let the portal die, and moved on to the seventh. She pulled a new knife —she only had two left, now—and this time gingerly stuck the barest centimeter of metal through. When no extreme force met her, she fed another inch to the planet, held for one minute, and pulled the knife back. Carefully, she held her palm an inch from the metal. She felt no emanating heat or cold, and tested it with short one-second taps against her skin before pressing it fully to her palm. It felt like a sun-warmed rock in spring. Warm, but not hot.

She let the portal close and the lake re-covered her in magic. She had to assume that these seven planets were the only ones available to her based on proximity to her current location, the only ones she was capable of reaching from this point. Which meant, if she portaled to one of the planets and reconnected to the constellation map, she should be able to see new options.

Maybe she had no idea where home was, but she could try to find *an* inhabited planet.

Number seven was her only viable option, and probably would have been the best one anyway. It was the farthest from her, so it should open up the widest range of options for future planets.

As she'd opened the previous portals, she'd tried to measure the amount of magic it cost to do so. It wasn't insignificant. The tiny bit she'd taken from the Shadow Market, or the bit she'd stolen from Laiveran, had been nowhere near enough to open a full portal, so it made sense she hadn't seen the map when holding magic, then. It had taken all the magic covering one of her arms to open a portal here, and the longer she'd held it open, the more magic it had eaten.

The magic *liked* clinging to her, so she could cover her body and take that with her, but it wasn't a very efficient means of storage. She managed to stuff a tiny bit into her pockets, like she had in the Shadow Market, but it still didn't feel like enough. Not when she had no idea where she was going, or where she might end up.

There had to be a way to condense the magic for storage—just *one* of the small arm bands Laiveran had worn had carried enough magic to open a portal for him, possibly even more than one—but no matter how she took the magic in her hands and tried to condense it into a ball, like packing powdered snow together until it became more and more dense, the magic wouldn't acquiesce.

Eventually, she gave up trying. She was covered in magic from head to toe, had two pockets-full, and that was going to have to be enough. It would get her maybe eight jumps? She didn't let herself think about what would happen if jump number eight landed her on a foreign planet with no signs of life, no resources, and no portal well to give her hope. She just opened the portal to the seventh planet.

No matter her conviction, as the planet's landscape appeared behind the rift, she stood there a minute longer, unwilling to step forward. She was so far out of her depth it was laughable. Staying where she was felt safer, but she imagined it was the kind of safe feeling that led to a slow death. The kind that told you the world was dangerous, and if you just stayed shut up inside your home, with no connections and no adventures, nothing would ever hurt you again.

It was a seductive belief, because it held some kernel of truth. Except in this case, it didn't. If she didn't leave here, she was going to die. She was already thirsty, hungry, and tired. The longer she stayed, the worse those three things would become. And the more time she had to dread leaving, the harder it would be to make herself go.

Nyx didn't believe in gods, but as she stepped through the portal, she almost wished she did. Having something to pray to in that moment might have been comforting.

11

———

Seth watched as one of the metal rings on Jevryn's arms pulsed, power flowing from it to the councilor. Magic spun around him and Griff in tandem, as if including the Avatar was not even a conscious thought, but simply something done out of habit. Then his magic circled wider to include Kaden.

"Where?" Jevryn prompted.

The three of them looked at the open air as if something was there. Kaden narrowed his eyes, walking slowly, sometimes forward, sometimes from side to side, pausing every now and then as if following points on a zig-zagging dotted line that no one else could see. Points Jevryn's magic was allowing him to see.

Seth's irritation spiked. This wasn't a game. This was Nyx's life on the line. Kaden was the one who'd gotten her into this mess in the first place, and if Seth had been the one to drag him back here out of necessity, he didn't trust him to complete this task unsupervised without causing more damage than he already had. "Do you want to clue in the rest of us?"

Jevryn flicked a dismissive hand, as if to say his concern was unnecessary. Kaden ignored him entirely. Seth didn't need the gentle, featherlight brush of Griff's wings, the one that clearly said, "Let it go, there's no point in arguing," to *know* there was no point in arguing.

Seth had never put much effort into convincing people of things. In his experience, most people *couldn't* be convinced of opinions other than their own. Not when they were as steeped in the belief of their own superiority as Jevryn and Kaden were.

Seth had always found that, far from having reasoned, verbal arguments, the swiftest way to get what he wanted, was to simply get what he wanted. Right now, he wanted to see what Jevryn and Kaden saw.

When the majority of the universe's inhabitants thought of Illusionists, they thought of what the word implied—the ability to make people see things that weren't there, or to hide from them the things that were. But illusion magic didn't actually make them see or unsee things—it worked off belief, off convincing a person's mind that a thing was or was not present.

That was the first and simplest use of the ability, and it was the most widely known. But magic that worked on belief could trick a person into more than simple sight, and no sub-branch of the Illusionist ability was better at that than the trickster class.

His power slipped out, barely a thread, as slender as a worn-thin fray on an old pair of blue jeans. So thin that if you rubbed it between your fingers, it would seem about to dissolve. A touch so insignificant it was beneath notice, especially to someone who had lived as long as—attained as much arrogance as—a member of the All Council.

Shields surrounded Jevryn's mind, but they were shields meant to withstand powerful frontal attacks, not insignificant ones that had no hope of causing damage.

A wall that had been built to hold against a catapult's assault might do that particular job well, and yet have cracks that would allow water through its facade. Seth was the proverbial water, his magic slipping through the cracks. He asked for so little, a tiny suggestion that perhaps Jevryn wished to include him in whatever he and Kaden observed. And because the request was asked so subtly, so insignificantly, it went unnoticed.

Jevryn's portal magic swirled out to encompass him. Glowing dots swam into Seth's vision, the air overlaid with the spheres. They hung around him, as if he stood in the center of space, the planets close enough to touch. Kaden passed between the points, pausing at one, then another, before continuing on to the next.

Jevryn's brow furrowed, but not at what Kaden was doing. That was the only warning Seth got, and it didn't come quickly enough. The councilor moved so fast Seth never saw it. One second Jevryn was standing quietly, the next the blade of his katana rested against Seth's throat.

"I have killed people for far, far less."

It wasn't the blade at Seth's throat that made the first sliver of icy fear ripple through him. It was the matter-of-fact tone of voice Jevryn used, the way he wasn't even angry, as if he'd drawn his sword out of a sense of principle rather than desire. That conveyed a level of self-assuredness Seth had never seen in all his years of working with and against some of the nastiest people the universe had to offer.

He swallowed, and just the simple movement was enough pressure against the sharp blade to break the skin and send a trickle of warmth running down his throat. He gave Jevryn his trademark, cocky grin. "If you wanted to kill me, you wouldn't have bothered to pull the strike."

He just didn't know if that restraint came because Jevryn had no intention of killing him, or if he'd changed his mind because Griff had thrown a wing in front of Seth as the councilor struck, and the katana's blade had sent four sheared feathers fluttering to the ground.

Councilor and Avatar stared at each other for a long moment, and then Jevryn re-sheathed his blade. "Perhaps," he replied. "But a smart man would not tempt fate in such a manner again.

Do you trust your friend so little that you do not believe he will find her without your aid?"

Seth laughed. "I don't trust him at all. And he isn't my friend."

Jevryn shrugged, but he did not remove the magic that allowed Seth to see the points through which Kaden walked. And, after a pointed cough from Griff, the magic spread out further, encompassing Morgen, Evra, and Kalvar as well.

"She's not in any of these places," Kaden said.

"You are certain?" It wasn't Jevryn who asked, but Griff, and the *way* that he asked implied he found it highly improbable that she wasn't.

Seth found it difficult to reconcile the gentle, father-like Griff he'd come to know in the last few months with Nyx's revelation that Griff himself was as old as the All Council. That he and Jevryn had history. History that apparently meant he'd seen the map they were looking at before, and understood what it represented.

For all that Nyx and Morgen had spent a great deal of time theorizing about portal magic, and how it might be used outside the typical bounds of spelling stones, Griff had never once mentioned that he had any firsthand knowledge of it. That Jevryn was a portal witch and that Griff had, in all likelihood, traveled with him in just such a manner as Nyx and Morgen had tried to puzzle out the theoretical mechanism for.

Anyone with eyes could see how fond Griff was of Nyx. Seth didn't think the Avatar would deny her much of anything she asked. But he'd never mentioned this. And when Seth had asked him about portal magic earlier, he'd said he *couldn't* answer.

"I am sure," Kaden said. "She's not on any of these planets."

Jevryn lifted his hand. He drew his thumb and middle fingers together and the map drew in on itself, as if he was zooming out on a computer screen. The original spheres were still there, only smaller, and new ones had populated around them.

Kaden walked through them for several minutes before stopping in front of one. "Here. She's here."

The point was far enough away from where Jevryn stood, his physical position presumably representing Earth on the map, that it gave Seth pause. Distance in the universe didn't—shouldn't—mean much of anything. The ley lines connected to planets far more distant than the one Nyx was on now. But because those planets *were* all on the ley lines, they had never seemed truly out of reach before.

Jevryn stared at the point Kaden indicated. Just...stared. It was unsettling.

"Jevryn? What planet is that?" Griff finally asked, taking the one step forward and to the right that brought him next to the councilor. It was another unconscious movement, like the one Jevryn had made when he'd included Griff in the sight of the planetary maps.

Like the one Jevryn made now, his hand coming up to idly rest on Griff's shoulder. Like the lie that rolled off his tongue next. "Just a dead one, Arradin. It is no cause for concern."

The softness that had slipped into Griff's manner disappeared with the brush-off Jevryn's words obviously were. Apparently, *Don't you worry your pretty little head about it, darling,* was universal across time, species, and relationships.

As was the response it inevitably inspired. Griff's shoulder twitched, shrugging off Jevryn's hand.

"Wait." Kaden tensed, following something only he could sense. "She's moving again."

12

———————

At first, Nyx thought everything seemed fine. No other species jumped out to attack her on her new planet, the air temperature was reasonable, and if gravity was somewhat less than ideal, well, she didn't mind a little extra bounce in her step.

The landscape was flat and barren, and stretched out in every direction as far as the eye could see. Though she hadn't really *expected* there to be anything useful here, based on what she'd seen through the portal window, it was still disappointing to realize there was no point in doing even a small exploration of the planet. Based on her line of sight, she could wander for days and never find a portion of the planet that bore signs of life. Much less of sapience, or a Station.

She needed to…

Nyx blinked, confused, trying to remember what it was she needed to do. Her limbs felt weak and rubbery, a state unhelped by the dizziness that claimed her next. She fought through a sudden bout of nausea, forcing herself to think, to remember what she was supposed to be doing. It was something important, something…

It hit her in a burst of momentary clarity. The temperature of the planet was safe, but that didn't mean the *air* was. In an oxygen deficient atmosphere, the body would continue to breathe, none-the-wiser to the fact that it wasn't taking in what it needed. That it was slowly dying.

She hadn't been here long. Had she? How many minutes could the brain go without oxygen before suffering permanent damage? She pulled desperately at the portal magic, half-forgetting why she did so even as the map of planets unfurled. She didn't have time for carefully evaluating the best option. She had to move before she forgot why she was moving. She picked the farthest point on the map and stuck her fingers through. When they didn't freeze or incinerate, she crawled through.

Nyx emerged into frigid water. There was no breaking of the surface because she hadn't fallen from air into liquid—it was as if the portal had simply opened into an ocean's depths. There was no light, no sense of up or down, and the pressure in her ears hurt, as if she'd swum to the bottom of a too-deep pool.

Her lungs burned. She'd already gone too long without oxygen. She had no idea if the surface of the water was within her reach, or which direction was up. Out of the corner of her eye, something glowing came into view, swimming toward her. She didn't know if it was real, or if it was a hallucination. But even if there was life here, life that could survive underwater, she couldn't.

She grabbed at the magic clinging to her legs and opened a new portal, picking a planet at random as her vision receded at the edges. There was no time to test it. As soon as the edges yawned wide enough, she swam through. Her hands and arms broke through onto dry land. She clawed forward, dragging her head through and gulping in lungfuls of air. Glorious, oxygen-containing air.

She slumped for a minute, halfway through the portal, willing herself to have the strength to drag the rest of her body through. Her hands didn't seem to be working right, but if she passed out with half her body in one world and half in the other, would the portal close and bisect her?

The thought was enough to get her moving again despite the fact that she couldn't feel her fingers. She was *freezing*.

She heaved her upper body onto dry land, then her hips, then her thighs. She was almost wholly through when sharp needles tore into her right calf. She kicked on instinct, fear of the unknown and the unseen adding weight to the strike, and her foot connected with a solid *thunk*.

Pain sliced into her leg, but whatever held her let go, and she scrambled fully into the new world. She flipped onto her back, her heart thudding wildly, and looked back. The sunshine of her new planet cut through the ocean depths of the other world, revealing a pair of glowing red eyes. They stared at her from a face that would look almost human, if it weren't for the serrated fangs in the alien's mouth, the gills just below its ears, and the body that tapered into a scaled tail at the hips.

It gave a flick of that tail and lunged forward. Its arm shot through the opening between worlds, reaching for her—and recoiled as the water on its hand froze instantly. It fell back, and Nyx hastily snapped the portal shut.

Holy fucking shit. She'd almost been dragged into the depths of an alien ocean. By a *mermaid*.

The mermaid bite didn't hurt and that seemed...odd. She tried to move, only to find she couldn't. She was *freezing*, her teeth chattering so hard the muscles in her jaw and neck and throat ached, and she couldn't feel her fingers or her toes.

The ocean had been cold, yes, but as she forced her head down to look at her injured calf, she understood the real problem was that this *planet* was cold. The water on her body had frozen to ice, the material of her clothes gone rigid. She tried again to move, but she barely managed to break the ice covering her arms.

Her teeth clicked together, her muscles spasming as her body shivered violently. She reached for portal magic, the planetary map coming up once more. Everything was blurry and unfocused. She blinked but her eyelids wouldn't actually move. They were frozen open, the dry, cold air stinging her eyes and making them water, her tears freezing solid as soon as they trickled out the corners of her eyes.

She reached for one of the points on the map but her hand wouldn't move.

Focus. She couldn't need to actually touch the planet point. It wasn't a real, tangible thing. Reaching for it was just a physical means of expressing her intent, of directing the magic. The same kind of crutch as a Hidden's promise.

She picked a planet and willed everything in her towards it. For a moment, nothing happened. It was if she strained against an invisible force, and that force resisted her. She gritted her teeth, realizing absently that her shivers had stopped and that was very, very bad. She screamed in frustration and desperation, and something in her snapped.

Magic flowed and wrapped around the planet point. As the portal coalesced, she gave the magic another silent plea. For the portal to open *beneath* her. Because she couldn't feel a single part of her body now. If she had to crawl even an inch to go through her portal, it wouldn't happen.

The ground opened beneath her and she fell through it, landing so hard it kicked the breath from her lungs, shattering the ice on her clothes. Her vision blurred at the edges and she was so, so tired. She blinked, managing the movement this time. Or half of it, anyway. Her eyes closed, but they were heavy and didn't want to open again.

Why should they? She could curl up, right here, right now, and sleep. Maybe when she woke, she would realize this had all been a terrible dream, and she was safe in her Station.

Her Station.

Griff. Seth. Morgen. Evra.

Laiveran had gone back to the Station for the Harvester, and her friends would be in his way. She had to get up. She had to get off of this planet and find a way home, to make sure they were alright.

Drowsiness dragged at her, calling with intoxicating power, but the momentary jolt in clarity told her this was the kind of sleep she might never wake from. She was in the grips of hypothermia, and she didn't think this planet was much warmer than the last. Not warm enough to raise her body temperature.

She strove to flex her fingers and managed that tiny bit. She sucked in a hard breath and called the map again, taking stock of the portal magic she had left. How many jumps had she done? Three? She'd thought she had enough magic for eight, but then she'd held the portal from the ocean world open for a while, so...

Her eyes shuttered closed. She drifted sideways, jerking back awake at the movement. She had to leave and hope for a warmer planet. Like every jump before this one, it was portal or die. Hypothermia might not be the worst way to go, but she didn't want to go at all. She picked a point and summoned the portal, expecting another barren, lifeless planet.

Instead, she was greeted with lush greenery, tall trees, and the movement of small, winged creatures flitting through a sky in which twin moons stared down.

Life. There was *life* on this planet. A choked sob tore out of her and she lurched forward, sliding through the portal and onto the blessed heat of a sun-warmed rock.

The planet thrummed with activity. The air swam with the chirruping calls of the bird-like creatures and the buzzing sounds of insects. Best of all, it was *warm*. Thick, suffocating heat wrapped around her like the softest of blankets.

She spotted a tree six feet away, its base wider than she was tall, and struggled to crawl to it, wanting the shelter and support of something larger than her. But she was so tired. Her limbs were too heavy, and what little adrenaline had fueled her died in the absence of a clear and present danger.

Her body simply gave out.

13

———

Seth had watched Jevryn follow Kaden's movements about the map as the ex-enforcer stopped at various points. First, at a planet seven points away from the one he had initially stopped by, then at another one only four points later. Though the second destination had been shorter in terms of planet numbers, it had been roughly equivalent in terms of how much distance separated them.

"That does not make any sense." Jevryn had said, sounding annoyed, but then he'd been cut off as Kaden announced Nyx was moving *again*, five planets away, then another nine, the latter points knit close together.

They all waited, but Kaden didn't move again.

"That *still* does not make any sense," Jevryn said.

"Why?" Seth asked. Naturally, it wasn't until Griff repeated the question that Jevryn bothered to answer it.

"Because no one who could travel this far in one jump" —he pointed from Earth to the first planet Kaden had stopped at— "would proceed to travel in short jumps to planets so insignificant they are only on the map out of a sense of thoroughness. It is the work of an amateur, it is—"

"Nyx," Seth finished.

"What?" It would have been amusing, having Jevryn and Kaden bark at him in tandem, had the situation not been so serious.

"You said it yourself. The first jump was the work of someone who knew what they were doing. It was made by the person who took Nyx. The other jumps—they're hers."

"Nyx isn't a portal witch." Kaden said it matter-of-factly, as if she couldn't possibly be something he wasn't aware of.

Morgen shuffled his feet, looking uncomfortable before he said, "She is, actually."

Kaden's eyes flashed. "How do you know that?"

Morgen sighed. "She stole a bit of portal magic from the well on—" He broke off, his gaze shifting to Jevryn. "From, ah, the well we all saw, and she managed to use it a little." His gaze flicked back to Jevryn and then away. "We spent some time looking into portal theory." Returning his attention to Kaden he added, "Which you might know if you'd bothered to get in contact with me at all."

Kaden, in what Seth was coming to view as typical Kaden fashion, ignored the part of that sentence that would have required any explanation or apology on his part. "Fine. If she's a portal witch" —the words sounded bitter in his mouth— "then why isn't she coming back here?"

"Because she has no idea what she is doing," Jevryn said, with all the haughty disgust Seth imagined it took centuries to cultivate. Or, who knew? Maybe Jevryn was just born that way. "She is fortunate she is not dead, playing with magic she hasn't the faintest understanding of."

Seth snorted. "What was she supposed to do? Sit around and wait to be rescued?"

"It would have been highly convenient, yes."

"In case you've forgotten, by All Council law, portaling is technically illegal. No one's supposed to know how to do it. Nyx must have realized she's not on a ley line planet by now, so as far as she knows, she's dead in the water and no one is coming for her. She's doing the only thing she can."

Jevryn grunted. "At least she seems to have hit her limit. If she had gone any—"

"She's moving again." Kaden walked a little further through the dots. "Here."

Jevryn's eyes closed. "Wonderful."

"Why do I get the feeling you don't actually think that planet's wonderful?" Seth asked.

"Because despite all evidence to the contrary," Jevryn said, "you are not a complete idiot."

Such high praise, and from a councilor, too.

"What planet is she on?" Griff asked.

Almost a full minute went by before Jevryn answered. "Amentia Furor."

Griff sucked in a breath. "You have to go for her. Now."

"I have already said that I will."

"What's wrong with Amentia Furor?" Seth asked, unease curling in his gut. Griff was about as level headed as they came. If he was worried…

Griff and Jevryn shared a look, and though it was brief, it was the kind of shared glance that spoke volumes without words.

"It is not a safe planet for humans," Griff said. "The indigenous life there is very large."

"Try again," Seth said. "Maybe without lying to me."

"I haven't lied."

"Then try again with the real reason you're worried about Nyx being there."

Griff simply stared at him, his eyes full of ancient weight, and sadness and secrets.

"*Say* something."

"He cannot," Jevryn said. "His tongue is bound by magic far older than you, and be glad of it. Because if he answered you, it would mean your death."

"And Nyx? If she stumbles onto whatever secret you're hiding on that planet?"

"It is a large planet. It is highly unlikely."

Seth laughed. "You don't know Nyx, so let me enlighten you. She is a trouble magnet. She *loves* secrets. If you leave her alone in a room for five minutes, she will go through all the drawers and cabinets just to see what's there." She'd known the very first time Seth had left their isolated pocket of Earth Between, even though he'd only done it for ten minutes, just to see if he could. She had used that time to snoop through his room. She hadn't found anything exciting, because he'd been thirteen and they lived in the middle of nowhere. Neither of them had owned anything anything exciting to find. But she'd looked, because she was Nyx.

They'd started sneaking out together after that. Once they'd discovered the Dead Earth tradition that was Christmas, and he'd seen the way the decorations and presents and ritual of it all lit up her face, he'd made a point to sneak into Dead Earth to get her a present every year. Said present inevitably never made it to the actual date of Christmas. No matter how well he hid it, she would find it within a matter of days.

Which was why, "The only highly unlikely thing to happen on that planet is her *not* finding whatever you don't want her to find. So I'll ask you again. What happens when she finds it?"

"Nothing happens," Griff said calmly, his eyes daring Jevryn to contradict him. "When you find Nyx, you will bring her home, *here*, to me. She will be whole and unharmed, and if she *does* discover the secret of Amentia Furor, you will ensure that she survives it. You will never tell a soul, and you will never seek to harm her for it."

"Or?" Jevryn prompted. It wasn't challenge in his voice, necessarily, it was more...curiosity. As if he liked this side of Griff, and he wanted to see more of it.

"Or I will finally find a way to do what I would have done

the day I woke chained to this Station, had you not stayed my hand."

Jevryn took a jerky step forward. "You would not." But he didn't sound convinced.

"I would. And know that nothing you could say or do would stop me this time. Bring her home, Jevryn. Prove to me that something is left of the man I once loved."

Tense silence stretched between them. "Do you honestly believe that I would not?"

"I have not known what to believe in a very long time," Griff finally answered.

Jevryn's shoulders did not quite slump—Seth thought the councilor had been born with perfect posture and was incapable of relinquishing it, even in the face of dire emotional blows—but he lost some of his arrogant rigidity.

Very well," Jevryn said finally. "If it is my word you need, then you have it. But you know how dangerous Amentia Furor can be, even under ordinary circumstances. These are not ordinary circumstances. The planet is in a century cycle."

Griff flinched.

"What does that mean?" Seth asked.

"It means that even *I* would be foolish to travel there alone," Jevryn said. "And given the circumstances, I can hardly take an Enforcer team with me. Or rather, I could take them, but I could not return them, and I believe Arradin would take issue with my executing an entire team, even if it *did* return Nyx here."

"You are saying you require volunteers?" Evra asked.

"Indeed."

Seth arched an eyebrow. "You'd have to kill your own Enforcers if you took them, but we're going to walk back out alive, free to go on our merry way?"

"Whether you return alive is entirely up to your skills and the planet. But should those two prove both sufficient and merciful, then yes. I am confident you will keep your mouths shut, because if any of you ever speak of Amentia Furor, you will only sign your own death warrants." He paused for a moment, considering, then added, "And possibly my own."

Seth shrugged. Different day, same high-handed, end-of-the-world doom and gloom. "I'm in."

"As am I," Evra said.

"It's Nyx," Morgen said. "Of course I'm in."

Kaden didn't answer. He didn't answer for long enough that Jevryn said, "Your participation is not optional, I am afraid."

"I never imagined it was," Kaden replied, bitterly enough—comfortably enough—that Seth wondered just how much experience Kaden had working for Jevryn.

Now that the problem of *how* to reach Nyx had been solved, Seth's anxiety subsided enough for him to recognize how wrong the dynamic between Jevryn and Kaden was.

Kaden had taken from the council what was possibly the most powerful object in the universe. Not only did Jevryn not seem to care about that fact *at all*, Kaden didn't look worried. He certainly wasn't warily watching Jevryn out the corner of his eye the way Morgen was doing. The way a sensible wanted fugitive would.

"I'm sorry," Kalvar said, reminding everyone in the room that he hadn't volunteered yet, either. "I *want* to help Nyx, but I have a promise to keep." He turned, over and over in his hands, the envelope the blue-haired girl had given Nyx just yesterday. He looked guilt-ridden by the choice, and he shouldn't have to. He was barely eighteen, for fuck's sake.

Seth clapped him on the shoulder. "Nyx understands promises, kid." *And she would murder me if I let you go to a planet a councilor thinks is too dangerous to go to on his own.* "Go keep yours."

The guilt eased from Kalvar's expression at having someone older—and presumably wiser—tell him he was doing the right thing. Seth wished *anyone* would have done the same for him when he was that age. The kid nodded and walked out the door.

"The planet is in a century cycle," Jevryn said. "This cycle is punctuated by a series of storms that come and go without warning. They are both magical in nature and disruptive to other magic in unpredictable ways. I suggest you bring with you whatever you find most useful outside of magical means. You have fifteen minutes to gather anything you require. If you have not returned to this location by that time, you will be left behind."

Classic arrogance from a man who, by his own admission, needed backup where they were going.

No one moved. Evra and Morgen were already carrying everything they thought they might need, prepared for this moment, and Kaden had presumably done the same. Just as Seth had.

"Are we ready, then?" Jevryn asked.

They...weren't. "One second." Seth ran back to his room. He'd packed everything he had thought he might need. But not everything *Nyx* might need. Because almost everyone she cared about in the universe was about to be traipsing about an unknown planet looking for her, and as thing stood, Jevryn A-Morridahn was the only person capable of getting them all off it safely.

If something went wrong, if they were separated, Nyx would never leave them. She didn't have it in her.

Seth flung the door to his room open and strode to the clear vase on his dresser. It was wide-mouthed, the base nearly a foot in diameter, narrowing to six inches at the top, and it was filled with stones. Hundreds of them. And every single one was spelled to bring its possessor back to Earth.

He'd come to Earth often over the last seven years. He'd never known why, when all the memories he'd retained of Earth had been unpleasant, he'd had such a drive to return here, over and over again. Not until Nyx's face had surfaced in his mind a few months ago. But even without knowing, every time he'd come, he'd left with a new handful of stones, and he'd paid a portal witch to spell them.

He plucked four stones from the jar, carried them downstairs, and distributed them, grudgingly giving one to Kaden as well. "In case we're separated."

Jevryn looked at the stones with distaste, as if their very existence offended him. But he extended his hand, palm up, and said, "If you wish those to return you here from where we are going, I am afraid they need a power boost."

14

Nyx woke to the shrieking call of an avian creature. She lay facedown on stone so hot she had gone from hypothermic to sweating through and through. The rush of wind heralded the arrival of a massive winged animal, and she rolled to her left on instinct. On the bright side, the talons the length of her forearm that bit into the stone an inch from her face were at least not biting into her soft human flesh. On the not-so-bright side, she rolled straight off a cliff.

She scrabbled, catching the lip on instinct, then screamed and nearly lost her grip as the blisters on her singed right hand burst open. She felt a commiserating sense of too-tight scorched skin on the right half of her face and neck, and recognized the feeling: sunburn. The serious, painful kind.

A rush of wings flapped above as a leathery, winged bird creature—she was *not* going to think of it as a *pterosaur*—alighted on the stone outcropping she'd previously occupied. Its foot-long beak darted forward, pecking at her right hand and she jerked it back, dangling from the precipice by her left. When her grip held, Nyx blessed Evra for every minute of the rock-climbing course the Amazon had made her repeat over and over.

The bird—okay, fine, *pterosaur*, for lack of anything better to call it—pecked again. Nyx replanted her injured right hand, gritting her teeth through the pain, and jerked her left away just before the bird's beak struck. She caught a glimpse of what lay behind it, of what she'd apparently been sleeping next to: a nest. Six taupe-colored eggs, each a little bigger than the size of her fist, were nestled together.

Shit. Nyx slid her way along the stone outcropping as fast as she could, hoping if she put enough distance between her and the nest, the mother would leave her alone. But the bird followed her aggressively, pecking and flapping its wings, making it difficult for Nyx to keep purchase on the smooth, chalky stone. Above, clouds descended, blotting out the sun, and thunder rumbled across the skies.

Nyx hit a curve in the stone. On her next handhold, it crumbled beneath her, leaving her hanging only by her left hand. Before her right could regain purchase, the *pterosaur* struck, beak biting into the flesh on the back of her left hand. She couldn't hold. Her grip faltered and she fell. Hundreds of lightning bolts lit the sky, and in their wake, portals opened. She fell directly into one…and landed with a hard thump on a dry, grassy plain.

Both of Nyx's hands throbbed—the burned fingers on her right, the beak-torn skin on the back of her left. The grass that surrounded her was up to her waist, thick stalks as big around as her wrists. Overhead, the sun remained hidden, but the twin moons she'd seen upon arrival still blinked down at her, reassuring her that she remained on the same planet. Thunder rumbled again, but no lightning followed this time. Instead, she heard the rip and tear and roar of creatures in battle.

She grabbed her bo staff with her left hand, flicked it open, and forced her right to make the two-handed grip, adrenaline seeing her through the worst of the pain. The sounds of snarling, fighting creatures grew closer, and only the waving of the tall grass indicated their approximate locations. Far to her right, maybe a thousand feet away, the plains improbably gave way to lush jungle.

Nyx didn't know what manner of beasts fought in the grasses, and she didn't want to find out. She wanted to get out of their reach. *Run to the jungle,* she order herself. *Climb a tree.*

She took off, although *took off* was perhaps an optimistic description of what occurred. Her calf throbbed from the mermaid's bite, and the thick grasses of the plain caught at her legs and abdomen, slowing her down. The stalks were too cloistered together to weave between and too thick to cut with anything save a machete, which she didn't have. Fighting past them was exhausting, like wading through mud, the thick stalks battering her skin.

But that wasn't the real problem. The real problem was that her movement did not go unnoticed. Being hunted had a specific quality to it, a distinct feeling of being sighted in on and chased. Nyx felt that now, and she had nowhere to run for cover. The edge of the jungle was too far from her current location. She clutched her bo staff in both hands and held it in front of her like a ward, a shield, a prayer, and struck on instinct as the first creature lunged for her through the grass.

The staff took the bite meant for her neck. The momentum of the creature's lunge bore her to the ground and Nyx twisted and heaved, throwing it off her. It was a small quadruped, maybe two feet tall with leathery gray skin, a short tail, and raptor-like claws. It looked like a prehistoric ancestor of the modern dog. A dinosaur mutt.

Nyx hadn't managed to throw it very far. It rolled to its feet, snarled, and launched itself at her. Midway to her, another mutt tore out of the grass and intercepted it. The two fell to the ground as a single roiling ball of fangs and claws, slashing at each other with abandon. They were...crazed. *Everything* around her was crazed. The sea of grass was awash with the sounds of fighting and pain and death.

This wasn't natural in any sense of the word. Predators in an ecosystem fought over food or territory or mates. They didn't all come out of the woodwork at once to engage in a frenzy of communal battle. It was madness. As if the storm raging around them—a storm that brought no rain, only darkness and thunder and lightning—was magical at its very core, inducing insanity in the planet's life.

Nyx braced, waiting for the same frenzy to overwhelm her. But the magic of the storms had no mental effect on her, as if its ability to induce temporary insanity was tied solely to the natural denizens of the planet.

The two mutts fighting each other had already forgotten about Nyx. Ahead, a massive herbivore went down under an onslaught of smaller predators. The boom as it fell shook the ground and sent Nyx to her knees.

Pain lanced through her calf where the mermaid had bitten her. She shoved back to her feet once the ground settled, but the vibrations knocked the fighting mutts apart and they took notice of her again. Hurriedly, Nyx went to trade the staff for a dagger, but the obstinate length of metal wouldn't let her go.

"Oh, you have got to be joking." She shrank the bo staff down to half its length to use it like a nightstick, one-handed, and pulled a dagger with her right hand. The pain from her burned fingers compromised her grip, and she wasn't certain how effective she would be if she had to strike.

A low, clicking trill sounded through the plains, and she had the distinct sense of more mutts joining the first two, of being closed in upon on all sides.

Sweat dripped down her spine. She was not kitted out to fight a horde of dinosaur dogs. She was injured, under-prepared, and the creatures amounted to a rabid pack. They would tear her to shreds in seconds. She had nowhere to hide.

Hide. Of course. You are an idiot, Nyx Fortuna.

Like she'd done on Arkadia when she'd hidden herself, Kaden, and Kalvar from the passing army, she held very still and said, "I promise to keep myself Hidden from crazed dinosaurs."

The words stuck a little in her mouth now that she'd remembered—and had a real-life example of—why Hidden promises could be so very hazardous. But she thought it would take less magic to convince non-sapient animals she wasn't standing here than it would to do the same if she was surrounded by a species of higher-intelligence. If she was wrong on that count, well, she thought dying by magical drain was probably preferable to being torn apart.

Except her promise to herself did nothing. She felt it *try* to, that innate space inside her that tied her to Hidden magic reaching for it. But her power failed to answer, as if something interfered with her connection.

The storm. It wasn't just magical; it was magically disruptive.

The thundering of hooves split the air, and she wondered what new terror charged toward her. Sadly, she didn't think she would be alive to find out. The eerie clicking and trilling of the mutts hit a fever pitch and they erupted out of the grass, lunging at her from all sides.

Events unfolded after that in an odd sort of slow motion. As the mutts flew toward her, the hoofbeats she'd heard grew louder. Unbidden, an image appeared in Nyx's mind of her ducking to the ground.

Ducking was about the dumbest thing she could do right now. She had no armor, no shield to hide under. Ducking would make her a conveniently huddled target for the pack that leapt toward her. She had a better chance of dodging them as they landed, trying to jump over them with her wounded leg, and then resuming her difficult flight through the resilient grasses.

But the image in her head was loud and clear and insistent, and she obeyed it on reflex. The creature that burst through the grasses did not remotely fit with the other dinosaur-like animals she'd seen. It was pure mythology, something she truly didn't believe nature could have cooked up without sapient imagining.

The beast was at first glance equine, its body the size of an exceptionally large draft horse. But where a horse had fur, this thing had scales. Tiny, glistening scales the color of dried blood that covered every inch of its body, and it had a row of sharp vertical spikes in place of a mane. A spiraled horn jutted from its forehead, and as the creature charged, it lowered its head and drove that horn straight through the body of one of the attacking mutts.

The need for Nyx's ducking became obvious when the creature's tail arced out in a semi-circle over Nyx's crouched form. It spun on its hindquarters, carrying that tail-whip in a full circle. The tip of the tail ended in small, wicked flechettes that carved into the mutts. They struck, biting deep, and where they landed sparks of flame leapt from the contact.

Nyx had once asked Evra if unicorns and dragons existed, to which Evra had replied with a distinct, "No," and an implied, "Are you an idiot?"

Nyx was one-hundred percent certain she was in the process of being rescued by a unicorn-dragon. With one sweep of its tail, it took out the mutts to Nyx's left. One or two stumbled to their feet, but they were so injured Nyx was easily able to dispatch them.

To her right, the unicorn-dragon wreaked utter destruction. It flung the mutt impaled on its horn toward two others, knocking them down like bowling pins. Two of the mutts leapt onto the creature's back, their claws sliding harmlessly off the hard, tight armor of its scales.

The unicorn-dragon kicked and gored. It struck with its tail. Wherever hooves or tail landed, flame followed. For its crowning finale, it opened its maw, the split of its lips going several inches further back than a horse's would, and revealed a double row of sharp, pointed fangs that bit the remaining mutt in half.

Overhead, the storm broke. Whatever part of it called the creatures of the land to madness broke with it, and the field around Nyx morphed from the insanity of battle to the chaos of animals fleeing.

The unicorn-dragon did *not* flee. It turned the whole of its terrifying visage upon Nyx.

She stood, but froze mid-crouch when its ears perked forward. Its eyes were distinctly reptilian rather than equine, a deep yellow with a vertical slit black pupil. It was a disconcerting difference. The unicorn-dragon looked at her with some degree of intelligence, she just didn't know if that was high-animal intelligence or actual-sapience intelligence.

"Umm…thank you?" she offered. When in doubt, be polite.

Carefully, as if wary of *her*, the unicorn-dragon stretched out its neck as far as possible, reaching its muzzle toward her without moving its planted feet. Nyx held very, very still. Its fine-scaled muzzle touched her chest, the great unicorn horn mere inches from her face. The second it made contact it jerked back as if it hadn't quite expected her to be real.

It made a noise that was somewhere between a snort, a squeal, and a roar, and jumped straight up, all four hooves leaving the ground in an undignified manner. Its tail flicked, showering the air with sparks and catching several of the nearby stalks of grass on fire. It landed, gave a half rear, then trotted a circle around her, making all manner of sounds.

Sounds her translator spell did not translate.

Had she scared the unicorn-dragon? Angered it? Excited it? It pranced back around to face up with her again, slowly creeping forward, forward, forward, until—

It shoved its face into her chest, only failing to gore her because the lower half of its face was so long that its horn went over her shoulder. Sincerely hoping she was reading the room right and not about to get herself killed—really, she'd had that hope entirely too many times since becoming a Guardian—Nyx went with instinct and reached up to scratch behind the animal's left ear.

A deep rumble, like a cat's purr on steroids, kindled inside the massive chest. It pushed its face harder into both her chest and her hand, the sheer power of the large creature forcing her back a couple steps. Its horn knocked into the side of her neck, but it didn't seem to notice.

Up close and personal, the unicorn-dragon was larger than a clydesdale, and apparently starved for affection.

15

Nyx stumbled back another step as the unicorn-dragon butted its head against her again. It was both adorably cute and hazardous to her health.

Large animals did not, typically, realize how fragilely breakable humans were. Nyx's childhood mare, Belle, had had a propensity to want to use her as a rubbing post as well, and never once considered she might damage the human girl.

If the unicorn-dragon had been a horse, Nyx would have nudged its face away and asked it to back up out of her space. What did she do with a unicorn-dragon? Already, she felt a bruise forming on the side of her neck where, with every vigorous rub of the creature's face, its horn knocked against her. It was also worth considering that the animal wasn't entirely equine. Half its genetic makeup was very much mythological dragon. What if it decided she smelled nice and got the urge to bite her?

Her vivid imagination conjured an image of the unicorn-dragon chomping her in half.

A second after Nyx had the thought, the animal gave what could only be termed an appalled snort and backed away from her, a quizzical look in its eyes. It tilted its head at her, and then a series of images launched into Nyx's mind: Nyx and the unicorn-dragon running together. Nyx throwing a stick and the unicorn-dragon chasing it. Nyx picking out the sticker burrs stuck in between the spikes on the back of its neck.

"You communicate with images?" she asked disbelievingly. Yes, she'd gotten the impression that the order to "duck" earlier had come from it. That it could project images into *her* mind wasn't necessarily that weird to her. She'd experienced stranger things since coming to Earth Between. But that Nyx could somehow project images into *its* mind? Or that it could just pick them up, as it seemed to have picked up on the one she'd had of it biting her in half? That was…weird.

In response to her question, the unicorn-dragon gave an irritated huff and sent her an image of them. It wasn't just an image, though, because alone, that image didn't mean anything. No, it was an image combined with feelings, a sort of irritated exasperation, as if the creature was saying, "Use your thoughts," in the same way an adult might say to a screaming child, "Use your words."

But how exactly did that kind of communication work? Images weren't words, and Nyx had always been utterly terrible at interpreting art. During one of her lonelier years in Dead Earth, she'd spent a lot of time in the Phoenix Art Museum. She'd gotten a terrible headache for being away from Tempe, but it was manageable, and she had tried, very hard and very diligently, to appreciate the supposedly impressive art there.

She had come to the conclusion that she didn't get it. She *liked* some of it, but whatever art history majors spent their extensive college careers interpreting and theorizing on was a complete mystery to her. She was so bad at it that she found reading graphic novels taxing. She spent far too much time feeling like she was missing the point, which was buried somewhere in the pictures, and it took her forever to get around to reading the text because, by the time she got to it, she felt like she'd still missed half the story.

"Okay," she muttered under her breath. "Use your thoughts." She'd felt something along with the unicorn-dragon's last image. So maybe she could send her own feelings back with an image.

She remembered the fear of being trapped in the circle of mutts, then the unicorn-dragon bursting in to rescue her. She sent that series of images and tried to imbue it with her gratitude.

The unicorn-dragon—she really had to come up with something shorter to think of it as—let out a pleased rumble and resumed its purr-roar. At least, Nyx hoped it was a pleased rumble. Really, how did something with an equine body purr?

Okay, refocus. Nyx had said *Thank you*. The unicorn-dragon had not yet run off. She considered the thoughts it had first sent her—which had essentially amounted to the two of them hanging out.

So it—Nyx ducked a sideways glance underneath it and came up with *she*—wasn't surprised or confused by Nyx—a human. Hope blossomed in Nyx's chest. If the unicorn-dragon had met other humans, or other species similar enough to humans that she wasn't weirded out by Nyx, then maybe this planet had other people on it.

She tried to imagine other people next to them. She wasn't good at abstract imagining, so she ended up sticking Morgen, Evra, and Seth onto the landscape. And, because she was a spoken language person at the end of the day, incapable of *not* saying what she meant, as she sent the image she asked, "Are there other people here?"

The beast shook her head and sent an image back. Empty landscape.

Nyx frowned. Did that mean there weren't any other people on the planet, or just that there weren't any in their vicinity? She crafted a new image, this time the landscape filled with other unicorn-dragons. "Are there any more of your people here?"

A wave of sadness hit her, and Nyx felt like she'd just bought a kid their favorite candy bar, only to unwrap it and stomp it into the dirt. Nyx received an image of the unicorn-dragon standing alone in the tall grasses while in the distance the sun rose and set, rose and set, repeating on an endless loop.

"You've been here alone?" Nyx didn't think she sent an image with that, but maybe her tone got the meaning across, because the unicorn-dragon nodded. A second later she perked up, sending another image back of the two of them together.

Not alone, anymore, she seemed to say, and sent back the series of images of all the things she apparently wanted to do. Things she had, perhaps, done with someone else?

Nyx didn't think the unicorn-dragon—okay, that was it, she was calling her Drago—was intelligent in the sense that the species that traveled the ley lines were. She got much the sense from Drago that she did from dogs and cats and other highly intelligent mammals. Drago wasn't dumb, but Nyx also didn't think she worried about things like inventing new technologies, accumulating wealth, paying mortgages, and so on. The things every other traveling species in the verse seemed to have in common.

No, Drago felt like a highly intelligent, designer pet. And she was out here, in the middle of nowhere, alone.

"I swear to every star in this universe, if someone *dumped you here* because they didn't want to take care of you anymore, I am going to find them and murder them."

She rubbed at the space between her eyebrows. Okay. She'd made a friend. This was good. She wasn't alone on a foreign planet anymore, and Drago had presumably been here awhile. That was also good for Nyx. Drago would know things she didn't. Like where there might be a safe space to try and figure out what she was going to do next.

She looked down at herself, taking stock of the remaining portal magic that clung to her, and her heart sank. She had enough—*maybe* enough—for one more portal. One more chance to get home. But if she'd made this many jumps already without landing on a planet inhabited with a species that could get her home, what were her chances of doing so on the next jump? Of doing so *blind* on the next jump, because she didn't have enough magic to risk opening portals to various planets to try and choose the best one?

The universe had a lot of planets. Nyx could be literally anywhere. If she jumped again, she could die, or end up on another planet as equally unable to help her as this one. But if she stayed, would she wander here forever, with only Drago for company?

A hysterical bubble of laughter rose in her throat as she was reminded of *Jumanji*, of Robin Williams' character. *In the jungle you must wait, until the dice read five or eight.* There was no board game sitting at home, waiting for someone to come along and roll the right dice to bring her back. While Seth, Morgen, Griff, and Evra were probably losing their minds trying to figure out what had happened to her, they couldn't hope to reach her here. Wherever *here* was.

Stars, she missed them.

So quit whining about it and do something. She took a step, wincing as she did. Her right calf, the one the mermaid had bitten, pulsed and throbbed painfully. Cuts and scrapes were not something Nyx had ever really worried about before. Because before, she'd always had access to things like soap and clean water and antibacterial gel and bandages.

"I will never take modern conveniences for granted again," she muttered. The bite had torn through the mercury boot, and she unbuckled it now, rolling the top of it down and pulling her pants leg up. The cloth was stuck to her calf with dried blood and didn't want to give. If it was coming off, she was going to have to rip it off, quickly and painfully. Then it would start bleeding again, and what was she going to clean it with? Her clothes were relatively clean, being the dirt-resistant Talorean cloth—thank the stars—but that also meant they wouldn't make very good bandages if she cut them apart.

She had a morbid curiosity to know how deep the gouges

went, but not at the expense of making things worse when she had no feasible way to then make them better. She needed to find water, though even if she did, she wasn't sure using it to clean a wound was the best idea.

There were very few bodies of water left on Earth one could simply drink out of and not come down with a bacterial infection or worse. Rinsing an open wound in potentially alien-bacteria-riddled waters sounded like a good way to lose a leg. Then again, so did letting infection set in because she *hadn't* cleaned it.

Of course, if she didn't get off this planet soon she was going to have to drink the water, at which point cleaning a wound with it couldn't be much worse. She hoped. Maybe she would get lucky and it would rain.

She slid the top of the boot back around her calf and re-buckled it, taking a tentative step. It hurt, but maybe as long as she kept moving, it wouldn't swell up and become an even bigger problem.

The sky, as if it had sensed her request for rain—or, more likely, as if it just felt like being problematic—darkened once more, the swell of thunder growing. A growl rose in Drago's throat, and an image flashed into Nyx's head of her on Drago's back. Pretty-as-you-please, the unicorn-dragon went to her knees in a little bow.

Having seen what the storms brought last time, Nyx didn't hesitate. She threw her leg over Drago's back and barely settled astride before Drago leapt to her feet. Nyx's right hand gripped one of Dragon's mane spikes. A pulse of pain went through her fingers, but she couldn't switch hands, because the bo staff was stuck to her left.

This time, what tore out of the grass toward them was not a dinosaur mutt, but a horde of something much more akin to *Velociraptors*. Drago whirled and sprinted into a gallop. Nyx nearly lost her seat at the sudden maneuver, her legs clamping down around scaly sides as long limbs ate up the ground.

They hurtled forward as the raptor pack emitted yips and

cackles in tandem, sending Nyx's heart into a primal sort of panic. Even being chased by the Kumir hadn't felt like this. However strange the Kumir were, they were still human and could, therefore, theoretically be reasoned with. They were hired assassins. Their hunting of her was methodical.

What was happening behind her was in no way methodical. It was the violent wildness of something intent on bringing her down and ripping into her. Drago was running for all she was worth, but the raptors were gaining on them.

The grass grew thicker and taller. Drago burst through a particularly dense section, stalks grabbing at Nyx's skin and hair. She felt the sharp stinging pull as a chunk of locks caught and ripped free of her scalp. It was impossible to keep track of the raptors on their heels, the grasses too tall to allow her to actually see them.

Suddenly, a loud rustle sounded to her left, and she brought the bo staff up just in time as one of the raptors leapt, its jaws closing around the metal of the staff instead of her leg. It clamped its jaws down anyway, the harsh jerk as Drago continued forward and the raptor dug in its heels lancing a bolt of pain up her shoulder. Just when she thought it was either drop the staff or fall off Drago's back, the raptor lost its grip on the slippery metal and its teeth slid off.

"Please tell me you have a plan," Nyx shouted, sending her words along with an image of a raptor-less landscape. Drago sent her an image back. It was of a forested area that abutted the grasses they now ran through. In the image, Drago and Nyx ran into the forest, and the raptors stayed in the grassy area, despite there being no physical impediments Nyx could see that would stop them from following.

Nyx heard another rustle and swung the bo staff in a wide arc, over her head and then down, slamming it into the skull of the raptor to her left. Now would be a find time for Drago to help out with a fiery tail-flick, but the whole of the unicorn-dragon's focus seemed intent on forward momentum, as if simply getting to the treeline would make them safe.

Nyx couldn't see any reason why the raptors would be afraid of trees, so it had to be something *else* about the forest. There had been a particular tree in the image, a different species than the others, and oddly silver. Nyx still couldn't see what it would do, but maybe it was what Drago was running for.

Nyx scanned the landscape ahead of them, and she could just barely make out what might be the silver tree. She just didn't hold out much hope of them getting to it before the raptors took them down. Only the two had attacked, the others waiting—waiting for Drago to tire, to stumble, to slow. Given the sweat dripping down her mount's scales—and Nyx was pretty sure scaled animals were not supposed to sweat, so that was weird—Drago would tire soon. The unicorn-dragon had already been sweaty when she'd first arrived to Nyx's rescue, as if she'd somehow sensed Nyx's presence and run a long way to reach her.

Combine that with this current all-out flight, and Drago had to be exhausted. Nyx needed to go on the offensive, to do something to keep the pack at bay, or they weren't going to reach the presumed safety of the forest. A memory popped into her head, Viktor teaching her what would be considered, by Dead Earth standards, a trick-riding maneuver. Tactically, it was most useful when one had a bow and arrow and was fleeing a battle. The rider flipped around on the horse so they faced their pursuers, and shot arrows at them when they wouldn't be expecting attack.

She hadn't done the maneuver in at least seven years. Hoping it was just like riding a bike—or in this case, a horse—she placed her hands on Drago's withers, awkward with the bo staff stuck to one hand, and hooked her right leg up and over, riding "sidesaddle" for a second before swinging her left leg around so she faced backwards. Her right hand slipped with the bo staff beneath it, and she overshot a little and unbalanced, digging her heel into Drago's side in a move that pulled her right hamstring muscle as she fought to stay astride.

She caught and rebalanced herself, reaching for the throwing stars at her belt just as one of the raptors lunged for Drago's right hind leg. Nyx gripped the star in her free hand and aimed for the throat. Between the jostle of Drago's gait and her limited recent practice with throwing stars, she didn't hit the target she'd intended. But that was okay, because instead of hitting the throat, the star embedded itself in the raptor's eye.

It went down with a cry, and Nyx felt twin pangs of relief and regret. She knew that nature wasn't always pretty and it was rarely kind, and it was a certain level of privilege afforded by advanced society that let most people go through life without sullying their hands with death of any kind. But she didn't have to like being the cause of that death. Maybe it was natural in the cycle of this world that a predator killed or was killed, but she shouldn't be a part of the natural cycle here. She was just in it, upsetting it, her stars finding target after target any time a raptor lunged.

It was almost too easy, because these were creatures that had no experience with humans, no understanding of avoiding ranged weapons. If they'd had that experience, maybe they would have backed off on their own. She gripped the last star between her fingers, readying it, when Drago gathered herself and leaped forward, and tree leaves brushed against Nyx's face.

Drago had barely passed the treeline when she skidded to a stop, and before Nyx could panic, the pack of raptors stopped short a foot from the trees, releasing high, keening screams. They clawed and shook their heads and then, as one, turned and fled.

Nyx and Drago stood right next to the silver tree she'd seen in the mental image, and as she looked farther down the treeline she saw another, and then a little ways farther, another. Brushing her fingers against the silver bark, she did not think it was entirely natural. It felt like it had once been a tree, but had been altered into something else.

Was it some kind of force-field or electric fence? Except it hadn't kept her or Drago out. Remembering the way the raptors had clawed at their heads, she wondered if it emitted a sound neither she nor Drago could hear, one particularly damaging to the other creatures on this planet. And if that's what it was—some sort of engineered perimeter fencing—then what was it guarding the perimeter *of*? More importantly, who or what had made it?

Uneasy, she slid off Drago's back and extended the bo staff back to full length, holding it like a walking stick as she turned to the unicorn-dragon. The great beast's head was down, her sides heaving. She was covered in white lather from her ears all the way down her neck, sweat dripping like rain from the scales.

She shot a nervous gaze back to the plains area. If there were *Velociraptor*-like creatures, and crazed dinosaur mutts, there was a good chance there were *other* things out there. Given the supersized nature of all the flora, it pointed strongly towards the likelihood of supersized fauna. She had zero desire to meet anything on the level of a *T. rex*.

"Hey." She lightly touched her hand to Drago's withers. The mare startled, then relaxed, turning to press her face once more into Nyx's chest, horn resting over her shoulder. Nyx rubbed behind her ears. "You did good, buddy. But I think we need to get moving." She sent Drago an image of the two of them walking. Drago heaved a great sigh and lifted her head, walking off to the right. She stayed within the treeline, but Nyx couldn't help but notice she hadn't ventured any further in.

"Does something else live in here?" she asked. But she didn't know how to ask that question via pictures. Drago just tilted her head quizzically at her.

If Nyx knew what creatures she was asking about, she could picture them in the woods and send it to Drago. But she didn't. It wasn't lifeless within this forest—the air was filled with the myriad sounds of buzzing insects and flying things, and dozens of other noises she couldn't identify, all fading into the background like a pleasant white noise.

Drago was clearly comfortable here. Unworried. Maybe whatever had built the perimeter defense was long gone? The prison on her first planet had been long-abandoned, after all. Maybe it was the same here.

The unicorn-dragon paused, muscles tensing, her head going straight up in the air, ears perked. Nyx stopped too, turning in a slow circle, looking around and above. She didn't see anything. But she noticed the sounds had stopped, every creature within hearing distance gone still and silent.

She felt it before she heard it, a vibration in the earth like the marching of hundreds of feet, speeding toward them.

"Run?" She sent an accompanying image. But Drago didn't run. She went to her knees, then her belly, tucking her chin to her chest so the tip of her horn rested on the ground, as if in supplication. Then Drago sent an image to Nyx in return, of her doing the same thing.

Nyx's pulse beat wildly in her throat, the thrum of the earth and the approaching roar of sound demanding that she move, that she run. But the only place to run was back out to the plains, where the raptors and who knew what else waited.

Drago was down. She was tense but she wasn't terrified. Rational thought told Nyx that if the creature who lived here was telling her to fold herself into a submissive posture, it was the smart thing to do. Her flight instinct told her to flee.

She hovered, caught between doing as Drago advised, running for her life, or pulling a weapon with an actual blade. The branches on the trees ahead swayed wildly. Hoping she wasn't making a monumental mistake by putting her faith in a creature she'd only just met, Nyx went to her knees. She still couldn't drop the bo staff, so she placed it on the ground in front of her, bowed her head, and squeezed her eyes shut.

Later, she would think that shutting her eyes had been the best possible thing she could have done. Because if she hadn't, she'd never have been able to stay on her knees, never been able to resist bringing her bo staff up. Wind created by the approaching force teased at her hair. The footsteps grew to a crescendo, then halted abruptly. Something whipped through the air, stopping just shy of her face.

Heart racing, Nyx opened her eyes to a stinger the length of her forearm, its curved, wicked tip an inch from her eye.

16

Nyx jerked back from the stinger on instinct, then froze at the feel of a faint, rough prick at the nape of her neck. She swallowed. Her eyes skimmed over the threat at her front, down a long segmented tail, to a body that was…that was…

She didn't know what it was. Insectoid, to be sure, but she didn't think insects had ever grown this large on Earth, even millennia ago. Its abdomen was easily six feet long, held aloft by eight spindly legs. From there, where the thorax of a similarly built insect would be, was something that *could* potentially be considered a thorax, but it rose straight up in the air, perpendicular to the abdomen.

The thorax stretched four feet before attaching to a head that was both ant-like and not. Antennae sprang from its forehead, double mandibles bracketing a mouth that towered above her. Its eyes were a pupil-less ink black. The smooth chitin of its exterior was a shining, glittering ochre that seemed to shift in tone.

It was beautiful. It was terrifying. It was monumentally pissed. And there were dozens more just like it surrounding her.

The one whose stinger rested in front of her face clicked its mandibles together furiously. Hissing, spitting noises emerged from its throat. The sounds had a cadence to them like language, but the translator spell on her wrist did not twist the words into something she could understand. But it was *definitely* language, which meant the creature wasn't an *it*, but he or she or they.

The hissing and clicking stopped and the creature's head pulled back, a weight to their stare that clearly indicated they expected her to provide an answer.

"I'm sorry," she said, "I don't understand."

Mandibles clicked and the insectoid head came forward again, dipping until it came level with hers. He—she decided to go with "he" for ease of reference—issued another stream of hisses and clicks that sounded almost identical to the first, as if he was repeating his question and somehow thought getting in her face about it would make her more likely to understand.

But the sounds didn't make any more sense to her the second time around. "I'm sorry, I still don't understand. I'm kind of lost." She smiled, trying to appear friendly before remembering that, at best, a smile meant nothing to someone who didn't have lips and, at worst, baring her teeth might be taken as a threat. "I didn't mean to come into your territory, if that's what this is, and I—"

She cut off as his head tilted abruptly. For a hopeful moment, she thought maybe he had some translator spell of his own, one that had simply taken a moment to kick in, and now he understood her. But he didn't respond to her words. His gaze was riveted on her chest. She dared a glance down. At some point in her mad journey, her necklace chain had come free, the Harvester of Worlds no longer hidden behind her shirt.

The stinger touched the side of her face and trailed down her cheek, her neck, before slipping beneath the necklace chain. *No, no, no.* He *couldn't* be seeing the Harvester, could he? Her magic hummed along happily, giving no indication that her Hiding had stopped working.

The stinger caught the chain and tugged, cleaving the necklace in half. The Harvester and Jevryn's ring, the two items she always wore on it, tumbled down. The stinger darted for the falling items. But it was Jevryn's ring it caught on its end, while the Harvester tumbled to the forest floor, unnoticed.

She reached for the Harvester, but that small movement had the stinger at her back pressing sharply into her neck. She froze and the pressure stopped increasing, but the wet trickle sliding down her neck told her it had broken skin.

Please, please do not let that be a venomous stinger. Given the size of the creatures, if the stingers could deliver venom, she would probably already be feeling it. Carefully, she pulled her hand away from the Harvester and dropped it to her side. The pressure at her neck lessened, until she once again felt only the barest touch.

The commotion over, the insectoid alien at her front drew his tail to him, holding the ring before his eye and studying it as a jeweler might inspect a diamond. A buzz of power arced from the alien to the ring, as if he searched for something. His tail whipped forward, shaking the ring in Nyx's face while he issued a new series of noises at her. He looked angrier than he had before.

"I don't know what you're asking. It's a ring, it's just a ring."

The stinger shook again, the ring twirling around its tip. This time when the alien spoke it was short, harsh, and demanding.

Did he...want to know where she'd gotten it? It seemed absurd, but he had clearly recognized the ring. Or...she thought back to the testing jolt of magic the alien had probed at the ring with. The ring belonged to Jevryn. Who was to say what kind of magic it held? Possibly magic the alien wouldn't like. Maybe Jevryn's ring was a magical stealth bomb that could explode at any time, and the terrifying being before her thought Nyx had personally come to deliver that threat.

Wait a second. It was *Jevryn's* ring. *Councilor* Jevryn, of the near-immortal All Council that everyone claimed had brought order to the universe.

"The ring was a gift," she said, even though she knew he wouldn't understand that part. But the next words she spoke slowly, careful to pronounce each syllable clearly. "From Jevryn A-Morridahn."

If she'd thought everything around her had been still and quiet before, it went more so now. It sounded like something in the alien's throat was rearranging and then, in an eerie, high-pitched tone that sounded like a maniacal mockery of her own, drawing out the syllables in strange places, he said, "Zhev-ryn 'ah More-ee-dahn. All Coun-sel."

Sincerely hoping that whatever Jevryn's relationship with these people was, it wasn't one that was going to get her killed, she nodded slightly. "Yes. Jevryn A-Morridahn from the All Council gave it to me."

The alien moved quicker than she could follow, his tail wrapping around her abdomen. The tail pinned her arms to her sides and jerked her up, like she was caught in the coils of an anaconda. She made a desperate lunge for the Harvester. Her fingers brushed the edge of its sphere but the alien jerked her airborne before she could latch onto it. Holding her aloft, her captor issued a series of clicks to the others, and they sped toward the inner forest, leaving the Harvester behind.

<hr>

Nyx noticed the columns first. Of a circular construction, maybe four feet in diameter, they were formed from thick, waxy leaves that had been pasted together, like some sort of bizarre nature papier-mâché.

She leaned back as much as she could in the confines of the tail's grip and craned her neck. But no matter how she squinted, she couldn't see past the dense canopy above to discover what the columns were for. All the movement and effort did was remind her that she hurt. The height of her adrenaline had worn off, dulling to a constant, low-level fear that gave her time to notice her injuries as the alien scurried through the forest with frightening speed.

Al, she decided. She was going to call him Al, because it was harder to be frightened of Al the Friendly Insect Being than it was to be afraid of the unknown giant insectoid monster. Al, though he might be friendly in the make-believe space in her mind, was not a smooth ride, each step jarring.

Nyx's calf throbbed in a way that made her suspect the mermaid's bite might have been venomous where the stinger of Al's buddy had not been. Or, if not venomous, at least infection-causing. Wasn't it supposed to be bad to go into the ocean with an open wound? Was she on the verge of an alien blood infection?

Her arms, trapped tightly against her sides, made her blistered fingers knock against her leg with each jostling stride, and the sunburn on her face was severe enough that even the light breeze felt unpleasant.

Al let out an eerie, high-pitched screaming noise that was either a we-have-arrived announcement or a war cry, and ran straight at the base of one of the columns. He was moving so fast, there was no way he could stop in time to avoid a collision. If Nyx had thought it would do any good, she would have loosed a scream of her own.

At the last second, she tensed her muscles, bracing for impact. It never came. The pincers on Al's front legs jabbed into the column's sides, pulled free and grabbed higher as pincers on his lower limbs gained purchase. Al ascended, back legs catching hold, his body flattening like a centipede's. He scurried up the vertical structure as easily and quickly as a horse galloped over smooth land. Up and up and up he went, and if it wasn't for the fear that closing her eyes would somehow get her killed, Nyx would have done it.

Part of her wondered why the aliens didn't simply climb the trees—why build these giant columns in parallel?—but most of her just wanted the trip to be over. All it would take was one accidental uncoiling of Al's tail and she would be free-falling with nothing to stop her. What if Al decided he *wanted* to drop her? She could practically hear him reporting the incident to whoever was in charge. *Well, you see, I did* find *a soft-skinned alien creature, but I'm afraid I dropped it. Tail cramp. Getting old is hell, you know.*

She started laughing—not a good sign given her current circumstances—and couldn't stop until they broke through the canopy and Al lurched over a ninety-degree curve, putting them on horizontal footing.

"Holy shit."

At her words, Al's upper body went vertical again. He swiveled to look at her with something that approximated wariness. But since he wasn't threatening her, talking at her, or moving, he was no longer interesting enough to wrench her gaze from the sky city that sprawled before her.

Swaying bridges stretched from post to post, criss-crossing and connecting in various directions as far as her eye could see. At least, Nyx thought of them as bridges. They didn't have the typical human construction of a swinging bridge, with planks and guide-ropes, but rather were like more flexible versions of the circular post Al had just ascended. In that sense, she supposed they were more like cables.

They were alive with movement and energy, the insectoid aliens zooming along the cables. They didn't appear to have directional lanes—if two of the aliens were about to hit a head-on collision on the same cable, they both shifted to the sides, the cables wide enough around to allow them to move on opposite sides until they were past each other.

As she watched, one of them hit an intersection and switched to a vertical cable. Nyx followed their progress and realized the tree city extended multiple levels higher. It was like the upward camera shot on a sci-fi film of a futuristic city, except instead of tech-fueled hover lanes, or other sky-based transit, this one was a criss-cross weave of cables and ropes.

Al started moving again, as if he'd finally decided his strange alien captive wasn't going to descend into a fit of madness with the potential to upset his balance, and it was time to move things along. This first level of the city appeared to be nothing but a transit center, the cables here primary lines like highways or interstates. As they moved deeper into the labyrinth, some of the city's insectoid aliens would descend to this level only to move a few cables over horizontally and then go back up.

There was also no place to rest on this level. As Al transitioned seamlessly to a vertical cable, carrying her up, up, up, with no end in sight, the differences between that initial level and the others became even more pronounced. She passed several levels that appeared business based, aliens congregating at various platforms and stations built between the cables, the air alive with the sound of their chatter. Some had patterns in bright colors painted onto their carapaces, and these garnered the most attention from their peers.

Other levels appeared more industrial. The aliens on these were smaller, more nimble, and they bustled about with near-feverish intensity, though Nyx couldn't tell what that intensity was directed toward.

Al caught a horizontal line and carried them to the city's very edge—an edge that was under expansion. Here, at least, Nyx understood what the aliens were doing. Workers carried large woven sacks filled with leaves that were larger than Nyx. They handed the leaves off to workers who clung precariously to inch-thin cables. These workers ran the leaves back and forth through their mandibles, coating them in a thick, viscous liquid and then molding them around the thin cable, building it out.

Al caught another vertical cable. The levels they passed now were less populated. They had a feeling of exclusivity and privilege, and she didn't see a single alien on them who didn't have at least some decoration or adornment. She also noted the presence of what appeared to be guards stationed around the perimeter of each level. These were all larger insectoids, like Al, and his crew. They were resolute and unmoving, where the aliens on the other levels were either industriously busy, or easy and relaxed.

Even these guards paid them little mind—which told Nyx either nothing ever happened here, or Al was high up in the chain of command—until they reached the top floor. At least, Nyx assumed it was the top because she couldn't see above. Where the other levels had been largely constructed of cable, with only small areas containing an actual "floor," this level was all floor. Or roof? She wasn't sure which word better applied. Unlike the transit cables, those above her were thinner and worked in a cross-hatched pattern, supporting a dense brown mat. Like the world's largest, flat hammock covered over with a cushion.

Two guards waited on platforms built just below a three-foot-wide opening. They clearly recognized Al, and their issue, as their tails crossed over the opening to deny him entrance, just as clearly wasn't with him. They broke into angry-sounding clicks, pointing their arms in Nyx's direction.

She was a little carsick, for lack of a better word, by this point, and it took her longer than it should have to put together that the guards didn't want to let Al through if he was still in possession of her. One's tail even swiveled toward Nyx—as if he intended to take possession of her—but Al drew himself up, the lower half of his body holding onto the cable while the front half went perpendicular to the rest. He held the arms on the upper half of his body wide, as if saying, "You think you can? By all means, go ahead and try."

The two guards hesitated, glancing at each other. A new series of clicks issued from Al's mouth. Nyx had a feeling they were in the "or" portion of the conversation. "Let me through, *or* this Very Bad Thing will happen to you." She thought she might have caught Jevryn's name, but Al was speaking so fast she couldn't be sure.

Just when Nyx thought Al was going to engage in a fight with the guards, a sound like soft thunder greeted her ears, and the floor above them rippled. The two guards went slack. Not quiescent, as if willing to let Al pass, but non-responsive, as if they didn't even see Al anymore. Al dropped his upper body back to the cable and ascended.

Nyx sucked in a breath, desperately wishing Al would put her down, so she could run in the opposite direction. The outer five feet of the floor was clear. After that, it was lined with the large insectoids she decided to label the warrior class. They stood in a neat row, enough space between to allow them to maneuver, but not so much that anyone would think of trying to dart between them. Another row of guards waited behind the first. Al carried them along the edge of the floor until they came to an opening in the line that was about four feet across. He slipped through it, turning left into a corridor made by living beings. He followed it down, around a corner, down again, to slip through another four-foot-wide opening and into the next corridor.

It didn't take many turns for Nyx to realize Al was carrying her through a living maze. He passed some openings by in favor of others, winding deeper and deeper, towards the center of the floor. She wondered what the point of the maze was—generally speaking, if you built a maze to keep people from finding something, it was because you didn't have the people to guard it. But this maze was *made* of guards.

Al took another turn and they fell under the shade of a great awning. This level was stretched between the very tops of the trees, and thus wasn't shaded by the tree canopy. She looked and saw poles stretching up from the floor, between which was stretched the awning that provided relief from the sun. It was made of the same leaves she'd seen the workers rolling and molding to make the cables, though in the awning they were stretched flat and pasted together.

They moved inward until they were nearly beneath the center of the awning, stopping in front of a row of guards packed so tightly together no space could be seen between them.

Al approached the tallest of them, who drew himself up in a clear defensive stance.

Al issued a series of clicks. The guard he spoke to jabbed a pincher at Nyx and retorted with a stream of angry sounds. Al clicked his mandibles together and pushed forward, into the other's face. Nyx tensed. If these two were about to get into it, she would prefer it if Al put her down first.

Then a new voice filtered out from beyond the row of guards, the clicks rolling out with a softer, somehow more melodious, edge. The guard before them absolutely did not look pleased. But he did step aside and back, as did the six guards to either side of him, forming a mini corridor with their bodies, and revealing what could only be the colony queen.

17

The queen lounged on a plush bed of soft mosses. She was bigger than all the others Nyx had seen so far, nearly double Al's size. Her coloring was exquisite, running the gamut from gold and silver on her face to indigo blue down her thorax, shifting to deepest purple on her abdomen. Patterns—words?—swirled within those bases in different colors—jewel-toned greens and blues, and metallic pinks and oranges. This, Nyx thought, was what the aliens on the other levels were trying to mimic with their body painting. This beauty, this color, this purpose.

But unlike the others, the designs on the queen did not look made from anything so common as paint. Nyx narrowed her eyes, feeling the power that swirled through the air on this level. Wild strands of color swam into her vision. For every color on the queen's body, a corresponding funnel of power connected to her, like mini tornadoes that fed in and out of her from something above.

Nyx craned her head, trying to see. A small circular opening cut through the shade awning high above the queen. The triangular tip of something vaguely crystalline jutted through the opening, like an enormous glass jewel suspended above them, and in its depths swirled...portal magic. Nyx grabbed for it with that innate part of her that was drawn to portals, but nothing answered her. So *much* nothing that she wondered if she was wrong, and whatever lay inside the crystal was only blue, but not magic.

Then the small bit of portal magic that still clung to her leg—all she had left—lifted away, as if the crystal called to it. She grabbed for it mentally, desperate to hold on, but all except a small, dime-sized piece tore away, disappearing into the crystal's depths.

Nyx stared down at the small piece clinging to her boot, her stomach sinking so hard it might as well be trying to exit her body. Before, she'd doubted she had enough to open another portal, but now? Now she had nothing.

The queen shifted. She had watched Nyx's struggle with a sort of bored interest, catered to on all sides by attendants rubbing ointment into her exoskeleton, others fanning her gently with a large leaf. Now, she gave a dismissive wave of her foreleg in a "leave us" gesture so human-like that it made Nyx wonder if she was simply interpreting the other species' actions through a human lens. But then the queen's attendants ceased their attentions and filed out of the maze.

Al's tail swung forward and uncoiled, dropping Nyx to the ground. She stumbled, landing with a crunch of the dried, coniferous-like needles that comprised the floor. His tail remained around her in a loose circle, ready to capture her once more should she prove problematic.

Remembering Drago's warning to her when the aliens had approached them at the forest's perimeter, Nyx tried to look non-threatening as she dropped slowly to her knees. The bite in her calf gave a painful throb of protest.

The queen studied Nyx, her black eyes inscrutable, before her gaze shifted to Al. He retrieved Jevryn's ring, which he extended to the queen with stately grace. He spoke.

Nyx's extreme desire to know what Al said had another flare

of effort coming from her translator spell, but it once again failed to make any sense of the alien language. Only when Al broke from his native speech to repeat Jevryn's name in that creepy, high-pitched mimicry of her own voice, did she understand anything.

The queen took the ring, rolling it between two pinchers. She looked at Nyx and spoke. The clicks were not accompanied by any bodily gesture or tonal change Nyx could pick up on to give any indication of what the queen wanted. She could have been saying, "Lovely weather we're having," for all the emotion that went along with her statement. Nyx wondered if that lack of emotion was a facet of the species—or, more likely, a lack of Nyx's ability to recognize what expressions and movements denoted emotion in the species—or if it was a matter of the queen's position, that she had trained all such tells out of herself.

"I'm sorry, I don't understand." Nyx wondered how many times she was going to say those words. She didn't speak them because she thought the aliens would understand her, but out of a desire not to be seen as belligerent or uncooperative. Did they have *no* translator here? These people must have seen a human before—or at least, the queen and the one beside Nyx must have —because they had been wary of her but they hadn't seemed surprised. Maybe they had met Jevryn himself, since his name clearly meant something to them. If they had, how had Jevryn communicated with them?

The queen let out a rapid-fire sequence of clicks and held the ring out, much as Al had done when they had first seen it. Nyx repeated Jevryn's name, along with the words "All Council." Then, on a stroke of inspiration, she said the names of every other councilor she could remember. The four who had come to her Station came easily to mind, and she pronounced them with care. "Kiev A-Morridahn. Alistair. Alora. Coral." She didn't know any of the others' last names, but the more names she said, the more grave the queen became.

When Nyx had been silent for a moment, the queen chittered

angrily, flinging two arms on the same side out wide. Nyx hoped her expression conveyed confused and apologetic as she repeated, for the eight-billionth time, "I'm sorry, I don't understand."

The queen's mandibles clicked together and her tail lashed toward Nyx. Nyx scrambled back, her instincts screaming that this was the moment she died. Al's tail clamped around her, preventing her from going anywhere. Which was probably a good thing, because the queen wasn't actually trying to kill her, while the row of guards behind her probably would if she stumbled into them.

Rather than the stinger at the end of her captor's tail, the queen's had something that more resembled the grabber claw in those game machines where you put a quarter in and futilely attempted to retrieve a stuffed animal. The grabber was comprised of eight segments, the points of which all met. They snapped open, and a ribbon of portal magic streamed from the crystal above, spinning into the grabber.

Nyx fought the urge to try and take it from the queen. It wasn't enough for a portal. The queen drew the magic before her, four upper arms weaving, and the now-familiar planet map came into view.

Except it wasn't the same map. Or, it was, but it was more extensive. Where Nyx's map had included only small sections, what she'd assumed were the planets in range of her ability to reach, this map spanned hundreds of planets, so large it filled the entirety of the room in which they stood.

Nyx stared around her, disbelieving. "Can you reach all of these?" she asked, wonder in her voice. And if the queen could, why had no one in the ley-line-connected universe ever met anyone from this species? Nyx had gone through the resources at the Station, trying little-by-little to correct her massive ignorance about the universe. While she couldn't recall every sapient species off the top of her head—there were dozens of subspecies for the human base alone—she was certain there hadn't been any insectoid species among them. To a one, every sapient species listed was either mammalian, avian, or reptilian, and the reptilian ones were fairly few in number.

The queen tilted her head, mandibles clicking in what Nyx could only interpret as a mutter. She waved two of her forelegs and the map changed. Some of the planets disappeared entirely, including what Nyx was pretty sure was one of the uninhabitable ones she'd briefly been on during her journey here. Of the ones that remained, some planets took on a purple tinge, while the rest took on a red coloring.

Another flick of the queen's legs and a white line traced through the space between, isolating the purple planets from the red. The queen pointed to herself, then to the purple planets. Then she pointed to Nyx and indicated the red planets. Understanding dawned even before the queen pointed to the white line, and mimed Nyx moving across it combined with bringing the sharp tips of her tail to Nyx's throat.

Well, fuck.

There was, apparently, a border zone in the universe, and Nyx had illegally crossed it. She suspected the only reason she wasn't dead already was that, having recognized Jevryn's ring, Al and the queen feared she might have an interpersonal connection to the All Council. As a general rule, illegalities or no, it was a bad idea to kill someone who might be of importance to the ruling members of the neighboring territory, if you didn't want to start a war.

The queen was minding her T's and dotting her I's, in case it turned out Nyx was the All Council's favorite pet employee, and killing Nyx might anger them. How long did she have before the queen realized Nyx *didn't* have that connection, and Jevryn was not going to show up to this planet to get her out of her current mess?

Or, worse, did the queen have a way to contact the All Council? Death might well be preferable to whatever the Council would do with Nyx if they *did* decide to take it upon themselves to come get her.

This time, Nyx didn't respond to the queen's gestures. Even though her words couldn't be understood, silence felt like the smarter option. The queen let out a sound that reminded Nyx of one of Griff's world-weary sighs, and waved her foreleg. The map disappeared.

Al and the queen exchanged a few more clicks, and then Al's tail curled around Nyx once more. He carried her out of the maze, and descended to the level below. He spoke to the two guards at the entrance to the queen's level, then carried her to the corner of the floor, where a room—or was it a house?—was built onto the platform.

She had seen many like it on the way up, large, sprawling enclosures formed of the same coniferous-like needles that formed the floor of the queen's level. This one looked like it was made for only one of the alien beings. Two of them would fit, but they wouldn't have much room to walk around.

Al deposited her against the far wall and chattered away at her, pointing to things as he did. A mound of soft moss on one side of the room that was probably a bed. A spout on the far wall. A section of the wall that, to Nyx, looked no different than any of the rest.

As he was talking, another insectoid clicked at him and Al ducked out, returning a moment later with three items held carefully in various pinchers. The first was a wide earthen pot she sincerely hoped held water. Her throat was so dry it hurt, and keeping her eyes open against tiredness and dryness was a challenge. The second item was a small cup, the third a flat wooden tray of...food?

He placed the items on the floor and left. Nyx approached them. Outside the entrance, two guards shifted, alert, as if they thought she might make a break for it. Zero likelihood of that happening. She was barely standing.

She licked cracked lips, wincing as the movement hurt the

severely sunburned side of her face, and peered into the pot. Empty, as was the cup. She frowned. Why give her two empty receptacles? Unless…

Nyx went to the spout Al had pointed out on one of the walls. She pressed her ear to the mat and heard the sound of running water—as if a pipe rested on the other side and someone on one of the lower levels was drawing off it.

Hopeful, she retrieved the cup with her free hand, mindful of her burnt fingertips and sincerely wishing she'd listened to Morgen's advice to give up on the bo staff. Holding the cup under the spout, she used the tip of the shortened staff to depress the spout, and water poured out.

She *whooped* in excitement and heard a corresponding shuffle outside as one of the guards peered in, drawn by her exclamation. She toasted him with the cup of water. "Here's to hoping I don't get alien Giardia."

She tipped the cup back and drained it in a few greedy pulls. The guard shared a look with his companion, exchanged a few clicks, and turned his back to her once more. She could imagine how that conversation went.

That creature's weird.

Uh-huh.

What do you think it's doing?

No idea, man.

Think it's dangerous?

Al didn't tie it up, so…no?

Do you think—

We're off in an hour, man, just guard the door like we're supposed to. I've got a date later.

She laughed to herself as she drank another glass of water, and realized she had another problem. She needed to pee. The room did not appear to have any restroom facilities. Nyx knew precisely nothing about insects, but if she had to go out on a limb, it seemed reasonable that they might not urinate.

She eyed the pot. Either they understood human physiological needs and had left it for that purpose, or she didn't know what they'd left it for. Since her only other option was peeing on the floor, which was permeable, and meant she would probably end up peeing on someone the next level down...yeah. Pot it was. If she grossed the aliens out with her necessary biological functions, at least she couldn't understand their language to hear them being disgusted by her.

She dragged the pot into a corner away from the fully open door—not that alien insectoid species *cared* what she looked like half naked, but still—and tried awkwardly to unbutton her pants around the bo staff stuck to her hand. Her fingers wouldn't come away from the metal enough to grasp the button, and trying to flex them made the *pterosaur* peck on the back of her hand hurt. The fingers on her other hand were burned. Continuing to stand made the mermaid bite throb, and for love of the stars, she just wanted to *pee* without a semi-aware weapon clinging to her tighter than a leech.

She shook her hand violently. Dried blood broke on the back of her hand and oozed fluid. The pain made her magic swell in response, and it suffused her voice as she lit in to the hunk of metal in her palm. "Look, I get that you are terrified of being alone again. We're *all* terrified of being alone. But if you cling to something too tightly and never let it go, it's going to climb the walls to get away from you no matter how much it liked you in the beginning.

"I *want* us to be partners, okay? Why do you think I keep picking you back up even when you're so damnably inconvenient? But if you don't let go of me right now and stop freaking melding to my hand, one of two things is going to happen. I'm either going to die on this planet, because having both hands when I need them is super imperative here, in which case you will be alone until the literal end of ever, because *no one else with opposable thumbs is on this planet*. Or, I am going to survive and get home, at which point we are done. I will drop you in the endless trunk myself and no one will ever take you out again."

She felt a little shitty about that last statement. But then she felt a cautious warmth from the staff. The metal shook, her fingers sprang open, and the staff dropped to the ground.

"Seriously?" All she'd had to do was *literally* talk to it with her magic shoving her intentions every which way?

She got the indelicate business of going to the bathroom over with, then hesitantly picked up the staff and clipped it into its holster. She wanted to trust it. She also didn't want to get stuck with it again right now. However, mindful of its potential feelings, she gave it a reassuring pat.

Exhaustion dragged at her eyelids. With the exception of passing out on the cliffside after arriving here, she'd been awake for over twenty-four hours. She knew she should look at her wounds and try to clean them now that she had water. But she was just so *tired*.

She crawled onto the bed of moss and fell asleep.

18

Jevryn's ultimatum that they be ready to leave in fifteen minutes, or else be left behind, turned out to be a hurry-up-and-wait situation. Jevryn had opened a portal, cursed, and held up his hand in a staying gesture, just in case anyone was thinking of making a break for the roiling mass of storms on the other side of that rip in space.

That had been four hours ago. Shortly after opening the portal, Jevryn had shrunk it to the size of a bowling ball, and they had waited.

Waited while the world on the other side of the portal only cleared for brief periods, the longest of which had lasted all of two minutes. Two minutes in which Seth had pushed for them to go through, and Jevryn had said it wasn't time. Two minutes in which Seth couldn't even go through on his own, because his body wouldn't fit through a space as small as the current portal.

Though it was small, Seth would have thought holding it open for so long would drain the glowing bracelets that ringed Jevryn's arm. But barely a quarter of blue had gone from the first, and the others remained untouched.

Just when Seth was convinced they would stand there forever, waiting, the storms on the foreign planet broke. Chaotic green and purple skies cleared, and Jevryn's already perfect posture straightened. His hands drew apart, the portal widening and stretching.

"Now," he ordered. Evra, Morgen, and Kaden went through first.

Seth turned to Griff. "You remember what to do?"

Griff tapped a talon to the small illusion-filled vial hanging around his neck. "It is breaking glass, it is not—what is that phrase Nyx always says? Rock science?"

"Rocket science," Seth corrected. The vial held a premade illusion tailored to Griff. If Seth didn't return with Nyx before the next scheduled Arrival in two days, Griff could break the vial and pass himself off as her to check the travelers through. It would last for a week once activated. If they weren't back before then, he suspected they all had bigger problems. "I'll bring her home."

"I know you will." Griff lowered his head and nudged Seth toward the portal. "So go and find her."

He was stepping through when he heard Griff say to Jevryn, "That one is mine, too. Take care of him."

Jevryn sighed. "You always did have a soft spot for strays, Arradin." He followed through the portal, practically on Seth's heels, the path back to Earth closing behind him.

Seth fingered the portal stone in his pocket like it was a good luck talisman and took in the lush jungle that swathed Amentia Furor. He hated the jungle. All jungles, every variation, on every planet. They looked pretty, but more often than not, they were filled with things that wanted to kill you.

Something small flew at his face and he swatted it, crushing the small body between his hand and his cheek. When he withdrew his hand, a small black and red smear marred his palm. Alien mosquitoes. Perfect.

"Well?" Jevryn said to Kaden.

A muscle along Kaden's jaw ticked, the only sign that he was perhaps not quite as happy to be commanded about by Jevryn as he pretended. But Seth felt the buzz of magic as Kaden called on his Hound abilities, and after a moment he pointed in one direction and said, "That way."

Jevryn's expression gave nothing away. "How far?"

Kaden shrugged. "It isn't a precise measurement. A few hours' walk, roughly. I'll have a better idea once we start moving."

A deep shadow fell across the land, and he looked up. Black clouds covered the skies. They swirled with light and chaos that could not be matched by even the most violent of storms he'd witnessed on Earth.

Chill wind swept in with the sudden darkness, and a bolt of blue lightning lanced down from the sky, striking a tree several hundred feet away. The massive trunk splintered in two, the cleaved half falling to the ground with a resounding crash.

Jevryn cursed and drew his katana. "The storms are disruptive to magic use. If you don't need it, don't use it. We get to Nyx as quickly as possible. Kill anything that moves, and pray you run faster than anything you can't kill."

<hr>

Seth's world quickly narrowed to three things: run, slash, stay hidden. He'd seen a lot of shit in his day. He'd been to a planet home to the lizard-people like Bryn's general, Essteria, where violence was the only currency that was worth anything. But at least there it *was* worth something. Prove yourself vicious enough, and you gained respect.

Here, the world looked unchanged by any civilizing influences. Nothing that he, Jevryn, or Kaden killed respected the violence or the brutality with which they did so. The creatures here did not learn and back down, because for every dinosaur-like beast they slew, there were ten more to take its place.

It was mayhem, and the only reason he could find for it was the storm. As if the chaos of the nature itself was inside the animals' minds, driving them to pointless violence. And it *was* pointless. Half of the creatures within sight were engaged in fighting each other to the death, in numbers there were no natural causes for.

On no planet he'd ever been on did entire species go to war with others unless they were of human-level intelligence. The creatures around him were only predators, and while predators might have packs and prides, and hunt for food when necessary, hundreds of lions did not suddenly congregate and pick fights with an equal number of other predators.

They slashed and killed and it was not personal. They fell into work as a unit, and if they didn't all have the years of experience working together that Morgen and Kaden did, they were all experienced enough in bloodshed to know how to take cues from each other. Things were going about as well as could be expected when the lightning that had been circling the skies for what felt like hours finally deigned to descend upon the earth.

Where lightning struck, portals opened. A fresh wave of frenzy came over the creatures. The tail of one of the larger beasts swung into Evra's side, knocking her into one of the portals. Morgen jumped after her, his hand closing over her wrist, and they fell through together.

Shit. Seth darted for the portal.

The storm abruptly ceased, clouds dissipating as if they had never been, and the portals vanished. The land around them was blood-soaked and body-strewn, and in the sudden calm after the storm, the maddened creatures regained some measure of rationality. They ceased their battles and fled.

Seth stared at the space where Morgen and Evra had vanished. The portal was gone. He *knew* there wasn't any finding them, but it didn't make him feel better about the fact that he couldn't.

They were both experienced fighters. They were together. If things grew dire, they could tap out and return to Earth at any moment. They were smart. They would make it.

Seth shook his head and focused on the here and now, on the things in his control. He stood near Kaden and Jevryn. He was still glamoured from sight—fighting things was unsurprisingly easier when they couldn't see you coming—and on instinct, he chose to remain that way.

Kaden moved for the spot where Evra and Morgen had disappeared, but Jevryn halted him with a simple clearing of his throat. "What are you doing?"

"Going after them."

"You will never find them," Jevryn said. "The portals open at random to other points on the planet. It is a large planet."

"I won't leave them out here alone."

"You can, and you will. That was the agreement. They understood the dangers when they came here. And they have the portal stones the Hawthorne boy so helpfully supplied them."

Kaden didn't look happy about it, but he didn't argue. "Where *is* Seth?"

Jevryn shrugged. "There were many portals. Presumably, he fell through one. Nyx?"

Kaden clenched his teeth, but he pointed in a direction and started walking. Seth pulled his magic more thickly around him. It whispered quietly, telling anyone who looked that the space he occupied was only empty air. That his breath was simply the sighing of the wind. That his footsteps, as he followed Kaden and Jevryn, were not there.

He was very interested to find out how Jevryn and Kaden interacted when they thought no one else was watching.

They walked for hours. So many of them that Seth almost dropped his glamour to ask Kaden if he was certain he knew where the fuck he was going. Eventually, they passed through a field of high grasses, coming out the other side at the treeline of another forest. When Kaden moved forward, Jevryn flung out a hand, holding him back.

"You are certain she is in the forest?"

Kaden nodded.

"Is there any chance she is simply on the other side of it?"

"That depends on how large the forest is. Why?"

Jevryn ignored the *why*. "It is perhaps fifty units across."

Kaden shook his head. "Then she's inside. I'd put her at eight units away, at most."

"Stay here," Jevryn ordered. "Under no circumstances are you to enter the forest. I will return when I have her."

"And if you don't?" Kaden asked as Jevryn turned away.

Jevryn lifted one eyebrow. "If I do not what?"

"If you don't return. I can't help but think it would be convenient for you if I died here, waiting for you."

"Did you have that realization late, Kaden Moor, or were you foolish enough to come with me having had it earlier?"

Anger flashed in Kaden's eyes. "I owe Nyx a debt I can never repay. A debt, I might add, that I owe because of you."

Seth crept a couple steps closer. *Now* they were getting somewhere.

Jevryn shrugged. "I gave you her mother's scent. I told you to find Elena Fortuna. That you have brought her daughter into this game is a move I had not counted on. One I did not appreciate being surprised with when I found her in Earth's Station. If you owe her a debt due to the action, it was your own poor judgment that did it."

Anger drew the lines of Kaden's mouth tight. "You told me Elena was on Earth. She wasn't. Nyx was the only option."

"Was she?" Jevryn asked mildly. "Or did you simply like the way she looked? She is a pretty thing. Like her mother. And unlike the rest of the Council, I am very aware that you spent two years on Earth. Tell me, did it take you that long to convince her to Hide the Harvester, or did you like her company?"

"It took me two years because she didn't have a fucking clue what she was."

Jevryn's eyes narrowed. "What do you mean?"

"I mean she had Hidden-induced amnesia. I mean her mother stole her mind and left her there to rot. I mean that maybe it wasn't kind to leave her with the Harvester, but if she'd stayed in Dead Earth like I thought she would, she'd never have come to any harm from it. And if *you* had done your part and kept the Council from going after Morgen, I never would have had to leave her in the first place."

Kaden advanced, his sword clenched in his fist, the blade still dripping blood, and for one moment, Seth thought he might actually be angry enough to level a strike at the councilor. "Where were you, when I rotted in Psionics for a year for carrying out *your* orders? Where were you the four years I spent on Arkadia?"

Jevryn's face remained as impassive as ever. "You never broke," he said lightly. "A year there, and a sentence to Arkadia, and you never told them it was me who helped you escape. Why? Death is kinder than Psionics, redemption even sweeter. They would have given you one or the other, had you given them my name."

"I thought about it," Kaden said. "Every night, I thought about it. Maybe I'd like to think I did it because I saw what was in Alistair's eyes when he pulled the Harvester from the Vault. Because I know whatever he would have done with it would have altered the Council in a way that wouldn't have been good for anyone."

Kaden spat to the side. "It's the noble reason, I guess. But the truth is, if I gave them your name, they wouldn't have stopped until I'd given them *hers*. I kept your secrets because of *her*. So I suppose you should be grateful 'she's a pretty *thing*.'"

Something flashed across Jevryn's eyes, too quick to read, and then it was gone. "Stay here," he said again. "If you cross into that forest, I will not be able to stop what happens to you."

He turned and walked, pausing just in front of the treeline. He did not look back but he said, "When you were rotting in Psionics, Kaden Moor, I was rotting there alongside you. Your silence is the only reason I once more walk freely. It was two years before they trusted me enough to allow me to portal again. Two more, before they quit following my every move.

"Believe what you wish, but I would have come for you on Arkadia when the circumstances allowed it. Had things occurred in that manner, the Council would never have known you left. Your existence, though still that of a fugitive, would have been of a fugitive no one knew to look for.

"I may have my faults, but I honor my debts. If you have hope of a future in which you are not hunted across the universe, then stay here. Do not enter the forest. You have my word that when I find Nyx, I will return for you."

Kaden, law-abiding, duty-sworn idiot that he was, actually just stood there and let Jevryn walk away without him. Seth shook his head. Then he pulled his magic tighter about him and slipped after Jevryn.

19

The councilor moved deeper into the forest, but all of Seth's attention was dragged suddenly to the right. The familiar feel of Nyx's power called to him. Close, so close. But he didn't see her.

He hesitated. If he wound up chasing ghosts and lost Jevryn —but Jevryn had stopped twenty feet into the forest. The councilor stood, his hands loose and relaxed at his sides, waiting.

Nyx's magic tugged at Seth again. Keeping one eye on Jevryn, he followed the pull until he stood on top of the beacon. But she wasn't there. He spun in a slow circle. Nothing. He looked up, peering into the vastness of the canopies above. Nothing.

He crouched, running his hand over the ground, until the feel of cool metal brushed his skin...and he closed his fingers around the Harvester of Worlds. His heart thudded in his chest.

She was here. The Harvester was irrefutable proof that Kaden hadn't led them to the wrong planet, the wrong place. But it was also proof that wherever Nyx was now, it wasn't of her own volition. Because she never would have left the Harvester lying on the forest floor if she'd had a choice in the matter.

A noise came, from far away at first, then closer, like he stood at the base of a mountain as an avalanche approached. The ground shook. Seth's gaze shot to Jevryn, but the councilor didn't look alarmed. Resigned, perhaps, but not alarmed.

Seth pulled illusion and shadow tight around him and took a couple steps back toward the treeline. Despite Jevryn's calm, Seth had the irrefutable sense that something terrible was coming, and he had a feeling he wanted to be nowhere near the councilor when it arrived.

The sky chose that moment to darken over again, the onset of a new storm coming as abruptly as the previous one had dissipated. Despite his personal dislike of Kaden, he glanced back to where they'd left him, just able to make out the short fall of golden hair.

Jevryn glanced back too, a frown tugging at his lips. Then he gave a slight shake of his head and turned back in the direction of the approaching force. That look told Seth two things: one, that Jevryn wasn't worried about any monsters outside the forest coming into it, and two, that he might feel a moment's hesitation about leaving Kaden to whatever fate awaited him in the storm, but he wouldn't do anything to prevent it.

The sound of steel being drawn, the thud and scuffle of battle, told Seth the likely outcome of what was happening beyond the forest. He tried to tell himself it wasn't his problem. But he *was* the reason Kaden was here.

He hesitated a moment longer—long enough to get a glimpse at what approached through the trees, something more terrifying even than the dinosaurs he'd left on the other side of the forest—then he slipped the Harvester into his pocket and ran back to Kaden.

He knew immediately it was a lost cause. Kaden was surrounded on all sides, and the only reason he wasn't dead yet was because of his admittedly impressive swordsmanship. If Seth dived into that fray, he would die. Besides which, playing fair had never been his first choice in anything. Playing fair had the predictable result of leaving a person in a terrible position because no one else was playing fair.

He needed to turn the tables, to give them an advantage far greater than two swords against a horde of dinosaurs. An idea popped into his head, bringing the curve of a smile to his lips. *Oh, yes, that was good.*

He'd have to drop his own cloaking to do it, because the creation would be a massive power drain. But it would be worth it. Especially to see the look on Kaden's face for a few seconds before he realized what he was *actually* seeing.

He drew the image up in his head, whispered it to his magic, and it formed beside him, power making real what Seth hoped did not actually exist on this planet, despite the rest of its natural inhabitants. He crafted until the pull on his magic turned into a painful burn, and when he had the shape of it, the whole of it, he made the creation visible.

A lot went in to making an illusion appear real. If you were doubling something that already existed—such as himself, as he often did—care had to be taken to get the details just right. To ensure it moved and talked as he himself did, that the shadows fell where they ought.

He wasn't constricted by reality in this making. Reality had given him the basis of the design, and imagination was all that was required to bring it to life. A new darkness fell over the land, over the battling hordes of maddened creatures, and they froze, sensing the threat of a predator far greater than them.

He had given the illusion form and presence, its bulk visceral and awe-inducing. It towered twelve feet above them, its left foot alone half his height. He grinned and the illusion grinned with him, its mouth gaping open. Large, wicked teeth gleamed in the storm-wrought darkness, and it roared.

The illusion was one of his finer works. The roar had weight and reverberation. It was illusion given sound, and that sound shook the firmament. It tore through the air and assaulted his eardrums, rattling his body to the bones, and in the wake of its overwhelming presence, the creatures around them scattered.

Kaden's nostrils flared, his eyes wide as he turned, looking up at the giant beast that had appeared less than ten feet from him. His grip on his sword was white-knuckled. Seth could practically see the cogs turning in Kaden's mind as he fought to reconcile what he saw and felt and heard with what rationality was telling him couldn't have appeared out of nowhere.

It was a waste of magic, but Seth couldn't help making the great beast lower its head to puff hot air in Kaden's face. The Hound drove his sword straight up through its jaw, piercing through all the way to the top of the skull.

Seth slow-clapped, stepping out from behind the dinosaur's leg. "Properly heroic," he said lightly. "But I think you would have died had it been the real thing."

With a snap of his fingers, the illusion vanished, leaving Kaden holding his sword, tip pointing to the sky. He lowered the weapon, though he did not, Seth noted, put it away. He could see Kaden wrangling with what to ask first, and what eventually came out was, "Where did you cook up that monstrosity?"

Seth laughed. "Earth's biological history books. *That* was *Tyrannosaurus rex*. Favorite childhood dinosaur of five-year-old boys the planet over."

"That thing actually existed?" Kaden growled.

"A long time ago. On a planet much like this one. You'd best hope it doesn't *actually* exist here, seeing as how all the little plants and animals here aren't so little, and might actually sustain a creature of that size."

Kaden made another non-verbal grunt in response. "What the hell are you doing here?"

Seth let out a put-upon sigh. "I believe the proper words are, 'Thank you, Seth. I was just about to get my head bitten off when you rode to the rescue.'"

"Why?"

"Why say, 'Thank you?' See, it's a time-honored tradition

among civilized people. The words are necessary for a proper continuation of goodwill and—"

"Why did you bother intervening?"

Seth shrugged. "Turns out Nyxi's bringing back my conscience. It's highly inconvenient."

A new thought seemed to occur to Kaden. "How close have you been this whole time?"

Seth grinned. "Close enough to know you're keeping even more secrets than everyone thought. Would it have been so hard to open your mouth and say, 'Sorry, Nyx. I did it all on Jevryn's orders?'"

The muscles in Kaden's arm bunched and the point of his sword came up. "Unlike you, I have a sense of loyalty. I wouldn't expect someone who made his living in the Shadow Market to understand that some things are bigger than *you*. Bigger than what you want."

Seth *tsked*. "She was right. You really don't take responsibility for anything, do you? Tell me, is it nice, getting to offload the consequences of everything you do under the excuse of taking orders? To not have to decide for yourself what's right or wrong, because the powers-that-be decreed it, so it must be just?"

"You know what? The next time you feel like intervening to save my life, do me a favor. Don't."

Seth snorted. "Noted." He walked to the forest's edge, pausing to look back. "Are you coming, or not?"

"I have orders to remain here."

"Yes, yes, I heard them. Did you know that Jevryn was well within distance of you when the second storm hit? That he certainly heard you being attacked, as I did? He chose to leave you here to die. You got him to this point, and that's all he needed you for."

Kaden's jaw tightened, but he just said, "That's the job."

"You aren't an Enforcer anymore, man. The only person you're fooling with your bullshit sense of honor is yourself."

"Jevryn will bring her back."

Seth shrugged. "I think he intends to. But while I didn't *see* what's inside that forest, I did hear it. And while I'd love to have faith in the all-powerful All Council which, from the bit I just heard you two discussing, sounds as if it's embroiled in either civil war or a long history of manipulative infighting, I just can't make myself do it.

"And I feel obligated to let you know that the beasties don't cross the treeline. I'm guessing the monsters inside are worse. Doesn't it just make you itch to know what Jevryn's keeping hidden in there?"

"You sure Nyx is the one who can't keep away from a secret?"

Seth grinned. "Well, she is exactly where I said she'd be, isn't she? Right smack in the middle of trouble? We're two of a kind, me and her." *And you'd do well not to forget it.* "I'll make you a deal. I'll keep us nice and out of sight. If we get in there and Jevryn's got everything under control, I'll let him handle things."

"And if he *doesn't* have everything under control?"

Seth thought he might hate Kaden more than ever in that moment. Maybe, if Kaden had been so convinced that a councilor could handle any situation that might present itself to them, convinced that his help was unnecessary, that there was no possibility that Nyx *wouldn't* come out of that forest, Seth could have forgiven him for staying where he was told to. He'd have thought him an optimistic fool, but he could have forgiven him.

But that single question said Kaden had always known there was a chance that no one was coming back out. Seth wanted to walk away right then and leave Kaden to fend for himself. If another storm hit, Kaden's life wouldn't be on his conscience. But he'd caught a glimpse of waited inside the forest, and Kaden had his uses.

He walked back to Kaden. "If he doesn't, then I do whatever it takes to get Nyx out. What will *you* do?"

Kaden didn't answer. He had shown absolute resolve when it had come to getting Nyx back from *Seth* in the Shadow Market, but throw the All Council in the mix, and he chose loyalty to an institution over her every time.

"Forget it," Seth said. "I'll get her myself."

One step. Two. Then, "You're certain you can keep both of us out of sight? Even after making that monstrosity?"

"Please. I could make a *T. rex* in my sleep." A slight exaggeration. Having never made a *T. rex* before, it had taken more out of him than it would have had he practiced it regularly. But he'd grown up a very bored child in the middle of nowhere. He'd had nothing to do but practice magic, and magic, like any muscle, bounced back more quickly when it was exercised regularly. He could do what needed doing.

"Then let's go get her," Kaden said.

Unfortunately, the planet had other plans. Thunder rumbled, lightning struck, and the ground beneath them shimmered, rearranging itself into a stormy blue. They fell through into open air, and Seth found the ground rushing up to meet him.

He tucked and rolled as he hit, mitigating the impact of the landing, and pulled his knives as he gained his feet. But the fickle planet produced no monsters this time, the sky clearing.

He stood on cold gray stone, the landscape craggy rock for as far as the eye could see. Kaden stalked toward him, his face grim.

"How far?" Seth asked.

"Between two-hundred-and-fifty and three-hundred units."

Seth did the conversion to miles—it was the unit of measure he'd grown up with, and it was the one that still made the most sense to him because of that. "Shit." The portal had dropped them over a hundred miles from the forest. "Which direction?"

Kaden pointed to his left. Seth started walking.

"You coming?" he yelled back.

Kaden caught up. "It will take us days to reach her. And that is if the planet doesn't helpfully relocate us a dozen times between then and now."

"Your point?"

"That Jevryn will likely have her off this planet before we traverse even half that distance."

Seth stopped walking. "You want to leave? Be my guest."

Kaden's inscrutable gaze swept over him, measuring. "Killing yourself for her won't help."

Seth laughed. "I'm difficult to kill. Remember that. And I'm not leaving this planet while she's on it. Your little Link tells you she's gone, then I'll go home. Until then, I'm walking towards her. You do whatever the hell you want."

He was thirty paces away before he heard Kaden move after him.

20

———

Seth hadn't realized how much he'd enjoyed the last three months of not being covered in blood and gore on a weekly basis until he was thrust back into it. He flicked his knife blade, flinging off the majority of blood that coated the metal, wiped the weapon on a mostly-clean section of his pants, and slid it back into its sheath.

At least Jevryn's warnings that the planet's storms interfered with magic hadn't proved accurate thus far. His illusion use hadn't gotten this much of a workout in months. He'd mostly stuck to making himself unnoticeable, and hadn't yet found another occasion to spawn a *T. rex*.

Crafting an illusion that large—with enough reality to make it terrifying enough to scare off the other beasties—required uninterrupted focus. He'd had that time, standing on the protective edge of the forest Jevryn had disappeared into. He hadn't found it again on the rest of the planet, where the storms started without warning, portals spitting out snarling creatures and the frenzy calling more of them to the fray.

Sometimes, they were positioned well enough that he could throw Kaden under an illusion with him and they could skirt the trouble. Other times they were smack in the middle of it and there was no time to breathe, just fight and hope they survived until the storm halted.

He walked through the bodies and caught up with Kaden, the sharp edge of adrenaline fading and leaving him feeling empty and irritated. Kaden didn't acknowledge his approach. That was typical of their interactions so far, but it was starting to piss Seth off. Maybe he didn't *want* to talk to the guy, and he certainly didn't want to be BFFs, but there had been half-a-dozen instances in the last hour where his chances of meeting an untimely end would have decreased dramatically if they'd had even a flimsy excuse for a working relationship.

Then again, Moor probably didn't give a fuck whether Seth lived or died. He was the expendable one on this expedition, and he knew it.

Abruptly, Kaden stopped and crouched. His fingers splayed over the ground, the scent of tracker magic spilling from them. It hit the back of Seth's throat and left an acrid aftertaste.

"What is it?" he asked, trying not to gag on the magic stench. His dislike of the magic, the affect it had on him, was psychological. He had a Pavlovian response to it because, in his youth, smelling it had meant one of two things. Either his father was abandoning him, yet again, to go hunting after a woman who treated them like her servants, or Seth and Nyx had run away, and they were about to be dragged back to hell.

He hadn't understood that Hound magic didn't *actually* smell bad until he'd gone out into the universe and realized no one else thought it smelled like anything. But knowing that hadn't made the reaction go away. If anything, it had gotten worse with time.

The scent of it now only added to his increasing irritation. When Kaden stood silently, magic dissipating, and turned in a different direction than they'd been moving all day, Seth's irritation spiked further.

"Where are you going?"

Kaden didn't answer.

"Did her location change?"

Again, no answer.

"Kaden."

He might as well have been talking to a rock for all the response he got. He stepped in front of Kaden, blocking his path, but Kaden just walked around him—or would have, if Seth's knife wasn't at his throat the second he dodged.

Kaden's eyes dropped to the knife, dispassionate and unconcerned, before flicking back up to Seth. "Go ahead and try, if you want. You'll find I'm also difficult to kill."

Seth didn't try. He also didn't remove the knife. "So he *can* speak. For a second there, I wondered if your brawn had completely overridden your brains and you'd regressed a couple steps on the evolutionary chain."

That expressionless facade cracked a hair and Kaden snarled, "Don't push me, Hawthorne."

"Or what? You'll run away? That's your default setting, isn't it? I'd be surprised you even showed up now, but then you Hounds are obsessive as fuck."

Kaden stepped in, getting in his face, the knife edge drawing a thin line of blood. "You should be thanking me for getting out of your way."

Oh, that would be the day. "Please, you're such a colossal pain in the ass, your presence would be far more of a deterrent to your chances with her than your memory."

Kaden put one fingertip on the knife blade, and Seth let him push it away.

"Then you aren't the least bit concerned I might decide to stick around when this is done?"

Seth laughed. Kaden didn't, and it was there in his eyes, that Hound's obsession he'd seen so many times on his father's face. "You honestly think she'll want anything to do with you?" he said harshly.

"I don't know. Do you?"

Seth's hands clenched into fists. *No. Yes. Maybe I don't know, either.*

Thunder rumbled to the north and Kaden's eyes tracked it, alertness rippling through his body. "Out of my way."

"Why? What's over there?" Why had Kaden suddenly decided to change course?

"Morgen and Evra."

Seth cursed and sprinted toward the storm beside Kaden. "Fucking use your words next time. If you'd told me it was them, we could have skipped the manly bullshit." *Even if I really would have enjoyed taking a swing at you.*

In response, Kaden put on a burst of speed and Seth doubled down after him. *Running headlong toward a certain fight. Just what I usually never do.*

He heard Evra's scream before he saw her. It wasn't a scream of pain or fear, but one of pure, unbridled battle lust and frustration. He crested a steep rise of gray rock and emerged onto a plateau blanketed by the storm's reach.

Evra was a blur of motion, spinning and striking, trying to carve a path through the madness. Morgen shouted something at her. She sank her blade into the beast before her, withdrew the sword and jumped back, retreating behind him. She spun so her back was to his, guarding.

Morgen opened his mouth and the eeriest sound Seth had ever heard came out of the half-Siren, something between a mourning wail and a demon's shriek. The dinosaurs on that half of the plateau, well over fifty in number, crumpled.

"Holy shit." Seth couldn't tell if they were dead, dying, or sleeping. As the sound went on, he resisted the urge to clap his hands over his ears, a move that was unnecessary, and would be futile even if he did need to block the sound.

He'd known Morgen was talented. But to compose, in a battlefield situation, the precise sound needed to incapacitate multiple species no one had ever encountered before, and have that sound not harm the humans present…that was on another level.

Seth forgot, for a moment, that he hated Kaden's guts. "Can he do that again?"

Kaden, his friend's life on the line, also decided it was a convenient time to forget his and Seth's mutual animosity. "Not for another ten minutes."

Ten minutes might as well be an eternity in this situation. "I can get us to them," Seth said. "Stick behind me, step where I step, and try not to sound like a rhinoceros."

Seth pulled illusion over them and dove through the mass of crazed, snarling beasts. Cloaking Kaden took all his focus. Covering someone *else* under illusion was difficult unless they were standing perfectly still. He had to account for every footfall, every breath and noise. It was virtually impossible unless they followed Seth's every instruction to the letter.

Mercifully, Kaden actually did. But despite his cooperation, Seth felt his control over the illusion slipping, his magic suddenly recalcitrant. He set his teeth and doubled down, spending illusion in waves, the kind of blunt-force approach to cloaking he hadn't taken since he was twelve.

"Something's up with the magic," he gritted out. A fine time for Jevryn's warning to prove necessary.

They were almost to Evra and Morgen, six yards to go, at most. He dove through a gap between two pairs of *Velociraptor*-esque creatures, and felt his magic vanish. In his grasp one second, gone the next, leaving him fully visible. He reached for illusion again, but it wouldn't answer. The well of his magic was still present, but he couldn't access it, like he'd left a room that locked automatically behind him, and he'd forgotten the key.

He shouted a warning to Kaden and dropped and rolled as the four raptors fighting each other decided he was a more appealing target than their own kind. He came up with two curved blades in his hands, reminiscent of Earth's kukri knives.

A mouth full of teeth snapped at him. He lunged sideways as

he gained his feet, bringing the knife in his right hand in an uppercut slash across the throat. The thick hide required extra force to penetrate, and the resistance that met his strike told him the enchantment on the blades, crafted to aid in scenarios just such as this one, had failed alongside his illusion magic. He'd broken through, but not deep enough to sever anything vital.

The creature screamed in outrage and Seth jumped back, dodging a swipe of talons. He nearly lost a chunk of his shoulder to the jaws that snapped at him from behind. He moved forward, dodged a bite from the raptor in front, and ran and launched himself onto its back. He drove his knife into the base of the raptor's skull. The enchantment still wasn't working, but the knife was the highest grade of Anduvian steel, and the strike had the full force of his body behind it. The tip split through the thick hide and bit deep, into the spinal cord.

He couldn't help but think of Nyx as the creature fell and he rode it to the ground. She'd always hated to see anything hurt. He'd hated it too, before he'd learned that hating it only made him feel more. That mourning the hurt of something that had to be done only made *you* hurt more. She'd never gotten that jaded, and he thought it had disappointed her when he had.

Then he'd lost her memory, and he'd lost all reason not to let that cold indifference take him over entirely. Now that he had the memories back, had *her* back, all of those repressed feelings kept creeping back in. This wasn't the first time he'd wondered if the girl she'd been when he'd last known her would have been willing to accept the things he'd done since he left. It was, however, the most inconvenient time he'd wondered it.

He leapt clear of the falling raptor just as something large and winged swooped from the sky. A pointed nose hit him square in the chest, knocking him to the ground…and under the legs of two quarreling beasts.

His legs came up protectively on instinct, shielding his abdomen. A clawed hand swept toward him and he slashed under it, severing the tendons between the wrist and claw. His other knife found the beast's vulnerable stomach, sliding through the softer hide and straight up. Hot entrails spilled over him.

He brought his knife up as the beast dove at him. He committed to the strike even as he knew the angle was wrong, the force insufficient, because he was out of options. Long, vicious teeth snapped toward his head.

He was going to die.

The whistle of steel cut the air and a sword cleaved through the creature's neck, severing it neatly. A spray of blood drenched him. He scrambled back, clearing the ground a second before the creature's heavy, headless corpse landed with a thud.

Kaden stood there, sword dripping blood, a hard smirk on his face. "Having performance issues, Hawthorne?"

Seth spat a mouthful of dinosaur blood and rolled to his feet. "Fuck you, Moor."

A winged beast dove from the sky, straight at Kaden's back. Seth felt the telltale flicker of magic at his fingertips and took a chance. He sheathed one of his knives, pulled a throwing star and took aim. He made a quick calculation for distance and angle, and let fly. The star struck true, in the throat, and the enchantment in the star caught. The weapon spun and chewed with magic's aid, biting through skin and tissue until it flew clear through the neck and the creature dropped.

"You know someone" —Kaden moved forward and slashed at an approaching threat— "recently told me" —another strike— "the correct response to having your ass saved" —final blow— "was 'thank you.'"

"Thank you," Seth said, picking his way once more toward Morgen and Evra. "But also, fuck you."

"Back at you."

They grudgingly fell into formation as they worked their way through the field, slowly at first, then with more urgency and recklessness. It was as if every beast on the field had sighted in on Morgen and Evra, the two nearly buried under the onslaught.

If they'd been any less skilled or any less in sync, they'd already be dead. They fought together like they'd been doing it for decades, a perfect complement of form. Somehow, Seth doubted they'd be arguing anymore when they got home.

When, not *if*. They were all getting out of here. This fucking storm needed to break.

He and Kaden cut through the final obstacles between them and their friends, adding their defense.

"About time you two got here," Morgen said, "You were going so slow I thought you'd stopped for a recess."

"I didn't want to cramp your style," Seth shot back. "You sang such a lovely tune earlier I thought you'd go for an encore."

Evra issued a fierce, guttural growl as her sword caught in a raptor's talons. She twisted the sword, stepped, stepped again, and drove the blade through its stomach. "This is not the time for you two to devolve into one of your sarcastic exchanges."

"Yes, sir," they shot back in unison.

"I hate you both."

"You love us." Seth felt that promising flicker of magic at his fingertips again. It sparked and grew brighter, brighter, begging for his attention. "Okay, everybody, here goes nothing. Stay as still as you can."

His magic enveloped them and they froze. The dinosaurs that had been focused on them halted, their quarry having disappeared before their eyes. One that had been lunging for Morgen forced the half-Siren to take two steps back. Seth compensated for the movement, his magic dogging Morgen's steps, and the dinosaur's jaws bit down on empty air.

The storm vanished. This wasn't the slow easing of storms he'd grown used to, where the clouds would part and it would gradually dissipate. This was an abrupt cessation, the oppressive weight of the storm lifting. As if something had reached out and caused the daylight to return.

Seth was now used to the way the animals all snapped to confused alertness, as if the storm had hypnotized them, and they didn't understand where they were or why. They turned and fled, only minor scuffles following their departure. He held the illusion until the rocky plateau was empty of anything not human, then let it drop.

"So." Seth wiped his knives on his pants. He was out of clean spots of fabric and settled for getting the metal mostly clean before sheathing the weapons. "What brings a nice couple like you to a place like this?"

"Three portals," Evra answered with no trace of humor. "What brings you here?"

"One portal and a lot of walking." Seth pointed over his shoulder. "Nyx and our fearless All Councilor are that way. I'm going. You coming with?"

Morgen grinned. "Can't think of anywhere better to go." He slung his arm over Evra's shoulders. She didn't take it off at the elbow, which Seth supposed answered the question of whether they were getting along again.

"Perfect. You wanna hold hands, Moor? I don't want you to feel lonely."

Kaden grunted.

So they were back to vague noises as a form of communication. He could work with that.

21

Nyx woke to the feeling of being watched. She pushed up and cried out in pain when the blisters on the tips of her fingers burst open. Her sleep-hazed brain had forgotten she was injured pretty much everywhere.

"*Fuck.*" She cradled her hand to her chest, looked out the door, and realized that feeling she'd had of being watched was because people *were* watching her. Two aliens with beautifully-painted carapaces, who looked like the pampered nobility of this alien species, tilted their heads as they watched her.

Nyx blinked and tried to stand. Pain lanced through her calf and she thunked back down. Apparently, adrenaline had deserted her.

The two gawkers—they were definitely gawking—watched her graceless fall with avid interest. One chittered excitedly to the guard on her left, who responded with a terse click. She spoke again, pulled something shiny out of a little bag, and offered it to the guard.

He moved a pincher forward as if to take it, but the other guard slapped the questing hand away, then waved all of his upper limbs at the newcomers. They must have paid off the guards for the privilege of leering at her, but whatever they'd tried to procure with the second payoff—coming inside, potentially—the other guard had drawn the line at.

Great. She'd traveled across the universe and nearly died so rich people could stare at her for amusement.

The second guard gestured again and the two onlookers turned around, clearly irritated. Then they froze. The guards froze, too.

The noises of the city changed. The buzz and hum of the city, the soft whisper of rustling leaves as the giant insects scuttled from cable to cable, leaf to leaf, room to room, ceased. The soothing white noise of a city at work vanished, the backdrop of sound going quiet.

She expected the sound to resume. For the four insectoids outside her door to begin moving and talking again. But the city remained as quiet as a tomb.

She pushed to her feet, braced for the pain this time, and walked to the open doorway. "Umm, excuse me?"

The guards gave no sign that they'd heard her. Given how reactive the first one had been when she'd gotten excited over water, she thought they would have reacted to her if they could.

Nyx pulled the bo staff, extended it to its full length, and stuck it out the door. Nothing. No reaction. They were completely frozen. And yet, just walking out the door seemed like a bad idea.

She clipped the staff back into its holster, backed up to the far wall and got a running start, just in case the aliens weren't as paralyzed as they appeared. She ran and leaped through the doorway, tucking her head and hoping that if she was wrong, she was moving fast enough not to get bisected.

Momentum carried her straight through the gap between the guards, and then between the two onlookers. When no tails lashed out to capture or decapitate her, she stopped and looked out at the city. It felt like she was in some kind of macabre horror story where time had stopped.

Every inhabitant of the city was as unmoving as a statue.

Some were frozen mid-stride, halfway up or down columns. A group of three, sitting on a little flat area and clearly sharing a meal, had mouths open, bites of food halfway carried to their mandibles.

Her first thought was that the city was under attack—that an outside force had done something to freeze the inhabitants. But in that case, she would expect to hear the sounds of an army infiltrating the city. She heard only silence.

So...maybe this was something normal that happened? A sort of reset for the colony? Except, if it was normal, routine, the two gawkers wouldn't have chosen this time to come look at her, would they? And the guards would have done something to prevent Nyx's escape in their downtime.

Unless, of course, they'd realized she had nowhere to go. Hundreds of feet stretched between her and the safe ground, and she had a bum leg and two injured hands. She didn't have a chance.

Still, if she was going to escape—and however decently she'd been treated so far, waiting around to find out what her captors were going to do with her sounded like the worst of all possible bad ideas—now was her chance.

She couldn't descend multiple floors, but maybe she could ascend a single one. If the queen's guards were frozen too, she could get within reach of the portal crystal, and this time, she would succeed in siphoning magic from it, because she had no other choice. She just needed enough to find her way to a new, hopefully safe planet.

She squeezed in between the two aliens who'd come to gawk at her and followed the cable back to the column that led up to the queen's level. The pain in her leg dulled the more she moved, until it receded to an ache in the back of her mind.

Nyx reached the column and realized her belief that she could climb it had been overly optimistic. The sides were pocked where the aliens' pincers had jabbed in as they climbed, but none of the grooves were deep enough for her to get a toe-hold, and they would just barely allow her fingertips to squeeze in. Which would absolutely destroy her burned fingers.

She was about to admit she should return to her room and wait when she looked down. *The mercury boots.* She looked up at the opening that let onto the queen's level. It was plenty wide, maybe six feet in diameter.

"This is smart in theory and dumb in practice," she muttered to herself. She steeled herself and said, "*Los.*" The buckles on the boots shifted from black to bronze as they accepted the command, kicking into what Nyx thought of as first gear.

She crouched and jumped straight up, the amplification from the boots letting her clear six feet. When gravity pulled her back down, she said, "*Losara,*" skipping *Losa*—second gear—and going straight to third.

Losa might have been sufficient, but she couldn't risk it. If a second jump on *Losa* didn't carry her to the queen's level, it would still carry her high enough she'd break her legs coming back down. She was better off with *Losara*, better off over-shooting than under.

She bent her knees, braced for the impact as she landed, and pushed off with everything she had. Like the way each bounce on a trampoline would take you higher than the last, the boots took the force of the six foot drop, combined it with her jump, and sent her hurtling skyward.

She'd been a little crooked on the second jump, and she ducked her head and tucked her shoulder as the opening approached, the right half of her body scraping the side as she went through. It arrested her momentum somewhat, but she traveled another five feet up before she started coming back down, and only barely remembered to shut the boots off with a hasty, "*Exa,*" before twisting to land just to the side of the hole in the floor. Thank the stars the side of her face that hit said floor wasn't the sunburned one.

She came slowly to her feet before the lines of frozen guards, listening for any sign that some were awake or soon to be. There was nothing from them, only stillness and quiet. But in the center, the vines of color Nyx had seen earlier were a mass of shifting lines, like a lightning storm concentrated on a single point, stretching from the portal crystal down to the queen.

Nyx focused on it, trying to call the magic inside the crystal, hoping her earlier failure had been due to the stress of the situation. But though she could feel the magic, she couldn't get it to answer her. She needed to get closer.

She moved, slipping through the spaces between the guards, heading in a more or less straight line for the queen's area. No need to solve the maze when the guards were out.

She slowed the closer she came, hiding behind insectoid bodies and trying to catch a glimpse of the queen. To see if she slept as the others did. If there *was* some problem here.

Two rows of guards from the center, she crouched and peered around a coiled tail.

The queen was indeed awake—and she wasn't alone. Four others of her kind were awake and flanked her—not guards, but...advisors, maybe? And standing before them, his back to her, was a man with long, silken black hair. It fell bone straight past his shoulders, resting against the black cloak that swept the ground. He held himself with perfect straightness, perfect poise.

Jevryn.

For all she'd given the alien race his name, she hadn't expected they would actually reach out to him—or that he would answer their summons. *Now* she understood why the colony was frozen. Maybe the queen hadn't been concerned about them seeing a single human brought in, but a councilor? She clearly wanted privacy, and all of it.

Jevryn spoke, but instead of words, Nyx only heard the hisses and clicks of the insectoid language. She frowned. Human throats could not make the range of noises coming out of Jevryn's mouth. But if he was using a translator spell, one different from hers that could make the translation for him, why wasn't Nyx able to understand what he was saying? The translator spells she was familiar with didn't physically change the words coming out of someone's mouth, they just made people hear them in their native language.

The queen cut him off abruptly with a wave of her foreleg and an angry click. Then she jabbed her foreleg in the direction of Nyx's hiding place.

Shit.

Jevryn spun, piercing blue eyes landing on the space where she crouched.

"Nyx Fortuna." He pronounced each syllable of her name with exacting precision, sounding anything but pleased. She had the urge to duck her head like a child who had disappointed an authoritarian parent.

Jevryn's hand flicked up, and as the arm of his cloak fell down she realized he was wearing bracelets similar to the ones Laiveran had worn. Portal magic flew from his fingers and wrapped around her like a ribbon. The now-familiar rift opened, and she found herself spat out on the ground at Jevryn's feet, between him and the hive queen.

You could do that with portal magic? Just hop from place to place? "I—"

"Silence," Jevryn ordered. Nyx snapped her mouth shut.

Jevryn turned his attention back to the queen, inclining his head to her in a brief bow. He resumed speaking to her, and Nyx once again heard only the insectoid language, devoid of any meaning she could interpret.

The queen let him finish, with obvious impatience. Her tail whipped out, catching Nyx under the chin and tilting her head up, as if she were being offered for inspection. Then the queen turned back to Jevryn and spat a single word.

Whatever she asked, Jevryn clearly didn't like it. A terse click was his response. Then he opened his arms in an un-councilor-like gesture that seemed to say, "What can you do?" He proceeded to expound upon his reply. When he was finished, the advisor at the queen's left started in, but she cut him off with a dismissive flick of her tail.

She drew herself up to her full height and began to speak with the air of a judge dispensing a sentence. She gestured to the crystal above her. Her words were quietly spoken, the hisses and the clicks having as soft an edge to them as such words could, like a piano note played with the dampening pedal engaged.

When she was finished, she gave Nyx what might be interpreted as a kindly look, and two of her arms reached out to draw Nyx to a standing position. Jevryn bowed again to the queen, then lifted his head, his icy gaze turning on Nyx. "Come. We are leaving."

Nyx scrambled to stick by his side, unable to believe they were walking out of here just like that. The queen gestured, and an insectoid from the first inner circle—Al—unfroze. He listened to his queen and then fell in behind her and Jevryn.

They were to have an escort out of the city, then.

"Jev—"

"Do not speak until we are gone from this place. I do not think I can converse with you without screaming, and I have gone to a great deal of trouble to appear calm and diplomatic."

She managed to observe the requested silence during the walk to the edge of the floor. She continued to observe it out of necessity when Jevryn portaled them, in rapid succession, from floor to floor. They barely landed on one before he whipped them down to the next, and by the time she stumbled out onto the actual ground, she was dizzy, a little nauseous, and thought she would have rather Al carried her down in his tail.

He'd managed to keep up with them, more or less, dropping from one of the columns a few seconds after Jevryn's portal spit her out. Nyx put her hands on her knees and breathed deeply, fighting the urge to be sick. "Couldn't you have just brought us from the top floor to here in one go?" she asked, breaking the moratorium on speaking.

"Yes," he replied.

She waited, but he didn't offer any other explanation. "Okay," she said, "then why didn't you?"

"Because I am deeply frustrated." He straightened the cuffs of his robe and began walking without another word. She followed. When the ache in her calf made her stumble for the fourth time in twice as many steps, Al's tail curled gently around her, and lifted her off the ground. She didn't mind.

Al had never hurt her, even though there likely wouldn't have been any repercussions for him if he had. He'd refused to hand off to other guards in the city, who likely would have treated her with less care. And he'd made sure, when she was confined to her room, that she had the basic necessities. She had grown oddly fond of him during their brief interactions. She patted his tail where it wrapped around her stomach, and hoped the gesture conveyed her appreciation.

They reached the edge of the forest, and Al stopped and placed her gently on the ground.

"Can you tell him thank you for me?" she asked Jevryn.

He gave her a strange look. "You do understand that when I arrived, they were debating wether to execute you or not?"

It did sting, but she made herself shrug. "He was nice to me."

Jevryn exchanged a few words with the big warrior, then turned back to Nyx. "He says you are welcome, and have brought excitement to an otherwise boring tenure. Let us go, now."

Nyx didn't move. She scanned the ground, looking for the Harvester. She didn't even know if this was the same place where she'd come into the forest. One of the large silver trees was there at the perimeter, but that didn't mean it was the same one she'd entered next to.

She felt nothing, no indication of the Harvester's presence. A faint flicker tugged at the edges of her awareness, and she realized that wasn't precisely true. She felt it, but it was very far away.

Al gave her a gentle nudge toward the perimeter, where

Jevryn was intent on leaving her behind. She trotted after him, a new worry occurring to her as she stepped out of the woods and into bright sunshine.

She hadn't seen Drago since she'd been taken. Was the unicorn-dragon alright? Nyx didn't want to leave the planet without her. She'd been so excited to see a person. Nyx remembered her joy, the images that conveyed delirious excitement at the possibility of having a companion.

Nyx stopped walking and started conjuring images, hoping whatever Drago's range was for receiving them, it was one she could reach. She looked at the trees, sending that image out. With any luck, Drago was near enough by, would know the landscape well enough, to follow her mental image to the space they occupied. As for convincing Jevryn to take Drago with them…well, she'd cross that bridge when she came to it.

"What are you doing?" Jevryn asked.

"I am thinking thoughts."

"Are you? That would be a refreshing change, as it appears you have not been thinking *any* since you left Earth."

There was enough irritation laced in Jevryn's words to snap Nyx out of her thoughts of Drago and the Harvester. "What I have *been*, since I left Earth, is abducted and dragged to parts of the universe I'm pretty sure *no one* knows exists."

"You very nearly broke a peace that has lasted a millennia!" he shouted.

"How was I supposed to know that?" she yelled back. Maybe yelling at a councilor wasn't the best idea, but she was at the end of her metaphorical rope.

He went on as if she hadn't spoken. "Do you know what happens to portal witches who accidentally come here, child? They are killed on sight. That is the treaty the Council has with the Minethrans. We keep our own to us, and they give us the same courtesy."

Well, that probably answered the question of why portaling was illegal. "Then why didn't they kill me?"

"Because you had my ring and my name, and you had the relative fortune to arrive when the planet is in its one-hundred-year cycle, when the storms come. Those storms are sacred to the Minethran people. This entire planet is sacred to them. They believe it has a soul, and these storms are the expression and rebirth of that soul. They were debating whether your arriving during them was some sign of the planet's favor towards you. Even so, they were leaning in favor of execution before I arrived."

"It's not like the All Council has a warning sign at the boundary that says 'Portal Witches Not Welcome' in large neon letters."

"Had you exhibited *any* sense of restraint before portaling all over the universe like a child with a new toy, you would not have found your way here."

She didn't like the way he kept referring to her as a child. Then again, she supposed that almost everyone must seem like a child to him, given how long he'd lived.

"What was I supposed to do?" Nyx demanded. "Stay right where my kidnapper put me? In a creepy jail that looks like it hasn't been used since the dawn of your precious peace treaty?"

Jevryn closed his eyes. Nyx would bet money he was resisting the urge to pinch the bridge of his nose in frustration. His eyes flicked back open and his next words were spoken in tight, even, controlled measures. "Explain. Everything."

"Everything is a very broad word."

His eyes shone with annoyance. "You do not want to try my patience. I was never graced with particularly much of it, and you have already consumed the majority of what I do possess. Begin with your abduction and continue until my arrival here. Leave out no detail."

Nyx considered her options. On the one hand, Jevryn had saved her from execution. Or, if she was a really untrusting person, he *said* he'd saved her from execution. On the other hand, he was a member of the Council that had nearly killed her and could do so at any time on a whim. She didn't really know why he'd come here for her.

"I'm…not entirely sure that's in my best interests."

"If your reluctance stems from the Harvester of Worlds, be assured I am already aware it is in your possession."

Nyx chewed on that revelation for a minute. "And how long have you known that?"

"I suspected it as soon as I realized what you were in that Station."

"I'm just a Guardian."

"If you were *just* a Guardian your Station would be in turmoil and Arradin would be dead. I will expect an explanation of *that* later. You are fortunate the other councilors who came with me that day are not as adept at recognizing Hidden as I am."

He said "fortunate" like she could have predicted the outcome of the councilors arriving at her Station, and neatly avoided the entire matter. He said it like she should have known what she was, and been prepared. Then again, if he just *recognized* Hidden, she supposed he wouldn't have any reason to suspect *she* had no idea what she was.

She glanced around at the field surrounding them. If this wasn't the same area she'd entered in, it was indistinguishable. Bodies littered the ground, remnants of the storms' effects. "Shouldn't we have this conversation somewhere else? Maybe on Earth, where we aren't at risk of being attacked by alien dinosaurs?" She really *really* wanted to be home.

"No. You are comfortable on Earth, and Arradin dislikes it when I interrogate people for information."

Charming.

"The queen has interceded with the planet for a temporary cessation of the storms, so there is no immediate danger." He said it like someone might say, "She asked the principal to delay the pep rally half an hour."

"And you think that has a high likelihood of working? That the planet really has a soul?"

"Whether the planet has a soul or not I cannot say. But the queen *is* the queen because she is intrinsically tied to the magic of this world. If she is confident in her ability to keep the storms at bay, then *I* am confident in her ability."

Nyx hesitated. She didn't necessarily have to share Jevryn's confidence. She was ten feet from the Minethrans' forest. If worst came to worst, she could jump back through. Even if Jevryn couldn't get her out again, death by execution was probably better than death by jagged dinosaur claws. She hoped.

She still didn't want to talk, but he already knew the damning bits—she had the Harvester, she was gone from her Station, and she was a portal witch—so she relented and filled in the finer details of how she'd ended up here.

Jevryn listened to it all with the air of a bored instructor. "That was all? You just…languished in a cell?"

She scuffed her foot on the ground. "Well, Laiveran might have rambled on with varying degrees of sanity."

Jevryn perked up like a bloodhound scenting a trail. "Laiveran?"

"It was the name he gave."

"What did he look like?"

Nyx described him. "Do you know him?"

"I would like to believe that I do not. What did he want from you? What did he speak of?"

"Mostly he just went on about his dead wife a lot. And…"

"And what?"

You'd already be dead if he wanted you dead, she reminded herself. "He's looking for the Harvester." She debated her next words but said them anyway. Because Jevryn was the person most likely to be capable of answering her questions about the Harvester. It was why she'd used his ring in the first place, even if she'd intended to extract some sort of promise before spilling her guts in the original plan. "I have reason to think he might be the person who made it in the first place. Do you know if that's true?"

"I could not say with certainty unless I met him."

Which sounded like a yes to Nyx.

"Come. We have wasted enough time. If it is Earth you wish to return to, then to Earth we shall return."

"Umm, about that."

"Yes?"

"I, uh, I sort of lost the Harvester here."

"What do you mean you—" He cut off abruptly, eyes widening at something over Nyx's shoulder. She turned just as joyful images bombarded her mind, and saw the unicorn-dragon running toward them. The equine was ecstatic, filling Nyx's mind with pictures of her and Jevryn. Drago was very, *very* excited to see them, and she was charging straight at the councilor.

22

———————

D rago barreled into Jevryn, head-butting him with the lower non-horned portion of her face with enough force to knock him back several feet. Nyx jumped in front of the unicorn-dragon, certain the animal was one second away from Jevryn's blade at her throat. "Please don't hurt her. She didn't mean any harm, she's just lonely and—are you *laughing*?"

He was. He was standing there, laughing with what sounded like actual happiness, an emotion she would previously have thought him incapable of. Drago decided Nyx was getting in the way of her fun, and darted around her to frolic a little circle around Jevryn before ramming the lower half of her head into his chest again.

Jevryn wrapped the unicorn-dragon's massive face in a hug, and she responded by sloppily licking at him. "Temerex, you clever girl. I did not think you would still be alive."

Nyx put two and two together. "Wait, she's yours? *You're* the one who dumped her here? Because that is really shitty. Do you have any idea how lonely she was when I found her?"

Jevryn recovered his decorum, putting a gentle hand on Drago's—Temerex's—forehead to back her up before turning a look on Nyx that reminded her that, despite how normal he seemed with Temerex, he co-governed the universe and likely hadn't been talked to like that in several centuries. He continued to stare for so long that she dropped her gaze.

"Sorry," she muttered.

"For the record, I am not responsible for Temerex's being here. Kiev brought her here while I was…indisposed. By the time I regained the ability to come here, other matters took precedence, and I truly did not believe she would still be alive."

"Whatever you have to tell yourself to sleep at night," Nyx said under her breath. If someone dropped *her* unicorn-dragon on a foreign planet, she would go find it the second she was physically able, and everything else could wait.

The look on Jevryn's face said he'd heard every mumbled word and he wasn't amused. Her brain chose that moment to remember that he *had* gotten her out of the insect city, and he was her only sure bet of getting home. She apologized in the only way she could manage, which wasn't really apologizing at all. "I find abandonment triggering. Personal experience, and all that."

Great, perfect response. Jevryn A-Morridahn, High Councilor, really cares about your mommy issues.

Except he did seem to, because he said, "Kaden told me your mother left you on Earth. That she Hid your memories. Is that true?"

For one stunned moment, Nyx was certain she'd heard him wrong. Then she thought he must be referencing things the All Council had learned when Kaden was in Psionics, except Kaden had said he'd never told them anything about her, and if she didn't fully trust what he said, she trusted in the fact that none of them had ever come to Earth looking for her before the Arkadia incident. She wasn't sure how many options that left.

"Kaden? Kaden *Moor* told you my mother left me?"

"I did require some explanation for why he brought the Harvester to you instead of Elena. So, yes. He told me."

It all fell into place then, the little things that had never made sense to her before. That Kaden had escaped with the Harvester in the first place. That he had so easily found her on Earth, when apparently no one else in the universe had known where the last Hidden were. Jevryn interceding when the Council had come to her Station, keeping Koral from digging into her mind. Jevryn giving her his ring, a boon granted on the flimsy excuse of a debt to Griff.

It had all been Jevryn, from the beginning.

She couldn't breathe. She bent over, hands on her knees, trying to suck down air that didn't seem to contain enough oxygen. Was this atmosphere oxygen deficient and it had finally caught up with her? Except, no, an oxygen deficient atmosphere couldn't sustain life as large as the creatures on this planet, and—

"Are you well?"

Laughter bubbled up her throat. "Am I *well*? My life since I came to Earth Between has been a chaotic up-and-down circus of insanity that I can now directly blame *you* for, and you want to know what the worst part of all of that is? It's still the best fucking year of my life, because the answer to your question is *yes*. Elena Fortuna took everything I was from me and threw me away.

"What little memories I've gotten back don't exactly paint a rosy childhood, and sometimes I hate her so much I can't sleep at night." She paused to suck down a breath, delighted to find that anger, heightened by the chaos thorns in her cheek, had made breathing a doable thing again. Along with thinking.

"Oh my god, it was you, wasn't it? You're the one who brought Elena to Earth." Who else but a councilor could have afforded to purchase a portal stone to every planet? Had they been some kind of escape insurance, should Elena have needed them? Jevryn certainly didn't require them to travel. "Were you the one sending her money, too?"

She didn't expect him to answer. She expected him to brush her off in that brusque manner he had and demand they return to a discussion about where the Harvester was. But he did answer.

"Convincing your mother to stay on Earth was not an easy task. Money was the incentive she required, and it was well within my reach to give."

Nyx absorbed the statement, as if the information he'd so casually delivered wasn't world-shattering for her. "Okay. So you did that. All so, what? You could have the last Hidden under your control?" So much for Seth's wealthy father theory. Like most things, it all just came down to power and money, and Nyx supposed she should just be grateful her mother had had enough humanity *not* to abandon her before she could legally make her own decisions in Dead Earth.

Jevryn's lips twisted. "That is certainly what Elena wished to believe. Far be it from me to point out that had I not intervened, she would have been hunted down and killed like the rest of your people."

"And you did that out of the kindness of your heart, I suppose?"

"I see you have her same talent for scathing sarcasm."

Nyx flinched. She didn't like the idea of being anything like her mother. It was strange, talking to someone other than Seth who had known her.

When she didn't respond, he answered her original question. "Of course I didn't. I am a councilor, am I not?" His lips curved in a bitter smile. "We do nothing out of the kindness of our hearts. Something you would do well to remember."

"Then why are you here? Why answer their" —she jerked her thumb back at the forest— "summons?"

"I did not answer the Minethrans' summons. I answered yours." He lifted the hand bearing the ring the Minethran queen had returned to him. "And I have answered more than enough of your questions. Where is the Harvester?"

Nyx blurted it all out like ripping off a bandaid. "I wore it on the same chain as your ring. The ring the Minethrans saw. They kind of broke the chain and the Harvester fell off, and I tried to grab it but I was a little too busy being abducted to manage it. I tried to find it on the way out, but I don't think it's in the forest anymore."

Jevryn absorbed all of this. "Then where is it?"

That was the question, wasn't it? Instinct tugged her inward, to the net of Hiding tangled around her, guiding her to a specific knot in the structure. She only hesitated for a second, then reached with phantom fingers and untangled the knot. She felt a sharp tear, like she'd ripped off an almost-healed scab, and memory rushed her.

Nyx stood outside the barn in the fading twilight, swatting at the mosquitoes that loved dusk this time of year. Seth stood next to her, loosely holding the reins of King, his bay gelding. King snorted and pawed, tail flicking over his side, not any happier about the mosquitoes than Nyx was.

Nyx's mother stood in front of her and held out a small brown marble. "Hide it," she ordered. "From everyone except him." She nodded at Seth.

It was Nyx's tenth birthday, and she didn't want to be out here, losing a pint of blood to insatiable insects. She wanted to be inside, with the Animorphs book Seth had somehow convinced his father to buy for her on his last trip into Dead Earth. But she knew better than to argue.

She took the marble. She didn't need the physical touch anymore to Hide an object, but it had been handed to her, so...

She drew a thread of magic and flattened it into a supple sheet, curving it around the marble. The exact form around the object varied from Hidden to Hidden, and was only important insomuch as it worked for them. Her mother always built nets of power. When Nyx was younger, she'd thought it was because her mother liked pretty, lacy things, and that's why her Hiding nets were always shimmering confections, gossamer thin, but so much stronger than they looked.

That was probably true—that her mother liked the nets because they were beautiful—but lately Nyx had started to think her mother liked them the most because nets captured things. Nyx preferred to think of her magic like a cloak, something that protected the thing it covered instead of keeping it caged.

She drew that cloak around the marble now, but she left a gap in the fold, one only Seth would be able to see through.

"Give it to him."

Nyx handed Seth the marble and her mother turned to him. "Take it into the forest. Then throw it as far away from you as you can. Do not note its location. I don't want you to have any idea where it is, am I clear?"

Seth nodded.

Her mother's eyes narrowed. "Help her, and you will both be out here all night. Understood?" Another nod. "Then go."

He shot Nyx an apologetic glance, but they'd both learned by now just how well things turned out when either of them tried to help the other against one of their parent's wishes. He jumped onto King's back. The gelding took off at the slightest squeeze of Seth's legs, eager to outrun the flying bloodsuckers biting him.

Her mother pulled another marble from her pocket and cast a net of Hiding over it. It took her less than a second, where it had taken Nyx a few minutes to do the same thing. At this point, the only way Nyx could manage that kind of instantaneous Hiding was via the Hidden promise she had learned was so dangerous.

"Look at the magic structure," her mother ordered.

Nyx slapped at another mosquito, the small insect smooshing between her palm and her neck. The bloodsuckers never bothered her mother. Probably magic of some kind, but Seth and Nyx liked to joke that Elena Fortuna was too bitter even for the mosquitoes.

Nyx squinted, the act of looking with physical sight helping to focus her magical sight, until the white-gold edges of her mother's Hiding became visible.

"Every Hidden is tied to their working," Elena intoned. "The connection is necessary for the continued functioning of the spell. If the link is severed—either intentionally, or due to the death of the Hidden who created it—the working will survive for a short time. Minutes,

hours, sometimes days, depending on the strength of the maker. But eventually it will fade.

"If something you have Hidden is ever lost to you, it can always be found again. You need only follow the link that connects you to it. This link will stretch across miles, cities, planets. It will always be with you, so long as you are committed to the working."

Her mother lifted her hand and there, dangling from her fingertips, was a delicate chain of magic. One end attached to the net. The other sank into Elena, drawing from the well of magic within her.

"Think of it as a vein." Her mother smiled. It wasn't a pretty smile —Elena's never were. "Because it will bleed you every second of every day that it is connected to you. And the more veins you open, the more you will bleed. Over time, the more you give, the more your capacity will increase. But the more you give—the more you can give—the more people will expect of you."

Her mother flicked her hand and the chain connecting her to the working vanished from Nyx's sight. Her cool, manicured fingers tilted Nyx's chin up. "Remember that, my daughter. That you can give and give and give, and it will never be enough. People will always want more, expect more, take more. The world is a leech, my daughter, and it will suck you dry without a second thought."

Her expression was almost tender in that moment. Nyx had caught little glimpses like this over the years. Short moments, where the part of her that desperately wanted her mother to love her, to accept her, could believe that maybe she did. Then the tenderness vanished. Elena dropped her hand, her expression hardening.

"Look inside yourself and find that connection. If you have diffi-culty, search for the feeling of that which belongs to you being siphoned away. Once you've found it, follow it, and find the marble. Do not come inside until you have it."

So Nyx settled against the barn wall and searched. Seth returned and settled next to her, eventually falling asleep as the hours spun out.

Looking for the connection was like swimming through an ocean trying to find a single drop of water. It took her far too long to realize she was looking for the wrong thing—looking for something terrible and ugly, because that was how her mother felt about her own power. But though Nyx didn't like being forced into these exercises, her magic was still beautiful to her, still wondrous, still an expression of her. And she didn't hate herself.

She stopped looking for the marble as if its hiding had been forced upon her, stopped looking for it as if it was something that had been stolen, and started looking for the thing she had chosen to protect.

Miles away, deep in the forest, the soft light of her power beckoned.

"Are you expecting to find the Harvester in the wind?"

Nyx blinked, coming back to the present. Had Jevryn A-Morridahn, lauded high councilor, mightier-than-thou, just lowered himself to engage in the very sarcasm he'd accused her of?

In all fairness, she had been staring sightlessly into the wind. She reached into the core of her power, feeling, as she had all those years ago, for the tether to her working. She grasped it, and her awareness of the Harvester snapped into place. She pointed. "If I were, I would inform you it's floating in the wind in *that* direction."

Jevryn frowned. "How far in that direction?"

"I don't know. It feels pretty faint, so...far?" She still had no idea how it had left the forest in the first place. Then again, she'd seen rocks bigger than the Harvester get stuck in the frog of a horse's hoof, so maybe some clueless creature had walked over it, gotten it stuck between their toes, and carried it off into the great beyond.

Temerex sent her an image of Jevryn and Nyx on her back as they raced across the plains, the picture suffused with excitement. Nyx stroked her forehead. "I'm really glad you want to help, but I don't think you should be carrying both of us around."

"You caught that?" Jevryn asked, his voice casual and neutral. *Too* casually neutral. Something about her catching Temerex's thoughts bothered him.

"What? She's very vocal with her thoughts, if that makes any sense. You'd have to be pretty dense to *not* hear them."

"Indeed." Jevryn said something under his breath, and he was apparently better at muttering than Nyx was, because *she* couldn't make out *his* words.

"She should *not* carry both of us," Nyx said. "Horses should never carry over twenty-five percent of their body weight. It's terrible for their backs."

Jevryn's voice practically dripped amusement. "While I am certain Temerex is delighted you have taken her well-being to heart, let me assure you that while she may have the predominant body of a horse, her skeletal and muscular structure is far more robust. She could carry ten times our weight and be none the worse for wear." At Nyx's skeptical look he continued, "However, it will not be necessary. Given the temporary cessation of the storms, there is no reason we cannot portal planetside."

Nyx wasn't entirely sure she hadn't had enough portaling to last her a lifetime. Especially when Jevryn unclipped one of the bracelets from his arm and held it out to her.

"It does not bite," he said, when she didn't take it.

She eyed it skeptically. "While I admit that having a super cool portal magic bracelet of my very own has a certain appeal—you know, in case you meet an untimely end or decide to leave me here—I would like to know what the catch is."

"The blundering attempts at portaling that led you to this planet are an embarrassment to the craft. You require instruction, and I find there is no experience like *necessary* experience to make instruction sink in."

It was official: Nyx had absolutely no idea what to make of Jevryn A-Morridahn. She could ask him why he would bother teaching her anything when portaling in this manner was illegal for anyone save a councilor. But however tired she was of portaling, she was more tired of being out of her depth, and if she asked why he was doing this, there was always the chance that he would change his mind about it.

She took the bracelet and clapped it over her wrist. It resized itself as it closed, fitting snugly without hampering her circulation. With the bracelet in her possession, curiosity got the better of her. "Could I ask you a hypothetical question?"

"Hypothetical, meaning the question involves your knowledge of illegal activities?"

"Maybe."

"Nyx, you and I are currently seeking to retrieve the Harvester of Worlds, which you are not supposed to know exists, and which I am directly responsible for delivering into your possession. There is nothing else you could admit to knowing that is more detrimental to your chances of survival than that. Not even knowledge of this planet."

He really knew how to comfort a person. "Right." She cleared her throat. "How do you keep all this secret?" She waved, indicating the planet. "Once I had access to enough portal magic, the planet map sort of just popped up for me. But the portal witches in the Shadow Market have access to enough magic, and they don't seem to realize you can travel this way."

"The witches in the Shadow Market are an embarrassment to the name of portal witch."

Okay, tell me how you really feel.

"They have been given a narrative about how portal magic works, and their gift is weak enough they will not find their way to that map without someone guiding them to it."

"But I did. Why?"

Jevryn waved his hand dismissively. "The talent runs stronger in some lines than in others. Now, in its atmospheric state, portal magic takes up a great deal of space, as you have already seen. The bracelet compresses that magic into a denser form that is capable of being more readily stored."

Nyx accepted she wasn't going to get anything else out of him and focused on what he was telling her. "So, like how you can condense a gas into a liquid form to store more of it?" She supposed that might be something they didn't *do* out in the wider universe—she had trouble picturing cryogenic storage tanks on the magic-heavy planets she'd read about.

"Yes, precisely like that," Jevryn said, leaving her to wonder if they *did* have cryogenic storage tanks and mechanically compressed gases, or if they compressed and stored it by magical means, or if they did neither of those things and Jevryn was just really well-informed about Earth's technologies. Since Griff was on Earth, Jevryn might have more than a passing interest in the planet.

"Your first step is learning to store and retrieve that magic. You have some small amount of portal magic clinging to your left ankle. You will find—" He cut off as his gaze traveled down to where the dime-sized tuft of magic clung to her leg, but she didn't think it was the magic he was staring at.

His voice came out a little too measured. "Where did you get those boots?"

23

———

Jevryn's hand twitched toward the mercury boots and Nyx took a defensive step back.

"They were a gift." It wasn't *exactly* a lie.

His gaze sharpened. "Arradin gave them to you?"

"Maybe," she said, drawing the word out.

"I have been looking for those for eight centuries." Then, more to himself than to her, "Damn it, I *asked* Arradin if he had seen them anywhere."

Yeah? How had that conversation gone? *Hey, babe, sorry about the whole you getting stripped of your freedom and identity thing and sentenced to an eternity of servitude, but have you seen my mercury boots lying around? Maybe under the bed?*

No wonder Griff had been so exasperated when Nyx decided to keep them after her little jaunt to Tenebris Umbra.

Jevryn held out his hand, imperiously.

Nyx crossed her arms. "They belong to me."

"No," Jevryn replied, a muscle ticking along his jaw. "They belong to me."

"I have no evidence of that. Besides, Griff told me they suited me."

"Did he? Clearly, he and I need to have a discussion."

Nyx would pay an entire month's wages to hear how *that* conversation went. But Jevryn looked militant about having the boots back, and she had the distinct feeling that his wanting them back had less to do with the boots and more to do with Griff.

"Let's say I *did* give them back to you now." She was not giving them back. Now *or* ever. She didn't know what had happened between Jevryn and Griff, but she did know she was firmly on Griff's side. "Unless your current shoes magically adjust foot size" —and she could tell from the look on his face that they didn't— "that would leave me barefoot on a planet full of dinosaurs and storms. Do you think that would help or hinder our current endeavor?"

Amusement sparked in Jevryn's eyes. "Tell me, did you learn that knack of speaking as if you were a children's teacher from Arradin? If so, he has taught you remarkably well."

"I will take that as the correct answer, which is, 'hinder.' Look, you've done without these boots for like eight hundred years, right? You'll survive a few more hours."

A few more hours, until she was back home, where Griff would undoubtedly make Jevryn give in to letting her keep them out of principle. Really, though, Griff could have warned her about where they came from.

"Now, you were saying something about me putting portal magic into the cool armband?"

Jevryn waved at the armband, letting the boots go. For now. "Storing the magic is not the difficult part. Pass the bracelet through the magic."

Nyx barely got the armband within touching distance of the small tuft on her ankle before it was sucked inside in a thin stream, the armband turning just a little deeper blue as what it held became packed more tightly together with the recent influx.

"How does that work?"

"The band is made of thalacite crystal. The crystal and portal magic have a naturally attractive relationship. Therefore, it is quite easy to store the magic, but retrieving it comes with some slight difficulty for novices."

At least he'd said "novice" and not "hopeless idiot."

"Okay, so how do I pull it back out? And how do I know how much to pull for a portal when it's condensed like this?"

"How were you measuring it before?"

"Uh…" She shuffled her feet. "You know, I just sort of covered myself in portal magic, and the first few portals I opened took about this much." She held her hands apart to show "this much."

Jevryn pinched the bridge of his nose. Actually pinched the bridge of his nose. She wasn't certain she'd ever seen anyone do that before in real life. "Please tell me you were not measuring use by sighted quantity."

"How else would I measure it?"

"By *feel*."

"Feel seems infinitely more subjective than quantity."

"Quantity is irrelevant in a substance that, as we have just seen, is compressible and expandable depending on atmospheric and environmental conditions."

His condescension grated on her. "It's not like anyone's ever explained this to me before. I was doing the best I could."

He shook his head. "Indeed, I suppose they have not. Very well. Feel is, as you stated, subjective. But it is only subjective between users. What I know is an appropriate amount to wield is not the same amount that you might use to accomplish the same feat.

"For instance, I traveled here directly from Earth. That required significant magic use even for me, given the distance between planets. It would take you ten times as much, and you would not be able to hold the use of it long enough to accomplish the feat. The more you practice, the more you will be able to hold, and the less magic you will need to accomplish the same tasks."

"It sounds like you're telling me I'm going to become a more efficient conduit."

"That is precisely what I am saying. That you could portal as far as you did—paltry though those distances are to the more-seasoned of our number—with so little training, speaks to the strength of your ancestral line."

Nyx's ears buzzed with excitement at the words *ancestral line*. He'd said it so matter-of-factly, without any curiosity or hesitation.

Ask him. Just ask him if he knows who your father is. But Jevryn was still droning on about limits and experience, and whether he did or didn't know her father's identity, now probably wasn't the time.

Jevryn snapped his fingers in her face. "Are you paying attention?"

She nodded dutifully.

"Then what did I just say?"

"You said to do this." She touched her left ring and middle fingers to the top of the clear part of the bracelet. Unlike the black thalacite crystal, the clear portion was extyll, a semi-permeable rock that, if enough force was exerted, allowed portal magic to be drawn through it in either direction. This permeability allowed the naturally attractive force of the thalacite to draw the portal magic inside the bracelet, where it remained contained until a greater force—the portal witch—extracted it.

Her fingers touching the thalacite, she reached with the part of her that had felt that unstoppable draw to the ley line the first time she'd seen the portal room of her Station. The part that had been so mesmerized by the portal well in the Shadow Market. The part that had felt halfway euphoric when she'd stepped into the lake on Lehine.

The magic within the bracelet was not an insignificant amount, however small it appeared. She felt its hum through the extyll and reached for it. But her fingers couldn't pass through.

Of course they couldn't pass through. Porous rock was semi-permeable to wispy magics, not solid human fingers. She wasn't supposed to physically reach into the bracelet, she was supposed to entice its contents into coming to her.

She sank into the feel of the magic again, of its presence inside the bracelet, and called to it. The magic responded by brushing against the inside of the bracelet, vibrating against her skin. It was interested, but not yet interested enough that it would pass back through the barrier.

She tried again, offering the magic a glimpse of everything they could do together—the portals they could spin, the places they could go—and this time, a slender thread of blue slipped out of the bracelet and curled in the palm of her hand.

"Passable," Jevryn said. "That part will get easier with practice."

Didn't everything get easier with practice? Wasn't that why instructors the world over were always pushing *practice, practice, practice?*

"Okay, what now? Is there, like, a local map I can pull up?"

"Portaling on-planet is not the same type of working as shifting planets. While range can eventually be extended to specific places you know well enough to picture, for the time being, you are going to be restricted to line of sight." He pointed to a large rock maybe twenty feet away. "Portal there."

It wasn't very far away. "Okay. How?"

"You said that when you moved between planets, you reached for those planets on the map. If that is how you instinctively use the ability, then it will not be so different here. Reach for the rock. Let the magic do the rest."

She felt silly as she stretched her fingers toward the rock, to where if she closed one eye, her fingers lined up with it in her vision. But then, she'd grown accustomed to feeling silly since she'd become a part of the wider universe. She concentrated on the rock and her desire to be there, and the magic against her palm itched and stretched, demanding, but not *doing*, and she knew she hadn't pulled the requisite amount of magic from the bracelet.

She teased another strand out and it twined with the first, opening the now-familiar oval in space, through which she could see the rock on the other side, now looking as if it were a foot away instead of twenty. She jumped through.

On the bright side, she landed on top of the rock, completing her first ever line-of-sight portal jump. On the not-so-bright side, the portal made her misjudge the distance. She stepped down too hard—like reaching the bottom of a set of stairs but still thinking you have one to go, so that next step is jarring. Her injured calf screamed in protest and her leg buckled.

Jevryn and Temerex blinked into the space next to her. "You did not mention you were injured."

She stared at him.

"Aside from—" He waved a hand to indicate her sunburned face and damaged hands.

She deadpanned. "Aside from all my other injuries?"

He had the decency to at least look mildly guilty. She eased to a sitting position. She needed to look at the wound on her leg, she just didn't want to. As long as she didn't look at it, she could pretend it wasn't that bad.

"Show me," he ordered.

There wasn't an easy way to show someone the back of your calf while sitting. And she was not standing again right this second. Nyx scooted back on the rock, gingerly stretching her leg out in front of her. It...didn't look great.

Jevryn frowned. "What bit you?"

"A mermaid."

"Mermaid?" By the way he carefully repeated the syllables, she could tell the word hadn't translated.

"You know, vaguely human creature that lives underwater and has very sharp teeth. I accidentally portaled to the bottom of an ocean."

Jevryn shook his head. "Trouble magnet, indeed." He waved at her calf. "Remove the boot."

"So you can run off with it? I don't think so."

He gave her a hard stare. It was a good hard stare, since he'd had a few centuries to practice it. "Remove the boot."

"This happened yesterday." Was it yesterday? Her sense of time was all out of whack. "The bite went through the boot upper, my jeans, and my sock, and now all the blood has dried and glued the fabric to my skin. Taking it off is going to hurt. It will also reopen the wound and expose it to more debris, and then it will probably hurt too much to put the boot back on. I'm not doing that just so you can stare at it."

He said something in a language that didn't translate. A small portal opened next to him, a square of space about two feet by two feet. On the other side, she saw shelving filled with neatly labeled containers, though she once again couldn't read the language. Jevryn frowned, and the shelf slid sideways. At least, it looked like that was what happened, but it made more sense that the portal was moving to a different location on the shelf.

Temerex sidled up next to Jevryn and stuck her head through the portal, her horn knocking a couple boxes off a row.

"Tem." Jevryn's voice was all good-natured exasperation, and must have been accompanied by him image-speaking to Temerex, because she pulled her head out looking contrite. She trotted over to Nyx and lowered her head, sniffing the rock Nyx sat on before huffing out a breath and sending Nyx an image of her scratching Temerex's ears.

"I would love to," Nyx said, "but my hands are shot." She held them out.

Temerex sent her the ear-scratching image again.

"I don't know how to tell you it hurts too much to scratch your ears." How could she convey pain via mental image?

Jevryn glanced over and must have conveyed it for her,

because Temerex stopped asking for ear scratches. Jevryn pulled two boxes to him and let the portal die.

Nyx watched him place the boxes next to her on the rock. "Where was that?" She pointed at the empty space where the portal had been. Was it some strange pocket reality?

He opened one of the boxes, sifting through the contents, and answered absently, "My home."

"So you just...opened a portal to your storage closet and grabbed what you wanted?"

He looked at her like he was afraid she might be a little dense. "As you saw, yes."

It hadn't occurred to her that someone might use portal magic in that way. That they could reach through to a room on another planet like they were reaching through a window. The implications—the *uses*—were astounding. "Can I do that?"

Jevryn, having presumably been doing this for centuries, answered with a bored, "In time, if you practice enough. It requires a sense of connection to the location, and the ability to visualize well. Also a singularity of focus. If you get distracted while you are reaching through and accidentally close the portal, you will sever whichever limbs are on the other side."

She shivered. "Has that...happened to people before?"

"Many times."

Note to self, do not try to retrieve items from another planet while distracted.

Jevryn selected a bottle, unscrewed it to reveal a dropper, and squeezed three dropper-fulls of viscous brown liquid onto her calf. It soaked through the fabric and had a numbing effect, taking the edge off enough for him to unbuckle the boot, peel the layers back, and make a more direct application.

"It will take a minute for it to sink through the tissue layers," he said. "Hands."

She was not about to argue. She held them out and he squeezed a drop onto her burned fingertips, then one to the back of her *pterosaur*-pecked hand. Now that she couldn't feel the pain anymore, she watched with interest as he drained the blisters, applied salve, and taped her fingers. The peck on the back of her hand he efficiently cleaned, then sealed with a thick coat of something that went on clear and dried white. She made a fist and opened it. The coating flexed with the movement of her hand, supple and feeling almost like her own skin.

"How long will this last?"

"A few days, depending on how rough you are with it."

"And the numbing?"

"A few hours."

Better than nothing.

"However, given the interference from the fabric layers, this is still going to hurt." He said it so calmly she didn't realize what he was doing until he'd sliced through the pants and sock covering the mermaid bite and ripped the pieces back.

Flesh tore, the wound broke open, and blood welled and ran over her skin.

"Son of a bitch," she yelled. He'd wisely pinned both of her legs down, or she probably would have kicked him in the face. She would also bet money he'd given Temerex instructions, because the unicorn-dragon had dropped her big, heavy head onto Nyx's shoulder, holding her steady.

"Go on," Jevryn said calmly, "get it out."

She did, which mostly amounted to seeing how many different ways she could say, *"Fuck, fucking, fuck,"* with great vehemence.

"Are you done?" he asked when she'd been quiet for all of five seconds.

She glared at him. "Yes."

He released her, generously applied another dose of the numbing liquid, gave it a minute to set in, and went to work cleaning the bite out. Curiosity got the better of her, and she looked at it, feeling a little queasy once she did. The mermaid's teeth had been long, needle-like, and they had bit deep. Any deeper, and Nyx might have lost an entire chunk of flesh to the creature. The skin around it also looked black.

"Is it necrotic?" Nyx asked.

"Beginning stages," Jevryn confirmed. He unscrewed a jar and dipped his fingers inside, digging out a glop of thick mint-green paste. He smoothed it over the bite, packing it under the torn flaps of skin that she was beyond grateful she couldn't feel. He pressed a piece of gauze into place over it, then covered the gauze in the same sealant he'd used on the back of her hand. "The salve will neutralize any toxins in the bite and prevent further damage, but you should see a healer as soon as you return to your Station."

No, I thought I would just let it fester until they had to take the leg off.

He handed her the topical analgesic and gestured at her face. She gratefully slathered the entirety of her sunburn in it, whimpering in relief as the pain subsided. She gave the near-empty bottle back and he packed up the medical supplies, returning them to their place on his shelf. She still couldn't get over the fact that he could just pop into his house whenever he wanted.

Her stomach squeezed painfully, so she asked, "Can you reach through to other places in your house?"

He nodded.

"Do you happen to have a sandwich lying around your kitchen for the woman who hasn't eaten since she left Earth?" She said it jokingly, but she was entirely serious. She hadn't been willing to risk the food the Minethrans had brought her, since she figured they might not know any better than her whether her system could handle their food. She was starving.

She hadn't been this hungry since before she came to the Station, and the tightening ball of her stomach closing over nothing wanted to bring an avalanche of bad memories back on her. Memories of a time when the conversation she was having right now would be impossible, because no one would see her. A time when she'd rationed cheap food like it was gold because she didn't know when she'd be able to get more.

She wasn't going back to that. She *couldn't* go back to that. She reached for the net of Hiding inside her, reassuring herself that she could still find its lines, its threads. That the cauterized edges held, and her mother wasn't about to wipe her from existence again. That she wasn't about to be *nothing* again.

"Put your boot back on," Jevryn said, oblivious to her internal brooding.

She reached deep inside herself and found a scrap of humor. "So you *do* admit they're my boots. I'm so glad we've come to that consensus."

He shot her a look that had probably brought an entire planet to its knees at some point in history, and opened a portal window to his kitchen. Her stomach growled. She focused on her leg, carefully tucking her cut pants back into the boot upper and buckling it on. She was impressed with how the material had held up, even with the tears, and hoped it could be repaired.

She finished the task and looked up to find that, not only was Jevryn comfortable enough with his skill with portals to risk one lost limb, he was comfortable enough to risk two. He had both arms stuck through and he was…actually making her a sandwich. She didn't recognize anything he was putting on it, other than the bread and something leafy that resembled lettuce.

He finished and pulled it through, thrusting it at her like its making had been a grueling, unpleasant task, and he wanted to be done with it.

She stared at it. "You made me a sandwich."

"You said you were hungry and wanted one."

Yes, well, there was asking a high councilor for a sandwich, and then there was him actually making you one.

"Is there something wrong with it?" Jevryn asked icily.

She took it, before he decided to toss it through a portal. "I'm just trying to figure out if there's a way I can put this on a business card."

"Business card?"

"It's like a resumé."

"You want to put a sandwich on a resumé?"

"No, I want to put, 'Jevryn A-Morridahn, High Councilor of the Universe, made me a sandwich,' on a resumé. I could put it under the Distinguishing Facts section."

"Why am I struck with the feeling that you were an exceptionally difficult child to raise?"

The reply shut down Nyx's sense of humor. "Yeah, well, for me to be difficult to raise, someone would have had to *actually* raise me."

He didn't respond to that because, shockingly, people found it awkward when you brought up your tragic childhood. She bit into the sandwich and stifled a moan. Say whatever else you wanted about him, the man made a damn fine sandwich. Temerex apparently thought so too, because her muzzle kept getting closer and closer, her upper lip stretching out toward the sandwich.

Nyx held the food out of reach while she chewed and swallowed. "Is she actually hungry?"

"She is always hungry."

That was horses for you. "Okay, but am I rudely eating in front of her while she's starving?"

Jevryn shook his head. "She is fine."

Nyx polished off all but a small chunk of the sandwich. Temerex had stared hopefully at it during the three minutes it took Nyx to eat. Nyx would not have previously said that reptilian eyes could look sorrowful, but Temerex's did. "Is anything in this bad for her?"

"No. She is omnivorous."

But leaning towards the carnivore side, if her sharp teeth were any indication. Nyx held the remaining bite of food out on the flat of her palm. The unicorn-dragon lipped it delicately into her mouth, and chewed as if it was the best thing in the world.

"Are you ready to continue?" Jevryn asked.

It took her a minute to realize he was talking about portaling. She was not ready to continue. She was tired and she just wanted to get home and see her friends. They were probably worried sick about her, while she was lounging around on a rock on a foreign planet, eating sandwiches and hobnobbing with councilors and unicorn-dragons.

But she didn't delude herself into thinking she would ever have a better chance to learn about this side of her magic. And given the number of times she'd already found herself on other planets in a disturbingly short amount of time, she wanted to be able to harness portal magic effectively.

She dusted off her hands and stood, pleasantly surprised when her injured leg held without issue. She was going to have to be careful not to overextend. Her inability to feel the pain didn't mean the leg wasn't still injured. If she forgot about it and took off running, it was going to hurt a lot more when the feeling came back.

"I'm ready," she told Jevryn. "Where am I going?"

He pointed to a spot beneath a tree some fifty yards away. She coaxed a tendril of portal magic from the bracelet and got to work.

24

───────

By the count of Nyx's watch, she'd been portaling for over an hour. Her nerves felt like they were physically on fire, and what had at first been a fun time of playing teleport had now become bone-grindingly repetitive.

She was currently doubled over with her hands on her knees, trying to catch her breath. When Jevryn opened his mouth, Nyx cut him off. "I appreciate your presumed faith in my stamina, but I am not opening any more portals for at least an hour."

Or maybe never. Opening a portal again *never* sounded really nice.

"We could have stopped any time you wished. I was merely testing your limits."

Nyx found the energy to raise her head and glare at him. "Generally speaking, if a person has sweated through every garment they are currently wearing, they're at their limit."

She'd gotten entirely too comfortable mouthing off to Jevryn. Perhaps because he had yet to put the fear of the All Council into her, or because he'd made her a sandwich, or because Temerex was all loyal puppy over him. He wasn't what she'd expected, and she kept having to remind herself that, since he was Griff's ex, she was honor-bound to leave Jevryn A-Morridahn in the category of Person To Be Treated With Extreme Derision At All Times.

"Ah," he replied. "How fortunate that I have you here to inform me of these basic properties of the human condition, of which I am woefully ignorant."

She glared harder. "Aren't you supposed to be too powerful and lofty to descend to sarcasm?"

Jevryn scratched absently at Temerex's shoulder. He'd gotten on her back around fifteen jumps ago. Nyx would have been irritated by him riding along like some literal overlord, were she not pretty sure he'd only gotten on because Temerex's enthusiasm for having him back meant she'd been about a second away from rolling underneath him.

The unicorn-dragon clearly thought he was the best thing since sliced bread. It wasn't that Jevryn was *un*likable, precisely, more just...unknowable. He'd been weirdly kind to her so far, but it was in the manner of an old god who found her vaguely intriguing at the moment, but might decide to kill her in the next if his mood changed.

"If we become bereft of all emotion, can we even be said to be a person, anymore?"

Nyx straightened fully, finally having caught some measure of her breath. "So, what? You're playing at sarcasm so a few centuries of existence doesn't turn you into a soulless automaton?"

The corners of Jevryn's lips twitched. "Something like that, I suppose. Is it convincing?"

Nyx couldn't figure out of it was a serious question or if he was just messing with her. "So far, you don't *seem* like a corrupt, impersonal ruler out to subjugate the universe."

"Oh," he said drily. "Good."

"But people aren't always what they seem. And just so we're clear, if you're being nice to me because you think I'll put in a good word with Griff, or whatever, I'm on his side."

"I do not believe any intercession in the universe would do

me any good where Arradin is concerned. And I am not being nice to you."

"If you're not being nice, and you're not trying to win bonus points with Griff, then why are you teaching me anything? Especially when what you're teaching me is illegal?"

Jevryn looked off into the distance, ignoring her question. "How far are we from the Harvester now?"

She sighed and checked, already knowing what she would find. "It's close." She hesitated, but she didn't have anyone else around to confide in. "I think it's been moving toward us this entire time."

At first, she hadn't been sure, but the closer they got to it, the more certain she was that it was also coming to her. Which was odd, since her Harvester-trapped-in-the-foot-of-a-wild-animal theory really didn't have an explanation for that wild animal heading unerringly in her direction.

Jevryn's hand, which had been idly stroking Temerex's neck, stilled. "Is there anyone, save yourself and Laiveran, capable of recognizing the Harvester?"

"What do you mean?" She knew exactly what he meant.

"Did you voluntarily leave anyone out of your Hiding of the object?"

Oh, shit. "Did you bring someone else here with you? Did you bring *Seth* here?" This planet was a nightmare when the storms were going. If Seth was here somewhere, alone, he could be seriously injured. Or dead. Or—

"You left the Hawthorne boy out of the Hiding? Not Moor?"

"Why would I leave—" She cut off as the implication sank in, and her voice dropped a few degrees. "Is Kaden here?"

"Yes."

Her hands clenched. "Is Seth here?"

"Yes."

"Is anyone *else* here?"

"Morgen Drahl and Evra al'Daemon insisted on coming as well."

It punched her in the gut. When Morgen and Evra had gone to Arkadia, it had been for their own reasons. Evra for Tamrin, Morgen for Kaden. Even when they'd accompanied her to the Shadow Market they'd had secondary objectives that didn't include her. But coming *here*? To an unknown planet with Jevryn? The only reason to do that, to risk that, was for her.

Tears pricked at the backs of her eyes. Six months ago she'd stepped off a bus in Phoenix, Arizona, dying right in front of people, and no one had seen her. No one had noticed.

And now, her friends had come for her. Morgen and Evra were loyal to their core—it was who they were—but she didn't think she'd fully accepted that she'd gained that loyalty, fully understood what it meant, until now.

Then there was Seth. Part of her—the part that expected everyone to leave, like her mother, like Kaden, like Seth himself once had—kept waiting for him to disappear again. To realize that even if she regained all her memories, she would still never be the girl he remembered. To realize the universe they'd always wanted to see together was still out there, and playing house with her at the Station was just a temporary past-time.

But he hadn't traveled this far across the universe for a memory.

Morgen, Evra, Seth—she understood them coming for her. But... "Why is Kaden here?"

They hadn't parted on good terms. She'd essentially told him she never wanted to see him again, and he'd seemed to return the sentiment. Hell, in the Shadow Market, she hadn't been able to get him to speak more than a sentence of explanation, and now he was here?

"Because I would have had no notion of where you were without him."

Nyx frowned. "You knew where I was because of your ring."

Jevryn spun said ring on his finger. "This is not a tracking device. It had the power to alert me to your call because I imbued it so. I saw no reason to have tracking capabilities on an object I gave to a woman who should have been bound to a single planet. Though I now fully recognize my hubris in such an assumption, the fact remains that the only way to find you was via Kaden."

She remembered Jevryn telling her that he had required an explanation from Kaden about why he'd brought the Harvester to Nyx instead of Elena. She had just assumed that he'd gotten that explanation earlier. Like, maybe when Kaden was in prison. Or after Kaden had left her in the Shadow Market. Any time other than literal hours ago.

She rubbed at her temples, trying to ease the strain there. "So you just...painlessly tracked down the person the All Council wants most to find in the galaxy and said—what? Don't worry about the whole treason thing, just find Nyx?"

"I did not have to locate him at all. Your Seth did that." Fortunately, Jevryn continued to explain without prompting, because Nyx's brain was working too hard at not imploding to ask further questions. "Did you know Hawthorne has a collection of portal stones to every ley line planet in the galaxy? Were it not that I am, for personal reasons, uninterested in the legality of your friends' activities, I suspect I could put everyone on your Station in prison for the rest of their natural lives."

"Why *are* you so uninterested in the legality of everything? Isn't legality your job?"

Jevryn smiled at her. It was not a pleasant smile. It was nothing a smile *ought* to be. It was a warning, sharp and simple. "If you believe that *any* councilor considers themself to have a job, to be beholden to an ideal or a set of ethics, you are most grievously mistaken.

"Power is never about morality. Government is never truly about peace or stability. Rule is rarely ethical. People will take what they can take. The institutions they create to cement that rule oftentimes grow out of their control, and to some measure do trap them.

"Those institutions are necessary, for it is the facade of beneficence alongside great power that enables any leadership to withstand the test of time. The belief that without that structure, society will fall into chaos."

"Society does fall into chaos without leadership," Nyx retorted. "If you're trying to preach anarchy, that never works. Topple societal structure and another will crop up in its place. People think an ungoverned world will be great until they realize that lack of larger society just leads to right of might on a smaller scale, with less protections for the people most easily abused."

"You are correct. But I am not preaching anarchy. I am merely demonstrating that my lack of interest in upholding the laws of society ought not be so unbelievable. The gears of the institutions we have built grind on in quotidian service to societal laws. I am required for them to function only as a figurehead. I spend my time to further my own ends. Among which is the fact that I do *not* wish the destruction of the current system.

"Should the Harvester fall into Laiveran's hands, or back into Councilor Alastair's, I do believe that destruction would come to pass. So you see, my motives are entirely selfish. And Nyx? Should you ever encounter another councilor again, do remember that lesson." He held out his arm, as if to help her onto Temerex's back. "Come. We have, as you pointed out earlier, had quite enough instruction for one day. I will bring us the rest of the way, and we may discuss what happens next in more amenable surroundings."

Reluctantly, she took his hand and clambered up behind him. She really hoped he kept Temerex to a walk. The necessity of hanging onto Jevryn if Temerex burst into a gallop did not appeal.

As she pointed Jevryn in the right direction, a new thought occurred to her. Earlier, before she'd told Jevryn that she'd lost the Harvester, he'd wanted to take her back to Earth immediately. "Were you just going to leave everyone here? Kaden and the others?"

Jevryn shrugged. "I informed them of the dangers of traveling to this place. They understood the risks inherent in the storms."

"I'm sure they didn't understand the risks of you just deciding to up and leave them."

"I could not possibly have found them in any reasonable amount of time. The storms here open portals to other parts of the planet without rhyme or reason, and Kaden is the only tracker in this group."

"Doesn't make you any less of an asshole."

"Perhaps not." But after a moment, he said. "Your Seth did not come unprepared. Each of your friends has a portal stone to Earth, and I ensured they have magic enough to get them home. Am I less terrible to you now?"

"Not in the slightest."

He smiled. She was kidding herself if she thought it looked a little sad.

"That is perhaps the smartest thing you have said since we met."

25

———————

Seth hadn't seen a hint of a storm in over two hours, and the absence was starting to weird him out. It was an itch beneath his skin, the certainty that this brief reprieve would be paid for later with overwhelming opposition.

It made him tense, and the silence that had fallen over their group half an hour ago wasn't helping. Nor was the fact that the only productive thing they could do was keep mindlessly trekking forward. "You're certain we're getting closer?" he asked Kaden. "Your little Link kink isn't messed up?"

Kaden didn't respond. After their brief confrontation earlier, he'd returned to his default setting of being as expressive as marble. Then again, maybe that was unfair to marble. In the right artist's hands, marble could be pretty damn expressive.

Morgen made a helpful, yes-do-tell noise, since he was the only person capable of getting Kaden to respond using actual words.

"I'm certain. In fact, she's moving faster towards us than we are towards her. Almost like she's the one tracking us."

Seth ignored the implied question. "You didn't think to mention she was moving?"

"You didn't ask."

"This is good news," Evra said, preventing Seth from saying anything overly rude in response. "It means she is likely with Jevryn."

Yes, it was good news. News he should have been apprised of the moment it started happening.

"I understand how we're tracking her," Morgen said, "but how is she tracking us?" He raised a questioning eyebrow at Seth.

Seth shrugged. "I picked up something of hers." His fingers brushed against the Harvester in his pocket. He'd known Hidden remained connected to their workings, wherever they were. He just hadn't known if Nyx remembered enough to know how to follow hers. "How far are we from her?"

"Not far. Maybe fifteen units."

Ten miles, give or take. Considering Kaden had estimated she was a few hundred miles from them when he'd first checked after the storm's durations, it shouldn't be possible for her to be that close.

"So they're portaling the distance," Morgen said.

Kaden shook his head. "Jevryn could have brought them that far in a single jump."

Seth grinned. "But Nyx would do shorter jumps."

"She wouldn't risk portaling here," Kaden said.

Seth snorted. "Right. Because of the two of us, you *definitely* know her better."

Kaden didn't get the chance to answer. The wind shifted, the skies darkened, and the air shimmered as portals coalesced all around, like they'd been thrust into a room of hanging mirrors.

They formed a circle on instinct, each of them with their backs to the others.

"There's high ground to my right," Evra said sharply. "If we fight our way there, we can hold them off."

Yes, Seth thought grimly, *but for how long?* He didn't reach for illusion—though a quick check showed his magic answered, for now—going instead for the enchanted throwing stars. If he was alone, he would go for illusion, but if it failed… "You should all leave," he said calmly. "Portal back."

"Take your own advice, mate," Morgen said.

Seth didn't answer.

"That's what I thought. If you're staying, we're staying."

"Agreed," Evra said tersely.

Kaden grunted, but he didn't pull out a portal stone, so presumably he was staying, too. Well, Seth had to tried.

The shimmering air condensed as the portals solidified, and out poured dinosaurs. Some flying, some flailing, every single one of them pissed off and out of its mind. "High ground, then. We'll hold it through the storm if we can. If not, we get out."

He might be stubborn, but he wasn't stupid. He had a handful of rocks from this planet in his pack. If the worst came to it, he'd portal out of here to the Shadow Market. He didn't care how many of Bryn's loyal subjects he had to terrorize before he made his way to a portal witch willing to spell them for him. He'd do it, and he would come right back here as many times as it took until he found Nyx and brought her home.

"Break right," Kaden ordered. They moved right in tandem. Seth threw stars like he had an endless supply, the enchanted discs burrowing through the creatures, each one sinking jagged teeth into vital points.

The seconds stretched into minutes. As they ticked by, it only became more obvious their efforts wouldn't be enough. They would have to portal out. He knew it even as the others redoubled their efforts, and he ran out of stars and switched to knives. There were simply too many crazed things to fight.

Then the strangest thing happened. The dinosaurs began to disappear. It was portal magic, obviously, but not the wild, unpredictable magic of the storms. It was calculated and precise, taking the beasts closest to them and moving outward, one by one at first, and then whole handfuls at a time. As if someone inexperienced had started, and someone more accomplished had joined in.

He spun in a circle, looking for her, for *them*, and found her. She jumped off the back of what looked like a unicorn-dragon hybrid. She had her concentrating face on, and whips of portal magic lashed from her hands. She was the most beautiful damn thing he'd ever seen, and she was grinning her head off, like she did when she'd had an idea and it was panning out exactly as she'd planned.

Then the magic in her hands sputtered and died, as if she'd run out of it, and the grin on her face died with it. A shadow flew over his head. He didn't have time to react—because he was staring at her like a fucking idiot—and thick talons pierced the protective layers of his Enforcer armor. Claws raked his shoulders. Massive wings flapped, claws stuck in the fabric, and he went airborne.

Nyx screamed his name, and all he could think was that he had a damn fine knack for screwing up at the worst possible moment.

N yx had thought she was being so smart, using portals to drag the dinosaurs off everyone. After all, the danger of using portals during the storms, of the magic failing, only posed a problem if she was portaling someone she cared about the survival of. If a dinosaur got lost in one somewhere, well, she didn't *wish* that fate on them, but it was better than watching her friends get torn to ribbons.

When Jevryn had joined her without comment, following her lead, she thought she might even have managed to impress him. For one blissful moment, she'd believed everything would turn out all right. Then the winged dinosaur had swooped straight for Seth and the magic in her armband had run dry.

"Jevryn." She hated how panicked, how pleading, her voice sounded. "Get it off him."

"I cannot portal only the one."

"Then bring them both." She would take the risk. She would live with the potential consequences, because the alternative was already determined. The creature's wings strained and it moved higher, higher, carrying Seth up and over the lip of the nearby cliff. "Just get him out of there."

Jevryn's focus drifted barely long enough to glance in the direction Seth and the winged dinosaur were moving. In that brief slip of time, the amount of sword-swinging Evra and the others had to do without Jevryn's aid notably increased. "I can save Seth or I can save them. Decide."

Fuck. "Keep doing what you're doing." She snatched a bracelet off Jevryn's arm and took off running, whispering, "*Los,*" to her boots. The kick up in speed took her a few strides to adjust to, but she'd been practicing at the Station. As soon as she had it under control she said, "*Losa,*" the boots amplifying her speed yet again. She stumbled over a rock, the scenery moving by her in a blur, but she caught herself and kept going.

She didn't dare go up to the fastest speed. Her body could barely keep up with what the boots were capable of now, and she could only do this for a couple of minutes, at most. But that was all she needed. Just to get in range of Seth, so she could make sure she portaled *all* of him and the creature. She'd never done this before. She'd been portaling in general for all of a day. Portaling moving targets had started five minutes ago.

What if she screwed up? What if she got something wrong and cut off Seth's arm, or his legs, or—

She was almost close enough to try when thunder rolled through the skies again, a new wave of portals opening. She ducked and dodged them, forced to turn off the boots and slow as the path between her and Seth became a minefield of new portals. Thunder shook the skies again and the portals closed as swiftly as they had appeared.

Above, two shapes plummeted. Seth struggled to free himself from a now-lifeless winged corpse. One of the portals must have opened half atop the beast, then closed. It was the only explanation for why the creature was suddenly missing its head and the upper portion of its body.

It was enough to make her realize he was falling too fast for her initial plan of portaling him from up here. She had one option, and if she'd had any time to really think about it, maybe she wouldn't have had the guts to do it. But in that heart-stopping moment of watching him fall, tangled up in claws and wings, all she knew was that she wasn't going to lose him again.

She worked the boots back up to *Losa* as she ran and then, a yard from the cliff edge, said, "*Losara*." Her foot struck the edge and she pushed off hard, hurtling straight for Seth's falling form. The boots, on their highest amplification setting, pushed her far from the cliff, far enough that for a terrifying moment, she thought she might have overshot.

Seth pulled the talons free of his left shoulder and the corpse, heavier than Seth's weight, separated from him a second before she hurtled into him. She tangled her arms and legs in his, determined not to lose him. The ground, so far away, was nonetheless rushing up to meet them too fast. Her chest felt numb with adrenaline, her hands and fingers shaking with it. For a moment, she couldn't think.

"What the hell are you doing?" Seth shouted.

His voice broke her out of her trance. The panic was still there, still in her, but she could think past it now. She pulled on the portal magic in the fresh bracelet, wrapping it around them both like a net.

She looked into Seth's eyes, familiar and just as scared as she was, and said, "I really hope I'm not about to kill us. But in case I am…"

Nyx kissed him. Then she closed her eyes, pictured the top of the cliff, and her magic dissolved the world around them.

They landed badly, but they landed. The portal had arrested most of their downward momentum, but not all of it, and she was clutched so tightly to Seth that when they landed, her on top of him, her forearms and her feet were curled underneath him, crushed by their combined weight.

She barely felt it, so gloriously grateful to be alive, and only noticed in an absent way that the fickle storm had halted. She yanked her arms out from under him, running them over his chest, down his arms, then turning to look behind her at his legs.

"Nyxi, darling, whatever are you doing?" he drawled the question in that slow, lazy way he had that only seemed to get slower and lazier the more unnerved he was.

"Making sure I didn't accidentally cut off your arms or legs or—"

"Lips?" he suggested.

She wheeled back around before her brain caught up and she realized that, if he was talking, of course she hadn't cut off his lips. She fixated on the ripped fabric at his shoulders.

"How bad is it?"

"Not bad."

Not bad? "That thing had talons the length of my hand."

"Yes, and they mostly hooked in the shirt. Some clawed skin but nothing punctured. I'm fine."

That seemed improbable. Yes, the shirt felt sturdy, but *talons the length of her hand.* She ran her fingers over the shirt-armor thing, looking for a zipper or buttons or any other kind of closure and having no luck. "What is this and how do I get it off?"

"Standard-issue enforcer field armor with some aftermarket modifications. As for getting it off, I'm receptive to mood-lighting, any and all comments on my exceptional hotness, and dirty talk."

She stared at him. "Are you seriously cracking a joke right now? Like *right now?*"

"I don't know." He looked at her, and she saw her own fading panic mirrored in his eyes, as if he also couldn't believe they were both alive and mostly whole. "Did you really just jump off a cliff for me?"

"I guess so?"

He tangled his hands in her hair, dragged her face to his, and kissed her. He drew back abruptly. "Wait, did you only kiss me because you thought we were going to die, or—"

"Seth?"

"Yes?"

"Shut up." She pressed her lips back to his, losing herself in the taste and feel and *realness* of him. He met her intensity, kissing her back with all the pent-up longing she'd hoped had been there the last few months, but been too afraid to find out.

His tongue slid past her lips, brushed against her own, as teasing and taunting as the man himself. His hands slipped from her hair and down her back.

A throat cleared. Loudly.

Nyx broke away from Seth and sat bolt upright. Jevryn A-Morridahn stared down at her from Temerex's back with a look that was half exasperation, half barely-restrained fury. Standing behind him were Evra, Morgen, and Kaden.

26

A *live.* The word practically rang in Nyx's head. Her friends were all alive and, if not unharmed, at least not mortally wounded. She disentangled from Seth, and was saved from saying something awkward like, "Well, this is awkward," because Jevryn had settled on fury over exasperation for his dominant emotion.

"Of all the foolish, asinine things you could possibly do, I admit you have exceeded even my wildest expectations."

Nyx was too exhausted, her body a juxtaposition of tired and wired, to answer him with anything but flippant sarcasm. "Are you upset over my near-death experience because then you wouldn't have anyone to Hide the Harvester, or because I would have gotten blood all over your favorite boots?"

"Need I bother choosing between the two? Let me assure you that when we return to Earth, we will be having a lengthy discussion on the virtues of thinking before acting. Now, let us go, before—" He broke off abruptly.

"Before me?" a raspy voice asked, finishing Jevryn's sentence.

Laiveran. He looked a little more sane than he had when he'd been her jailer, though the change did nothing to make him feel less dangerous. If anything, it had the opposite effect.

Clearly, he had been to her Station, discovered the Harvester wasn't there, and come looking for her again. His gaze shifted between Nyx and Seth. "I do not know which one of you I need, and that is odd." He tilted his head. Magic pulsed from him and wrapped around her. It didn't hurt, it…searched.

"A Hidden," Laiveran said. "And something else, too." His magic gripped her tighter, and this time it did hurt, like a spear trying to cut to the very center of her. She gasped.

Jevryn jumped from Temerex's back and placed himself in front of Nyx and Seth. Morgen, Evra, and Kaden flanked him, and Temerex came to Nyx's side, a cascade of worried images dropping into Nyx's mind.

Her friends' presences didn't physically halt the flow of Laiveran's magic. It simply moved around them like water around rocks.

"Let her go," Jevryn commanded, "and play with me instead. You always wanted to know what lurked inside my soul. Find out, if you think you have the skill."

"Why? Are you concerned about what I might find in hers?" Laiveran asked. But his magic released her. He shook his head at Jevryn. "I do not need to search your soul to know what lives inside your heart. And I do not wish to waste time on games."

His gaze slipped past Jevryn, to Nyx and Seth. "Give me what is mine."

The power drawn from her to keep the Harvester's Hiding surged from a trickle to a flood. She was already on her knees and she still had to throw a hand out to steady herself.

"Nyx? What can I do?" Seth asked.

She couldn't answer him. She couldn't breathe, and magic was pouring out of her too fast.

Kaden unsheathed his sword. "Jevryn?"

"Hold," the councilor ordered.

Nyx wanted to scream at him to *not* hold. Morgan and Evra

clearly came to the same conclusion. They ignored Jevryn and attacked.

Portal magic flickered from Laiveran's hands and wrapped around them. Nyx tried to lunge for them but her stupid body wouldn't work. They vanished.

Please let them be alright. Please let Laiveran have sent them somewhere safe.

A muscle ticked along Kaden's jaw. His hands flexed where they gripped the sword, but he didn't move.

Jevryn eyed Laiveran. "You have driven the universe to madness once before. Was it not enough?"

"No. Not until she is returned to my side."

"Nyaera is *dead*, Laiveran. Let her go."

Laiveran's focus lapsed, and for a moment, Nyx could breathe again. She sucked in a lungful of air but could still only manage a whisper to Seth. "Kaden. I need Kaden."

"Moor!" Seth barked.

Kaden shifted his stance, really looking at her for the first time. He backed away from Jevryn and Laiveran, keeping his focus on them, until he stopped by Seth. "What's wrong with her?"

"I don't know."

"Promise," Nyx whispered.

She saw the fear flash across Seth's face as he understood. "The promise you had her make to Hide the Harvester. Release her from it."

"Why? What's happening?"

"There aren't any brakes on a promise like that. No amount of magic in the world can convince Laiveran the Harvester isn't here right now, but that promise is making her try anyway. Release her, or she's going to die." *And if that happens, I swear on every star in this universe that you'll follow her.*

Kaden looked at her, and there was…*something* in his eyes. "I release you from any promises you have made to me."

The tether between Nyx and the Harvester snapped. The

squeezing pressure on her lifted. Her magic was hers again. *Only hers.*

Laiveran broke off whatever he'd been saying to Jevryn. He inhaled deeply, like he was breathing in the scent of fresh-baked cookies. "Ah, *there* it is."

Laiveran's left hand snapped out, fingers curved as if he gripped an invisible sphere. The Harvester tore through the pocket of Seth's jeans to nestle in Laiveran's palm. Kaden moved —and vanished as portal magic wrapped around him. It reached for Seth next.

"No!" Nyx scrambled to her feet but Seth was already gone, vanishing in a twist of portal magic. She swallowed, wondering if she would go next. And Laiveran tried, but his magic hit her and bounced off.

"Interesting," he said. "You learn quickly, it seems." He turned back to Jevryn. "You will not consider my offer?"

Jevryn remained quiet. What offer? What had Laiveran said while she'd been busy trying not to die?

"Reacquisition will be difficult," Laiveran continued, "given the mess you have made with these 'Stations.' With your help, it will go more quickly. Once it is done, Nyaera and Arradin will be whole again."

Unease crept down Nyx's spine. Laiveran was insane—oh, he was speaking in whole sentences and grounded in time again, but he was still talking nonsense—and Jevryn had to know that, right?

But as little as Nyx knew about Jevryn, she knew Griff was the one person he wanted above all else. And Laiveran had just promised to give him back.

The silence in the air had a weight to it. Blue lightning crackled between Jevryn's fingers. "Living is loss," Jevryn finally said. "We have all suffered it. That does not give us the right to massacre in its name."

Laiveran shrugged. "If you will not help me, one of the others will. Our kind was not meant to live as long as we have.

The burden weighs on a mind. When next you see your lover, be certain to tell him that once again you could have saved him, and failed from cowardice."

A torrent of portal magic tore through him, but before he could blink out of existence, Jevryn flung a hand toward him, his own portal magic roaring through the space between them. His other hand snaked out, grabbing Nyx's wrist.

He pulled on her, but it wasn't a physical pull, or rather, not one on her body. It wasn't a pull on her magic either, nor the portal magic that still remained in the second bracelet on her arm. It was a pull on her *ability*. On that innate part of her that allowed her to channel the magic itself. Jevryn had tapped into it somehow, harnessing it as if it were his own, using the combined might of his and her abilities to stop Laiveran from portaling.

Competing dominance, she remembered Morgen saying, when he'd explained why you couldn't portal inside a Station— because the Station's ability took dominance. Jevryn was borrowing from her to manufacture that same dominance to hold Laiveran in place, and it *hurt*.

It felt as if someone had jabbed a giant fish hook into her stomach and tugged, hard, but the hook had caught on the cage of her ribs and refused to let her go. Her legs went out. She dropped to her knees, gasping, still held somewhat erect by Jevryn's iron grip on her wrist.

Temerex let out a small whicker of concern, and Seth's voice whispered in her ear. "Nyxi?"

Her heart slammed into her chest. *Not gone.* He'd just made everyone think he was.

"I'm fine," she managed, even as she couldn't stop another gasp from working its way up her throat. "It's necessary. To hold him here. But we aren't going to last much longer."

Jevryn and Laiveran were both frozen in place, the magical contest keeping them from engaging in a physical one. Seth or Temerex could strike, but she had no idea what the disruption would do to the portal magic. Seth could stab Laiveran in the heart and end up on another planet. Or half of him could.

"Don't attack him," she said. "Just get the Harvester."

She felt Seth's smile against her cheek. "Too easy."

In Laiveran's hand, the Harvester began to spin and glow, as it had that day she'd given it free rein against the Kumir. But far more terrifying than that day, it also began to grow. And she knew from up-close, personal experience that she did not want to be in its path when it hit its zenith.

She also knew, from the increased pain that tore through her as Jevryn fought to hold Laiveran, that the councilor was not going to let go. Whatever had happened so long in the past, this was personal for Jevryn. If given the choice, he would stand in the wake of this fire and let it burn him to ash. He would let it burn them *all* to ash.

She felt a brush of air at her side. "Got it," Seth whispered, and she felt the weight of the Harvester drop into her pocket. Nyx stared at Laiveran's hand, where the Harvester, to all appearances, still spun. Damn, Seth was good. She built a new cloak of Hiding around the true Harvester, sealing it tight. So long as Laiveran didn't realize he had a fake, he wouldn't search for it, so it wouldn't kill her to keep it Hidden.

She wrenched her arm from Jevryn's grasp. Or tried. He was far stronger than his slender frame made him appear, and her arm moved approximately four inches. His fingers clamped down so hard she felt a swollen, squeezed sensation in her fingertips, like a tourniquet had been tied on. Did he work out specifically for hand strength, for stars' sake?

She could try and pry his hand off her but that would just piss him off and not work. Stabbing him in the arm would also piss him off. It would work, but the repercussions probably wouldn't be to her liking.

There was a third option. It would still piss him off, just hopefully not to a lethal degree. She got her feet underneath her, grabbed onto Jevryn's arm with her free hand, whispered, "*Losara*," and shoved as hard as she could.

They hurtled up and backwards, the force strong enough she barely managed to hold Jevryn in the initial abrupt departure. As it was, she lost him soon after they went airborne.

The connection he'd had to her broke. Laiveran vanished. She managed, "*Exa*," so a stray footfall wouldn't send her hurtling off again, before she hit the ground. As fate would have it, her left hip hit first, the rest of her following, head connecting to the ground with a whiplash strike.

She had a sudden memory of falling off a horse in her childhood and landing in near-exactly the same manner. Now, like then, the impact stunned her, air rushing from her lungs as if a vacuum had sucked it from her.

For a moment, as she stared up at the sky and realized nothing was broken, she thought she was fine. Then her throat grew tight, each breath harder to drag in, the action audible as she wheezed against the constraints of a body unwilling to perform. Her vision degraded into brighter and brighter spots of intense white.

In so many books, when a character passed out from physical trauma, the world just went dark for them. That was not Nyx's experience. *Eventually* it would go dark, sure. But the trip there was filled with blinding brilliance so intense that the first time it had happened to Nyx—that first fall off the horse—she'd thought she'd broken something in her neck and was going blind.

She fought for consciousness, determined that if she wanted it badly enough, she could will herself not to pass out. But in all likelihood, no will in the world would have saved her had Seth not appeared as she was stubbornly trying to climb to her feet, the world weaving back and forth. Or maybe *she* was weaving, she wasn't sure.

"Lay your ass back down," Seth ordered.

Nyx chose to believe she did as told because she wanted to,

not because she was physically incapable of achieving a vertical position. Her head dropped back against the ground, and the white in her vision was a kaleidoscope of sparkly fractals that obscured any and all sight of the real world.

And as she was sitting there, thinking that passing out would actually be really lovely, Seth's words struck her as extremely funny. She tried to laugh but she didn't have the air. "Bet you" —she wheezed in a breath through her constricted throat— "say that" —another wheeze— "to all the girls."

Seth snorted and picked up her feet, resting the soles of her boots against his stomach.

"What are you doing?" she managed.

"Elevating your legs so you don't pass out."

"Who does that?" Miraculously, it seemed to be working. The pressure in her throat eased, breaths coming easier, and her vision started to clear.

"Everyone who knows anything about not passing out from a head injury. Better?"

"Getting there."

Jevryn A-Morridahn's glowering visage appeared in her newly-returned sight as he loomed over her. He wasn't angry. Oh, no. If the cold, hard lines of his face and the bright luminosity of his eyes were any indication, he was monumentally *furious*.

"Do you have any idea what you have done?"

"Seth?" In the shadow of Jevryn's fury, Nyx's voice came out as barely more than a squeak. "Put my feet down. I think I'd like to pass out now."

"I am attempting to make concessions for the impetuousness of youth, for the fragility of such short years in existence, but the level to which you have erred leaves me powerless to make excuses for you."

"Have you *seen* the Harvester work?" Nyx asked. "Because I have. He was going to use it and he was going to kill us, and it wasn't going to be pretty. You were just too stubborn to let him go."

"Did it never occur to you that I had a plan for *not* dying?"

"Yeah? What was it?" If he had some natural defense against the Harvester of Worlds, she was dying to hear it. *Ha. Dying.* Clearly, elevating her feet had kept her conscious, but it hadn't done much for her lucidity.

"Laiveran is the Butcher of a Hundred Planets, the Enslaver of Souls, the Father of Genocide. Letting him go was not an option."

She noticed he had not once in that string of doom and gloom mentioned what his brilliant plan to survive the Harvester of Worlds had been. "Maybe, if the All Council didn't hide its dirty laundry, someone would know all of those very scary-sounding things you just mentioned. But since the wider universe has never heard of Laiveran" —here, she glanced to Seth for confirmation and he nodded— "I had to assume letting him get away and us living was better than us dying and then letting him get away by default, on account of us being dead. You're overreacting."

"*He is mad.* And now he is reunited with an object whose power rivals his madness."

"No," Nyx said, "he's not." She retrieved the Harvester and waved it at Jevryn. "See? Laiveran may be mad, and he may be gone, but he is not currently in possession of the Harvester of Worlds."

Jevryn looked at Seth. "You made a copy? A *believable* copy?"

Seth shrugged. "Everyone underestimates an Illusionist."

Jevryn's eyes narrowed. "That is because most Illusionists do not know their craft down to a minute enough level that they could fabricate something so complex without preparation."

"I had an extraordinarily dull childhood."

Nyx tugged her feet free of Seth's hands, and he let them go reluctantly. Now that her ability to intake oxygen had been normalized, the severity of the situation sank back in. Yes, they had avoided the worst possible outcome, but that wasn't exactly saying much. Laiveran was still out there, he still knew exactly where to find the Harvester, and she didn't think any ability of hers to Hide the object would keep the knowledge from him again.

All magic is will-based, her mother's cool, dispassionate voice intoned. *A Hidden's, yes, but others as well. Hide from a person what they desire most in the world, and you may succeed if the Hiding comes unsuspected. But should they catch a glimpse of that thing again, should something remind them of it and they remember, no working you can conceive will ever keep them from it again.*

She pushed herself up, wincing. Her upper thigh and hip were swelling, her palms bleeding from shallow cuts. "How long do we have before Laiveran recognizes he has a fake?"

Seth grimaced. "The illusion of the object itself will hold for a few hours. But he'll probably realize it's not the real thing long before that. The double worked so well here because I could shift the signature the actual Harvester gives off to the fake. Now that the two aren't in the same place, the illusion will lose potency."

Nyx struggled to stand, and she couldn't decide if she was annoyed or charmed when both Seth and Jevryn held out a hand to her. She went with the practical response, placed one hand in Jevryn's and one in Seth's, and let them haul her to her feet.

She gave Jevryn a suspicious once-over. "*You* don't look like you got hurled backwards by magical boots."

"Being a councilor has its privileges." Apparently, those privileges extended to not feeling like your leg had tripled in size and gotten waterlogged. "Need I remind you that, had you given the boots back, you would not be experiencing your current discomfort?"

"Given them back?" Seth asked.

"He's under the mistaken belief that they're his. A misunderstanding I'm sure Griff will be happy to clear up when we get home."

"Then let us return there."

A portal yawned into existence, the familiar grounds just outside the Station's borders appearing. She swallowed her rising fear. If Evra and the others weren't at the Station when she got back…

She straightened her shoulders. If they weren't there, she would find them. Somehow, she'd find them. They'd traveled past the known universe for her. She wouldn't do any less for them.

27

The skies above Kaliaris were dark and roiling. Nyx stepped through the portal just outside the Station's border, facing the front porch and the griffin fountain. Seth, Jevryn, and Temerex followed, the unicorn-dragon nearly goring Nyx with her horn in her excitement to be off Amentia Furor. She licked Nyx sloppily on the cheek in apology, unconcerned with the juxtaposition of bright sunshine where they stood, and the sleet that rained down from massive thunderclouds a foot away.

"Nyx?" Seth asked quietly.

"I don't know." Either Kaliaris or Griff was upset. Or both. She stepped over the invisible line that separated Station from Earth Between.

Pain erupted in her skull. She gasped as the hot knife of agony tore through her, doubling over. It only took her a handful of seconds to sort through the information roaring at her through the bond—but a handful was too many to keep Seth, Jevryn, and Temerex from following.

Seth's arms wrapped around her, holding her up. "Nyx?"

She struggled to blunt Kaliaris' senses—it was their fury and agony drowning her—and found her voice. "Get away from the Station. Now."

Too late.

The ground opened and swallowed them. Jevryn cursed, Temerex let out a panicked whinny, Nyx braced for impact, and Seth pulled her tight against him.

They didn't fall so much as slide, skidding down a steep earthen incline. She sank deep into the Station's senses to keep from panicking as the hole they'd fallen through closed over, sealing them in. It was pitch black, but she felt the dimensions of the tunnel through the Station's senses. It was wide enough in diameter to allow Temerex clearance without injury.

If the smattering of images jumping into Nyx's mind from the unicorn-dragon were any indication, Temerex had stopped panicking and decided to enjoy the ride with an easy acceptance no horse would have had in the same situation.

The earth of the tunnel flor was packed so smooth and tight it might as well have been the metal of a playground slide, and they slid down it with increasing speed. The tunnel took a sharp curve and bright white light glowed up at them from below.

What do you know, there is a light at the end of the tunnel.

She strained through the bond, through sluggish senses, for whatever lay beyond that light...and her heart leapt as she felt three familiar presences. Temerex cleared the tunnel, then Jevryn, then Nyx's stomach dropped out as she and Seth went airborne. She landed on top of him for the second time in less than an hour.

"We really have to stop doing this," Seth grumbled. "If you're going to throw my back out, I can think of more rewarding ways to do it."

She rolled her eyes and gained her feet, not relaxing until her eyesight confirmed what she'd felt. Evra, Morgen, and Kaden stood in the center of a barren and—as the tunnel opening sealed behind them—doorless room.

Morgen grinned at her. "Hey, little Guardian. Fancy meeting you here."

She shook her head. Morgen and Seth could humor their way through the damn apocalypse. Which they might well be on the verge of.

"Laiveran sent you guys home?"

"No," Evra said, "he sent us to a creepy prison full of skeletons."

"Been there, got the t-shirt. What happened when you portaled here?"

The three of them shared an uneasy look. "It was…quiet," Kaden said. "Almost like the Station was just a building. We couldn't find Griff. Then it was like an earthquake went through the place and we dropped in here."

Jevryn's eyes sharpened at mention of Griff. "You could not find Arradin, and yet he brought you here? Why?"

"Griff didn't do this," Nyx said with certainty. She closed her eyes, trying to feel for where he was.

"The Avatar is the control," Jevryn said. "That is how the Stations were built."

"Mm-hmm. And no one's ever made aftermarket modifications to a car before."

"What does that mean?" Jevryn's voice held a note of low warning, enough that Nyx snapped her eyes open.

Oh, wow. He was pissed. She thought she'd seen him angry on Amentia Furor, but now he was incandescent, in both senses of the word. He was filled with rage, and he was glowing. The lightning that had danced between his fingers earlier now arced up his arms, crackling over the rest of his body and bathing him in a deep, blue glow.

Morgen, Evra, and Kaden took a step back. Seth moved closer to her side.

Jevryn hadn't been this mad when he'd thought she'd let Laiveran escape with the Harvester. Which told her precisely where Jevryn A-Morridahn's true loyalties lay—ever and always with Griff.

"Griff is fine," she said quickly.

"How can you be certain, and where is he?"

"You asked how I was able to leave the Station without it driving Griff mad. I bound myself to it. Much in the same way he's bound to it, and then him to me as well."

Jevryn cursed.

"It was that or we really would all be dead. So if Griff died, I would know."

The lightning drained back to Jevryn's fingers. "Where?"

"I don't know. The Station is being difficult." Except she didn't think Kaliaris was the one being difficult. Their senses were blunted, numbed, like they were…asleep. Griff had told her Kaliaris slept, but they hadn't felt like this before she left. This felt deeper, almost drugged. Even if Griff could do that to Kaliaris, he wouldn't. "Could Laiveran take control of a Station?"

No answer.

"Jevryn?"

"I do not know."

"The Council built them. How can you not know?"

"We did not build the first. And the pattern with which they were made was not our own."

She stared at him. "Laiveran? He built Calista?" At Jevryn's confused expression she said, "The Station in the Shadow Market?"

"Yes."

Fuck. The guy who had designed the computer code now had free access to it. She finished searching through the Station's numbed senses, coming up with the answer she'd already expected. Griff wasn't anywhere in the Station that she could feel —no one else was anywhere in the Station that she could feel— and there was only one part of the Station where her senses and Kaliaris' senses didn't overlap.

"They're in the Station's Heart."

Jevryn frowned. "Its what?"

"Heart," she repeated. Maybe the word got muddled through translation. "What do you call it?"

"What is 'it'?" He looked like whatever patience he'd managed to recoup was spending fast.

Umm...well, for Kaliaris it's a creepy vine room straight out of a horror novel, and for Calista it was a bright pastel cotton-candy wonderland. "It's...like the center of the Station's consciousness?"

His expression did not clear, so she was doing a shit job of explaining. "You know, how at the ley line platform, if you don't access the ley lines you can go to that between place where you can talk to the Station?"

"Such a place does not exist."

Evra cleared her throat. "It does, actually."

Jevryn turned to her, eyebrow raised.

"We all saw her come out of it. She coughed up black ooze, it was truly disgusting."

"Kaden?" Jevryn prompted.

Nyx crossed her arms. She hadn't had time to get used to this new development—to the knowledge that Jevryn had sent Kaden to Earth with the Harvester.

"I can't speak to what she saw while she was there, but yes. She did go somewhere through the portal that wasn't the ley lines."

Why did it irritate her so much that Kaden had answered? Maybe because he'd refused to explain anything to her in the Shadow Market, but he answered Jevryn without hesitation. Without even a single glance to Nyx to confirm if she minded him telling Jevryn things that might have ramifications for her.

Granted, she had told Jevryn about the Heart herself, and Kaden's response only verified what she'd said. But she suspected it wouldn't matter what Jevryn asked, Kaden would answer.

"Very well. If this...Heart is where Arradin is, then take us there."

Yes, Your Majesty, if only I'd thought of that myself. "Kaliaris is difficult to manipulate at the moment. If I open a path to the Arrival Room, I don't know how long I can hold it open. We may not all make it. If we do, you should know I can't force Kaliaris to let me in. I've been trying to talk to them for months and they've refused to acknowledge me. If they do, they may not let *you* through. I have nothing to do with that."

Jevryn's eyes sparked. "Let me handle that." He said it with the kind of confident arrogance born of centuries of being at the top of the hierarchy, certain that nowhere and nothing was barred to him. She had a deep suspicion Kaliaris was about to knock him down a peg.

"Right. We have one other problem." She looked at Seth.

"This problem?" He held his right hand out, palm up, the Harvester resting on it. "Or this problem?" His left hand mimicked his right, holding another Harvester.

Nyx patted her pocket, where she'd stowed the Harvester, and came up empty. Someone had been practicing his pick-pocketing again. She looked between the two Harvesters he held, pretending to debate it. "This one." Nyx followed the pull of her magic, dug into his left pocket and pulled the actual Harvester out.

He grinned at her. "Cheater."

She rolled her eyes and turned back to Jevryn. "Right now, Laiveran doesn't know it's here."

"How can you be certain?"

"Because my magic isn't sucking the life out of me trying to Hide it." She could, fortunately, turn that tap off now that she'd built an ordinary Hiding around the Harvester as opposed to making it via a promise, but the magic pull was a good indicator of Laiveran's awareness. If he actively looked for it, he would know it was here, and she would feel it. "He probably suspects we're the people he just trapped in this room, but he doesn't know."

The Station didn't have eyes, so he couldn't see them, but three people with a hoofed animal was pretty much a dead giveaway. "I'm guessing his focus is on subduing Kaliaris." *And Griff.* She didn't say the last part because she didn't want to set Jevryn off again. "If I can reach the Heart before he takes full control, I think Griff and I together can free Kaliaris from him."

"Or he will simply reach through that bond and subjugate you both alongside the Station," Jevryn countered.

Nyx smiled. "I'm very stubborn."

"An inherited trait, no doubt."

Nyx's memories did not paint Elena Fortuna as stubborn. Haughty, aloof, self-involved? Yes. But not precisely *stubborn*. But then, maybe Jevryn wasn't talking about her mother.

She didn't have time to ask him about it now. But he was not leaving this Station before he told her whether or not he knew her father's identity. Given that he was the one who'd brought Elena to Earth, he was the person most likely *to* know it.

"I'm going to move us to the portal room and convince Kaliaris to let me through. Getting there is going to be a struggle, and it will draw Laiveran's attention, at which point he'll probably realize the Harvester's here. Even if he doesn't, he'll probably be pissed and come after you via the Station's control.

"I'll do what I can to hold him back, but I don't know how long it will take Griff and I to get a handle on this." She looked at Jevryn. "If we take control back from him and he flees, can you stop him?"

He just looked at her.

"*Will* you stop him?"

"Yes."

That was the best she could hope for. She closed her eyes again and sank back into Kaliaris' senses. It was like wading through mud as she pinpointed where they were—directly beneath the library—and asked the Station to open a pathway of stairs up. Kaliaris was sluggish in their response. The wall before Nyx broke open and closed several times in succession before she grabbed the flux of the Station's will and held, stairs forming like a video of falling dominoes being played in reverse.

"Everybody up!" she yelled.

Where the humans hesitated, Temerex saw the stairs and charged them like they were an open battlefield and she was going in for the kill. Nyx had forgotten about the unicorn-dragon, and she struggled to morph the steps into wider, shallower versions more accommodating to hooves. The Station moved like molasses in wintertime, but by the time Temerex hit the stairs, she had no trouble navigating them. Her powerful hindquarters drove her up, and she let out a bugling cry worthy of any warhorse.

"What *is* she?" Nyx asked.

"One of a kind." Jevryn answered. He followed the unicorn-dragon, Morgen, Evra, and Kaden on his heels. Nyx and Seth came last.

Sweat beaded on her forehead, and with every step she and Seth took, she allowed the tunnel to collapse behind them, until they finally burst into the library.

She led the way to the portal room. It waited in darkness, the only light coming from the six silver spheres atop the hexagon's posts. The space between them was not the smooth, solid cosmic floor that showed when the portal was inactive, nor was it the swirling cosmos it was when the ley line was disgorging travelers.

It was the open path to Kaliaris' heart. Jevryn strode up to it, then over it, but he didn't fall through the opening. It was as if a glass floor lay over the path, and it would not break for him. He looked at her as if it were personally her fault, and she could fix it.

"I told you Kaliaris might not let you through," she said. "You can try and follow me, but I don't know if it will work."

She took Seth's hand and pressed the Harvester into his palm. "Keep it safe. Whatever happens, don't let Laiveran get it."

A smile crinkled the corners of his eyes. "He'd have to find it first." Copies of the Harvester sprouted from his hand and tumbled onto the ground. The copies made copies, spilling from each other like coins from a bag and—dear stars, he'd even copied the magical signature of her Hiding on them. Even she couldn't tell which was the real one at first glance.

Nyx snatched one at random and tucked it into her pocket. She backed away but Seth's hand snaked out. He gripped the back of her neck and pulled her in, his lips finding hers in a hard, hot kiss.

"Come back," he said when they parted, his voice uncharacteristically serious. "Come back to me."

"I will. I promise." She turned and ran, jumping onto the path that led to Kaliaris' Heart and fell.

28

As it had the first time Nyx fell to the Station's Heart, the air turned viscous. Pressure built inside her head, and she fought not to inhale, until she was starved for oxygen and her mouth opened against her will. She gulped in a lungful of thick, liquid coolness and the pressure in her head vanished. She landed on the vine-covered floor with a soft *thunk*. The vines didn't move in response to her presence, did not ensnare or otherwise try to restrain her. They hardly seemed alive at all.

Except they had moved at some point, because Griff was buried in them up to his shoulders. He was trapped in front of the pedestal in the center of the space, where the Heart itself rested—where the chaos thorn Nyx had plunged into that Heart, the one that had saved Kaliaris' and Griff's lives and bound her to the Station, rested—and on the other side of it stood Laiveran.

Laiveran didn't turn at her entrance. If he noticed her presence, it did not show. Griff's head was slumped over, his eyes closed, but at the scuff of her foot on the vines he startled awake. His gaze landed on her, eyes widening.

"Nyx?" Griff whispered.

"Hey," she whispered back. "I'm alive. I missed you."

"I missed you too. I am glad you're alive. Please leave here."

Griff watched Laiveran. "Before he notices. Get out of here and leave the Station."

"Are you okay?"

"I am delightful. Leave."

"That's not going to happen. Kaliaris?"

Kaliaris did not respond. Nyx reached Griff's side and tried to peel the vines from him, both physically and via the Station's control. Neither approach worked, and her fingers were heavy and fumbling on the vines. She felt…muzzy. Confused. Like she —like the Station—was being drugged.

"What is he doing?"

Laiveran just stood there, his hands on the Heart's pedestal. He didn't appear to be doing anything at all. She was not a kill-first-ask-questions-later type. But she decided, given the circumstances, she could maybe be a maim-first-ask-questions-later type.

Her hand fell to the bo staff—and jerked to a halt, one inch away from the smooth metal. She tried to flex her fingers and couldn't.

Laiveran's eyes snapped open. "Ah. Now I understand. Two bonds to the source, instead of one."

Nyx's arm slammed against her side and she found herself walking forward in strange, jerky movements, as if she were a marionette guided by an unseen puppeteer. She fought against the control, but her body wouldn't answer. Laiveran pulled her and Griff forward, until they stood only a few feet from him on the other side of the dais.

"You were kind to me," he said, "when I came here first and was not in my right mind."

Was he in his right mind now? And if so, what had caused the change? "I was. And you abducted me."

"It was necessary."

"Because of your wife?" She braced for the question to set him off, but he only nodded. She couldn't reach Kaliaris, and right now she couldn't even control her own body. The only thing she could do was try to understand, and hope that understanding would give her the answer to this situation. She licked her lips. "Tell me about her. Your wife." What had he told Nyx her name was? "Tell me about Nyaera."

Pain flashed across his features at her name. But he spoke. "There is much to understand, if you are to understand her. What happened to her. My people were called Soulspeakers. That is not, of course, what we called ourselves. We had different words for what we do, but they do not translate so well.

"Our gift was to look into the essence of a thing, into its heart, and speak to it, like I speak to your Station now. It was a beautiful gift. It was *meant* to be a beautiful gift. It is why my kind mate for life. If you can look into a person and see every part of them, it is not so hard to find the one who complements you, and whom you complement, in every conceivable way. Two souls, to use that term, that can weather any storm together, that can grow and adapt in similar ways, can change without doing so in ways that will drive them apart.

"It is a very real bond that is not unlike the one you have with Kaliaris. Though your bond was born of different means, it has much the same result. We call it Heartsworn. Two Heartsworn can survive being separated for a time, though they do not bear it well. But if one Heartsworn dies? Well, that is a separation for which there is only one cure. In all the history of my people, none who bonded in this way ever lived more than a handful of days past the death of their Sworn.

"The only ones capable of surviving it were those rare groups in which three or more were bonded. Even then, the survival rate depended on the type of bond. Whether they were *all* bonded to each other, or whether they were connected as a group in different ways, by one who was connected to all, and those others only bonded to the central, and so on.

"Even in the true universal bonds, while the others might survive the death of one, they would never be quite the same again after. They were meant to be a whole, after all, and a part of them was now missing.

"I was not in such a bond. I belonged only to Nyaera, and she to me. In truth, I would not have wanted to survive her death. I should *not* have survived it." He trailed off, staring into the distance, as if he'd forgotten why he was talking.

She thought she understood everything he'd told her up to now. His people's marriages came with physical bonds, whether they were monogamous or polyamorous units, and they didn't handle the severing of those bonds well.

"And Nyaera?" Nyx prompted. "What happened to her?"

Laiveran shook himself, his eyes refocusing on her. "We were scientists of a sort, she and I, and neither of us ever more excited than when the first visitors from another world arrived on our soil. We were young then, barely old enough to be allowed to make our bond official. The opportunity to be at the forefront of a discovery as monumental as the existence of life on other planets—and not just *life*, not just bacteria and plants, but people who were not so genetically different from us—was over-whelming in its excitement.

"Especially when these visitors led us to a wonder on our planet that we had not yet discovered. A portal well. Nyaera and I were instantly entranced. We made our first jump that very afternoon. Foolish, perhaps, but Nyaera's enthusiasm was infec-tious, and I could never deny her anything.

"We joined with some of the first visitors who had come to our planet, and together we found other planets. Eventually, our unit became official, and we spent the next ten years that way. Exploring and making new connections, welcoming other civi-lizations to the growing map of the heavens. Each day was an adventure.

"Not all of them were good." His visage darkened. "It...is not so great a thing to be able to look into the hearts of those who cannot do the same. There is no reason to overcome darkness, if none can see it in you, and so there exists madness in the other races that would never have gone unnoticed in one of my own kin.

"Madness in our own people, if caught early enough, could be corrected, though some were too foul and had to be ended. In truth, I was horrified when I met Jevryn and Kiev. To allow one soul, split into two bodies at birth to continue existing in such a tortured state…" Laiveran shivered. "It is unnatural."

Nyx wondered what the Soulspeakers saw when they looked at those supposed souls, that they believed identical twins unnatural. She did not doubt they saw something very similar, something that might, at birth, be mistaken for a soul split in half, in the same manner that an Earth scientist looking at the DNA of identical twins at birth would see the same genetic material, and only notice the minute differences upon closer inspection. Every culture, it seemed, had their irrational beliefs, their unrecognized biases towards that which they did not have an easy explanation for.

Laiveran waved his hand dismissively. "We learned to work alongside the twins, after some time. There was so much to explore, so much to learn, and they were fearless in their exploration. Time and repetition made us fearless, too, made us believe that nothing was beyond our reach. We sometimes landed on planets with people too hostile to be brought to know the other planets, of course, but the solution there was simple: we left and did not return.

"Then we found Amentia Furor. It was in the midst of the same storms that rage across its surface even now." Laiveran's face twisted, pain shadowing his features. "The portals appeared and Nyaera fell through one. But she was already portaling as she fell. She portaled within a portal, and where she went, I could not follow. I could not even *find*.

"I only knew she was not dead because I could feel her." He went quiet, and when he spoke again his voice was soft. "I could feel *everything*. Her fear. Her horror. Her pain. No one—*no one*—was willing to find her. It spoke to reason that the portals born in the heart of the storm bore an excess of power, an amount of magic that one person could not perhaps channel. They only move one from place to place upon the planet, but because Nyaera was already portaling, the natural one must have boosted her range. She became trapped in an infinite loop.

"I thought we could reach her. If the strongest of us, those who had been portaling since the beginning, the most accomplished of our number, could do so together, we had a chance of reaching her. But they refused. I felt her pain as she died. I felt every day, every hour, every minute, of her suffering until she was finally gone.

"And I was ready to follow her, when the answer came to me. When I understood how it could all be reversed and that— that gave me the strength to continue on." His tortured gaze focused on her. "I am not a bad person. I only want her back."

The grip he had on Nyx through the Station relaxed a touch, and when she spoke, it wasn't without compassion. She understood his pain. "You can't cure death, Laiveran."

"No," he agreed. "But I do not need to. I need only to return to a time when she was alive, and keep her that way. With this" —he held up his hand, and Nyx's copy of the Harvester flew to him— "I can do that." The shining sphere spun in his palm for a moment, then disappeared.

Laiveran's hand clenched into a fist around the empty air. The look he turned on her was void of mercy, of any of the emotion that had been on it moments prior. "You thwart me still? After everything I have told you?"

She felt the shift in the Station, a deep, shuddering drag as Laiveran bent Kaliaris to his will. Nyx reached for Kaliaris, but it was as if her mental fingers slipped right through them, unable to find purchase. Unable to stop the direction in which Laiveran sent the Station's resources: Toward Seth, and the hundreds of Harvester copies filling the Arrival Room.

29

S eth's experiences in life had led him to one irrefutable truth: that if you prepared for the worst and it didn't come, you should wait longer. Because the second you relaxed, the second you let go of that preparedness, the thing you feared would strike the moment you let your guard down.

So even though the Arrival Room had been quiet since Nyx's departure into the Station's Heart over thirty minutes ago, Seth held ready. He waited, copies of the Harvester lazily dripping from his fingers as they multiplied.

He'd made so many that he and the others were knee-deep in the bright spheres. Evra narrowed her eyes at the ones piled around her. She swept her leg in a slow half circle through the Harvesters. They moved with her motion as if they were real. Temerex took great delight in this, and started nudging at the Harvesters with her muzzle, pushing them around.

Evra watched the unicorn-dragon, then shot Seth an accusatory glance, as if the realness of the copies was worth some measure of censure. "How?"

He grinned. "What can I say? I'm good."

Her gaze narrowed further. "My mother hires one of the best Illusionists in seven sectors. She isn't this good. To make one or two copies feel and react as if they were the real thing? Yes. But not hundreds."

He shrugged. He didn't feel like explaining that he wasn't anything special, he'd just had to figure everything about his ability out on his own, and he'd had eighteen boring years to do it in. At least Nyx had had Elena, unpleasant as that tutelage had been. Seth hadn't had anyone who understood illusion magic, and Earth was sadly lacking in schools for the magically inclined.

Once he'd made it to the wider universe, he'd learned quickly how much of what he could do wasn't in the usual range of an Illusionist's ability, and he'd tamped down his public displays, not wanting to draw attention. The simple answer to why he could do so much that other Illusionists couldn't, was that no one had ever *told him* he couldn't. He'd never had a block in his mind about what was or was not possible. His only blocks had been his imagination and his willingness to stare at a brick wall until he found a way around it.

He'd been highly motivated to be inventive, because his illusions making Nyx smile or laugh or jump in surprise were the only rewards he'd ever gotten for his troubles. Ones he'd grown addicted to. But she was so good at figuring out his illusions that he'd been constantly having to one-up himself to get those reactions. Tutors the universe over might be shocked at how much effort they could get out of a teenager trying to impress the only eligible paramour on what might as well have been their own private island.

Or hell. Definitely private hell.

Evra was still frowning at him. She opened her mouth, no doubt to press him on the subject, when he made a dozen Harvesters swirl around her like she was caught in the middle of a wind funnel. It distracted her—or, more accurately, it distracted Morgen, who then distracted her—and no one asked him anything else. Stars knew Moor wasn't interested in knowing more about him, and Jevryn was…

Was there a refined, delicate way to say the councilor was throwing a fit? He stood in the center of the floor between the portal's hexagonal posts, a look of infuriated concentration on his face. Sweat had broken out on the sides of his temples, his jaw was clenched, and power surged from him, aimed at the floor. Twice, the center of the floor had turned pliant, only to snap back to glassy impenetrableness less than a second later.

It did so again now. This time, when the portal snapped back into rigidity, Jevryn dropped to his knees and hammered a punch into the surface. Power suffused the hit and it rippled through the floor, shockwaves traveling out…and then slowing, cresting, turning. The tides of power reversed and shot back to their origin, culminating in an explosion that threw Jevryn into the air.

It took Seth a moment to realize that Jevryn's midair halt ten feet above them was not the result of mystic councilor powers, but the result of the Station gripping and holding him. He knew the moment the others recognized it too, because three swords simultaneously cleared sheaths. Morgen, Evra, and Kaden fanned out equidistant around the perimeter of the room.

"Jevryn?" Kaden asked.

The councilor waved an irritated hand, dismissing him. "A moment."

Seth knew, from what Nyx had told him, that the councilors had *some* control over the Stations. Nothing near the level the Avatars did, but they could override ley line permissions and enter any of the Stations' Dens, so it stood to reason they had some small measure of physical control.

The irritated expression on Jevryn's face intensified and he descended, one slow foot at a time, until his feet touched the ground, and Seth felt a hardened shell of air around the councilor shatter.

In response, something rippled through the room. Not a physical force, but an awareness. Another consciousness.

Laiveran.

Seth felt the other presence brush up against the hundreds of Harvester copies in the room and pause, tugging at them and the reality Seth had built into them.

He buckled down, his magic spreading through the copies, reinforcing the belief in their existence, in their realness. Laiveran turned all of his focus on a single copy, searching for something specific. When he didn't find it, his belief in the existence of the copy faltered, taking that copy with it.

A funnel appeared next to one of the silver posts and sucked the Harvesters to it in great pulls, dozens disappearing into the funnel's mouth. The same intense scrutiny that had befallen the first copy was now bestowed upon the ones inside the funnel. As if Laiveran had built an automated magical program designed to sort through the copies in bulk and dispense of them.

That was fine. Seth cracked his knuckles and buckled down, Harvesters pouring from his hands at triple the speed as before. The name of the game was no longer creating the most realistic copies, but the minimum viable product in the largest quantity.

He overwhelmed the first sorting funnel and a second popped up, then a third, then a fourth.

"How long can you keep this up?" Morgen asked.

A fifth funnel appeared in the room and then…nothing. Laiveran had hit his limit on what he could handle. Seth hadn't, his copies crowding the funnel mouths. Seth smiled. "Longer than he can."

Laiveran recognized it, too. The funnels stopped sorting and vanished, all attention turning to Seth as Laiveran recognized that the simplest way to sift through an Illusionist's creations was to kill the Illusionist.

"Well, shit."

The Station flung Morgen, Evra, and Kaden into the walls, steel bands erupting from the painted surface to latch over arms and legs and torsos, holding them tight. Seth's feet sank into the ground, as did Temerex's, the floor solidifying around his ankles and the unicorn-dragon's fetlocks. It tried to do the same to Jevryn but failed to take hold.

A block of metal rose out of the floor, melting and twisting and taking shape into something vaguely humanoid, but with two blades for arms. It turned a sightless face on Seth and charged, and no illusion in the universe was going to move him from its path. He reached for the knives at his belt. If he was lucky, Laiveran's control over the construct would be limited, and he could hold it at bay.

Jevryn stepped in front of him, looking bored as the silver humanoid flashed toward them. "I have had about enough of this," he said coolly, flicking his hand in a lazy gesture Seth was now coming to associate with the man.

The lightning that so often crackled between Jevryn's fingers was no longer blue. It had turned a deep, bruised purple, so dark it was almost black, and it streaked out, striking the construct in the chest.

The Station screamed, in the only way that something without a voice *could* scream. The floors and walls shook, trembling, lights flickering on and off in various colors, and the construct fell. Its metal body jerked and spasmed before going limp.

Seth had known the Station was alive—that the parts of it that were ever-changing were a part of that living lifeform. But he hadn't fully embraced the fact until now. Until he'd watched part of the Station die, and felt as it emanated its pain.

Everyone stared at the councilor.

"You don't think that little ability would have been useful on Amentia Furor?" It was, of course, Seth's own stupid voice asking the question. Trying to break the tension.

Jevryn didn't turn. "On a planet where magic is unpredictable, death magic is something only a fool would set loose."

Seth didn't have anything clever to say to that. *Death magic?* He would say that such a thing did not exist, if he hadn't just seen it.

They waited in tense silence, but Laiveran did not throw anything more from the Station at them. It was as if he'd accepted there was no point with Jevryn present. He sealed the Arrival Room shut and his attention spiraled away, as if he'd decided they were a problem best dealt with after he dealt with the one in the Station's Heart.

The floor did not release him or Temerex, nor did the walls release the others. They simply held and waited, and Seth knew the only way they were getting out of this room intact was if Nyx and Griff came rising back out of that portal.

30

The Station's pain reverberated through Nyx. Funny, how she could feel it, feel everything, and yet be unable to respond through the Station. Unable to help Seth.

Jevryn had helped him, had stopped the thing Laiveran had sent for him—but he'd done it by killing part of the Station. Kaliaris' pain reverberated through her, a small but sharp wound that ached deep inside her.

"Salyrians," Laiveran said. Distaste dripped from the single word, and it took Nyx a moment to place where she'd heard it before. Laiveran had said it on Lehine, when he'd thought the skeletons in the prison were a result of a Salyrian's work.

What exactly *was* Jevryn?

Nyx made another push to reach Kaliaris, but the fog surrounding the Station's mind was too dense. But Laiveran didn't send anything else after Seth. He sealed the Arrival Room with all of its occupants inside, as if he'd decided it was only a matter of time before the Harvester was his once more, and he could wait.

He returned his attention to her, picking up the thread of their conversation as if they'd never left off. As if he hadn't just tried to kill the people above. "Of everyone that I have met since waking, you of all people should understand. You gave much to save what *you* loved."

Vines rose from the Station floor, curling around Nyx. They lifted her into the air, moving her across the room until she hung before Laiveran, her face even with his. His long fingers brushed across the chaos thorns in her cheek.

"Too much, some might argue. And yet no one hunts you across the galaxy for it. Why is your sacrifice acceptable but mine is not?"

Was Laiveran really comparing her giving away two of her chaos thorns to the mass destruction Jevryn had accused him of? "Because the only person I hurt was myself."

He frowned. The vines carried her back to Griff's side as genuine confusion creased Laiveran's face. "And to whom have I caused harm?"

Nyx didn't know how smart her next words were. Probably not very. But even if she was certain Laiveran should not end up with the Harvester ever again, she preferred to hear both sides of every story. "Jevryn called you the Butcher of a Hundred Planets. And you did make something called the Harvester of Worlds."

Laiveran looked startled. "Is that your only qualm? I can understand how you might view that as problematic. But Jevryn understands better. He has given you a false impression of what occurred. Yes, the Harvester has consumed planets, and yes, those planets are gone now. The people who inhabited them gone as well. But I am going to spin the universe backwards. What was done to get there will yet be undone."

Spin the universe backwards. She remembered a vague bit about Einstein's theory of time travel. It was something like that, wasn't it? That if you could travel fast enough, you could go backwards in time. A lot of people thought he might even be right about it, except no one could actually generate enough energy to do it.

If the Harvester could contain that kind of energy...she

needed to understand how it worked. She needed him to tell her how it worked. "Even if the Harvester actually harvests worlds, nothing that small could contain the kind of energy you would need to do what you're talking about."

He gave her what, on anyone else, she would have considered an amused look. "You still think you will survive this interaction." His certainty that she *wouldn't* made her cold. "So you want me to tell you about the Harvester. How I made it. What it *is*. Do you think that knowledge will allow you to control it?"

"I don't want to control it. I want to destroy it."

Laiveran shook his head. "It cannot be destroyed. It *is* destruction. Long before I trapped and chained it, that was yet all it knew. It was born in destruction, and it lives for destruction, but it will never die from it. It cannot die."

"Everything dies."

"So believes everyone who has lived either too short or too long a time."

He was so serene, so unruffled, as if everything he was talking about—as if literally destroying entire worlds—was a purely academic thing, rather than something he'd actually done—that it woke a furious anger in her. "You can't kill billions of people to save one person who's already dead," she snapped.

He did not immediately obliterate her, though she couldn't bring herself to be grateful.

"I find," he said slowly, "that when people say you cannot do something, what they mean is that they do not *want* you to do that thing. I very demonstrably can. I already have. What makes those billions of lives more valuable than Nyaera's? Why do they deserve to live instead of her?"

"It isn't about what's deserved. I'm sure your wife didn't deserve to die. But neither did any of the people you killed. The difference is that what happened to Nyaera was an accident. What you did to everyone else was murder."

"Murder is...personal. Stab a person in the heart, strangle them, beat them, feel their life fade beneath your hands—*that* is murder. I do not believe you can properly term my actions murder."

"Do you prefer genocide? Atrocity?"

He shook his head. "At least, in what I did, their deaths were peaceful. And once I went back, it would all have been undone. Those people who died—they would never have been born. You believe I am a monster. But I am not the one currently benefiting from my so-called genocide."

Why did it sound like he was implying that *she* benefitted from it? "I don't know what you're talking about."

He sighed. "In my youth, my teachers were fond of reminding me that ignorance is no excuse. I never particularly cared for the wisdom, but I find it fitting now."

What was it with the older generations feeling the need to pass on their own trauma in the form of vague advice? "You may find it fitting, but if I don't know what you mean, it will never change anything."

"I built *one* Station, as Jevryn calls them now. Only one, and it was never meant to be permanent."

"Calista."

He nodded. "I would have reclaimed it before I went on. I simply needed a space to finish the last of my equations, a space where time was not an issue. And had Jevryn and his newly-formed Council not interfered, I would have made everything right in time. Instead..." Laiveran waved his hands and the vines inside the room undulated. "The soul of a planet is a powerful thing. Rip it from the moorings of its world, take it from the inhabitants who kept it in harmony, and it becomes an angry, dangerous thing. So it is no wonder, when the All Council copied my design, that they chained an Avatar and a Guardian to those souls to keep them in check."

Nyx felt like the floor had dropped out from beneath her. Which, considering she was still held aloft by Kaliaris' vines, wasn't too far off the mark.

Kaliaris. They weren't—they *couldn't be*—the soul of a planet. Could they?

She heard Kaliaris' voice, as if from far away, groggy and barely coherent. <It has been long since I was what I was born to be.>

Kaliaris? She didn't speak their name out loud, didn't want Laiveran to hear. *What is he doing to you?*

But Kaliaris didn't answer. She felt them dimly against the back of her mind, still there, still alive, but as if they'd been forced into a deep sleep and had only managed to wake for a brief instant.

A soul. She was bound to the *soul* of a planet, and Laiveran the Soulspeaker was controlling that soul. He was reaching through her bond to it to control *her.*

She could understand now why Kaliaris had been so angry toward her. What must it be like, to have been made against your will into something other than what you were? To then be controlled and used for centuries, and Nyx simply the next in a long line of such controllers?

She hadn't known, hadn't even been given the choice of becoming the Guardian here, even if she probably *would* have chosen it. But she had known, since going into the Station's Heart, that the Station was sentient, and maybe she bore some responsibility for not trying harder to reach Kaliaris. To find out what they were before she found out in *this* way.

She had been consumed with her need to find out what the Harvester was, with her hope that Kaliaris would tell her. She'd only wanted answers from them. They had terrified her in their first meeting, and because of that fear, she hadn't wanted to know them more.

Admittedly, they had not been particularly pleasant or desirous of knowing *her.* But she couldn't help but feel now, in this moment, that she should have tried harder. Was all her manipulation of the Station since her new bond to it nothing different, nothing better, than what Laiveran was doing to them now?

She didn't know. But she did know that even if Kaliaris considered both her and Laiveran to be evils, she was definitely the lesser of the two of them. After all, she'd never killed them, if that was what Laiveran had done to acquire their soul. She had, in fact, saved whatever was left of their life, irrevocably tying hers to theirs in the process. They hadn't wanted to die. They had allowed the bond she'd made to them. They'd chosen it. They'd chosen her, in the end. Maybe they didn't like her, but they didn't have to.

They just had to want her more than Laiveran. She didn't think that would be a problem. If Laiveran gained full control of Kaliaris, Seth's trick with the false Harvesters would be up. He could simply hold Seth here until he burned his magic out. Even if Seth could run, Laiveran had proved he could find the Harvester easily enough. More easily than before, if Nyx was dead.

She felt for the rage that always pulsed through the chaos thorns in her cheek. Wondered again—as she had strictly forced herself *not* to wonder in the past, for fear of driving herself mad —what they were. If the Stations were planetary souls, were the ley lines a part of them as well, and thus the chaos thorns too?

Wonder later, live now, she ordered herself. She opened herself to the influence of the chaos thorns, and as months of repressed rage inundated her, she grabbed onto that fury and followed it to the two other thorns that existed outside her body. That formed the basis of her bonds. She felt Griff's steady presence, then the cold *otherness* that was Kaliaris.

She took all the rage inside her, all the fury and chaos and confusion, and shoved it out of her, through that link, *in* to Kaliaris. She had done something similar the last time she'd been in Kaliaris' Heart. Where the chaos thorns had an unhinging effect on her, they had seemed to calm Kaliaris, as if they—or their influence—was some missing part of the Station.

It just hadn't occurred to her, at the time, that maybe they were *literally* a missing part of them. Kaliaris stirred as Nyx poured the energy of the thorns into them. Laiveran let out a hissed breath and the vines around her grew tight, constricting.

She pushed back. She reached for Kaliaris with everything she had, even as she felt Griff doing the same. They both ordered the Station's vines to release them and shudderingly, tormentedly, Kaliaris embraced their command. Control slipped from Laiveran, shifting to Nyx, and she made a request of Kaliaris.

Her Station delivered. Nyx grabbed her bo staff, flicking to extend it as the vines lifted Nyx and flung her directly at Laiveran.

Too fast. Kaliaris had thrown her too fast, too hard. A blow to the head with this much force could kill Laiveran. Could kill the only person who knew precisely how the Harvester worked.

She reached for the Station's air, trying to slow her approach, but Kaliaris refused. They *wanted* Laiveran dead. She couldn't blame them, but she couldn't let it happen, either. She also couldn't abort, because she didn't think they'd get this chance again, and she couldn't afford to let the Station fall back under Laiveran's control.

Nyx altered the angle of her strike and pulled the blow—but in the split second before she connected, the chaos thorns in her cheek flared, sending a surge of anger and power through her.

She didn't pull the blow. She hit the Butcher of a Hundred Planets with everything the Station and the chaos thorns could give her.

He crumpled, his hold on Kaliaris vanishing. Nyx landed beside him, her hands trembling on the staff, Kaliaris' satisfaction staining the air.

31

____

Nyx dropped to her knees and pressed two fingers to Laiveran's neck, relief flooding her when she felt the pulse. She'd barely ascertained his living state before Kaliaris gripped Laiveran in a mass of vines, and he woke. A vine around his neck squeezed, cutting off airflow, and he did not remain conscious for long.

"Kaliaris," Nyx said softly. She didn't have to say any more than that.

<He deserves to die.> But the vines loosened a fraction, letting the unconscious Laiveran breathe again, as if Kaliaris was, for once, willing to entertain her requests. <You have heard, by his own admission, what he has done.>

"I'm not here to preach mercy at you. He had none. For anyone, it seemed, even himself." Nyx might not *want* to kill him. But in this particular instance, knowing the mass harm that Laiveran had caused, that had less to do with what she believed was deserved in the situation, and more to do with her own desire to not be the hand that did the killing. That, and one other very important thing. "I've wanted to ask you a question for a while now. One Calista said you might know the answer to. Can you tell me how to destroy the Harvester of Worlds?"

Kaliaris was silent.

"And if you can't, do you want his death more than you want the answer to that question?"

<I do not know how to destroy the Harvester,> Kaliaris finally said.

"Why did Calista think you might? I'm not asking to be difficult," she added, when she felt Kaliaris' irritation. "I'm asking because I don't think she would have said you might if she didn't have a good reason for it. One that might help us figure out the answer."

Laiveran stirred, and Kaliaris promptly choked him back into unconsciousness. That could *not* be good for a person's longterm well-being. Somehow, she didn't think Kaliaris cared.

Kaliaris' sigh was a ripple of wind through the room. <Because I was the first. I do not have the answer you seek. You wish me to spare Laiveran's life, for the Harvester's destruction. Let me show you what was, what *I* once was, so you may understand why you ask such a difficult thing. And why I will ask a far more difficult one in return for his life.>

Nyx blinked and the world disappeared. Sight, in the way Nyx conceived of it, was replaced with a different kind of awareness. Her body, if she could even think of it as one, was immense. Her awareness was of the people, the lives, her existence made possible, but also of the other planets around her. They existed, not in isolation, but in a network.

But there were other things in the universe aside from planets, other things she felt the force of. Things like the Souleater. It was close to her, and someday, as time went on, it would come for her soul, too. But that day was many eons distant, and its inevitability did not trouble her.

Then one day something new came to her corner of the universe: a man with a strange affinity for souls. Laiveran. He chained the Souleater, binding it to his will, and aimed its hunger toward her. What should have been a distant future became a present reality. Her body was sucked into the

Souleater's insatiable maw, ripped apart, the lives she had spent so long growing, nurturing from barely-aware cells to beings capable of conscious thought, destroyed in an instant. Everything gone, until only her essence remained, and she was forced to watch and endure as one after another, her brethren joined her in the Souleater's depths.

But the more the Souleater consumed, the more powerful it became, until the cage could no longer contain it. For Laiveran had underestimated the Souleater's strength, and that of she and her brethren as well. So the man removed Calista's soul, a single withdrawal to restore the cage's stability.

She was forced to watch—and feel—as Laiveran split Calista's soul, weaving and stitching it into the stone of another planet, until Calista existed there like some butchered parasite on the back of another of their kin.

She felt it as if it were her own experience, felt Calista's pain and horror, all the while unable to act. This remaking of the natural order did not go unnoticed. Other humans came to Calista, taking the caged Souleater from Laiveran. She and her brethren listened as this new council of man determined what was to be done with them, and this thing they called the Harvester of Worlds.

They spoke, in endless debates, about the Harvester's instability. About the looming threat of war in the universe. They all agreed that what had been done to Calista was a terrible thing, but... *but*, might it have been a necessary thing? They studied Calista, marveling at the transformation Laiveran had wrought —at the possibilities that could be realized, for Calista was the start of a bridge.

And when they were done with theory and ready for practice, it was Kaliaris' soul they plucked from the Harvester's depths, Kaliaris' soul they stitched onto a planet they cared nothing for, because its evolutionary path had diverged so drastically from all of their own.

The pain was excruciating, her soul torn into pieces and

reformed, forced into a shape it was never meant to hold. It drove her to the edge of madness. Not only the pain, but the solitude. She was a planet built for life—her soul was not meant to live bereft of it.

She did not know if she managed to communicate that pain —that need—or if Kiev discovered it by other means. But he bound another being to her and their soul, their life, tethered her once more to an existence she no longer wanted. Then she watched as, one by one, her kin were subjected to the same fate, until they were stretched and joined physically across the universe in ways they were never meant to be, their souls turned into undying conduits for the traffic of the universe.

She blurred through the next several centuries. Guardians coming and going, tangentially connected to her but not *truly* connected. All lost and alone and steeped in too much of their own misery to ever wake up and wonder where their new sanctuary had come from. What it might be costing someone else.

Griff, the only constant in her life, the only thing tethering her to sanity, and he a man who had endured so much pain he lost himself, and she couldn't protect him. He was treated so much like a thing, a mere interface of a building, that it was easier for him to forget and believe that was all he was. Until a woman came to the Station. A woman without her own memories, who gave him a name when he could no longer remember his own.

Gradually, her sense of self changed. She was no longer a sightless being of great immensity, but simply Nyx again, sitting in the Station's Heart, slumped against Griff's side, tired and hurting and furious about things she couldn't change because they'd already happened.

<I will always be grateful to you for bringing Griff—Arradin —back to himself.>

Nyx could tell, by Griff's lack of reaction, that Kaliaris spoke only to her. So she answered to them alone. *You kind of tried to kill me.*

<I was angry.>

I've been trying to talk to you for months and you've refused to admit I exist.

Another ripple of wind through the room. <You awakened the object which ended my existence as I knew it, and began my incarceration here. I needed time to come to terms with it.>

Have you? Come to terms with it?

<With you, yes. With Laiveran…>

Nyx felt a blink in her consciousness, and knew Kaliaris had dialed Griff back in to the conversation.

<I do not need to tell you how dangerous it is to let him live. If you wish it of me, I need something in return.>

"What?"

<Freedom. For me and all my brethren. An end to our agony even if that end can only be a death.>

"You…want me to kill you?" She recoiled from the thought. "When I offered you the chaos thorn, you didn't want to die then. What changed?"

<I would have welcomed death, even then. But I did not want Griff to die. A planet is meant to protect its people, and he and you are the only people I have. As things stand now, neither of you can survive my death.>

For some reason, when Kaliaris put it in those words, it hit harder than her previous knowledge that she could never be free of the Station without dying. She was in a three-way symbiotically dependent relationship and it weirded her out. The knowledge that her life wasn't fully her own anymore. That it was dependent on theirs, and theirs dependent on her in turn.

If Kaliaris noticed her mini-crisis, they didn't comment on it. <You seek from Laiveran the knowledge to destroy the Harvester. I will allow him to live, but you must make me a promise in return. That once you have your answer, you will do nothing with it until you have also found a way to free us and the other Stations. Give me your word, and I will do as you ask.>

Nyx had to stop herself from giving a blanket agreement. She had just lived through Kaliaris' destruction and subsequent rebirth and unending torture. She wanted to promise them everything. She could give Kaliaris her word, and she could even mean it. But that didn't mean she could *do* it.

"What if I can't find a way to free you?"

She didn't think Kaliaris meant their next words cruelly. The Station that was a soul that had once been a planet simply viewed existence through a different lens than she did.

<While you reside within this Station, you have eternity, and if you do not reside within this Station, you have a death that will take Griff and I with you. Perhaps you will discover the answer next week or next year. Perhaps you will not discover it until the next century or ten has passed. But you *will* discover it, or you will know freedom no more than I or any other of my kin. I believe it is sufficient motivation.>

Great. Her Station was a fatalistic optimist. *You will achieve X! There is no other option.*

"You ask much of her," Griff said.

<Much has been asked of you, and yet you never complain.>

"I am beginning to think perhaps I should."

Kaliaris' vines rustled together like laughter, and Nyx patted Griff's side. "It's fine," she told him. "Kaliaris isn't wrong. They just might end up being disappointed in my ability to deliver." She took a deep breath. "You have my word, Kaliaris."

<Excellent.>

Now she had another problem. "How do we hold Laiveran? Without you suffocating him every thirty seconds?" She'd been trying to ignore it but she couldn't take much more. "If we take him above, I'm pretty sure Jevryn's going to kill him."

<I will keep him here.> A pair of cuffs materialized through the floor, a bronze set with delicate silver inlay that Nyx remembered cataloging in the Den inventory project. According to Griff, the cuffs prevented whoever wore them from accessing their magic. They had some other...unpleasant side effects. Ones Kaliaris no doubt did not care about.

"Is that safe?"

<I was unprepared before. Now, I am not. He will not escape my control again, and so long as he remains within my Heart, not even the councilors may reach him.> The cuffs clamped onto Laiveran's wrists. <Go now, Guardian. You have much to deal with above, and the councilor grows restless. I have no interest in having pieces of myself blown apart because Arradin's former chosen is prone to fits of violence.>

"But—"

<I will not bar the path to my Heart again. I will answer when you call. Laiveran will be here when you wish to speak with him.>

"Okay." She struggled to her feet. It felt like her body weighed a thousand pounds. The analgesic on her wounds had lost its numbing effect. She was tired.

She took a step toward the center of the room, where the path back to the portal room lay. Her feet were so heavy her toes dragged. She tripped and would have gone sprawling, but Griff's arm shot out, catching her.

"I feel obligated to point out that you are in no condition to handle anything," Griff said.

You are correct, sir. "You heard Kaliaris. If I don't get up there, your ex is going to throw a fit."

"Which is something *I* can handle."

"Nope." Nyx shook her head, and would have gone sprawling again if Griff's talons hadn't closed gently around her. "You don't have to talk to him."

"Your concern is touching. But I am not as emotionally fragile as I was when I first came back to myself. Rest, Nyx. I will deal with Jevryn."

Rest. It was a great word. A fantastic word, really, and sleep sounded awesome. "I can't just pass out and let him go. I have to talk to him. And make sure everyone is okay, and—"

"Jevryn will be here when you wake up. I will make sure that everyone is fine."

"But—"

"You are bleeding through your bandages and you can barely stand. I trust you do not want to speak to the councilor with your eyes half-closed and drool coming out of your mouth?"

She wiped her mouth. "I'm not drooling."

"No, but you checked, which means you're tired enough you thought it was a possibility."

"I'm fine. Beam me up, Kaliaris."

<There are no beams in here.>

"If you can see through my eyes, we're watching *Star Trek* when this is over. Send me back to the portal room."

She felt something pass between Kaliaris and Griff, then Griff said, gently, "I'm afraid you've been overruled."

He picked her up in one massive clawed foot, and the combined will of Griff and Kaliaris surged into her through their bond.

She fought the drowsiness that swamped her. "We are going to have a serious" —her eyes closed and she forced them back open— "discussion about" —her body went suspiciously pliant — "autonomy when..."

She passed out.

32

———————

The floor and walls of the Arrival Room released Seth and the others as the portal churned. Griff rose from the center, Nyx's limp body in his arms.

She couldn't be—Seth would *know* if she had… He stepped forward. "Is she…?"

"She is fine," Griff assured him. "Merely at her limit and too stubborn to accept the fact. Why don't you take her upstairs?"

"I can wake her," Jevryn said.

Griff turned a scathing look on him. "Wake her, and I will not speak to you for another eight centuries."

Jevryn's mouth opened, clicked shut, opened again. "My time here is not infinite, Arradin."

"No. But I imagine even a schedule as important as yours can find eight hours for my Guardian to rest." Jevryn started to respond, but Griff cut him off. "Imagine that she is someone important to you. Someone as important as I am, and *find* the time."

Griff deposited Nyx into Seth's arms, and he carried her to her room. She was *out* out, didn't even stir when he laid her on the bed. Griff followed a few minutes later, as Seth was peeling the mercury boots off Nyx's feet.

"Those damn boots," Griff grumbled. "You know he went on for a full minute about me giving them to her?"

"He's, uh, territorial about his stuff?"

"Not precisely. I had them made especially for him. A gift."

"So this is like, what? Taking the ring back when you end the engagement?"

"No. I let him keep the ring. The boots I snuck into his quarters to steal back before I left." Griff shrugged. "It's time they saw some use, and Nyx manages them well. I told him as much."

They lapsed into silence as Seth inspected the abundance of bandages on Nyx's person. The leg wound was the worst, blood seeping through the field bandage.

"I don't suppose he told you what her injuries are?"

"I had him write them down." Griff held out his front claw. A piece of paper appeared in it, and Griff handed the page to him. Seth read through the list, frowning when he got to the last line. "What the hell is a Kirathanu?"

"You know," Griff waved a hand, "half-human, half-aquatic?"

Seth stared at him.

"What was the word he said Nyx used? Mermaid?"

"She got bit by a mermaid? Where did she find a fucking mermaid?" He hadn't known they existed. They weren't listed on the official registry of species, and frankly, the idea of a human-fish hybrid was really preposterous.

"Apparently she portaled to their homeworld before she landed on Amentia Furor. I don't recommend it. Jevryn and I landed there by accident once ourselves. There isn't a drop of dry land on the planet, and the Kirathanu attack invaders to their territory with extreme prejudice."

Seth had no words to respond to the calm, logical voice Griff had used to describe *mermaids*. He excused himself to get a medical kit and returned, spraying the edges of the leg bandage with the adhesive remover. He let it soak in until the bandage came away easily under his fingers.

The wound that greeted him was clean but the tissue was jagged. Jevryn's note said the venom causing the necrosis had been neutralized, but the dead tissue would need to be removed.

"How out is she?" Seth asked.

"Kaliaris and I can hold her under. Do what you need to, she won't feel it."

Seth sighed. Griff filled him in on what had happened in the Heart while Seth washed his hands, put on gloves, and came up with a sterilized scalpel. He was a doctor by no stretch of the imagination, but the amount of magic soaked into the enforcer emergency regen kits could and did work miracles. Which was why Seth was very good at stealing them.

He got to work, and though he knew she wouldn't hear, he couldn't stop from shaking his head and saying, "A fucking mermaid, Nyxi?"

She really was good at finding the strangest trouble out there to be had.

Seth couldn't sleep. He'd managed maybe two hours, tops, lying on the bed next to Nyx. But he kept waking up, thinking she was gone, and not liking how still she was.

She never slept quietly. She was always tossing and turning, stealing all the covers and then waking up to complain that they were an uncomfortable mess.

Griff had assured him her stillness was because her slumber was Station-induced, but Seth found himself watching obsessively for the rise and fall of her chest, for the reassurance she was alive. He gave up trying to sleep and paced, every worst-case-scenario running through his mind.

Nyx not waking up. Laiveran escaping the Station's Heart. Jevryn having some alternative endgame even Griff couldn't guess at. The Council wondering where Jevryn was and tracking him here.

"You are going to wear a hole in the floor." Griff's great golden eyes opened at the foot of Nyx's bed. He stretched and sat up. "Go take a shower, eat something, and come back when you're calmer."

"I'm perfectly calm."

"Then why are you holding a knife?"

"I'm not—" He looked down. He was holding a knife.

"Shower," Griff repeated. "Food. I would like you to sleep but know better than to ask for miracles."

Haha. "You'll stay with her?"

"I will."

It was still harder than it should have been to leave her room for his. The last time he'd walked out on her when she was so dead to the world she didn't stir, he hadn't come back for seven years. The guilt clawed at him, leaving cuts that didn't want to heal.

He stripped and climbed into his shower, but the soap and water wouldn't wash the feeling away. The feeling that she never should have forgiven him. That he didn't deserve it. That he wasn't any better than Kaden. That if she finally got all of her memories back—if she remembered *all* of them—his leaving would hurt her more, and she'd resent every moment she'd spent with him since.

He leaned his forehead against the tile shower wall and closed his eyes, remembering her lips on his. Knowing he didn't deserve it and wanting to feel it again just the same.

He shut the shower off. The waterproof bandages he'd applied to his shoulders at Griff's insistence had held, so he dressed and went down to the kitchen to fulfill the food require-ment of Griff's orders. He would never admit it aloud, but he liked the way the griffin fussed over him. He would have given anything, as a kid, for his father to notice if he had or hadn't eaten. To notice if there was even food in the fucking house when he abandoned Nyx and Seth to go track down Elena Fortuna, *again*.

In three months, Griff had become more of a father to him than his own had ever been. And he didn't deserve that, either. He closed the refrigerator door he'd been staring into for the last five minutes and reached into the cabinet above it. The one Nyx would never put anything in because it was too tall for her to reach, and spaces that high and that out of the way "creeped her out" because they tended to see little use and collect cobwebs.

It was literally the only place to hide anything from her, and because of her connection to the Station's senses, he'd had to go the extra mile. He pulled a canister full of sugar down and dug around inside until he pulled out a rectangular box the size of a deck of playing cards.

He carried it outside, walked to the back boundary of the Station's grounds, and leaned against a pine tree. The same one he'd pinned Nyx against the night after he'd spoken to her in the bar in Dead Earth.

He flipped the cardboard box open, shook out a cigarette, and lit it with the lighter that was always in his pocket. He took a long drag, the harsh burn hitting his lungs, and held it before he exhaled the stream of smoke.

He'd never gotten addicted to nicotine. Nyx had never *let* him get addicted. She'd caught him on the second cigarette of his life and promptly launched into a tirade about cancer. Which had been hilarious, because neither of them had spent enough time in Dead Earth at that point to even know about cancer but she had, apparently, read the warning on the package and determined both cigarettes and cancer were bad, and she wasn't going to let him have either of them.

He'd only smoked after that when he'd needed, desperately, to be reminded that someone gave a shit about him. He'd light one up, conveniently in her vicinity, and wait for her to find him and go off. After he'd left, after he'd forgotten her, he'd found himself back on Dead Earth a year later, buying a pack.

He'd taken one drag and heard her voice. He hadn't known it was hers, hadn't even known it was a real person's voice. But it had meant something to him, that someone—even a person he thought he might have made up—cared enough to yell at him for the sake of his stars-cursed health.

He'd smoked sparingly over the years, chasing that voice, chasing the high he got from hearing it that was better than any drug on any planet. He needed to hear it now. He took another drag on the cigarette.

The door to the Station's back door opened and Kaden walked out. Now where could he be going? Seth pulled illusion over himself, fading into the background. Kaden walked straight for the area where Seth was.

Seth didn't think he'd been seen, so there was only one other reason for Moor to be heading in this direction. The same reason Seth had chosen this exact point for his meeting with Nyx months ago. It was the farthest point from the Station building, the most secluded, with the most coverage. If someone wanted to enter or leave Station grounds without being seen, this was the best spot to do it.

He waited until Kaden passed by him to drop his illusion. "Going somewhere?" he drawled.

To his credit, Kaden didn't look surprised. Mostly, he just looked annoyed. "Shouldn't you be happy? I'm getting out of your way."

"You're leaving her without a fucking explanation. Again."

"Are you pissed at me, Hawthorne? Or are you pissed at yourself for doing the same damn thing before I ever did?"

Seth wasn't even aware he'd moved until his fist connected with Kaden's face.

33

———

Nyx felt somewhat human again after taking a shower and putting on clean clothes. Kaliaris had even kindly sent up a bottle of the same analgesic Jevryn had used, so she could coat her extremely painful sunburn in a fresh layer.

She finished the application and stared at her reflection in the mirror as the numbing effects kicked in. She looked ridiculous, half her face its usual warm, olive color, the other half an angry red. She hadn't sunburned the entire time she'd been in the Arizona desert, but she passed out once on a foreign planet, and this was what happened.

She shook her head and stepped into her room. Griff rested on her bed. "Not a single word," she warned him.

His tail thumped. "It is not so bad, really."

"I look like I'm auditioning to be the lobster version of Two-Face. Never mind," she added at Griff's confused expression. She wasn't actually into *Batman* enough to suggest they watch it just so he would understand the reference. She plopped onto the bed next to him. "Okay, I'm showered, clothed, and medicated, as per your orders. Spill. What happened after one of the people I trust most in the world knocked me unconscious?"

A plate of cheese and crackers appeared on the bed, and Griff nudged it at her. Knowing a losing battle when she saw one, she started eating.

"You mean, what happened after the person who cares deeply about your well-being ensured you got adequate rest?"

Nyx snorted. "Sure. After that."

"Very little. Seth brought you here, and I told Jevryn he would have to wait to speak with you."

Nyx swallowed a barely-chewed bite of cheese and crackers. "That's it?"

"Yes."

"You're certain nothing else happened?"

"Quite certain."

She drummed her fingers on her thigh, debating whether to ask what she wanted. But if she didn't, it would eat at her. "Griff…why didn't you tell me about any of this? Portaling, the Harvester, Kaliaris?" He'd known she wanted answers, known she was trying desperately to find them.

A pained expression crossed his face. "I wanted to. But there were many things I was bound not to reveal when I was bound to Kaliaris. And some things, I did not know. There was a span of time, between Nyaera's death and my coming to this Station, where I was…indisposed. I am sorry, Nyx."

"It's not your fault." She could tell he was still uncomfortable, so she changed the subject. "Where's Jevryn?"

"He is resting on the main floor until you are well enough to speak with him."

"Resting?" Jevryn didn't seem like the type to wait patiently.

Griff shrugged. "Close enough to it."

"And everyone else is okay? Like, really okay? No one's missing limbs or dying of alien poisons?"

"They are fine. No one is—oh dear."

Nyx straightened so fast she knocked the cheese plate askew. "What? What's wrong?"

"I think you'd better get to the east quadrant. I *can* restrain them, but it is probably best to let them work out some aggression first."

Nyx tapped into Kaliaris' senses and immediately felt what he was talking about. She groaned. "I leave them alone for two damn minutes."

Like she had the first night she'd chased after Seth, she jumped off her balcony onto the fireman's pole outside her room and slid down, then reached for Kaliaris and folded the space between where she was and where Seth stood.

Back then, she'd almost passed out from the strain. Now, it was like the ability was ingrained in her, like it was nothing. Like Kaliaris had stopped fighting her.

She stepped from the ground outside her window to the Station boundary, where Seth and Kaden were busy beating the shit out of each other.

"Are you two fucking kidding me right now?" She punctuated the question by sinking them up to their knees in the ground, then moving that ground away from each other.

Seth dragged the back of his hand across his mouth, wiping away a trickle of blood. "Hey, Nyxi."

Oh, he had *not* just *Hey, Nyxi'd* her right now. She was going to mur—

She sniffed, leaned closer to him and sniffed again. "Have you been smoking? How many times do I have to tell you that shit is going to kill you before it permeates your thick skull?"

He smiled at her like she'd just told him he was everything in life that mattered to her. "At least one more time."

"Do I even want to ask?" Morgen's familiar voice was on the hoarse, raspy side, like he'd spent a straight day screaming—or using the half-Siren side of his abilities. He strolled up, taking in Seth and Kaden restrained by the ground. "I like what you've done here. Going for living statuary?"

"Potentially. Your best friends are intent on killing each other."

Morgen sighed. "Why is it that when they misbehave they're

suddenly my best friends instead of your exes?" His friendly expression cooled a degree as he looked them over. "You two good?"

Seth and Kaden ignored him to give each other their versions of hard stares. Perfect.

She heard the thunder of hooves and turned. Temerex charged at them with Evra on her back. The unicorn-dragon trumpeted a war cry and sent Nyx an excited image of Seth and Kaden on fire.

"*No*," Nyx ordered, "No fire." She accompanied this order with an image of herself spraying a fire extinguisher all over Temerex, which probably didn't make any sense to the non-Earth unicorn-dragon. Temerex did seem to take it as a personal affront, a wounded look in her big yellow eyes as she skidded to a halt before Nyx, showers of sparks spraying from her hooves.

Nyx raised an eyebrow at Evra as the Amazon dismounted. "Is there a war I missed?"

"One would think so. This marvelous beast" —Temerex made a pleased snorting noise at the clear admiration in Evra's tone— "forced me onto her back at horn-point and charged directly here."

"Did she tell you why?"

"I do not believe she is capable of human vocalization or high language function."

Nyx waved her hand. "You know, did she send you an image?"

Evra pressed the backs of her fingertips to Nyx's forehead. "Strange, you do not *feel* feverish."

"Ha. Ha." Nyx batted her hand away. "Never mind." They could discuss Temerex's image-speech some other time. She released Seth and Kaden. "Let's go inside."

Kaden didn't move, and Nyx finally put together that they were at the edge of the Station.

"You're leaving," she said flatly.

The seconds ticked by before he answered. "You're here.

You're safe. And I believe someone told me to never come back to Earth, so…"

Nyx flushed. Yes, she had definitely said that.

"You aren't leaving here without talking to her." Seth sounded genuinely pissed, and it took a lot to get him to that point.

She also didn't understand it. She understood the two of them not liking each other. But she was having trouble feeling any anger of her own toward Kaden, when by Jevryn's account he was the only reason they'd found her. Seth knew that, because he was the one who'd sent for Kaden. So why would he care if Kaden left?

Kaden looked at Morgen. "This isn't going to help."

"Sorry," Morgen said, "but I have to agree with Seth on this one." Evra backed him up with her arms crossed and a stone-faced expression.

It suddenly hit Nyx what this must all be about. "Look, Jevryn already told me he's the one who sent Kaden to Earth with the Harvester. It's fine. We don't need to have a discussion about it."

"That's not what this is about." Seth's eyes never left Kaden. "Tell her, or I will. But if I do it, it's going to be in the worst light possible."

Kaden looked like he had a bad taste in his mouth. He muttered something under his breath and jerked his head at her. "Let's get this over with."

Well, that was a great attitude to start a conversation with. "I'll meet you in the library," she told him. He could use the walk there to cool off. He opened his mouth, presumably to argue with her, and she cut him off with a pointed glare.

He wisely nodded and stalked back toward the Station building. Nyx crossed her arms. "Do any of you want to tell me what this is about?"

Three heads shook in unison. She narrowed her eyes.

"Oh, is that the time?" Morgen asked innocently, looking at

the watch he was not wearing. "I just realized I need to be somewhere."

"How coincidental," Evra said, "I find myself in the same situation."

"Cowards!" Nyx called as the two of them beat a hasty retreat. She turned on Seth. "What is this about?"

Seth swallowed. "He'll tell you."

"And if I want *you* to tell me?"

He just shook his head again. Great. They trekked back to the Station in silence, Temerex trotting happy circles around them as they walked. She gave an offended snort when they left her to enter the building, then whirled and galloped off across the grounds, once again trumpeting a call to whoever was around to hear it.

Seth remained quiet all the way to the library. When she reached for the door he reached for her, pulling her back, wrapping her tight against his chest. He buried his face in her hair and breathed her in, long and slow.

She relaxed, hugging him back. He was warm and real and *here.*

"I thought I was going to lose you," Seth whispered.

She swallowed. "I thought I was going to lose *you.*" The image of him plummeting from the air flashed in her mind. She had a feeling that image was going to haunt her for a long time.

She lifted her head and pushed onto her toes. Seth drew back, avoiding the brush of her lips. The sharp sting of rejection tore through her.

"Seth?" He hadn't let go of her. But he hadn't wanted to kiss her.

He closed his eyes. "Just talk to him, first." He pressed a kiss to her forehead and walked away, leaving her to wonder what Kaden could possibly have to say to her that affected her and Seth.

She stared at the door for a long minute, not quite ready to go in. She was still having trouble wrapping her head around the fact that Kaden was here. She'd been so angry with him in the Shadow Market. He'd been angry with her. It had been easy to break from him, then. Clean.

Now she was faced with the knowledge that the only reason she was here, standing in her Station again, was because he'd tracked her down. Because Seth had asked him to find her, and he'd done it, even though he hated Seth and was probably still mad at her.

She didn't know how she was supposed to feel about that any more than she had any idea why her friends thought it was so vitally important Kaden talk to her before he left. So she quit trying to make her feelings fit into a mold and shoved the library door open.

Kaden stood in front of the fireplace, his back to her, staring up at a picture of an angry, caged lion Nyx had never seen before. The rest of the library's decor had shifted to match that tone, everything gone rough and rustic, with a vaguely tortured feel.

Kaden didn't turn. She waited. The silence stretched. She thought she could fill an ocean with all the silence that had passed between them, and she was tired of it. Tired of feeling like it was somehow her fault, like if she could just say the right thing, *be* the right thing, he would open up.

He could travel across the universe for her, but he still couldn't talk to her. She didn't understand it. But she didn't have to, anymore. She could say what *she* needed to, and leave it. "Thank you, for coming for me." She hadn't meant it sarcastically, but he must have taken it that way because his shoulders tensed, like the words were a blow. She forged on. "Jevryn said he couldn't have found me without you, and I wasn't getting home on my own, so..." She trailed off, not quite willing to say, *You saved my life,* though it amounted to that.

Still nothing from him.

"Look, I get that everyone wants us to talk things out and be civil. It's awkward for Morgen, being in the middle of this, and maybe I was a little hasty banning you from the entire planet and all. We're both adults, so we can—"

"I shouldn't have been able to find you." His hands clenched into fists. "It isn't *normal* for a Hound to be able to track someone through a portal. That's what they wanted me to talk to you about."

She frowned. "They felt it was vitally important I know you're some kind of tracker savant?"

He finally turned and looked at her. "I'm not. Yes, I'm a good tracker, one of the best, but…I couldn't have found anyone else like this. If the same thing had happened to Morgen, I'd have been useless to find him."

Uneasiness reared its ugly head. In Nyx's experience, being the special exception was never a good thing. "Then why could you find me?"

"Because I Linked to you."

The uneasy feeling in Nyx's stomach intensified. "And that means what, exactly?"

"More or less what it sounds like. My magic is linked to you. There is nowhere you can go that I can't find you." He shoved his hands in his pockets. "It's how I found you in the Shadow Market after the storms. It's why Seth sent for me when you went missing."

"Seth knew about this?" That hurt, more than the rising panic at the knowledge that Kaden apparently had limitless stalking privileges where she was concerned.

He rubbed at the back of his neck. "He suspected."

And he hadn't told her. She swallowed that bitterness down to deal with later. "This…Link. What is it?"

The red that flushed Kaden's cheeks told her even before he said, "It's something trackers typically do when they marry. A reciprocal exchange."

"And you thought you'd just do it with me, without even *telling me*, much less asking for permission, because…?"

"Because you went to Arkadia because of *me*. It was my fault you were there, my fault you were in danger, and I needed to guarantee you wouldn't die there because of me."

All her old frustrations rose up. "I made my own choices when I went to Arkadia," she bit out. Kaliaris took the depth of her emotion and made it a literal force in the room, the walls groaning under the weight of her voice. "I didn't need you to make choices about what was necessary for my safety somewhere *I chose to go*. I'm not a child, Kaden, but you can't seem to stop treating me like one."

He inhaled, exhaled, closed his eyes. "You're right."

Two words she'd never expected to hear come out of Kaden Moor's mouth. But they were good ones. A good first step. They quieted the rage in her chest. "Then undo it."

His eyes snapped open. "What?"

"You admit you shouldn't have done this, right?"

His mouth tightened, but he nodded.

"Then undo it. Un-Link us."

"I can't. Once a Link is made, it can't be severed."

The world spun. She was *not* going to accept Kaden having ultimate lifetime stalking privileges. Not even if he promised to never use them.

Think, think, think. There was a lot of magic in the universe. Surely something could be done. "This Link. What happens if the person you're Linked to dies?" Kaden blanched and she said, "Oh, don't flatter yourself. You're not so terrible I'd commit suicide to get away from you, I'm asking how the magic works."

He hesitated. "There's nothing to Link to, so it fades."

Nothing to link *to*. Perfect. "Track me."

"You're standing right in front of me. There's nothing to track."

Shit. She needed his magic to activate. "Would it be helpful if you closed your eyes and I hid somewhere?"

"Yes, actually."

Great. She was going to play hide-and-seek with her ex-boyfriend. But this would be a better test, anyway. "Okay. Count to twenty, I guess."

He closed his eyes and she rounded the bookcase stacks, drawing on the Station just enough to hide her footsteps, so he couldn't listen to where she was going. She felt the tug a moment later. It was light, so light she wouldn't have noticed it if she hadn't been waiting for it. She latched onto the pull and felt around the edges of the connection. Then, like she'd done when Maruca had been pulling energy from her in the Shadow Market, Nyx Hid the place where Kaden's Link connected to her.

She felt the connection die—and that was what it was: a death. The threads stitched into her from his magic withering as the thing that gave them life disappeared.

"Nyx?" There was a note of genuine panic in Kaden's voice she'd never heard before, and something in her heart constricted at it. Rationally, he might know better, but his magic was telling him she was gone.

Quickly, she slipped two rows of bookcases over, where she could see the place she'd been standing when she broke the Link —the last place he would have felt her if this had worked. He broke into a run, slamming to a stop at the spot where she'd stood. He looked...sick, something wild in his eyes, his breathing shallow and fast.

She wondered, then, what it felt like for a tracker to lose a Link. If it hurt. The old instinct to comfort him rose in her. The need to ease any hurt he might feel. She acknowledged it and let it go. If breaking the Link caused him pain, it wasn't her responsibility. This had been his choice, not hers, and she wasn't living with it for the rest of her life.

But she could put an end to his current fears. She stepped into the main aisle. "I'm fine."

His gaze snapped to her, like he couldn't believe she was actually alive, like every sense he had was telling him she was dead. But at the end of the day, he was still Kaden Moor. She didn't think there was a single emotion he *couldn't* shut down, if he wanted to, and he did that now, his face going flat and expressionless.

But he stared at her a long time before he spoke. "So this is done. *We're* done." It was a question disguised as a statement.

She didn't want to answer it. But she deserved to move on, and so did he. "Yeah," she said softly. "We're done."

He gave a jerky nod, and walked away like he'd been dismissed. *Oh, for fuck's sake.*

"Kaden."

He stopped.

"I don't hate you."

He turned around, his expression wary.

"I'm not happy. I know you well enough by now to know you never would have told me about the Link if you didn't have to. I disagree with you making it, and especially with you not telling me."

He waited. "But?"

"But I think I understand why you did." At his core, Kaden was a protector. He'd been that way with her in Dead Earth. She'd seen it on Arkadia, the way he'd taken the most vulnerable under his care. The way he'd done everything he could to get them out. The way he'd grieved for Lana and Fari because they didn't survive, and he felt like he'd failed them. "I still disagree with it. But I wouldn't be alive right now without it and I…I can't hate you for that. We're done. But I can't hate you. I don't want to."

Some of the tension eased from his shoulders. "I know I didn't do anything right with you—at any step of the way—but I did care about you. I *do* care about you." He swallowed. "If you ever need help, you can ask, and I'll give it. Not because I think you're incapable, not because I think you're a child, or because I know I owe you, but because I want to."

It was officially the longest speech she'd ever heard him make. "Thank you."

He nodded.

"If you want to visit Morgen here, you're welcome to." She gathered up all the maturity she had and made herself say, "Maruca, too, of course."

A ghost of a smile teased his lips.

"So, uh, take care of yourself," she added lamely.

"You too." He hesitated, like he might say something else. Then his lips pressed into a firmer line, and he turned and opened the library door.

A stern-faced Jevryn A-Morridahn on the threshold.

34

Nyx had felt the councilor standing outside the library for the last five minutes. He'd probably come as soon as he'd learned Nyx was awake, and what her location was.

"Councilor," Kaden said.

Jevryn looked at him. "I owe you a debt, and I always pay them. If you want a better life for you and your sister than the one you are living now, wait for me."

Kaden hesitated, but it was brief. He nodded and walked out. The door closed behind him, leaving Nyx alone with Jevryn. He had packed away the bits of humanity that had shown through on Amentia Furor, and he was once more a councilor—aloof, inscrutable, unknowable. Then he sighed and that exterior broke again, and he just seemed like a man —tired and with the weight of the universe on his shoulders.

He sat in one of the two massive wingback chairs that had appeared before the fireplace and gestured to the one opposite him. She took it.

"Tell me what happened."

She didn't know what she *should* tell him.

As if he could sense that she was trying to parse out which

pieces to reveal, he added, "The truth, if you will. It has been an exceptionally long day."

The truth. "Kaliaris decided to keep Laiveran."

Jevryn straightened. "Keep, not kill?"

Well, that explained why Jevryn had been willing to wait around while Griff insisted she be allowed to rest. He'd thought Kaliaris had killed Laiveran, and the immediate danger was gone. The way Jevryn looked now…she didn't think telling him Kaliaris had kept Laiveran alive at *her* request was a smart idea.

But fortunately, there were other truths at play than her own. "I think Kaliaris has a few centuries of deep-seated animosity to work out where Laiveran is concerned."

"And you allowed your Station to do this?"

"Allowed is a strong word. Kaliaris has the most power within their Heart, and we are talking about attempting to get between the soul of a butchered planet and the individual who did the butchering."

Jevryn sighed and leaned back in his chair. "I see Laiveran was feeling loquacious." He didn't sound particularly pleased about the fact, but then, she probably knew more about the Stations now than anyone save the All Council.

"Are you going to kill me for my newly discovered knowledge on how the current universal transit system was built?"

Jevryn's lips twitched. "No."

"Lock me in a dungeon?"

"No."

"Because those things would kill Griff?"

"*No.* Shocking though you may find it, I have no desire to end your life, whether it is tied to Griff's or not. But I do not think you fully grasp the severity of this situation."

"I grasp it just fine. If the rest of the council figures out Laiveran is here, I die, and Griff and the Station die. If the council figures out I have the Harvester, I die, and Griff and the Station die. I just don't see what I can do about any of it."

He steepled his fingers, measuring his words before he

replied. "I have made many mistakes in my life. That the Harvester came to you is one of the more egregious ones."

Ouch. Thanks for the vote of confidence.

"I correct my mistakes. This is a burden you were never meant to carry. Return the Harvester to me, hand over Laiveran, and I will handle them."

It was tempting. So, so tempting. To hand it off and wash her hands of the whole business. If she was going to give the Harvester to anyone, Jevryn didn't seem like the worst option. He had been, if not necessarily kind to her, at least kinder than he had to be. But she didn't know what he would do with the Harvester once he had it—especially if he had Laiveran, too. She didn't know it wouldn't simply end up back in the hands of the other councilors, whom she didn't trust at all. And she had made a promise to Kaliaris.

"I can't."

"It was not a request."

"Look, for one, Kaliaris is not going to let Laiveran go, so I can't give him back, and two, I don't trust you with the Harvester. Laiveran used it to butcher planets, and the rest of you used it to enslave them."

"Is that how Laiveran framed what we did?"

"It's how Kaliaris did. And since they're the one living with the results, I think they have the right to frame it however they want."

Jevryn was quiet for a moment. "I will not claim that we did what we did out of benevolence. I have never been particularly adept at lying. But I will say that we saw no other choice. You think, perhaps, that because the councilors have lived so long, we ought to have known better. But at the time we made the decisions that we did, most of us were not much older than you are now.

"Imagine that when the Harvester came to you, it was so bloated with power that it was on the verge of releasing *all* of it in an explosion that would destroy half of the universe that remained. Imagine that those remaining planets were already on the verge of being subjugated by a force who believed we were too irresponsible to continue being allowed to flit about the universe."

Nyx didn't *want* to see it from his perspective. She wanted to be righteously indignant about it and have everything be clean and simple. But she thought it through, and said, "The Minethrans?"

"Yes. They discovered the path to other planets long before we did. Consider them cynical or wise, but they chose not to interact with others, but to instead colonize uninhabited planets as their species swelled in population. At the time, they numbered dozens of planets, and though they did not make themselves known to us, they did keep an eye on us. They were not unaware when we discovered the delights of galactic travel.

"When we stumbled our way onto Amentia Furor, they were not…hostile, precisely, but neither were they welcoming. They did not wish us to visit the other planets in their network, but they allowed us a political outpost of sorts on Amentia Furor, that we might exchange knowledge with them.

"They warned us of the magic storms that hit their planet. They believe they stem from the planet's very soul. Laiveran and Nyaera, having an affinity for such things, wished to study the storms. They wished to reach that soul, and commune with it. They understood the dangers. It was a tragedy, when Nyaera was lost to one of the storm's portals, but it was one she chose to place herself in the path of.

"Experiencing her death drove Laiveran mad. He killed eleven of the queen's guard before he portaled off-world. The fallout was catastrophic." Jevryn's face went blank, as if remembering a time he still couldn't believe he'd lived through, and mostly chose to forget. "Only by promising to apprehend Laiveran and deliver him to the queen for trial did we escape immediate retaliation.

"But before we could do so, he built the Harvester. Planets

were destroyed. I believe the only reason Laiveran did not harvest Amentia Furor was because he believed Nyaera might yet be there. The Minethrans viewed Laiveran's atrocities as proof that we could only sow chaos and discord. The universe went to war."

Nyx frowned. "Griff never mentioned a war."

"No. Arradin…never experienced it. When Laiveran harvested the first planet, I understood well enough what would follow if he could not be stopped. I did not want Arradin in the middle of that. He is a scholar, not a warrior. But I also knew that if I told him the truth—what Laiveran had done, and what was to come—that he would refuse to leave my side. So I made him choose to leave by other methods."

Nyx groaned. "You *broke up with him* rather than tell him what was going on?"

He looked at her sharply. "Judge me if you wish. Stars know that I have done so myself far more harshly than you ever could. I believed he had returned to his homeworld. Given the terms of our parting, I was unsurprised that I did not hear from him.

"So when Laiveran harvested Arradin's homeworld, I believed I had lost him. Lost him, and that it was my own fault. It was not until this Station was built that I learned Arradin left me that day, only for Kiev to take him."

"Is there a reason your brother hates you so much?"

"Yes."

"And, let me guess, it's none of my business?"

"Precisely."

"So you hate Kiev for what he did to Griff, except that if he hadn't, Griff would be dead."

"The point," Jevryn said, very *pointedly*, "is that by the time we finally ran Laiveran to ground, we were exceptionally short on options. We wrested the Harvester from him and we believed him dead. We brought this news to the Minethran queen and informed her of the Harvester's instability, and what would likely occur if we could not find some way of dispersing the power it contained."

He'd told the queen they'd killed the person she was mad at in the first place, and that they were in possession of a ticking time bomb her troops were right in the middle of. Smart.

"We came to a temporary agreement, and the Minethran troops withdrew from our planets. Once we built the Stations, the Harvester was no longer an unpredictable threat. The Council was established and we returned to Amentia Furor to broker a lasting peace. One we achieved solely because Laiveran destroyed nearly all of the portal well planets in our system, and because we convinced the Minethrans that our supply of portal witches had died with them. That the All Council itself was all that remained of us."

"And they bought that?"

"Only portal planets breed portal witches. The Minethrans knew Lehine remained, but that planet had not sustained life in centuries, even then."

Nyx shivered, remembering the giant, abandoned tomb that was the prison of Lehine. "What happened there? The people in those cells—you just left them there to die?"

Jevryn's lips twisted. "What happened on Lehine was an atrocity."

"What *was* Lehine?"

"A prison for those who committed crimes off their home-world, when neither planet—theirs, or the one where the crime was committed—was willing to give up jurisdiction over the case. They were held on Lehine until a joint tribunal could be called.

"We—those of us who pioneered portal travel—were all familiar with the prison's protocols and safety measures because we helped design them. When Laiveran fled Amentia Furor in the wake of his murders, he fled to Lehine, and he used his knowledge of those protocols to lock the prison down. There he stayed, until he built the Harvester. We were not able to re-enter

Lehine and discover fully what had happened until after we obtained the Harvester. By then it was too late."

"But you just *left them there*. Their bodies. They had family, friends, who would have wondered what happened to them, who never got to know."

Jevryn's voice was gentle. "No, Nyx, they did not. Because when we made the decision to Hide the Harvester and the history of its making, Lehine was Hidden with it."

Nyx struggled to accept that. "You Hid an entire planet?"

"Yes."

"How many?"

"I do not understand."

"How many Hidden does it take to do that? How many of us were there?"

"Thousands."

Thousands, and now only she and her mother remained.

"Keeping the Harvester will only ensure you meet the same fate as your predecessors. Return it. Live your life here."

She shook her head but avoided the argument, picking up the thread of their previous conversation, and the part of it that didn't make sense. "If your peace treaty with the Minethrans was dependent on no one accidentally discovering them again via portal magic, why leave the Shadow Market alone? Aren't the portal witches there a threat to your big secret?"

"I told you that our treaty was in part dependent on convincing them that our portal witches were gone, save for the Council and those directly in our employ. We...lied. Many portal witches had settled on other planets, had had families and therefore descendants who might inherit the ability. Too many to track down, and no foolproof way of doing it.

"While we Hid the knowledge of portaling as we knew it, those original witches almost certainly had objects of stored portal magic that would be passed down through their family, until some curious great-grandchild inherited the ability and stumbled upon it. In such a scenario, we needed there to already be an inherent belief about how portal magic worked—so we bent portal magic to spell foreign matter from another planet, and we established a set of portal witches on Tenebris Umbra to instill the belief that this was the *only* way the magic could be used. It has kept the overly curious from finding what they should not. At least, until you."

Nyx frowned. "Then what did you tell the Minethran queen to get her to let me go?"

Jevryn hesitated, a mere fraction of a second, before he said, "I told her you were the descendant of a portal witch in our employ. A line we believed the ability had gone out of."

You, Jevryn A-Morridahn, are a shit liar. But she couldn't for the life of her think what he would have actually told the queen. The need to know the answer was an itch beneath her skin, but she knew he wouldn't tell her. When you boiled it all down, he was a councilor, and she was just Nyx.

She had to mentally work her way back to remember what the point of this brief history of the universe was. "So the Council was in a really tight spot and enslaved the souls of some already-wronged planets to prevent half the universe from going *boom*. What part of this is supposed to convince me to give you the Harvester?"

"The part where councilor Alistair has grown bored with eternity, and decided that perhaps using the Harvester to rekindle the war we worked so hard to avoid is the thing that would once again bring joy to his existence."

Nyx swallowed. She had a feeling she did not want to know what it looked like when planets went to war. "I would say, in that scenario, that the Harvester is safer with me than it is with you."

"For how long? You do not want this burden for an unending lifetime. Take my word on that."

"I'm not going to have it forever. I'm going to destroy it."

He smiled, looking amused. "Of course you are. And how,

precisely, are you going to destroy something powerful enough to consume worlds?"

"I'm going to get the madman who made it to tell me *how* he made it, so I can *un*make it."

Jevryn shook his head. "Even could such a thing be done, what you speak of would only destroy the cage which houses the Harvester. Dissolve that cage, and you unleash what lies within. Do you have a plan for what you will do with what is inside?"

"No," Nyx admitted, grudgingly. Because until she'd talked with Kaliaris, she hadn't realized it was a *something* inside as opposed to just a dangerous magical object. "But I'll figure it out."

Jevryn sighed, as if he was disappointed and had hoped she had an answer.

"Look," she said hurriedly, because if she didn't convince him, she had no doubt he would do his best to take the Harvester back from her. "Do you know what's inside the Harvester?"

Grudgingly, he said, "No."

"Then let me find out. You said you recognized what I was when you first came to my Station with the other councilors. You had to have guessed then that Kaden had given the Harvester to me and not my mother. You didn't come back to try and take it."

"No. But then I did not understand the manner in which you were bound to the Station. To Arradin."

"And that makes a difference because...?"

"Because now it means that the risk you put yourself in by harboring the Harvester is a risk to Arradin as well. If you die, he dies."

The words were a bucket of ice water dumped on her head. Nyx had never before been in a position to understand how it would feel to have someone discuss her life in front of her as if it didn't matter. She'd thought Jevryn felt some measure of responsibility toward her, for her coming into possession of the

Harvester. An impression he'd no doubt sought to instill, so she would trust him.

She had thought, when he'd taken the pain of Koral's fire from her mind, when he'd given her the ring and the promise of aid, that he was a decent person. That he was, perhaps, the *only* decent person on the Council. Because he obviously cared for Griff.

But the capacity to love didn't make someone a good person. Terrible people were capable of the emotion. Jevryn had helped her then because Griff hadn't wanted to see her in pain. She was like Griff's adopted daughter, and Jevryn was playing nice with her on the surface in hopes of repairing past errors of action.

She really hoped Griff was too smart to fall for that.

Griff. *He* was the only thing that moved Jevryn. "You should let me keep the Harvester," she said carefully, "because if you do, I might be able to free Griff."

Every line of Jevryn's body went alert. "How?"

She had to be very careful here. If she over-promised and under-delivered, well, Jevryn wouldn't *kill* her, but he could probably make her life very unpleasant. "Kaliaris wants freedom. For them, and the other Stations. Kaliaris wants them untethered to the planets they are bound to. They think the way to that is through the Harvester, and I agree. But I won't do it unless I can find a way to free the Guardians and the Avatars as well."

"That is an explanation thoroughly void of specifics. And it necessitates the destruction of the universe's entire transit infrastructure."

"Do you care? If it frees Griff, do you care about anything else?" She already knew the answer.

"No." He stood. "Very well. I will return in six months. Show me that Laiveran has been useful and you have some hope of accomplishing what you claim, and I will allow you to continue. Fail, and I will force Kaliaris to relinquish Laiveran" —the floor beneath Jevryn's feet trembled ominously, but he simply glared in response— "and I will take back the Harvester. I do hope you succeed."

He turned for the door, was nearly to it when Nyx remembered.

"Wait!"

He paused, angling his body slightly back towards hers.

"You brought my mother to Earth. Do you know..." Her heart rate sped up. She didn't think the mere possibility of asking a question should dump so much adrenaline into her system, but her chest felt light and over-expanded, her head dizzy, until she managed to blurt out, "Do you know who my father is?"

Something unreadable flickered across Jevryn's face. "Yes."

Her heart beat faster, faster, until she could barely breathe. "And?"

"And I do not think you would care to know him. He is not a good man, Nyx."

Anger sparked in her chest. "Don't you think I have a right to make that decision for myself? To know why he cared so little about me that even knowing what my mother was like, he left me with *her*?"

"Perhaps he thought that, as difficult as your mother can be, the life she offered you was yet better than the one he could have given you." He forestalled any response with an upheld hand. "You will get nothing else from me on the subject. Your father chose to have no part in your life. Believe me when I say that if he *had*, you would not have survived this long. Sometimes what seems like cruelty can be the height of kindness."

"That's easy for you to say. It's not your life."

He studied her. "What do you think knowing him would accomplish? As you have already stated, he left you to a woman no one would consider kind. He is not a father, Nyx. He is a man who abandoned you. Let it go. You will find no comfort in the knowledge, should you attain it." He pushed the portal room door open and strode out.

She followed. "Whoever it is you're protecting, I'll figure it out."

Jevryn did not so much as acknowledge the statement. He walked into the kitchen, where Griff, Morgen, Evra, and Kaden were gathered around mugs of coffee. Seth was conspicuously absent.

She inhaled the aroma of fresh ground espresso. Sweet, delicious coffee. She would kill for—

Morgen thrust a mug into her hand. She took it, blowing across the steaming surface. "Have I told you I love you?"

"It's a curse, being this perfect, but do try to restrain yourself, little Guardian."

She rolled her eyes.

Jevryn's gaze fell on Griff. "Arradin. A moment of your time?"

Nyx opened her mouth to tell Griff she didn't think Jevryn deserved a moment of his time, but the look the councilor shot her reminded her she was already on thin ice with the most dangerous person in the room. Besides, Griff could make his own decisions, and he'd apparently decided talking was fine.

He rose, still in large form, the spaces between walls and furniture widening to accommodate his bulk as he passed Jevryn, leaving the councilor to follow. They were almost out of sight when Griff paused and said, "Nyx, some privacy, if you would?"

She sighed and killed her awareness of the Station.

35

I t took Nyx a few minutes of searching to find Seth without tapping into the Station's senses, but after she struck out in his room and Morgen's lab, she found him on the back porch. He sat with his long legs stretched out in front of him, his back resting against Temerex's. She was sprawled out flat like a dead horse, her eyes closed.

Seth saw Nyx and stood up, taking pains to be quiet, but Temerex woke anyway. Her head and neck lifted up, eyes sleepy, and she sent Nyx two images. The first was Nyx and Seth on the porch, Temerex sleeping. The other was the three of them walking off.

Nyx sent the first image back to her. "Go back to sleep. We'll keep watch."

Temerex let out a soft groan and her head flopped back down, eyes shutting. Her mental images had been filled with the kind of bone-weary exhaustion that came from being on high-alert for years and finally feeling safe enough to collapse.

Nyx wondered how many of her physical needs and responses were similar to the equines buried in part of her DNA. While horses could sleep standing up, they couldn't enter REM sleep unless they laid down, and most didn't feel safe enough to lie down without a herd, even if it was only a herd of two. This might be the first time Temerex had *slept* slept in years.

"What is she?" Seth asked.

"I'm not sure, other than Jevryn's. Apparently, his brother dumped her on Amentia Furor as a not-so-subtle *fuck you*."

"He sounds charming."

"Oh, he is." *He killed two girls who'd already lived through hell, and every time I remember it, I wish I'd killed him instead of just scarring his face.* "Seth…"

A muscle twitched at the corner of his eye. "Kaden told you?"

She nodded. "I thought we didn't keep secrets."

"We don't. I didn't *know*."

"You clearly suspected."

"I did, but I thought…I thought I was just jealous. I didn't think he'd actually Linked to you. Hardly any tracker does that anymore. Even when you disappeared, I didn't honestly believe he could find you. I just needed something to hold onto to hope that you *could* be found. I couldn't lose you." He looked away, turned back, his eyes bright. "I don't *want* to lose you."

She took a deep breath and asked the question she'd been afraid of every time some random memory came back and brought a light into his eyes. "Is it me you don't want to lose, or the person I used to be?"

Because she could rediscover that person now—she could and would remove the Hiding Elena had placed on her—but recovering the old her wouldn't unmake the *her* that she was now. She was a product of the experiences she'd lived. Recovering her other memories would just make her *more* her.

If Seth was holding on to some remembered version of her… she'd changed since then. Would have changed whether or not she'd lost her memories.

"I don't want to lose *you*," he repeated. "I like *you*. Yeah, I like the memories I have of you—of us—but you're still you without them. Of course you've changed. So have I. But we're still the same people. We still fit."

"Then why does it feel like you've had me at arms' length since you came back?"

"I didn't know if you *wanted* to still fit. I didn't know if I just felt like we did because it was what I wanted. And I..."

"What?" she prompted softly.

He swallowed. "I left you."

"I know that."

"Intellectually, yeah. But right now you're the woman who was alone for a long time, who thought no one cared about her, and found me. What happens when you remember being the woman I was there for, who I was supposed to *always* be there for, but then I wasn't?"

"I don't know." She understood what he was trying to say. That she—the person she was now, with the memories she had now—didn't hold what he'd done against him. But the her that remembered her life might. "But we can find out. Something... happened, on Lehine."

She explained about finding the net of her mother's Hiding. Seth listened, his expression inscrutable.

"So you can remember? Everything? Like right now?"

"Maybe not this exact instant but, yes."

"What do you need from me?" he asked. No questions, no hesitations, no comments about how this might affect him. Just, *What do you need?*

"Patience. You said taking your memories back knocked you out for a day? Was that the only side effect?"

He shook his head. "Had a bitch of a migraine and I was kind of...dazed for a week or so. It's hard to explain. Nothing serious, but..."

But Nyx didn't know if she could afford to be dazed for a week—and she doubted it would only be a week for her. Seth hadn't forgotten his whole life—just the parts of her in it. "I have a lot more memories to shove back in my head than you did. I don't know what will happen if I rip off the bandaid all at once."

"Then we'll go slow." He took her hand, squeezing. "As slow as you need to. Take something small back and find out how it affects you."

Start small. She could do that. "There's one other thing." Something she'd been thinking about since she'd realized her mother was aware of her, of the Hiding and how Nyx interacted with it. "We still don't know why she did this to me. I know she's the devil incarnate and all, but…what if there was a reason for what she did?"

Some part of her still didn't want to believe her mother could have done this to her simply out of spite. She wanted to believe it had been for a reason, even if she couldn't fathom what.

Seth's eyes took on a hard glint. "Then she can drag her ass back here and explain it. You can throw her in the dungeon with Laiveran."

"Kaliaris' Heart is not a dungeon." But she smiled. He could always make her smile. "Okay. Slow, then." She threaded her fingers through his and lifted their hands. "What about this?"

"We take it slow, too. I told you before—I don't ever want to be something you regret. I don't want to be a mistake."

"You'll never be a mistake, Seth." She pushed onto her toes and brushed her lips across his, trying to convince him of the one thing her words—no one's words—ever seemed to: that he mattered.

For a moment, he was still. Then he kissed her back, hard and needy and possessive, with what felt like years of pent-up longing.

She suspected 'taking it slow' would have taken a fast dive off a cliff if Temerex hadn't startled awake. Nyx broke away from Seth as the unicorn-dragon jolted to her feet and took off at a dead gallop.

Nyx ran after her, heart pounding, furiously searching the Station's senses for what could have caused the mare's panic.

She folded space across the Station's grounds to keep up, arriving at the front border as Temerex skidded to a stop by Jevryn and Kaden.

No danger, then. Nyx couldn't see whatever images Jevryn sent the unicorn-dragon, but she didn't need them to know what was happening.

"You're leaving her? Again?"

"Arradin has agreed to care for her. I cannot take her with me."

"She *loves you*." Temerex's heartbreak was washing over Nyx in a drowning collage of gray and night.

"If I take her, Kiev will know where I have been. And he will not stop poking around until he discovers precisely *why* I was there."

Temerex nudged Nyx, sending her an image of Nyx, Jevryn, and the unicorn-dragon that needed no translation: family.

"You've been alive for nearly a millennium and you're telling me you can't find a way?"

"I *have* been alive for a millennium. And you are young, Nyx Fortuna. Perhaps too young to understand that the risk cannot be taken." He patted Temerex's neck. "I am sorry, my clever girl."

He turned, crossing the Station's boundary with Kaden. Temerex let out a heartbroken whinny that cut Nyx to her soul. Nyx put her hand on the unicorn-dragon's chest, gently stopping her from following.

"You're a heartless bastard, you know that?" she called.

"Yes," he replied without turning. "Of that, I am fully aware." Magic swirled, a portal opened, and Jevryn and Kaden disappeared.

Temerex cried, plaintive whinny after whinny, and no image or soothing noise Nyx made could ease the animal's heartbreak. She saw the unicorn-dragon's life in a flood of images. In Temerex's mind, Jevryn was her father, her best friend, the man who had raised her, trained her, loved her, until the day Kiev dumped her on Amentia Furor.

She had waited, faithfully, fully expecting he would come for her. And she thought he had, except now he was leaving her again.

It was too much grief for Nyx to take on top of everything else. She hugged Temerex's neck and cried with her.

<hr>

Nyx stared through red, puffy eyes at a fresh latte. It had taken a full hour for Temerex—and therefore Nyx—to stop crying. Griff had built the unicorn-dragon the luxury stall to end all luxury stalls, easily six hundred square feet and piled a foot and a half deep with bedding. That bedding was loose, heated rock, because that was apparently what unicorn-dragons wanted out of life, but the accommodations were still undeniably plush.

Temerex had wandered into it at Nyx's urging, her head hung low, and collapsed, utterly spent. Nyx was spent too. The sleep she'd gotten had only taken the edge off her exhaustion, and the crying jag hadn't helped.

Griff was equally morose. He'd reverted to housecat size and curled up on the chair next to Nyx, his tail flicking idly against the seat. Seth was quiet, too, which left Evra and Morgen desperately trying to bring up the cheer in the room.

"Can you believe it?" Evra demanded, distaste dripping from her voice as she waved that day's copy of *The Daily Between* at Nyx. "Team Six won."

Morgen made supporting noises of agreement, while it took Nyx a minute to realize Evra was talking about the charity competition. It seemed like it had happened a lifetime ago. Trust Evra to have the energy to be upset about who'd won after everything they'd been through.

Of course, she was laying it on thick enough—her voice a

little too irate, her hand gestures a little too flamboyant—that Nyx wasn't fooled. Evra al'Daemon was trying to take Nyx's mind off recent events in the only way she knew how.

That, or the Amazon was trying to ruin her hearing.

The cafe door opened, interrupting Evra's detailed analysis of Team Six's shortcomings, which were apparently legion. A familiar face greeted them, looking as tired as Nyx felt, enough so that faint stripes were showing on his skin.

"*Kalvar?*" she asked incredulously. She darted glances at the others, but they didn't seem surprised, so he must have come with Kaden. She didn't ask, because the blue-haired girl who'd given Nyx the note walked in behind him, and she had that flight look in her eyes like she might bolt at any moment

Nyx smoothed her voice into something upbeat and cheerful and hopefully non bolt-causing. "We missed you around here," she said, like she hadn't been completely shocked to see him. "Who's your friend?"

"This is Liya." He put his hand on her back and gently guided her forward. "Liya, this is Nyx."

"Hi." Nyx gave an awkward hand wave. At least, it felt awkward. Did hand waves ever *not* feel awkward? "We met briefly."

"Yeah," Liya said, barely loud enough to hear. "Hi." Her gaze darted around the room, never settling directly on Nyx.

Kalvar cleared his throat. "I was hoping she could stay here for a little while? Just until she gets some stuff sorted out."

"Of course!" Nyx might have put too much chipper enthusiasm into her voice, because Kalvar winced. "Griff? Could you show Liya to a room?"

Maybe having something to do would cheer him up, so he would stop looking so dejected. He straightened, found his spectacles and a smile. He was as polite and endearing as ever when he escorted Liya up, but his eyes were a million miles away.

Nyx waited until they were out of earshot to ask, "Do I need to be on the lookout for angry spouses, parents, or unscrupulous characters?" she asked. "It's fine if I do, I just want to be prepared."

Kalvar shook his head. "No, it's...no. That shouldn't be an issue. She just needs a place to stay while she figures things out."

Nyx nodded. "She can stay as long as she needs to."

"Thanks." He was quiet for a beat. "So, I've been thinking." Kalvar scuffed the toe of his boot on the floor, looking younger. He was at that age where he could bounce effortlessly between the lines of adult and kid. "I learned a lot with the Moors, and I got to see a lot of...interesting places," he said diplomatically.

Nyx made an encouraging noise.

"But I was thinking a slower pace might be nice for a while, and I was wondering if I could maybe have my old job back? And my old room?"

Nyx resisted the urge to squeal and jump up and down, because it would probably terrify Kalvar. "Your room's exactly how you left it, and I'm sure Liya will feel better having you here."

"And you're welcome to absolutely all of my shifts at the cafe," Seth chimed in.

"Don't you think you should engage in *some* form of gainful employment?" Nyx asked.

Seth shrugged. "Guess I could plant a garden in the back or something."

Oh, sure, that would be the day. Still, if he was even remotely considering it... "Plant some okra."

He grumbled. "If I do that, you and Griff will have me making gumbo every damn week."

"We'll try to restrain ourselves to every other week." Turning back to Kalvar she said, "You're going to love gumbo. Job's yours. It's great to have you back."

"Thanks." He ducked his head. "I—I really appreciate it." He headed for the stairs. Seth bumped up against her back, his arms folding around her.

"He looks sad."

"Yeah." She would bet hundred-to-one odds Kalvar's morose state had something to do with a certain redheaded Moor sibling. "That seems to be going around."

She leaned back against Seth, trying to figure out if there was anything else requiring her immediate attention, or if she had leave to fall apart for a few hours. Her leg hurt like a sonofabitch —both the bruise along her hip and the mermaid bite—and she really just wanted to take a bath.

She needed to have a more lengthy discussion with Kaliaris about Laiveran, too, but that could wait. She wanted to check in with Griff, but figured she'd give him some time to sort through his feelings. Kalvar and Liya were settled, and Evra and Morgen were on good terms again if the way they were flirtatiously arguing over whether Morgen had or had not put enough foam on Evra's cappuccino was any indication.

Seth got in on the argument, playing devil's advocate like only he could do. Seriously, there were *not* that many talking points about cappuccino foam. Nyx smiled, listening to them bicker good-naturedly. She sank back onto one of the barstools and laid her head on her arms, convinced that if she just rested for a moment, she'd find the energy to go upstairs.

But it was so nice to be home, to be surrounded by the people she loved, that she couldn't make herself get up. She fell asleep right there, the sounds of their voices soothing the jagged edges of her recent adventure.

EPILOGUE

ONE WEEK LATER

Nyx sat in the Arrival Room. The spinning silver orbs on their posts slowed as the portal wound down, the cosmic floor smoothing and hardening until it looked liked painted glass. The last traveler exited, but Nyx didn't leave. She sat on the chair behind the podium, legs drawn up to her chest, chin resting on her knees, staring at the portal.

Today had marked her first Arrival since she'd learned what Kaliaris truly was, and she'd had to work to be polite and professional to the travelers arriving in Earth Between. She hadn't offered her usual refreshment platter of cookies, and she'd struggled to take an interest in the town's visitors.

All she could remember was Kaliaris' pain as they were torn apart and reforged. When she saw the travelers, she no longer saw the wonder of the wider universe, but their feet tromping on Kaliaris' beaten body.

Griff strolled into the room, wings tucked along his sides. He was taking to his housecat size less and less often, and currently took up space roughly equivalent to that of a Shetland pony. She was glad that he was more comfortable taking the size *he* wanted to be—that he didn't feel the need to make himself smaller because he thought it was what others expected, or what would make them comfortable.

He took one look at her and said, "Kaliaris is not in pain anymore. The Arrivals do not harm them."

Trust Griff to know exactly what she was thinking. "Am I that transparent?"

"You care. And the pain you experienced at Kaliaris' transformation is recent and raw to you. But for Kaliaris, it was a very long time ago. They have come to terms with what they now are."

Nyx lifted her head. "They want to die. That hardly sounds like coming to terms."

Griff sighed. "They dislike existing in a mold outside of what they once were. It creates some dissonance for them, and they will never be truly at peace in this form. But they are not in constant misery every hour of the day. In truth, they are more content than I can ever remember them being. Having the others here—living in the Station—it makes them feel more like themselves, having people to care for. They are alright, Nyx."

"And you?" she asked.

"What about me?"

"Are you okay? You've been distant since you spoke with Jevryn."

Griff sighed. "He gave me a gift. One that brought me great joy, but also great sorrow."

There was more to it than that. She was certain of it. "I haven't seen you carrying around anything expensive enough to qualify as a sorry-I-was-a-dick-for-a-few-centuries apology gift."

Griff was quiet for a moment. "He restored me to my true form. For a few minutes, while he was here, I was *myself* again. I would not trade it for anything, and yet it is difficult to return to this form."

Oh, wow. "And he…couldn't make it permanent?"

Griff shook his head. "That is impossible, while I remain bound to the Station."

The weight of guilt settled more heavily onto her shoulders. "I'm sorry," she said, "I'm trying."

She'd spoken with Laiveran twice, but he'd lost much of the lucidity he'd gained when he'd been connected to Kaliaris' soul. It had taken her nearly an hour both times to bring him into the present, and then he had, predictably, refused to tell her anything useful. She hadn't expected him to, but she *had* hoped to come away from the conversation with some idea of how to reach him.

"There is no need for you to apologize. You will figure it out."

"What if I can't?" What if there wasn't even an answer?

"Then nothing has changed."

She lifted her head from her knees. "How can you say that?"

"Before you were tasked with undoing a madman's vision, you, I, and Kaliaris were three beings tied together for all infinity. What are we now?"

Reluctantly, she said, "Three beings tied together for all infinity?"

"Precisely. The only difference is, now we have hope."

Her heart squeezed. "Sometimes hope makes things harder."

"In the short-term, perhaps. Difficulties can be easier to bear if one is not being constantly reminded that something better is just within reach, and yet paradoxically seems impossible to attain. But existing without hope is not truly living—it is only enduring.

"Before you came to this Station, Nyx, that is what Kaliaris and I were doing—we were enduring. I chose to forget so much of my life because it was easier than being reminded of what I once had and no longer do. But I have hope again."

She hesitated. "Did Jevryn give you that?"

"No." His golden eyes turned on her. "You did. You breathed life into me again. You ignited a spark I had all but forgotten existed, and no amount of painful memories would make me change the things that have happened since you came here.

"I want you to know—though it is perhaps presumptuous of me to say, given I had no input in how you turned out—that you are the daughter I always wished to someday have. The family that, once I came to the Station, I believed I never could have. *You* are my hope, Nyx."

Her heart gave another painful squeeze, and she burst into tears. She hadn't realized how much she'd needed to hear those words until he'd said them.

"Nyx?" He sounded alarmed. "I am sorry if I overstepped, I—"

"You didn't," she managed, her voice thick with tears. "Hug?"

He opened his wings and she flung her arms around his neck, burying her face in his feathers. His wings wrapped gently around her, and he held her and let her cry. He was the strong, steady presence her life had lacked. And, because he was Griff, when she finally stopped sobbing, he produced a handkerchief.

She wiped her eyes and blew her nose, attempting to be delicate. She was relatively certain that, no matter what any etiquette guide might have to say on the matter, it was impossible to blow one's nose with decorum.

She stuffed the handkerchief into her pocket and shuffled her feet. "It'd probably be weird if I started calling you Dad, though, right?"

"Yes, probably."

"But...would you rather I called you Arradin, instead of Griff?" His true name no longer caused him the distress it had when Jevryn first used it, and the name she'd chosen for him now seemed lacking.

"I like Griff."

She gave him a skeptical look.

"I do," he insisted. "It is like a nickname. I have never had a nickname before. And it is the name you chose for me, when I could not remember my own. When no one else thought I deserved one. For that alone, I will always cherish it."

Nyx was saved from bursting into another crying jag when Temerex plodded into the room. Though the unicorn-dragon adored her new enclosure, she had disliked being cut off from everyone else, so Nyx had made a door from the enclosure to the Station. Temerex could open it by pushing a large button on the wall with her horn, and once Seth had seen it, he'd accused Nyx of being a pushover.

She probably was. But Temerex had been in a state of undeniable depression since Jevryn abandoned her, and Nyx was unable to refuse her anything that would bring her even the slightest amount of joy.

She ambled to Nyx, barely lifting her hooves the necessary amount to attain forward mobility. She shoved the side of her face into Nyx's chest and, as she always did, sent Nyx an image of Jevryn. Nyx scratched Temerex's cheek and sent her the image back without Jevryn in it. She wished she knew how to say, "I'm sorry your father is an asshole," with images.

Since she didn't know how to do that, she said, "Come on, girl, I'll get you your favorite," and sent Temerex an image of *qualtez.* An eel-like fish found on roughly thirty-percent of the ley line planets, the fish was Temerex's favorite food, and the only thing Nyx could get her to eat on bad days. Today was a bad day.

The unicorn huffed out a resigned breath and followed as Nyx and Griff led her back to her enclosure, where Kaliaris helpfully delivered a tub of *qualtez.* The unicorn-dragon dropped her head into the tub, and Nyx tried to ignore the disturbing slurping noises that ensued.

Omnivorous unicorn-dragons. Who would have guessed?

She leaned against the wall, closed her eyes, and sank into Kaliaris' senses, searching for her friends, needing to remind herself that they were alive, and safe.

Morgen and Evra were in his lab. The Amazon had been spending a lot of time there since returning from Amentia Furor, and both she and Morgen seemed happy.

Kalvar was in the cafe, closing down for the night, and Liya was with him. Nyx didn't know much more about Liya now than she had the day Kalvar brought her in. The girl wasn't precisely terrified of Nyx, but she wouldn't make eye contact, and never spoke to her unless she had to. Despite Nyx's attempts to make her feel welcome and include her in the Station dynamic, Liya still wasn't truly comfortable around anyone except Kalvar. Even so, she was perfectly polite, enough that she'd overcome her discomfort with Nyx to offer, no less than four times, various forms of payment in exchange for her lodging at the Station.

Nyx had refused them all. She didn't need money, and as much as she might want to know what the blue-haired girl's story was, she didn't *need* to know that, either. Kalvar had perked up a little over the last few days, and she thought having Liya around was good for him. Their relationship didn't seem to involve romantic interest from either party. They were just friends, and they needed each other right now.

Finally, Nyx searched until she found Seth. He was on the western part of the Station's grounds, on the acre or so he'd set aside for his garden. Nyx had almost choked when he'd gone out three days ago to start on it.

Seth hated farming. When she'd told him to plant some okra, it hadn't been serious, because she hadn't thought he would actually plant anything. She knew, without any specific memory surfacing, that he'd hated every minute they'd spent planting and tending and harvesting.

He'd spent the first two days of his garden project staring out at empty space and sketching furiously in a notebook. Unable to contain her curiosity, she'd snuck a glance at it yesterday, and things had made a little more sense. He wasn't planning a vegetable garden, but a botanical one. Areas differentiated by theme and type and feel, separated by walking paths and shady alcoves.

And yet there, at the edge of the carefully constructed design, was a patch labeled, *Okra.*

She wanted to ask him about it but was afraid that if she did, he'd stop. She didn't want him to stop. Not when this was the first thing he'd seemed genuinely interested in—aside from her —since he'd come to the Station.

He hadn't said a single word about when she might dismantle her mother's Hiding, as if he knew the surest way to get her to do something was to say nothing about it. He probably *did* know that about her. She wanted to know that about herself, too. Wanted to know things like that about *him,* more than just little snatches of things here and there, and feelings she couldn't remember the foundations of.

But each time she reached for a section of Hiding to undo it, fear stopped her. Fear that regaining who she used to be would somehow undo the person she was now. For the first time in the life she could remember, she was happy. Yes, she was terrified of what might come to pass with the Harvester, and Jevryn, and the Stations, but she was happy with the people in her life. With Seth.

What happens when you remember being the woman I was there for, who I was supposed to always *be there for, but then I wasn't?*

She didn't want to be angry with him again. She didn't want to feel betrayed again. What if all her memories came back, and they changed her? What if there was nothing in her past but unhappiness, and everything she'd wanted so desperately to know would bring her nothing but misery?

What if she was, at heart, a coward who didn't even know how to face herself?

"Nyx? Are you okay?" Griff asked.

She opened her eyes into Griff's concerned, golden-brown ones.

Fuck it.

Right here in front of her she had someone who'd become like a father to her, who had cared for her and still did. She had friends she'd traveled across the universe for, and who had done the same for her.

She had a—boyfriend? Yes, she had a boyfriend willing to ruin his beautiful vision of a walking garden with a patch of okra because she'd asked him for it. She had people in Earth Between who respected her.

She might not remember the person she'd been, but the person she was now—the person who'd made all those connections—was still built on that previous version of herself.

Nothing she could remember, nothing she could learn, could fundamentally change who she was. It could only make her whole.

"I'm okay," she told Griff. "But I think I'd like to remember some things now. Could you…would you wait with me?"

"Of course."

She left Temerex, who'd finished downing her *qualtez* and decided to sleep off the meal, and went up to her room. She settled onto her mattress, leaning back against a pile of pillows, Griff keeping guard at the foot of the bed.

Nerves hit again and she forced them back. *You'll always be yourself. Nothing can change that.*

She swallowed. "I want to go in small batches, since I don't know what kind of physical effects mass memory regaining could have. I figure I'll try for five sections of the net and see how that feels, but I don't know how much time that will take. If I haven't stopped in four hours, could you wake me up?"

Griff brushed his wingtips against her cheek. "Yes. I will be here, Nyx Fortuna."

He would. He was Griff.

She let the fear go and closed her eyes. The glowing, bright white lines of her mother's net swam into her magic sight. She reached out, touched the closest knot of magic, and lost herself in the swell of memory as it unraveled.

WONDERING WHAT GRIFF AND JEVRYN TALKED ABOUT?

Do you want to read the super-angsty Griff/Jevryn bonus scene? It's available exclusively to my newsletter subscribers. You can get it by signing up for my newsletter at:

https://michellemanus.com/newsletter/

If you enjoyed the book, it would be beyond super awesome of you to leave a rating and/or review at your retailer of choice. Reviews really are one of the best ways you can help support authors.

Thanks so much for reading!

ALSO BY MICHELLE MANUS

The Aspect Society Trilogy

Siren's Song

Valkyrie's Call

Truthfinder's Promise

The Nyx Fortuna Series

Guardian of Chaos

Guardian of Shadows

Guardian of Madness